**DAUGHTERS BORN OF PASSION,
BOLDLY BURNING WITH DESIRE . . .**

Her limbs, it seemed, turned to liquid as she felt
the length of her body pressed to his. The
pressure increased, forcing her lips apart, and as
she opened to him, her breath coming in short
gasps, she felt every inch of her come alive. She
returned his kisses savagely, delighting in the
new sensations that coursed from the depths of
her. Then he lifted her and carried her to the
pillows by the hearth, his mouth still wedded to
hers. Pulling away the blanket, he laid her down
gently as he undressed her until she lay naked
before him. . . .

Other Books by Aleen Malcolm

**THE TAMING
RIDE OUT THE STORM**

THE
DAUGHTERS
OF
CAMERON

Aleen Malcolm

A DELL BOOK

Published by
Dell Publishing Co., Inc.
1 Dag Hammarskjold Plaza
New York, New York 10017

Dell ® TM 681510, Dell Publishing Co., Inc.

ISBN: 0-440-12005-5

Printed in the United States of America
First printing—August 1983

PART I

~~~

The Great Lakes Region
March 1782

Ae fond kiss, and then we sever!
Ae farewell, and then forever!
Deep in heart-wrung tears I'll pledge thee,
Warring sighs and groans I'll wage thee.
Who shall say that fortune grieves him,
While the star of hope she leaves him?
Me, nae cheerfu' twinkle lights me,
Dark despair around benights me.

Fare-thee-weel, thou first and fairest!
Fare-thee-weel thou best and dearest!
Thine be ilka joy and treasure,
Peace, Enjoyment, Love and Pleasure!
Ae fond kiss, and then we sever!
Ae farewell, alas, for ever!
Deep in heart-wrung tears I'll pledge thee,
Warring sighs and groans I'll wage thee.

ROBERT BURNS
"Ae Fond Kiss"

CHAPTER ONE

"Put your hands up!"

Alexander Sinclair stared down at the untidy urchin who aimed a large gun at him. A pair of bright emerald eyes glared up from under a tangled mop of streaked golden hair.

"I said put them up!" And a shot whistled by his ear. Alex slowly raised his arms and grinned down at what he guessed was one of his five children, though which one he wasn't quite sure. Only his son Rowan had inherited his hair color, and this ferocious lad was too young to be Rowan.

"What in darnation is going on out there, Kess?" growled a deep voice from the barn.

So it was his youngest daughter, Kestrel, he realized.

" 'Tis some hairy old man!" answered Kestrel in disgust. "And he seems to think I'm a joke," she added, as Alex forgot his exhaustion and leaned back in his saddle roaring with laughter. "I said keep them up!" And another shot ruffled his hair.

"Hold on there, bairn," puffed an old man. " 'Taint right to shoot yer own father," he chortled, leaning his great girth against the barn wall and wheezing out his mirth.

"Well, thank you, Wee-Angus, I'm forever in your debt." Alex bowed. "To survive six and a half years of war to be shot on my doorstep by my own child would be too shaming. Well, what is it, son or daughter?" he teased as he swung his lean, tired body from his horse.

Kestrel stared up at the man and, upon realizing it was indeed her father, her green eyes flashed as she fought her impulse to run into his arms.

"What, no hug or kiss for this hairy old man?" he added gently, hiding his shock at the hard bitterness that marred her young face.

"Help your father, Kess," urged Wee-Angus, and silently Kestrel swung herself onto the tired horse's high back and rode him down to the lake to drink. Alex watched her proud, straight back and his eyes filled with tears. His youngest child was her own mother all over again.

"She'll be leading some puir mon a song and a dance one day," he laughed huskily.

"Aye, just like another we ken," agreed Wee-Angus.

"Where is she?" he asked, feeling suddenly afraid.

"Inside," answered the old man cryptically.

"Is she all right?" Something in the man's voice intensified his fear.

"Now you're home, I'm sure on it."

Alex quietly entered the house. He had thought of this moment a million times during the war. In his mind he had smelled the warm fragrance of the wood fire, heard the warm happiness of his children's voices, and tasted the sweet, hot passion of his wife. At last that moment was here, but in place of his dream there was a strange, cold silence. He stared around the large central room that was hung with the symbols of two great cultures, Scottish and Indian. Bagpipes and drums, claymores and bows, tartans and furs. He walked slowly around, touching and savoring each. He ran his fingers over the rough carving on the wall that proclaimed his children's births.

"Raven and Lynx Sinclair, born December thirty-first, 1762. Rowan Sinclair, September fourteenth, 1764. Rue Sinclair, August sixteenth, 1765. Kestrel Sinclair, May first, 1766," he read out loud.

"Alex?"

He turned slowly toward the soft, husky voice. Cameron stood in the doorway of their bedroom. To his brimming eyes she seemed almost ethereal.

"Is it really you, my love?" he whispered, afraid to blink for fear she would disappear and he would find himself back in the bloody slime of the battlefield.

"Aye," she breathed, moving slowly toward him. No words were spoken. There was nothing to say. There was just an aching tenderness, a painful joy as Alex enfolded Cameron in his arms and held her tightly. He had forgotten how petite she was, her head barely reaching his shoulder. She seemed more frail than he remembered. Strange sighs and sobs mingled with tears and laughter as they felt each other's faces, rubbed their hands across each other's bodies as if to convince themselves that each was really there and not some wished-for fantasy.

"I need to wash."

"Aye," agreed Cameron fervently.

"Are you implying that I smell, woman?" teased Alex.

"Aye, and I love it, I love everything that's you, my darling," cried Cameron, tears of joy pouring down her face. "Let me get Angus to help heat some water for you."

"I've no time for fancy baths. Let's go to the lake. It has been six long years since I've kissed you. I've dreamed of making love to you each night," he said, passion making his voice deeper.

"Aye, so have I," breathed Cameron. "But the lake water still has some ice. Remember, 'tis still March."

"Just fetch the scrub brushes and you can scrub me till we both tingle and then we can warm each other in our bed."

Kestrel sat under the low-hanging branches of a tall fir tree by the far edge of the lake watching her parents play like young otters, Alex in the water and Cameron on the shore. Two large hounds bounded back and forth beside Kestrel, adding their voices to the happy squeals and giggles that sang over the water. From the house Wee-Angus could be heard singing lustily as he piled wood on the blazing fire in the master bedroom and prepared two steaming mugs of hot whiskey and wild honey for the intrepid bather.

"Brr, enough! Enough!" laughed Alex. "Stop, woman. I'll hae no skin left and a certain important part of me is in danger of freezing!"

The girl couldn't hear what her mother answered as Alex swung the slight, ebony-haired woman into his arms and raced toward the house. They had no room for anyone else, she thought as she whistled for the dogs and walked pensively around the lake, her moccasins angrily kicking anything in her way. This man wasn't the father she remembered. Her father had been like a golden god, a mountain lion, as the Ottawa Indians named him. This man seemed worn out and weary: the gold of his hair less vibrant, the gold of his skin yellow and sickly, the gold of his eyes somehow tarnished. She walked through the forest, oblivious to the dogs who chased each pebble and stick she savagely kicked, until she came to a small glen where she sat on a large rock and stared at the cairns that marked each grave in the family plot.

Cameron watched her husband's sleeping face. She softly traced the new lines and stroked the silver hairs that glinted among the rusty gold of his beard. He lay stretched out upon the furs of their sleeping platform, the blazing fire reflecting along his lean rangy body. Cameron examined every once-familiar inch of him. He was like a stranger. Six and a half years had done more than etch cynical lines upon his face and change his hair color. It wasn't his weight loss or the new scars, she decided. Something indefinable had changed. Even in sleep he wasn't completely relaxed—there was a coiled tension about him as though he was about to spring. Tenderly she covered him and in an instant he sat up with a cry, imprisoning her wrist in a painful grip.

"Alex, 'tis all right. 'Tis me, Cameron," she soothed, afraid of the maniacal cruelty she saw harden his amber eyes. "Hush now and sleep," she comforted, pushing him back.

"Stay wie me. Dinna leave me, lass," he pleaded, pulling her down with him and holding her so close she found breathing difficult. Cameron lay still, feeling the rapid beating of his heart slow to an even pace. Carefully she tried to disentangle herself, but he slept so lightly the slightest movement wakened him and he sprang up in a panic, certain that danger lurked. She lay quietly, the pressure of his hard arms digging into her soft body and mingling with the aching joy she felt at his safe return. Her mind whirled with conflicting emotions. How could she have forgotten her sorrows even for so short a time? she worried. How could she not have told him of the losses that were his as well. It was best. Let him sleep, soon enough to share the heartache. She swallowed hard, trying to stifle the racking coughs that ached her chest, not wanting anything to disturb his homecoming.

"Och, Wee-Angus, there was many a day I dreamed of your cooking," stated Alex, leaning back in his chair. "I canna eat another morsel."

"But you've barely eaten any," protested Cameron.

"Gie him time. The puir mon's belly has to learn to stretch," growled Angus. "When was the last proper meal you ate?"

"I canna remember." Alex grinned sleepily, feeling full and content. He had slept for over sixteen hours, holding Cameron so tightly she dared not move.

"Now why is this house so quiet? I've had my rest so there's no need for tiptoeing," rallied Alex, the look he intercepted between Angus and Cameron sharpening his mood. "Are there no rowdy bairns' voices?"

"The lads aren't back yet," replied Angus, seeing Cameron at a loss for words.

"Back from where?" probed Alex.

"War!"

Alex silently digested the piece of cryptic information. His warm whiskey eyes had hardened as he stared at the large old man and then back to his wife.

"They are but bairns!" he protested. "Wee bairns!"

"Nay, Alexander, they are braw men like their father," corrected. Angus gruffly.

"My babies whether braw men or nay," whispered Cameron.

"When did they leave?" questioned Alex.

"The twins in 'seventy-seven."

"But fifteen years old," intoned Alex numbly.

"Rowan in 'seventy-eight. He was but fourteen," informed Angus.

"No word from any?"

"Aye, we've had word of the twins a few times and Rowan was home for a few days in 'seventy-nine but have had no word about him since," replied Cameron numbly.

"What of Rue?" Alex queried of his firstborn daughter whose blue-black hair mirrored her mother's but whose large wide-spaced eyes matched his own.

"Raped and dead!" a voice intruded.

Shocked, Alex stared in the direction of the challenging voice. Kestrel stood at the top of the stairs.

"Nay! You'll not say so!" contradicted Cameron savagely.

"I was there!"

"That's enough, Kess!" warned Angus. "Alex, we never found the lass's body," he whispered hoarsely, unable to meet Alex's anguished eyes.

"But you found Jemmy's, did you not?" clipped Kestrel. "Rue is dead!"

Alex stared up at his defiant young daughter and back to his wife, who fought to control her own fury. He looked from one face to the other, feeling the pain that emanated in the brittle silence.

"Kestrel, come here," he ordered softly. Kestrel looked down at her father and mother. She could not descend to their level. Once again at mention of her sister's name, the terrible crack of a rifle had shot through Kestrel's head, paralyzing her with fear.

"Why can't you accept death?" she challenged.

"Kestrel, I'm not asking you, I'm telling you to come down here!" Alex retorted.

Angus tensed, knowing the girl would inevitably do the opposite.

"No!" stated the predictable Kestrel before turning and disappearing from their sight. Cameron saw the telltale tic of fury work her husband's lean cheek and she drank deeply of a mug of water to stop a paroxysm of coughing.

"Are you all right?" asked Alex sharply, his brow furrowed as he saw his wife's frail shoulders shake.

"The water went down the wrong way," choked Cameron, taking a deep breath and hurriedly hiding the stained handkerchief from his eyes.

"We searched for Rue but there was no trace," offered Angus, answering the silent plea that he saw in Cameron's tear-filled green eyes.

"Where is Kestrel? I'll have no such rudeness from a child of mine!" roared Alex, confused and upset by the tension in the room.

"Alexander, please?" begged Cameron, grasping his arm as he would have stormed after his daughter. "Kestrel is hurt, gie her time. Sit back and listen, for 'tis not an easy thing to tell."

Alex allowed himself to be pushed back into his chair even though fury still pounded through him. He felt impotent as he stared from Cameron to Angus uneasily. Something was being withheld from him.

"I thought my loved ones were all safe," he muttered. "Protected by our sons and Goliath and Angus. Where is Goliath?" he added sharply, referring to Angus's equally enormous brother. "No!" he protested with anguish, seeing the answer mirrored in Angus's gray eyes that brimmed with unspilled tears.

"Aye," answered the large old man, blowing his nose loudly.

"Meron?" Alex asked almost timidly, afraid of what he would now hear about his wife's twin brother.

"We dinna ken. He left wie the twins to keep them safe," replied Angus. "We heard rumors that the war was over last summer. . . ."

"And here it is March and our sons still have not returned," whispered Cameron hoarsely.

"There's been nothing of any consequence this far north since 'seventy-nine when Clark took the fort at Vincennes," added Angus.

"And still our bairns have not come home," cried Cameron, gripping Alex's arm. Alex stared down into his wife's green eyes and almost recoiled from the burning intensity. Her cheeks were hollowed and the exquisite bones of her face finely etched. He reached out his large calloused hand and gently stroked the frail softness of her face.

"Are you all right, my love?" he repeated.

"Is the war over?" asked Cameron impatiently. "We were told that combined American and French forces in Virginia under Washington defeated Cornwallis. Is that correct?"

"Aye, I was there," replied Alex wearily. "Except for tying up loose ends the war is over and we won," he added flatly, not feeling the least victorious.

"Last summer?" probed Cameron.

"Aye, August."

"And now 'tis March! Seven long months! Why aren't my bairns home? Why dinna you return to me sooner?" fretted Cameron, choking on the anguished words.

"I came as soon as I could, my love. Do you think I could stay away from you one second more than I had to?" groaned Alex, holding her close and feeling the coughs and sobs shake her whole frame. " 'Tis a vast country and sadly the war could be over and the treaty signed and yet the killing continue . . . each side not knowing. . . ." Alex's voice trailed off as he felt Cameron's coughing subside, and she froze in his arms. "Why are you so frail?" he asked. Cameron laughed faintly and pushed herself away from him, flashing Angus a warning look and busying herself by removing plates from the table.

"You maun be joking. 'Tis wartime and food was as scarce for us as for you. Look to yourself, Alexander. You're nothing but skin and bones, yourself!" she laughed, banging the pots together.

Alex sat silently watching Cameron and Angus fiddling around, sensing that they were avoiding his eyes as they tidied the already tidy room. Several times he opened his mouth to speak but something he sensed kept him quiet. A terrible sadness hung in the air, thwarting him, and he could feel a building tension. Finally he stood, unable to bear the prickly intensity yet loath to ask the million painful questions that stung his brain.

"Tell me of my daughters," he demanded, and Cameron froze with her back to him, her thin hands clenched to her sides as though holding herself together. After a long still moment, she turned slowly, shaking her head.

Alex watched her walk numbly into their bedroom and close the door. Angus breathed heavily and took down a large jug of whiskey and thumped it on the table.

"Sit, lad," he said, and Alex obeyed.

"I left a warm loving house full of children and return to this?"

" 'Twill be so again," comforted Angus gruffly, pouring two generous mugs of whiskey.

"My wee Kestrel, as bright and beautiful as a butterfly. Like an enchanted pixie-child, flitting here and there, lighting up the gloomiest day with her smiles," remembered Alex, the stern lines of his face softening as he recalled. "Who is that bitter sullen stranger that speaks so rudely to her mother?"

Angus sat back, allowing the disappointed man to vent his spleen.

"No sons, no Rue. Where's Jemmy?" ranted Alex. "Jemmy!" he bellowed, banging on the table. "Where the hell is she?"

"Dead," answered Angus gruffly, and Alex groaned aloud with the pain of it.

"Tell me all from the beginning, Angus."

"Aye, sir, that I will. It was the autumn of 'seventy-eight. A group of . . ." The old man lost his voice. Alex replenished the mugs and they both drank deeply. After a minute Angus blew his nose loudly and cleared his throat. "A group of Redcoats from Fort Detroit—"

"A group of Redcoats came *here*!" interrupted Alex, afraid that their hidden valley known only to a few had been discovered.

"Nay! Hush your tongue! 'Tis not easy telling!" reprimanded Angus, taking another healthy swig. "We did our part in the war. Reporting British troop action, carrying messages, and the like. Providing food and clothing. On that awful day Goliath, Rue, and Jemmy were returning from taking some provisions for Clark's men at Fort Pitt. . . ."

"All the way to Fort Pitt? That's near a hundred miles!" exclaimed Alex.

"Nay, they rendezvoused wie some boats on Lake Erie half a day's ride. They were nearly home, just the other side of the west forest when they were ambushed. Goliath was shot in the back. Rowan was hunting and heard the shot and the lassies screaming. When he found my brother, there was no sign of Jemmy or Rue." Alex waited patiently for the old man to continue. "The ground was very dry and it was dusk, so tracking was difficult even wie the hounds."

"Kestrel said she was there?" probed Alex, recalling his daughter's angry words.

"Aye, apparently she wandered off aiming to meet up wie Goliath. She had wanted to go wie them but was told she was too young."

"Twelve," calculated Alex. "And my puir Rue not even fourteen."

"Aye. It seems Kess saw Goliath killed and followed the soldiers. We found her at dawn by Jemmy's body on the plain near High Tor. She was just sitting and rocking, singing one of the lullabies Jemmy used to sing to her when she was a wee bairn. Wouldna tell us anything, couldna's more like it."

"What about Rue?"

"Nary a sign."

"If Kestrel was there she must've seen what happened to her sister," protested Alex.

"Would seem as so but I think the lass was too shocked by what she witnessed. 'Twas like a part of her mind closed and she dinna see. You should've seen Kess, like one possessed, building cairns, three of them. When Cameron saw three she went wild and tore down the third. The wee lass dinna say one word. She just watched her ma tear down the cairn and then build it up again. Ten times or more that cairn was built. Since that day there's been a rift between mother and daughter."

"What of those animals?" roared Alex. "Did you track them down?"

"We found their carcasses about thirty miles south," hissed Angus. "All scalped. But no sign of Rue."

"What tribe was responsible? They could've taken our lass," exclaimed Alex.

"Gie me some credit, Alexander! That was the first thing Rowan and I thought on. That's why the young braw lad joined up with General Sullivan," answered the old man wearily.

"But it couldna have been Mohawk, Onondaga, Cayuga, or Seneca, as those tribes of the Iroquois fight wie the British. If it were one of the Iroquois it would have to be—"

"Tuscarora or Oneida," interrupted Angus. "But we spent months riding out to all those villages to no avail. When Rowan joined wie Sullivan he hoped to glean news as well as wreak vengeance on the Redcoats. He was no longer a boy when we next saw him. They slaughtered and burned over twenty villages. No Redcoats, just Iroquois men, women, and children."

"Aye, I heard of General Sullivan and Clinton's raids. It was reprisal for the massacres to the Colonist settlements. But if it wasna Tuscarora or Oneida, what other tribe could it have been that would slaughter and scalp Redcoats and take a girl captive?" persisted Alex. Angus shrugged and splayed his broad gnarled hands in a gesture of defeat. The two men sat in dejected silence.

"'Tis sorry I am that your homecoming is so grievous," said Angus quietly, as Alex stood and stared into the fire until his eyes were burning and dry.

"Aye," nodded Alex numbly before walking slowly to his bedroom. He opened the door gently so as not to disturb Cameron and closing it quietly behind him, he leaned back against it watching the firelight play on his wife's high cheekbone as she stood staring out the window at the moonlit night.

"Hear that?" she whispered without turning to him. Alex shivered as he heard the distant lonely howling of hungry wolves.

"Sometimes I think it is our child calling to us. I think of her lost out there," she whispered.

"It has been three years. . . ." comforted Alex.

"She is not dead!" insisted Cameron. "She is not dead!"

"Then we'll find her," soothed Alex, taking his wife in his arms, his tears dropping onto her cheek and mingling with her own.

CHAPTER TWO

As the sun rose, fingering the eastern horizon with bars of light, two riders cantered across the grassy plain, crackling the frost and misting the crystal spring air with their warm breaths.

"Not much farther now!" sang out the younger of the two. "Just up there," he laughed, pointing to the thickly wooded side of a mountain. Nick MacKay smiled at the boy's enthusiasm.

"How long since you were home, Sinclair?"

"End of 'seventy-nine after the Clinton Sullivan advance," replied the boy shortly, his childlike excitement rapidly changing to withdrawal. Nick stared at the closed stony face as the youth stared straight ahead without blinking.

"I heard it was ugly," he said softly.

"Aye," spat Rowan savagely. "But it was a good introduction to war, everything else was tame in comparison."

"How old are you?"

"No harm in telling now," replied Rowan, trying to dispel his gloom and trying to recapture his joy at going home. "I'll be eighteen in September. I wonder if the twins beat me home," he added, kneeing his horse to a faster pace.

"That poor nag'll never get you home unless you curb your impatience," remarked Nick MacKay. "The poor animal's ready to drop."

Rowan eased up his pace with a rueful grin. Leaving the plain, they rode silently through a thick forest and Nick marveled at the lushness of the vegetation.

"I dinna think spring would ever come again," he breathed, appreciating all he saw and smelled.

"I know what you mean," agreed Rowan as they walked their horses slowly, threading in and out among the trees.

Suddenly a shot kicked up dirt and pine needles in front of Nick's horse, which reared and frightened Rowan's mount.

"What the hell!" cursed Nick, reaching for his gun and trying to control his mount.

"Drop it!" ordered a muffled voice. "Now! Both of you!" And another shot kicked up the dirt. Rowan and Nick threw down their guns and wheeled round and round, trying to soothe their horses and locate their attacker.

"Kess? Is that you, Kess?" shouted Rowan.

"Rowan?"

"Aye!" rejoiced the young man.

There was a still moment.

"Kess?"

"Take off your hat!" said the young voice, which now sounded very vulnerable. Rowan removed his hat and even in the forest's filtered light his golden hair shone. Nick watched in amazement as a lithe figure dropped agilely to the ground from a thick fir tree. He frowned. Who was this young lad whose hair matched Rowan's? he wondered. Hesitantly, the small figure approached them, still holding the gun.

"Put the gun away, Kess. This is a friend of mine," said Rowan, dismounting stiffly and limping toward his sister.

"You're hurt?" she whispered.

" 'Tis better, just stiff from riding," he laughed, swinging her in his arms. "Och, Kess, 'tis good to see you."

Nick watched the two bright heads and the open joyful faces as the two young siblings greeted each other.

"Nick, this is my sister Kestrel Sinclair," Rowan announced. "Kess, this is Nick MacKay. Dr. Nicholas MacKay."

Nick smiled down at her small delicate face. What a little beauty, he thought, catching his breath. Her thick wavy hair was streaked with countless different shades of gold, her wide eyes an even brighter green than her brother's. He could tell she was tiny but there was no ascertaining her figure underneath the bulky leathers and furs that she wore.

Kestrel stared up at the tall man on the chestnut horse. She estimated his age to be about twenty-five or twenty-six. He had black hair and very dark brown eyes. His face was lean and bony, like a hawk's, she decided. She let her eyes fall lower so she didn't see the glint of amusement in Nick's eyes at the girl assessing him so openly.

"Kess?" her brother warned, embarrassed by his sister's staring. Kestrel reluctantly tore her eyes away from Nick's long muscular legs in their tight buckskins.

"He was looking at me like that," she said airily, wanting to touch the tall dark man and yet feeling the excitement of danger prickle.

"Kess?" protested Rowan, totally shamed by his sister's behavior. "I'm sorry, sir."

"Dinna apologize for me, Rowan Sinclair!" snarled Kestrel, picking up the guns. "Here." She threw Nick his and tucked Rowan's in her belt before turning and running fleetly into the forest.

"Kess?" yelled Rowan but she had gone. He turned, shamefaced, to Nick. "I am sorry about that, sir."

"Aye, that's a strange greeting after being away so long," answered Nick absently, his dark eyes narrowed in speculation, still staring after the young figure.

Rowan swung himself into the saddle. "Aye, that is very strange behavior. I hope all's well at home," he worried, fear knotting his belly.

Nick was thankful for the thick trees that slowed Rowan's pace. They rode in silence, wending in and out of the pines that thinned until they broke free of the dark forest into a valley bright with sunlight that reflected off a lake. Nick reined his horse to appreciate the beautiful tranquillity of the spot, but Rowan gave his tired horse a kick and galloped headlong across a small meadow toward the large wooden house.

Wee-Angus watched the rider through his sights and lowered his rifle when he saw the golden head.

" 'Tis Rowan! 'Tis our braw bairn home safe and sound!" he roared, his great stomach jiggling up and down with excitement.

"Rowan?" breathed Cameron, fearful that she wasn't hearing

right. She walked slowly toward the door and took a moment before opening it.

"Mother!" shouted Rowan as he saw her slight figure. He disentangled himself from Angus's great bear hug and limped toward her. Cameron couldn't move. She stood holding onto the door frame for support, her green eyes shining with unspilled tears that welled.

"Mother, och my own wee mother," whispered Rowan huskily.

Nick watched the reunion still astride his horse. His own vision was blurred as he watched the boy pick up the frail woman in his arms. The two disappeared into the house and he was left with the enormous old man who sniffed, aimed his gun, and then bellowed:

"Who on God's earth are you?"

"Nicholas MacKay," he answered, raising his hands in surrender.

"A Scot are you?"

"Aye."

"That's some braw lad," sniffed Angus, his cheeks wet with tears.

"Aye," agreed Nick. "Can I dismount?"

"I dinna ken, can you?" snapped Angus sarcastically, unaware that he still aimed his rifle. Nick nodded wryly toward the weapon and the old man looked down at his hands with surprise. "Och, what you doing there? Tsk!" He lowered the gun and Nick swung stiffly down. "Who are you, laddie?" hissed Angus, realizing he still did not know if the stranger was friend or foe. Nick felt the gun pressed into his back.

"I brought the lad back," he answered easily. "I'm Nick MacKay and you must be Wee-Angus MacLeod."

"Aye," agreed Angus laconically, lowering the gun and wiping the tears from his cheeks. "What was the shooting from the top woods?" he added, pointing the rifle in the direction of the forest they had just ridden through.

"It was Rowan's sister. Kess or Kestrel. Hair and eyes like his," answered Nick.

"Well, no point standing around like this wie these puir creatures about to drop," stated Angus, indicating the two lathered horses. "The barn's over there," he added, leading Rowan's mount. Nick followed him, stopping to allow two very large hounds to sniff and thankfully accept him, before continuing.

"Then I guess you're friendly," said the old man, offering his hand. "I'll shake no man's hand that a dog will bite. They see deeper than we can . . . sense, like wee bairns," he rambled as he

unsaddled Rowan's horse and rubbed down the winded animal.
"Where did he find such a sorry excuse for a mount?" he wheezed.

"They're all we could steal," answered Nick, taking care of his
superb chestnut stallion.

"Seems you got the better of the two!"

"Well, being a might heavier and older, I had the advantage,"
replied Nick. The old man turned and assessed MacKay.

"Black Scot. I hear a Highland touch," he concluded, his eyes
traveling up and down the well-built six-foot two-inch frame of the
young man. "Where?"

"Tain," replied Nick, naming a town in the northeast Highlands.

"MacKay land is further west."

"My mother was a McCulloch."

Angus nodded and went back to tending the horse.

"Raven? Lynx?" called a voice, and Nick turned as a tall thin
bearded man entered the stable. "I'm sorry, I thought wie your black
hair you were one of my sons."

"You must be Sir Alexander Sinclair," responded Nick. "I'm sorry
to disappoint you but I did bring another of them home."

"Rowan!" Angus burst out, unable to contain his joy.

"Rowan?" mouthed Alex. "I have not seen him since he was
eleven years old." Angus and Nick watched Alex almost sleepwalk
out of the stable.

"Darn flies, another flew into my eyes!" lied Angus as the tears
once more ran down his cheeks.

Alexander Sinclair was more afraid of opening the door to meet his
son than he had been in all six years of the war. He quietly let himself
into the house and stood at the door watching Cameron and Rowan
talking earnestly together. Every few words one of them stopped and
stroked the other's face and burst into tears.

"Son?" he said after watching for a while. Rowan straightened and
stood so Alex could see how tall his son had grown. He was still a
boy, he realized, looking at the thin legginess. Only in body, he
amended, as Rowan limped toward him and he saw the premature
lines on the seventeen-year-old face. *My son has suffered,* he thought,
and he cursed violence and war as he held the lanky youth close,
feeling tears wet his neck.

Cameron watched father and son. She rejoiced at Rowan's
homecoming. *Please let me live to welcome all my children home,* she
wished, as she wondered how long she could keep her illness a secret.

"Mother, Father, I feel a fool. I brought someone home with me and I forgot," burst Rowan and he looked so young that Alex rejoiced as he realized that no matter what his youngest son had endured, he was still a boy. "He saved my life in prison. He's a Scot and I know you'll like him. I wasna strong enough to come home alone. . . ." bubbled the boy, and Cameron and Alex exchanged loving glances as the joy within them ached.

"Nick? Nick?" called Rowan, out of the open door. "His name is Nick MacKay . . . he's a doctor," he added over his shoulder to his parents, who held each other tight. Cameron felt a pang of fear. A doctor? What if he could tell something was wrong with her, she worried.

"Nick?" In the stable Nick and Angus heard Rowan's husky youthful voice.

"My name's not Nick," stated Angus sarcastically.

"Nor's mine," chorused another voice from above, and Nick stared into Kestrel's green eyes before striding out of the barn into the crisp bright sunlight of the clean spring day. Kestrel leaped agilely down from the hayloft and Angus roared with laughter at seeing the scowl that creased her exquisite face.

"What so funny!" she demanded.

"You've met your match, my lass, and it's just in the nick of time," he chortled. "Get it? The lad's named Nick and the—"

"Nick of time," sneered Kestrel. "Angus, you're getting old!"

"Respect your elders!" warned Angus, stung by her quick tongue.

Nick knocked at the wide wood door, which was quickly flung open by Rowan who virtually hauled him inside.

"This is Nick . . . I mean Dr. or Major Nicholas MacKay," he proclaimed, embarrassing Nick with the obvious hero-worship.

"Nick will do," he corrected, extending his hand, first to Alex. Each man sized the other up and instantly liked what he saw.

Alexander Sinclair looked like an old tired lion, Nick decided as he stared at the tall lean man in his late forties or early fifties, his once sable hair touched with gray. He noted that the older man's chiseled face was tired and drawn and marred by a scar that ran from one grizzled eyebrow straight down his face disappearing into a full beard.

Alex, for his part, appraised the twenty-five-year-old lad, a dark, saturnine male with eyes deeply set under forbidding black brows and cheeks sharply defined beneath prominent bones. The young man's most arresting feature was his piercing eyes. This man could be ruthless, he decided.

"I'm Cameron Sinclair," smiled Cameron, offering her hand. "I'd like to thank you for the care you took of my son. . . ." Her voice trailed off as she felt the magnetism of Nick's nearly black eyes.

"Nicholas MacKay," said Nick, politely bowing over the frail hand he held. His eyes narrowed as he noticed the pallor of her almost transparent skin and the burning intensity of her green eyes, which seemed to plead with him. He frowned and then nodded, silently acquiescing, knowing somehow what she demanded of him.

"Are the twins back?" asked Rowan excitedly and Cameron shook her head numbly and turned away. "Meron?" added the boy, staring at his father, fear of what he might hear widening his eyes.

"Not yet," answered Alex. "But I'm sure 'tis just a matter of time now that the war is over. Now enough talk of war. We should be celebrating your safe return, Rowan!"

"We met Kessy in the top woods. . . . Is she all right?" asked the youth.

"What do you mean?" Alex replied, setting out some mugs and lifting down the jug of whiskey.

"She acted, well, strange," explained Rowan, embarrassed and not quite sure how to describe his sister's behavior—or even if he should.

"That's because she *is* strange, brother dear!" jeered Kestrel, standing in her favorite place at the top of the stairs. "Right, Mother?"

Nick sat at ease, his long legs stretched out, staring at the willful girl who challenged her mother so cruelly. He observed the fury that tightened Alex's cheek.

"That's enough, Kestrel. We have a guest who I'm sure doesna appreciate your rudeness!" he said scathingly, and Kestrel, meeting Nick's piercing eyes, flushed before retreating into the shadows.

"Drink, MacKay?" offered Alex and Nick nodded his thanks as he accepted the generous mugful.

"Rowan, get Wee-Angus so we can toast your homecoming," suggested Cameron, determined to dispel the awkwardness Kestrel had caused. " 'Tis a time for rejoicing!" she declared and proceeded to load the table with home-baked breads, pies, and cakes.

Kestrel sat upstairs in the shadows, listening to the happy chatter of the noisy meal below and wishing she was part of the festivities. She lay on her stomach and peered through the railings at the dark stranger who sat saying little but obviously appreciating Angus's gruff humor,

Rowan's youthful exuberance, Cameron's husky lilting voice, and Alex's terseness.

"Will she not eat with us?" she heard her brother inquire.

"To welcome her brother home she will!" stated her father, his voice tight with censure. "Kestrel!" he called.

" 'Tis best to leave her alone," replied her mother.

"Aye, when she's in one of her moods there's no telling what she'll do," agreed Angus hastily. Kestrel seethed as they discussed her.

"What is it with Kess?" asked her brother. "She's changed."

"Aye," concurred Alex. "It would seem she minds no one but herself. I dinna think I've ever seen such bitterness on such a young face before. It hurts to see it etched upon my own flesh and blood."

Cameron's anguished eyes met those of Nick MacKay as she tried to suppress the painful coughs that welled as the discussion successfully dampened the welcoming-home festivities.

"She's not a bad lass, just a might willful," comforted Angus lamely.

Kestrel strained her ears during the ensuing silence, not knowing whether they were whispering. She stared down between the banisters at the silent table, noting the sad tension as people stolidly ate. Her eyes narrowed as she saw the stranger, Nick MacKay, reach out and touch her mother's hand.

Cameron smiled gratefully at Nick as he raised his glass and proposed a toast to the speedy homecoming of the rest of the Sinclair family.

"She was always a spirited lass wanting to do what the oldest did and ofttimes managing, but she was never cruel," worried Alex as soon as he had set his mug down, and Cameron shook her head sadly, knowing there would be no changing of the painful subject. "She was never, ever cruel," he repeated.

Kestrel felt her eyes and the back of her nose ache as she remembered how things used to be.

"She's not cruel, Alex," protested Cameron. "She's just a confused child. 'Tis the war . . ."

"She's just run wild. Spends most of her time wie herself. Sometimes takes off for days on end. We used to worry but she has always managed to land on her feet," struggled Angus, clearing the table so Kestrel had to strain to hear over the clatter of plates and pots.

"Sounds like she needs reining," stated Alex. "She's no longer a wee bairn, Cameron. She's a woman."

"How old is Kestrel?" Nick asked, and Kess's heart skipped a beat at the sound of the deep strange voice.

"Near sixteen," answered Rowan. "She doesn't look it or act it, running wild dressed in that bundle of rags."

Kestrel didn't want to hear any more. She felt ugly and humiliated, hearing herself discussed in such a manner in front of a stranger. She crept away to the back of the house where she silently climbed out of a window and made her way to the barn.

Cameron heard a furtive rustle and looked up sharply, her green eyes trying to pierce the dark shadows at the top of the stairs. She sighed deeply as she realized that Kestrel had probably been a witness to the previous discussion. Nick, following her gaze, frowned, not understanding. He saw Angus and Cameron exchange knowing looks before he stared thoughtfully back at the stairs.

"Before the war started we talked of sending our sons back to Scotland for schooling. Remember, Alex?" said Cameron. Alex nodded.

"Maybe Kestrel should go to school, too. Never having gone to school myself I dinna ken much about it. Is she too old?" she asked.

"Mother, most girls are married by sixteen," offered Rowan.

"Not most," laughed Alex. "Quite a few, but by no means most."

"Mother was fifteen," Rowan insisted.

"And even more headstrong," teased Alex lovingly. "So there's hope for Kestrel yet."

"Maybe that's why we fight so," Cameron said sadly. "I try to reach her, but she makes me so angry I have to sit on my hands or I'd hit her."

"Maybe that's all she needs, a good thrashing," yawned Rowan, his eyelids drooping.

"I'd not try that, young fellow-me-lad," warned Angus. "Or you'll have a spitting wildcat in your hands. Could lose an eye," he laughed, helping Rowan to his feet and up the stairs.

Kestrel sat on a half wall in the stable, scratching the forehead of Nick's horse.

"You certainly are a beauty," she admired. "Nearly as beautiful as my mother's stallion Torquod used to be. Och, there's no need to get jealous, old beastie, I still love you best," she added, staring lovingly at an old black horse who docilely chewed and switched his tail. "I wonder what you're like to ride," she whispered and swung herself down onto the chestnut's high back. The horse sidestepped and tossed his head, not used to the strange rider. "It's all right, big one," she crooned as she rode him out into the afternoon sunshine.

"Whoa there, Kess. You canna be helping yourself to other people's—" protested Angus, but Kestrel dug in her heels, spurring the large horse to a gallop. "Oh, no. More trouble," groaned the old man as Alex and Nick came out of the house in time to see horse and rider splashing through the shallow water at the edge of the lake before disappearing from sight. The three men stood in silence. Alex waved his hands impotently, not knowing what to say about his youngest child's behavior.

"Puir beast was tuckered out, too," moaned Angus. " 'Tis a wild streak the lass has. I'm glad you're home, Alexander. She needs a strong hand. I've done my best but I'm too old," he gabbed, noting the set angry face of the dark man.

"You say sometimes she is gone for days?" said Nick cryptically, looking from one man to the other. He was exhausted. Every bone in his body ached and he was looking forward to a long sleep, not chasing across the countryside after a spoiled child.

"Well, Angus?" queried Alex.

"Well what?" asked the baffled old man.

"You know more of my child than I do. Is she sometimes gone for days?"

"Aye," replied the unhappy old man. "Sometimes," he added. "And sometimes weeks. . . ."

"What?"

"So maybe 'tis better that I get you tucked into a nice warm bed like Rowan," suggested Angus helpfully. "You'll not catch her, and wouldn't be safe if she's gone visiting," he finished unhappily.

"Visiting?" ejaculated Alex. "Visiting who!"

"Shush your mouth!" hissed Angus. "You want your poor wife hearing more things to worry on?"

"Visiting who?" insisted Alex, propelling the enormous old man into the barn.

"I don't rightly ken," prevaricated Angus.

"Dinna gie me that!"

"You'll not like it," warned Angus.

"I dinna expect to," replied Alex severely. "I dinna like what I see of my daughter's behavior, either."

"Tuscaroras," whispered Angus unhappily.

"Tuscaroras?" frowned Alex. "What are you talking about, old mon?"

"She's been riding wie them."

"Go on," ordered Alex.

"Raids and the like. Intercepting supplies for Fort Detroit. . . ." explained Angus.

"But surely there's no action now?" protested Alex, very conscious of MacKay's silent scrutiny.

"Clark has been waiting on reinforcements to attack Detroit for the last three years," interjected Nick. "He's been made brigadier general of the western forces and still he waits for Virginia to send the reinforcements that they promised. While he waits he's planned an offensive against the Shawnees in the Miami valley, which I sincerely hope my horse will not be a part of."

Angus and Alex turned anguished eyes and Nick almost felt a pang of guilt. There was no way the child could overtake or even catch up with George Rogers Clark's force, but he decided to let the two men worry a bit. That would teach them to raise a docile child. He breathed heavily and left them to their worrying.

Nick let himself into the main house and a tender look crossed his stern features as he saw a dozing Cameron seated by the fire. He allowed himself the time to evaluate her. She dressed like a native in buckskins and but for her green eyes could have easily passed for one. Like her daughter, she wore fringed trousers and moccasins but there the resemblance ended. They had the same vibrant green eyes and wild spirit, but Cameron's spirit now seemed to be weighed down. He ran a practiced eye over her smooth face, estimating her age accurately as late thirties and noting the deep brown that rĭnged her eyes like kohl and the tightly drawn skin that sharply delineated her fine cheekbones. Her eyes flew open and Nick was astonished not only by the intensity of the unusual color but by the depth of pain.

Cameron stared up at the tall dark man whose nearly obsidian eyes seemed to pierce right through her.

"What has my daughter done now?" she whispered with a rueful smile. Nick grinned back, surprised at her perception. "I know that look of fury. Only Kestrel could have caused it," returned Cameron impishly, in answer to his unspoken question.

"I prefer to talk about you," said Nick gently. "We are alone," he added when she looked worriedly about and her anxiety caused her to breathe with difficulty. Nick watched her frail shoulders shake as the violent hacking coughs tore at her body. As the spasms passed and she lay back exhausted in her chair, he held out his hand silently for the rag she had pressed to her mouth. Cameron stared down at the bright blood that stained the white linen before flinging it into the fire. She closed her eyes, feeling at ease with the strange young man.

Nick felt his professional objectivity desert him as he stared at Cameron's beautiful tired face. He ached with sorrow, knowing he looked upon a most precious human being who was dying. Her eyes flew open and he saw that she knew it.

"I know I am dying," she said, and almost as though to comfort him, she reached out and touched his hand. "But I will not die until my house is put to rights," she said fiercely and Nick saw how she must have been when she was young and rebellious. "Will I have time?" she added, allowing her fear and vulnerability to show.

"I've seen people defy death until they were ready," replied Nick huskily, his eyes mirroring hers as they welled with tears.

"Stay wie us as long as you can . . . or want," she said, and he felt a stronger appeal than the words and knew she pleaded with him to stay until the end.

"I will stay as long as you need me," he promised.

"And my family?"

"And as long as your family needs me also."

Cameron reached out and softly touched Nick's face. "You are so tired. You should be tucked in bed like Rowan. Soon I shall sleep. When my brother Meron returns with my twin sons. . . . But maybe he'll not return with two. Oh, I have dreamed such pain," whispered Cameron, getting frantic as a nightmarish feeling flashed through her. She struggled to her feet. Nick reached out to help her but she firmly shook her head. "I must be doing things or I'll brood," she stated. "Get you to bed while I get on with living."

Nick gently touched her soft cheek and for a moment he felt like an olden-day knight pledging allegiance to a lady. He had never understood until this moment such things and now he did. He, the archcynic Nicholas MacKay, felt he could promise this human being anything.

"Before sleeping, I need to bathe." He grinned engagingly and Cameron saw the boy beneath the man. "I'd not abuse your hospitality even though I doubt you'll ever get the grime off the sheets your grimy son is sleeping on," he laughed. "Unfortunately we both were detained by the British for several months and save for a quick dip in some frigid water we've not really been cleansed for . . . well, I'm shamed to tell you. Just tell me where to find soap and brushes . . . for I'll not disturb your fine Wee-Angus. Pretend I'm one of your . . . family and let me fend for myself." He was loath to say "one of your *sons,*" because he knew the feelings he felt were certainly not familial and because to have borne him she would have had to be eleven or twelve as only that number of years separated them.

Cameron smiled gently, knowing all that he felt, and gave him directions to find soap and brushes. A calmness had slowly enveloped her and she felt at peace for the first time in six years. Now she knew there was someone who'd be there for Alex and her children so that they would not be alone and without care when she was gone. She sat back in her chair beside the hearth and closed her eyes. She daydreamed and Nick's face merged with Alex's and she loved them both. She smiled softly. It was odd to think that if she were ten years younger and had not met Alex, she might have given herself to this virile dark man. Even if she had met Alex, she amended roguishly, she might have been tempted.

Cameron's comfort in Nick's presence deepened during the following days. When Kestrel still had not returned with Nick's horse, he thought to approach Cameron about it, puzzled as to how such an intelligent, caring woman could be mother to such a seemingly uncaring child.

"She's not uncaring," corrected Cameron as she stared across the lake that mirrored the setting sun. "I don't know what words to use but she cares."

"Certainly not for anyone but herself!" interjected Alex, eaten up with anxiety for his frail wife, whose coughing kept him awake although she tried to steal out of their bed. Each night he lay in the darkness hearing her trying to stifle the painful spasms.

"Remember how I was?" pleaded Cameron, reaching out to her husband.

"That was different. You had none but an embittered Highland outlaw to teach you love, but our child has had a loving home. . . ." ranted Alex.

"Not for the last three years. Not since Rue disappeared. Not really since you went off to war. Six years of war is a long time, Alex," strove Cameron.

Nick listened to the exchange between husband and wife and when he tried to leave to allow them the privacy of their conversation, Alex detained him.

"What do you think, MacKay?" he challenged and Nick shook his head silently, knowing Alex's fears as he looked at his exquisite wife, who seemed to be fading before their eyes. "Kestrel has no thought for any but herself! She's wearing you down to skin and bone wie worry," he continued.

Later that night Nick walked around the still lake, lured by the calls of the nocturnal animals. To his surprise he came across Cameron, silhouetted against the moonlit water as she sat quietly watching his approach. In the distance was the lonely howling of a pack of wolves, the haunting cries echoing down from the surrounding mountains. They sat in silence for several minutes.

"Don't judge Alex too harshly," said Cameron abruptly, feeling anger emanate from the tall young man.

" 'Tis Kestrel I'm judging," returned Nick.

"She needs your understanding not your judgment. I am afraid for her. What if none can reach her?" whispered Cameron. "I love her but she will not let me near. She hasn't since Rue disappeared. Who'll care enough when I am gone? There's so little time to undo everything," she grieved, rocking her body back and forth.

"Undo what?" probed Nick gently.

"I robbed them of their heritage. Alexander gave up everything for me. His title, lands, country. When I'm gone he must take our sons back to Scotland so they can choose where and who they are to be. You'll help Alexander, won't you? He'll need your help, Nick, though he'll not ask for it or admit he needs it."

Nick squeezed her hand comfortingly to reassure her and nodded silently before an attack of coughing rendered her speech impossible. Nick carried her back to the house, appalled at her weight. There was no physical substance left to her although her spirit burned fiercely. The sadness of it weighed heavily upon him.

CHAPTER THREE

Nick scrubbed his body briskly, perversely enjoying the cruel sting of the icy water. He was impervious to the antics of the male otters as they tried to win the attention of the females. He didn't see the comical courting dances of the stately heron and pheasant; he was too immersed in his own brooding thoughts. It had been two weeks since he had ridden onto Sinclair land and two weeks since the wild child had ridden off on his horse. No one seemed troubled about the girl's safety. She was probably behaving as she usually did, he surmised. He, of course, was worried about his horse who had been ready to drop when the brat had absconded with him, but as long as Cameron stayed serene about her daughter, Nick knew the girl was at least safe. His poor horse could be crippled or dead, but Kestrel, at least, was all right.

The back of his neck prickled warningly, but he attributed it to the temperature of the water, and he hurried his bath as his stomach growled with hunger. Actually, to be honest with himself, he was enjoying his stay in Sinclair country. There was something infinitely healing and soothing about planting and tilling the earth after long years of destruction; a cleansing rhythm to walking along the furrows tending and cultivating after years of standing still, taking aim, and ending lives. Life instead of death. It was a good feeling. *Death*. He pushed the ominous word away and breathed deeply of the fresh new morning as he thought of Cameron so tenuously holding onto life. He thought of the haunted pain mirrored on Alex's gaunt face as now he knew his precious wife was slowly and inexorably slipping away from him. Nick splashed the water furiously as he was filled with an impotent anger at not being able to do anything to help, and at Kestrel, whose absence was no comfort to her mother.

Kestrel dismounted painfully and peered across the lake toward her home. She recoiled and hid in the underbrush as she heard the telltale splashing. Craning her neck further, she recognized Nick MacKay. Why was he up so early? She seethed, staring at his muscular brown body. It was barely dawn and she had ridden all night, determined to arrive while the household still slept so she wouldn't have to face questions and anger. She was dead-tired and her neck and arm throbbed from a deep knife wound in her shoulder. The sunlight on the lake made her dizzy and she closed her eyes.

Nick rubbed himself briskly and pulled on his pants, sensing somehow he was being watched. A horse whinnied softly in the undergrowth to his right, and leaving his boots, he crept barefoot up the bank and circled in a wide arc. Parting the thick bushes he recognized his own horse: in a sorry state, covered with mud and burrs and nearly dropping from exhaustion. Where was the girl? he wondered as he patted the poor animal, his hand sticking to the sweat that had the horse shivering in the chill morning air. He cursed out loud. Where was the little devil? Her brother was right, she needed a thrashing. He scanned around and seeing the sunlight glinting on a golden head, lunged quickly, catching her by the scruff of her neck. Kestrel screamed as pain knifed through her.

"You need a lesson you'll not forget!" he said, his voice dangerously low and controlled. "But first you'll see to my horse that you've so sadly abused."

Kestrel kept her head bowed as she fought to keep from screaming again. She wanted to fight free of his iron grip but she hurt too much. Maybe if she went limp he'd relax his hold, she thought, as she was propelled along. Her legs felt leaden and her head light and dizzy as she fought to stay conscious.

Nick stared ahead as he strode, leading the poor horse with one strong hand and propelling Kestrel with the other. Kestrel concentrated on putting one heavy foot in front of the other as she stumbled and tripped. She couldn't raise her head, the pain was too intense and the distance to the barn seemed miles.

"Rub him down well," Nick ordered. "You'll not rest or eat until he is warm and fed, you ken." And Kestrel staggered as he released his iron hold. Taking a deep breath she raised her head, her face drawn and pale.

"Aye," she spat.

Nick stood watching her tend to his horse. He saw how she favored her right arm, holding the shoulder higher, and tilting her head to one side. He frowned and walked around the horse the better to see her face. Kestrel glared at him and he noticed the whitening of the skin around her mouth as though she kept her lips clamped tightly together.

"Are you hurt?" he asked brusquely, but Kestrel ignored him.

"Nick? Nick?" bellowed Angus from the house. Something was wrong. Nick forgot his concern for the girl and raced out of the barn.

Kestrel walked slowly back to the house. She knew something was terribly wrong. A heavy feeling of dread weighed her down and she knew it had to do with her mother. She stood for a moment outside the house, afraid to enter for fear what she might encounter. Steeling herself, she took a breath and hardening her expression, she pushed open the door. She froze on the threshhold, her eyes fastened on her mother in her father's arms. Cameron struggled against the spasms, gasping for breath, as she saw her daughter in the doorway, but the violent coughs would not be suppressed. She waved her hands impotently, reaching out to the seemingly detached girl, tears of pain and sorrow flooding her eyes.

Kestrel tore her eyes away from the bloodied handkerchief in Nick's hand as he gently dabbed her mother's face. She was filled with a sharp panic, somehow feeling responsible for the deep wound that caused her mother to suffer so. Just like Rue, she thought frantically, as she heard a sharp crack of a rifle again cut through her head, and she stared about the still room at the other people who stood frozen like statues staring at Cameron's frail body cradled in Alex's arms. Her brother Rowan's eyes were wide with fear and sorrow, his large young hands open and reaching as though to help. Angus gripped the edge of the table, his burly old face crisscrossed with tears. That wasn't her mother, decided Kestrel, looking back at Cameron. Her mother was big and strong and very imposing. That was a child in her father's arms. A fragile, skinny child.

"Kessy?" mouthed Cameron. Kestrel tried to back away but the wall was behind her. "Kessy?" •

Alex turned to look at his daughter and Kestrel recoiled from the fury in his eyes.

"Obey your mother, girl!" he snapped harshly. Cameron groaned with pain and weakly tried to soften Alex's tone by plucking on his sleeve.

"No!" shouted Kestrel, her young face showing terror. "I'm sorry. I didn't mean to hurt you so."

"Oh, Kess. Oh, Kess, dinna, please . . ." begged Cameron, tears streaming down her face. Nick crossed to the white-faced girl and taking her arm, pulled her toward her mother. Kestrel fought to detach herself until she felt like a sleepwalker, her eyes pinned on the bloody handkerchief clasped in her mother's hand. She felt her father's angry eyes boring into her.

"Kess, look at me, bairn," whispered Cameron. Kestrel stared into her mother's eyes fighting the need to throw herself upon her breast and cry as she had done as a baby. "I love you, Kestrel."

Kestrel fought the tears, and hardened her expression as fear flooded in.

"You dinna know me!" she spat, and would have rushed from the room but she was held firmly by Nick. Rowan gasped at his sister's apparent callousness.

"Oh, Kessie," grieved Cameron lovingly, squeezing Alex's arm warningly as she felt him tense angrily at Kestrel's remark. "Nick?"

"I'm here," he reassured, his deep voice reverberating through Kestrel's coiled body as he held her tightly.

"I want you to take care of Kestrel," stated Cameron. "I want you to marry her, Nick." Kestrel's green eyes widened with shock.

"No!" she shouted. "I don't need anyone. I can take care of myself."

"We all need someone," returned Cameron, staring lovingly at Alex. "Oh dinna cry, my darling," she said, reaching up and tracing the tears that ran into his beard. Cameron stared back at her daughter's mutinous face. "Kestrel, dinna hate me. One day you'll understand," she added. "Nick?"

"Aye," he answered, emotion making his voice husky. "I'll take care of her. She'll be my wife."

"I'll not!" yelled Kestrel, breaking the hushed sorrow of the still room.

"I'm too weary to do battle right now," answered Cameron with a smile. "Maybe after a wee nap," she added, closing her eyes and cuddling into her husband as she felt him tense to retaliate against their willful daughter. Alex lifted his wife into his arms and carried her to the privacy of their bedroom.

Kestrel stood staring at the closed door, unaware of Nick's strong arm until it released her.

"You knew she was this ill? Why didn't you tell me it was so serious?" cried Rowan, wanting to hit someone, anyone, as the pain welled in him.

"She dinna want you to know," sniffed Angus.

"There maun be something you can do? You're a doctor!" demanded the boy, staring up into Nick's stone face. "Do something!"

"I'm sorry," he said tonelessly.

Kestrel's mind whirled with a million things. She didn't know if she was asleep or awake. Everything had a nightmarish quality.

"I better finish seeing to your horse," she stated in a flat emotionless voice.

"What's wrong wie you?" snarled Rowan, catching her by the shoulder and swinging her around roughly. "Our mother is in there dying and you dinna care, do you?"

Kestrel bit her lip to keep from screaming as her brother's hand bit cruelly into her injury. She glared at him, unable to speak or cry. Rowan's cheeks streamed with tears. He shoved his sister away in disgust. "Why didn't you stay away!"

Kestrel took a deep breath and walked out the door. Nick frowned at the way she was holding herself as she walked unsteadily toward the barn.

"You shouldna be so hard on her, lad. Everyone has different ways of dealing wie grief. She hurts but 'tis all locked up inside," said Angus gruffly.

Nick wanted a long walk to clear his head but was loath to venture too far from the house. Alex was still in the bedroom with Cameron, and Nick had a feeling that the brave woman was just hanging on by sheer willpower, waiting for her sons and brother. He walked around the lake, trying to sort out his thoughts. He had made a promise to a dying woman. Marriage! He groaned and wondered at his sanity. He didn't want a wife, let alone such a wife as Kestrel Sinclair, the untamed brat. He sighed, knowing that he'd make the same promise again if Cameron asked, just so she could die in peace. He sat on a rock, thinking and idly skimming pebbles across the calm surface of the water. An image of Kestrel favoring one arm nagged his mind and he stood and headed back to the barn.

His horse contentedly munched hay, his coat gleaming. Nick ran a practiced hand down the legs and checked the hooves. Kestrel had done a very thorough job. His horse seemed none the worse for wear. Whatever had hurt Kestrel couldn't be too bad, he decided as he strode back to the house.

Angus and Rowan sat glumly at the kitchen table, silently eating breakfast, their eyes glued to the main bedroom door.

"Did Kess come in?" asked Nick.

"I dinna see her," answered Angus. "But that don't mean she dinna come in. She's as silent as a cat, is that one."

Nick walked slowly up the stairs to Kestrel's room. He lifted his hand to knock and thought better of it. He pushed the door open and walked in. Kestrel lay sound asleep still fully dressed, her breathing even and healthy, but her cheeks flushed. Nick stood still and looked about appreciating the bare but attractive room. Usually girls' rooms were cluttered and frilly; Kestrel's room was almost stark. Two woven Indian blankets added the only colors beside the browns of the wooden floor and walls. A gun and several daggers were casually thrown on top of a large chest. Nick turned back to the girl who lay on her stomach cuddled into the pillows on her sleeping platform. He stood looking down at the telltale rusty mark that stained the deerskin behind her shoulder. He gently felt her head. She was a little warm but not enough for concern, he decided as he left the room. Sleep was a good healer. Later he would examine her.

Angus and Rowan sat glumly amid the remains of their meal. Cameron's door was still closed. Nick sat and helped himself to bread and meat.

"Did you find her?" asked Angus and Nick nodded. "She looked a might peaky. Is she all right?" worried the old man.

"She has some sort of injury to her shoulder."

"Bad?"

"I don't know. I decided to let her sleep while I figure out how to handle her," replied Nick.

"Aye," chuckled Angus softly. "Och, I wouldna be in your shoes. I would have thought tired, hurt, and asleep she'd be easier to handle, but you're the doctor."

Nick took his time eating, trying to ease the tension in the room as the old man and boy sat staring at the closed door.

"I'll take a look," he said, patting the youth on the back and knocking softly at the door.

Cameron lay peacefully sleeping. Alex looked up at him and smiled wanly. Nick felt so useless; there was nothing he could do for Cameron. "Would you like something to eat?" he whispered, but Alex shook his head.

Cameron's eyes opened and for a moment they were two pools of suffering, which she quickly covered. "You promise?" she rallied, her proud spirit challenging the tall young man.

"Aye," he nodded and left, closing the door behind him.

"Sure you don't need help?" asked Angus as Nick climbed the stairs carrying hot water and his bag of medical equipment. Nick grinned and shook his head.

Kestrel slept fitfully. Terrifying images pounded her heart causing her to twist and turn, hurting her shoulder. She moaned softly and sat up as Nick entered her room. Still half-asleep she didn't react to him. He put the basin of steaming water on the chest and turned to face her. Kestrel frowned, bewildered.

"Take off the jerkin," he ordered, but she just sat, not understanding if she dreamed or not. "Or I'll take it off you," he added, hoping to challenge her. Kestrel backed away from him, holding her injured shoulder.

"You'll hurt yourself more," warned Nick, blocking the door. "I mean to see your shoulder."

"I'll take care of myself."

"How? You canna even see it. Now stop being a spoiled child. You'll be no help to your mother if you get sick," said Nick, losing patience. "So stop thinking of yourself."

"I canna get it off. I tried already," answered Kestrel, hating to admit a weakness.

"Then I'll cut it off," replied Nick tersely.

"It's just a scratch. It needs to heal, that's all. Now I'm sorry I took your horse, but he's taken care of and I'm very tired and want to sleep," chattered Kestrel, feeling a mixture of conflicting emotions. She felt feverish and despite the pain she moved her head back and forth to avoid looking into his compelling dark eyes. Nick's large hand cupped her chin and held her head still, forcing her to look at him.

"Now you'll listen to me, Kestrel Sinclair. I don't care one whit whether you're hurt or not! I happen to think you're a spoiled selfish brat, but I do care for your mother. Right now she deserves to rest in peace, not having to worry about you. So I'll see to your arm for her, because if it was up to me I think you deserved whatever you got!"

Nick's cold words cut Kestrel to the quick, but she hid her humiliation behind an expression of disdain. He turned her around roughly and she winced once and then stood perfectly still as he cut the leather of her jerkin from neck to hem, exposing her tan straight back. The deerskin fell off her left shoulder but was stuck fast to the wound on the right.

" 'Tis best to pull it off quickly," he muttered. "It will hurt." But he was somehow loath to hurt her despite his anger at her behavior. Her naked back made her look very vulnerable. Breathing hard, he wrenched the material so it pulled free and Kestrel shuddered but made no sound. It was a deep jagged cut that immediately welled with blood. Nick picked her up and she kicked out resisting. He dumped her facedown on her bed.

"Keep still!" he ordered. " 'Tis filthy, infected. When did this happen?"

Kestrel refused to answer, gritting her teeth to stop from screaming as Nick cleaned the gaping wound with boiling water.

"A few days it seems." He answered his own question as he worked efficiently, knowing he was causing her incredible pain. But she made no sound. "There's something unnatural about being too stoic," he muttered, wishing she would give a slight moan or gasp. "Strapping it up is going to be awkward. Sit up!" But she made no movement. He knew she was conscious so he assumed she was embarrassed about her nakedness.

"Come now, Kestrel, don't tell me you have maidenly modesty?" he teased.

Kestrel took a deep sobbing breath and attempted to turn over. The gash welled blood again that ran down her back.

"Stubborn child, let me help you!" said Nick, swearing under his breath at his stupidity.

"I can do it," insisted Kestrel. "And I'm not a child!" she stated, managing to sit up and face him.

No, she was not a child, Nick agreed silently as he lost his professional distance. She was an exquisitely formed young woman. Not only was her glorious hair many shades of gold from deepest auburn to lightest ash, but her skin was also a creamy gold. She sat straight and proud, her firm young breasts heaving slightly. Beads of perspiration under her eyes and along her forelip told him the agony she suffered.

"If you stand, it'll be easy to bandage," he said hoarsely and Kestrel obeyed like a marionette. "Put your right arm out a wee bit," he directed and he wound clean cotton gauze about the injury.

Kestrel stood, feeling pleasure at the touch of Nick's strong warm hands, and she was confused.

"There. 'Tis the best I can do for 'tis a very awkward place. Now have you a . . . night attire? Gown? Nightgown?" he asked, wondering why he felt callow and awkward.

Kestrel frowned, not understanding what he asked for.

"Are your clothes in there?" He pointed to the chest.

Why was he talking to her as if she didn't understand English? she wondered.

"Kess," he said decisively, "you should go back to sleep but you should wear a sling to keep your arm as still as possible so. . . What do you sleep in?" Kestrel still looked delightfully confused, and he found himself questioning his own reaction.

"I sleep here in my bed," she retorted.

"Aye, but what do you wear to sleep," repeated Nick, disconcerted by her golden nakedness.

"Wear? Nothing. Why, what do you wear?" she replied, feeling strangely aroused despite the constant pain.

"Then it'll have to be a sling around nothing," declared Nick, noting the hardening of her nipples and feeling a familiar stirring in his loins.

"There," he proclaimed huskily, tying the finishing knot of the sling. He stared into a pair of devilish green eyes, and smiled ruefully at her victorious expression. The little she-cat knew what she was about, he realized. She knew she had somehow successfully turned the tables. He had to admire her, he grudgingly admitted. There weren't many men who could have withstood the pain she just endured without a sound and come out a victor in a battle of wills.

"Sleeping's not going to be too comfortable for a while," he informed her as he packed his bag and picked up the basin, preparing to leave.

"Well, it's just what I deserve, is it not?" she said softly, throwing his own words back at him.

Nick put the basin back down and sat on the bed beside her. "Tell me, why you behave as you do?"

"How do I behave?" she challenged, the soft lines of her face hardening. "Because I don't bow and scrape and kiss my mother's feet?"

Nick looked at her long and hard. The bitterness that spurted from her young mouth shocked him. What had happened between mother and daughter to cause such a rift?

A sudden shouting from downstairs ended the silent scrutiny.

"You should sleep," he ordered, taking his bag and striding swiftly to the door, worried that Cameron needed him. A hoarse cawing added to the commotion.

"It's my uncle and brothers. They're home!" cried Kestrel, pushing past him.

CHAPTER FOUR

"Lynx! Ven!" yelled a happy voice and Kestrel, naked to the waist, clad only in buckskin trews and a sling, hurtled down the stairs and threw herself into her twenty-year-old brother's arms. "Lynx? Is it you or Ven?" she laughed, adrenaline and joy numbing the pain of her wound and thought of her mother.

"Lynx," replied her brother huskily.

"Oh, I'm so glad you're home at last," she bubbled over, tears very near the surface. "Where's Ven?"

Lynx held her close but she pushed free and stared around seeing the sorrowful faces of Angus and Rowan. "Meron?" she pleaded fearfully to her uncle, but he silently wrapped her in his lean, hard arms. "No!" she howled. "No! Ven's not dead, too?"

Nick watched the painful family reunion from the shadows, not wanting to intrude. A large old raven roosted on a rafter also witnessed the heartrending scene, bobbing his enormous head and shifting his weight from one leg to the other.

"Where's Mother and Father?" asked Lynx, fear shooting through him at his sister's cryptic words. He followed Rowan's anguished gaze to the closed door of their parents' room.

Meron walked slowly to the door. He knew his twin sister was ill. He had felt it in the deepest part of his soul and that was why Lynx and he had traveled virtually without sleep for five days. He opened the door and when Omen the raven cawed, he waited until the great bird had launched itself into the air, and preceded him into Alex and Cameron's room.

"What is it?" asked Lynx as the door closed behind his uncle. Angus and Rowan shook their heads sorrowfully, unable to speak.

"Mother's dying!" stated Kestrel, her young face showing no emotion.

"No!" shouted Lynx and Nick felt the youth's raw pain cut through him. Angus reached out to comfort but Lynx looked frantically about the large room that he had dreamed so often about during the violent, lonely war years. "Where's Rue and Jemmy?" he demanded angrily. "Where's Goliath?" he added when no one answered. Angus put a heavy hand on Lynx's lean shoulder but the young man savagely brushed it aside. "Where are they?" he demanded.

"Dead!" stated Kestrel when no one answered.

"Dead?" echoed Lynx, staring into his sister's furious face.

"Dead!" she repeated.

"And you don't care, do you?" yelled Rowan, appalled by what he felt was his younger sister's callousness. The door to their parents' door was thrust open and Cameron stood there.

"Mother," breathed Lynx as his eyes filled with tears. "Oh, Mother," he repeated as she stood proudly.

"I waited for you to come home. I'll not die in bed," she informed him. Lynx approached her almost reverently and when she wavered, he picked her up in his arms and carried her to her chair near the fire.

He knelt beside her holding her delicate hand in his calloused one. It felt like a cobweb to him. Although she was but a faint shadow of the woman he remembered, her spirit burned brightly through the enormous green eyes and seemed to dominate the whole room. Her twin brother Meron stood with Alex, his arm about his brother-in-law as he grieved at the tragic news that had been exchanged: his news of Raven's death and her news of Rue.

"Angus, pile the table high and break open the jug as we maun celebrate our loved ones' safe return," ordered Cameron with effort. "Och, my puir wee Ven," she added, her voice breaking as she thought of her dead son. "He dinna suffer, did he?" she sobbed. Lynx and Meron shook their heads, unable to speak as tears poured down their faces and stopped their voices.

Kestrel watched from the shadows as the table was piled high with food and drink and Nick was introduced to her brother and uncle. She sat on the stairs, unable to be part of the enforced gaiety.

"Angus, gie us a tune on the pipes," ordered Cameron, and after a rusty start the large Scot wheezed a sprightly tune on the bagpipes and the raven sat on the back of Cameron's chair nodding his head in time with the music.

"What is the sickness?" whispered Lynx.

"Consumption," answered Nick.

"Is there no hope?" pleaded the young man.

" 'Tis a miracle she's lasted this long," he replied, watching Cameron who sat straight and proud, dwarfed by the chair, gazing about at her family.

Cameron stared at the faces of her children, sadly noting how the war had marked them all. The firelight flickered on Kestrel's high cheekbone and vibrant hair where she hid in the shadows. *Oh, my puir wee Kestrel,* she grieved. *Nick'll not let you fly alone. He'll not be afraid of your sharp beak and claws.* Her loving eyes traced the premature lines of suffering on the faces of her two sons.

"Alex?" she called fearfully, not seeing him.

"I'm right here beside you, my darling," he reassured. "You look tired."

"I have all eternity to sleep so I'll not waste what little time is left. Lynx and Rowan maun go home to Scotland. To Glen Aucht. 'Tis their birthright," she worried. Lynx opened his mouth to respond but was stopped as his mother's agitation increased and a violent fit of coughing stopped her words. He stared in horror at the fresh bright blood that issued from her mouth.

"We've gone all over that, my love," soothed Alex.

"And Nick will take care of my wild Kestrel," she choked.

Kestrel moved closer, trying to hear as the feeling in the room intensified.

"I shall take care of Kestrel," promised Nick as Cameron's frail hand reached up to stroke his face. Kestrel shook her head mutely, wanting to reach out to her mother and beg her not to go. She edged nearer.

"Meron?" whispered Cameron.

"Aye," breathed Meron, taking one of her small hands between his large ones.

"Find my little Rue. She canna be dead, she canna or I'd feel it," she pleaded. "Look for her. Find her."

"Aye," agreed Meron, trusting his twin's intuition.

Kestrel felt panic claw into her at the mention of her sister's name. She wanted to rush away into the darkness outside, away from the feeling of death that seemed to hover above them on heavy wings like the presence of the raven.

"Alex, you gave up everything for me. Country, home, friends, lands . . ." coughed Cameron.

"You *are* everything to me," replied Alex, his heart nearly breaking as he felt the end closing. "Dinna go, I canna live without you."

Kestrel listened to the exchange between her parents. She wanted to scream and beat at them with her fists. She was filled with conflicting emotions. She turned, wanting to escape from the cloying sorrow that threatened to suffocate her. Maybe if she were alone she could release some of the terrible aching pain that consumed her. *You are everything to me. You are everything to me*, she repeated in her brain as she backed away from the tight-knit group that surrounded her mother. *Was there ever room for me?* she wondered. She stared up into Rowan's face. He and Lynx had a birthright. They were going back to Scotland with their father, while she had been foisted off on a stranger.

Rowan frowned as his sister seemed to stare at him with undisguised fury. He reached out to comfort and be comforted but she pushed him away.

"Kess, I'm sorry I was hard on you," he apologized, but she made no sign she had heard, just stared at him with dull eyes before stalking past him and then rushing up the stairs.

Nick caught the exchange between brother and sister and debated following Kestrel but instead turned and looked at Cameron, who lay back exhausted in her chair, her hands holding Alex's and Meron's as though to root herself to life. Her eyes opened and she and Nick exchanged a silent farewell before he quietly let himself out into the chill night air. He knew the end was very near for Cameron and he ached for her family as they waited for her death. He strode slowly around the lake until he found her favorite spot under the sweeping limbs of a large fir tree. He leaned against the rough trunk listening to the lilt of Angus's pipes mingle with the nocturnal life: the incredible loneliness in the howling of the distant wolves, the boom of a solitary heron, the haunting hoot of an owl. Such grieving calls wafted and blended over the still water. He allowed the aching to build within him and spill over as he realized that no matter how carefree and sprightly a Gaelic tune, there was always a throbbing lament beneath. He stared up at the clear sky as the sound of the pipes petered out and a stark silence took over. It was as if the night and all nature were holding its breath when Cameron died.

The next day was gray and overcast. As gray as the stones of the two new cairns. One for Cameron and the other for her son Raven. As gray as the silence between them all, thought Nick. There was an aching void where a vital person once had been.

Kestrel watched the men silently build the stone monuments. She sat in the bushes, hugging her knees and feeling as stonelike as the boulders that were stacked one on top of the other. Dispassionately, she observed her father, uncle, and brothers as they worked, ignoring the fine drizzle that beaded on their clothes and mingled with the tears on their cheeks. One by one each man put his last stone in place and stood back until only Alex remained methodically heaving the blocks. The rain increased until it drummed against the hard earth, plastering back the grasses and bowing the trees, and still Alex built Cameron's cairn, higher and higher, stumbling and slipping as he tried to stack the large rocks. Kestrel watched her father fall and lie with his arms embracing the monument.

Alex howled out his pain, trying to drown out the rushing wind and torrential rain that beat against him. Beneath the wet, cold pile of rocks lay his warm, vital Cameron. He had to release her. He had to cuddle her in his arms so she'd not be lonely, cold, and afraid. He clawed at the boulders, dislodging the topmost rock. He fought the hands that tried to stop him.

Rowan wept openly as he saw his father distraught with grief, fighting Nick, Meron, and Lynx as they tried to stop him from tearing down Cameron's cairn. Angus wrapped a large arm about the youth and led him back to the warm dryness of the house where they sat staring into the fire, their wet clothes steaming, unable to stop the hot tears that streamed.

At last, Alex stopped struggling and he stood still and stared about at the men who held him. He nodded, trying to communicate that he was all right. He could not talk, the pain was too fierce, hollowing out the most enormous chasm within him. Hands dropped from his arms, and he stared blankly as though he did not recognize his son or anyone else. He turned back to Cameron's cairn, the pounding rain and his grief bowing his shoulders and once-proud back.

Lynx, Meron, and Nick walked silently back to the house, leaving Alex.

"Where's Kestrel?" asked Nick.

"She was here," replied Meron, his keen eyes having caught sight of a glimpse of her golden hair. They entered the house and stood numbly, the water pouring off them and puddling on the floor. The fire burned noisily in the large hearth but there seemed no warmth, just a cold aching void.

Angus lumbered to his feet, opened his mouth to try to remonstrate about the dirtying of his clean floor but found he was unable to say anything as a lamenting sound issued from his mouth. He sniffed, wiped his wet cheeks, and then mopped the wet floor. He clattered about the kitchen making hot whiskey drinks, talking to himself as he grumbled about this and that in between great heavy sobs.

The rain sheeted down all day and still Alex sat as bowed and gray as the stones of the cairn. As the gray day darkened to night, he stiffly unfolded himself and slipping in the mire, made his way back to the house. He stood back looking at the warm squares of lighted windows, angry at what he saw. How dare there be warmth and light, he raged.

"No! No! Put out those lanterns! Put them out!" he roared, rushing furiously toward the door. He stood dazed on the threshold, looking at the silent tableau of men who sat wrapped in their own grief. "How dare all be the same," he whispered, losing his anger as he stared about seeing the spaces where Cameron should be. Her chair sat vacant by the hearth. Everywhere he looked he could picture her. Everything he looked at she had touched. He shook his drenched head before walking quietly to the room they had shared so intimately.

Rowan stood as his father swayed in the doorway. He had wanted to rush into the strong golden arms for comfort as he had done as a small boy, but there was no father, he realized. There were no strong arms. He was not a boy any longer. He shrugged off Angus's arm that reached out to him and laughed. Nick frowned at the derisive sound and looked inquiringly at the youth.

Alex sat in his room, unaware of his drenched clothes or the cold that seeped into his bones as he relived the years that he and Cameron had spent together. His mood alternated between an overwhelming sense of loss and violent anger in which he would curse the war that had robbed him of the last six years of her life. He threw himself down on the bed, emotionally and physically exhausted, only to smell her fragrance still captured in the bedding. His tortured mind would fill with hope and he'd reach for her in vain and howl at his empty arms. He couldn't imagine life without her and only his remembrance of the promise he had made to her, to take their sons home to claim their birthright, gave him any purpose at all. He would go home, after being away twenty years, to his estate of Glen Aucht on the Firth of Forth. Who was left there? What kind of life was left for him anywhere? The future seemed bleak and pointless. He stared at the gray ashes of the cold hearth, feeling empty, devoid of everything except his loss. Scotland his native land, once so precious, now seemed remote and comfortless.

Rowan and Lynx stared at their father's door, hearing him rant and rave and then sob piteously. It had been three days since their mother's burial. Three days since they had seen their father and three days since they had set eyes on Kestrel.

"Let him be," said Meron quietly as Lynx lifted a hesitant hand to knock on the door.

Alex, hearing the whispering and feeling his family's presence outside, finally steeled himself and wrenched open the door and stared into the shocked faces of his two sons. He groaned aloud as he saw Lynx's and Rowan's emerald eyes, so much like their mother's.

Nick exchanged glances with Angus as the gaunt man emerged from his room, still wearing the muddied clothing from the burial.

"There's food, Alexander," offered Angus gruffly as the man stared with anguished eyes about the homey room. Alex nodded and abruptly left the house, intent on a cleansing swim.

For the next few days, although Alex was no longer closeted in his room, he was closeted within himself as everything he did and saw, every place he went, held Cameron's presence. He couldn't even have a bath or eat without feeling that half of himself had been ripped away.

Angus watched the grim, bitter man, knowing the grieving time was not over. He wondered if Alex would ever smile again, and he frowned when he saw how the man avoided his two sons who themselves were still raw from the loss of their mother and brother.

Nick watched the humorless man and grieved for the Sinclair children whose childhoods had been prematurely curtailed by war, and who were now completely orphaned by their father.

"Is there nothing to be done?" he asked Meron as they sat staring over the lake.

"Time is the healer," returned Meron lamely. "There's nothing we can do. It is between father and sons."

"What about father and daughter?" pursued Nick. "She's not been seen since her mother's burial. He's not asked after her once."

"He canna even look at his sons, why expect him to look for a daughter who'll remind him of his loss even more? It took Alexander Sinclair a long time to learn to love again after losing his parents and two sisters to the English. Now he's hurting once more because he loved. Maybe there's only so much pain some men can bear," replied Meron.

"He spoke of leaving soon for Scotland. Surely he'd not just leave without his daughter?"

"You made my sister a promise," reminded Meron.

"Aye," nodded the younger man ruefully. "But 'tis strange to entrust one's child to a total stranger nevertheless," he added.

"Cameron knew what she was about."

"I guess. But where was my sanity in agreeing to such a thing?" wondered Nick wryly as they made their way back to the house.

They opened the door to the fragrant aroma of bread baking and rabbit stew bubbling over the hearth. Angus put one thick finger to his lips and rolled his eyes heavenward indicating the top of the stairs. Nick frowned, not understanding, but Meron grinned, his white teeth gleaming in his tanned face.

Kestrel peered down through the banisters at the men eating and her mouth filled with saliva at the appetizing smells that drifted up. Her mother's chair sat at the end of the table and her father sat turned away so he didn't see the vacant seat. All she could hear was the clatter of cutlery and crockery. Suddenly there was a crash as Alex pushed himself back from the table.

"I canna stay here longer," he cried brokenly. "There's nothing here for me but memories . . . nothing but heartache! 'Tis not right that the sun still rises and sets and the world still goes about its business!" he lamented. "We shall leave for Scotland at first light!" he stated.

Kestrel stood and looked down at him.

"What about me?" she challenged.

"Where have you been?" Alex demanded.

"What about me?" repeated Kestrel.

"Come here!" ordered her father, the sight of her cutting him to the quick as her rebellious stance reminded him of Cameron.

"What about me?" screamed the girl.

"Come here, Kestrel," he reiterated and when she made no move to obey, he shook his head in resignation.

"What about me, Father?"

"I canna be your father. I hae nothing to gie you. I can barely cope wie myself," he said brokenly. "Come here," he repeated, trying to make an effort.

Kestrel heard her father's words and fear flooded in.

"You wish it was me who died, not Mother, don't you?" she spat, covering her terror with fury.

"STOP!" roared Alex, brandishing his fist as his own anger erupted. Kestrel backed away into the shadows and then turned and fleetly ran to the back of the house and hid in the darkness. She would not be left behind, she decided, as she heard the soft deep rumble of the men's voices as the journey to Scotland was planned. Furtively she packed her saddlebags and then waited for the men to go to bed so she could raid the larder and sneak into the stable to help herself once again to Nick MacKay's chestnut horse.

Kestrel dozed, lulled by the deep male voices and the warmth of the house. She opened her eyes, suddenly disoriented, until she realized where she was. She shifted her cramped position and peered through the banister railing. The fire burned low, reflecting a deep red glow. All she could hear was an occasional crackle from the hearth and Angus's sonorous snore from one of the downstairs back rooms. Slowly she stood and tiptoed down the broad wood stairs, knowing which steps to avoid. She padded on bare feet to the pantry and helped herself to cold meats and bread, which she stowed into the saddlebags. Unable to resist, she dipped a crust into the big stewpot and ate hungrily before silently making her way out of the warm house into the chilly spring night. Keeping to the shadows she crept to the stable. One of the hounds growled low in his throat but after sniffing the girl, he thumped a heavy tail in welcome. Her heart beating in triple time, Kestrel felt her way in the pitch-black, toward the stall where Nick's horse was stabled, hoping her eyes would soon get accustomed to the dark. One of the horses snorted and whinnied loudly and she froze listening, but nothing else stirred. With her two hands held out in front of her she inched her way blindly until she pushed against a warm immovable object. She recoiled, stifling a scream of dismay as she realized it was a man's hard chest.

"I've got her!" cried Nick MacKay, grasping the small fists that beat their fury against him. Kestrel exploded, kicking and biting as she desperately tried to fight free.

"Sheath your talons, little sparrow hawk," laughed Meron, lighting a lamp. Kestrel stopped fighting, and breathing hard, she stared at her uncle. She was too angry to speak. Nick released her hands and stepped back. She looked glorious, lit by the warm light, her riotous hair seeming on fire, her tawny skin flushed with fury, her young breasts heaving. Meron smiled at the young man's appreciation of his niece.

"I wouldna relax your guard quite yet, MacKay," he warned as he saw Kestrel's lithe muscles tense. Nick sprang aside just in time to avoid a kick aimed at his groin. His face lost its wry humor as he caught her bare foot and brought her tumbling down into the straw.

"That's enough!" he roared, hauling her back on her feet. Kestrel showed no fear at Nick's icy rage even though she was terrified. She defiantly looked from one man to the other, knowing she wasn't strong enough to fight her way free as her quick mind planned her next move. Meron grinned as he saw her expression change.

"Meron?" she appealed to her uncle.

"Dinna try your little girl wiles on me," he laughed. "I'm for bed," he added, to Kestrel's dismay and Nick's consternation. They both watched Meron's silent departure.

"Now what?" challenged Kestrel, very aware of the masculine scent of the tall man who held her in a tight grip. Nick looked at her full petulant mouth and caught the cunning gleam in her eyes. The little vixen was trying to seduce him, he realized, and he wondered how far she would go to achieve her own ends. Kestrel stared up at Nick's hawklike face and shivered as his nearly black eyes seemed hooded. "Are you going to hold me all night?" she whispered, huskily hiding her intimidation at his stern appearance.

Nick didn't answer, but she thought she saw a slight smile come to his lips. Every nerve in her body came alive as she stood on tiptoe and pressed against him. Nick let go of her wrist and leaned casually against the wall waiting to see what she would do next. Kestrel was confused by what she was feeling. Her heart pounded and her breasts tingled. She stepped back from Nick, breathing hard, fighting to control these new sensations.

Nick watched her softly parted lips and curbed his desire to kiss her. He would take Meron's advice and keep his guard up, he decided. He watched her slowly back away from him, her eyes wide and bewildered. He moved toward her gradually, not wanting her to turn and run out of the stable. As his black eyes captured her wide green ones, Kestrel felt she was being stalked. She stepped back and was trapped against the opposite wall and still he approached, his head bending until she felt his lips softly touch hers. She stood mesmerized, not knowing what to do as the pressure of his mouth increased and he lifted her until her straining nipples were crushed to his hard chest. It was as though liquid fire raced through her limbs, culminating in the central part of her which she thrust against him, panting and writhing, not quite sure of who she was and where she was.

Nick drank of Kestrel's sweet young mouth, his own breathing matching hers, his broad hands cupping her firm young buttocks as he ground himself against her.

Kestrel opened her eyes and tried to remember her priorities. She pressed her hands against Nick's chest and tried to get perspective. She gazed into his fathomless dark eyes as she fought to catch her breath. A horse whinnied and she remembered her purpose.

Nick watched Kestrel's expression change from soft melting passion to hard resolve. He kept his eyes open and his senses aware as she thrust against him and offered pouting lips. Once more his quick reflexes and his instinct for survival saved him from a painful injury when, aware she was about to try something, he felt her leg muscles tense.

Kestrel's head was pulled back painfully as Nick grabbed her by the hair. She fought without calculation or thought, motivated by white-hot rage. She kicked, bit, punched, and clawed, determined to be free. Little animal noises of pain and effort burst from her mouth. Despite his superior strength, Nick had a difficult time keeping hold on the frenzied girl who thrashed about as though she fought for her life. It was as though she were possessed, he thought, marveling at her endurance in spite of the damage her sharp teeth caused his arm. Her fighting gradually slowed as she lay exhausted in his arms, sobbing from her frustrated efforts. He felt her labored breath and thundering heart reverberate through him as he held her close, not trusting her sudden quiet.

Her breathing slowed, hiccuping with the residue of her past stormy fight. Her flushed face rested in feigned trust on his broad chest as Nick leaned against the stall, knowing it was going to be a long, uncomfortable night. *Here we go again,* he thought wearily, as once more her wild fight started. This time her head crashed against the hard wooden wall, and he stared down, seeing the blood run and mingle with the sweat-dampened golden hair.

Nick carried Kestrel's limp body out of the warm stable into the cold night air. He sighed loudly with exasperation and fatigue as he wearily trod toward the sleeping house. To his surprise the door was opened for him, saving him the trouble of shifting Kestrel's weight. Meron held the door wide. His keen ears had heard Nick's approach.

"She cracked her head," he explained tiredly, laying her down on the fur-covered settle near the hearth. His experienced fingers examined her. "She's got a thick skull," he muttered. Meron silently handed him a wet rag and Nick cleaned Kestrel's sweat- and blood-streaked face. "Never thought I'd survive the war to become a nanny to an undisciplined child."

"Here," said Meron, handing him a mug of whiskey. "I think you've earned it."

"She's a strange one," worried Nick after a long swallow that burned and warmed his tense body.

"Aye," agreed Meron. "She was always a spirited child."

"Spirited?" laughed Nick. "That's an understatement. She's completely wild. Has no one ever curbed her?"

"I've not seen her for five years or so. She was ten and, as I said, a high-spirited little girl always competing with her brothers. Now there is a change. There's an anger," brooded Meron.

"Anger? She's a ball of fury! What happened between her and her mother?" probed the young doctor.

"Why? What did you see?"

"Just Kestrel's bitterness toward Cameron," Nick answered.

"It might have something to do with Rue's disappearance," mused Meron. "From what my sister managed to tell me, Kestrel is probably the only one who can really tell us what happened."

"How?"

"Apparently she was there. She saw her sister and Jemmy raped.

She was found by Jemmy's body and there was no trace of Rue," recounted Meron gravely.

"My God!" exclaimed Nick. "Rowan told me of the tragedy but he dinna mention Kestrel being there. How old was she?"

"It was three years ago."

"Twelve or thirteen years old," estimated Nick, shaking his head and falling silent. *It's no wonder Kestrel's strange*, he thought. "Three years? Is it conceivable that Rue is alive?" he added.

"My sister thought so," answered Meron.

"Maybe wishful thinking?"

"Maybe, but I doubt it."

The two men fell silent as they sipped their whiskey, each lost in his separate thoughts. Meron piled more wood on the dying fire and kindled it into a healthy blaze. Nick watched him idly as the heat from the whiskey and hearth relaxed him. Kestrel stirred and burrowed into his side and he wrapped a strong arm around her, holding her close. He listened to her even breathing, knowing that she had drifted from unconsciousness into a deep sleep.

"What are your plans?" Meron's soft voice made him start and he realized he had been dozing.

"Besides this encumbrance?" he replied cynically, indicating Kestrel. "I've not really decided."

"No family?"

"I've a grandfather and older brother still in Scotland," yawned Nick.

"No parents?"

"Both dead. My mother in childbirth and my father in war. I was raised by my grandfather."

"Which war?" probed Meron.

"In New France when I was four," answered Nick, stretching his long legs out in front of him as he tried to get more comfortable. Kestrel moaned and stirred, changing her position until she lay with her head pillowed on Nick's lap. Meron raised a quizzical brow at the young man's expression as he stared down at the golden hair fanned across his groin and the small hand that curled around his firm thigh.

"Why don't you try to catch some sleep, MacKay?" chuckled Meron. "You'll need all your energy and wits for when she awakens."

Nick grinned ruefully and wondered if he risked disturbing Kestrel by shifting her weight higher. There was no way he could relax with her warmth pressed to his most intimate spot. Carefully he lifted her head and rested it on his chest but she protested sleepily, twisting and turning until she was comfortably back in her former position.

"Even in sleep she has to have her own way," he murmured and Meron laughed softly.

CHAPTER FIVE

"Kess? Wake up, Kessie lass." Angus's gruff voice broke through Kestrel's sound sleep and she opened her eyes to bright sunlight. Where was she? She sat up, disoriented, and stared around at the large central room. How had she got there? she wondered, rubbing her aching head. She winced as she found the bruised cut.

"Your brothers and father will be on their way any moment," said Angus softly. Kestrel frowned at him, her young face still flushed from sleep. "They're outside wie Meron and Nick," he added, seeing her confusion. Kestrel stood and walked slowly to the door. She wanted to scream. Her mother was dead and now her father was taking her brothers away and she had only just got them all back. Seemingly devoid of all emotion she stood in the yard watching her brothers and father.

"Kessie?" whispered Rowan, reaching out to hug her.

"I hope you drown!" she spat vehemently, wanting to beg him to take her with him. "All three of you can drown in hell!"

"Oh, Kess, don't," begged Lynx, taking her tense body in his young arms.

"Don't touch me!" she screamed, fighting free, her flailing hand cracking his cheek.

"I'll be back as soon as I can," said Lynx sadly, knowing how hurt his sister was despite her rebellious stance. "Take good care of her, Nick."

"Aye." The tall dark man nodded.

"And I'll deliver the letters to your grandfather and brother just as soon as we get to Edinburgh," reassured the youth. "Try and be good, Kess."

Kestrel watched her two brothers embrace Meron and Angus before mounting up. She felt panicky. It was a bad dream. They couldn't just ride out of her life.

Alex walked slowly toward his daughter and froze in his tracks as her stormy green eyes took him back more than twenty years to the wild Scottish moor where he first met Cameron. Blankly he shook his head, trying to erase the memory and quiet the pain. He swallowed hard as his scalding tears welled and choked his throat. *Forgive me,* he wanted to say. *Forgive me, but I canna help you. Angus and Meron are better able to see to your needs.* Alex shook his head, unable to speak, and then turned sharply away from his daughter and mounted his horse. For a split second Kestrel looked childlike and vulnerable as she lifted her hands and stepped forward to detain him, but he wheeled his horse and galloped away. The two boys hesitated, looking from their sister to their quickly retreating father before awkwardly waving good-bye and riding off.

Kestrel stood silently looking after them. It was a mistake. In just a moment they would realize and come riding back for her and she had to be ready, she thought. She turned and ran back to the house. Where was her saddlebag? She remembered packing it. She raced up the stairs to her room and frantically looked. It wasn't there. She forced herself to try to think logically. The stables, she remembered, and dashed down the stairs.

"Whoa there, slow down!" growled Angus as she ran headlong into his wide girth.

"I have to get it. It's in the stable. I have to get it," she muttered, frantically trying to push him away, but he wrapped her in his arms and held on. "You dinna ken. They'll come back for me. I must be ready," she babbled, trying to get him to understand. Her head ached and she felt dizzy. The room tilted at an alarming rate.

Angus stared down at the muttering girl whose face was chalky-white.

"Nick?" he roared. "Nick?"

"Shush! No, you mustn't, you mustn't," hissed Kestrel. "Don't tell him." She fought to see straight, but Angus's concerned face doubled and trebled, receded and zoomed in.

Nick and Meron hurried in just as Kestrel broke away from Angus. She faced them, trying to keep her balance as she held out one hand as though to ward them off. She frowned and squinted her eyes, trying to get the two men in focus.

"I'm . . . I have to . . . I . . ." She strove to speak her

thoughts but couldn't remember what she had to do. "I have to . . ." She stopped and looked very confused.

"What? What do you have to do?" asked Nick, walking toward her.

"No . . . no," muttered Kestrel, shaking her head and backing away. "It's very important. I have to . . . I have to." Nick caught her and she struggled, muttering and pleading with him.

"It's all right," he soothed.

"No . . . no," protested Kestrel. "It's in the stable. Yes, it's in the stable. No, I mustn't tell you that." Everything receded and, terrified, she clung to Nick. Everything spun. "The room's moving! Stop the room from moving!" she screamed, her eyes wide and frightened in her pale face.

"She's delirious?" suggested Angus.

"More like a concussion," answered Nick shortly.

"A concussion?"

"Gave herself a nasty crack on the head last night. Along with a lack of sleep, her mother dying, and the rest of her family abandoning her . . ." Nick trailed off bitterly. He was angry but had no right yelling at the old man. "Sorry," he apologized.

"What can I do?" asked Angus, his eyes full of pity for the terrified girl who struggled wildly in Nick's arms.

"Stop it moving!" she pleaded.

"Shush, close your eyes. That's right. No, keep them closed," he soothed as he carried her to the master bedroom. "No, it's all right. Let go," he crooned as he tried to pry her clutching hands off his shirt. But she wound her fingers even tighter into the fabric and held on for dear life. "Shutter the windows and give me cooling cloths," he called urgently and Meron and Angus hurriedly complied.

Kestrel felt as though she were being sucked into a whirlpool, the world spinning round and round. She clung desperately to Nick.

"Close your eyes," he would gently say and she would for a second, only to feel suffocated by blackness. "Take deep breaths," he ordered, trying to get her to still her panic.

"Can't breathe," she gasped.

"You can! Take deep breaths!" shouted Nick firmly, knowing the girl had crossed into hysteria. He wrenched her hands off him and sat her up, raising her arms above her head.

Meron and Angus silently watched the pale girl obey Nick's stern voice. Her eyes were still wide with terror and her nostrils flared, but she breathed deeply, calming herself.

"There," sighed Nick as Kestrel lay back exhausted on the pillows, her eyelids drooping. He exchanged an ironic look with Meron as they watched the stubborn girl fight to stay awake. Each time they thought she had succumbed, her eyes would fly open and her body would tense.

Finally Kestrel slept soundly, and leaving the door open, the three men sat around the table.

"Will she be all right?" worried Angus as he kneaded bread dough furiously to soothe his own jumbled emotions. Nick shrugged absentmindedly, lost in his own brooding thoughts. Meron stared off into space. "I dinna ken what the world is coming to. I couldna wait for the war to be over and everyone home," mourned Angus, punishing his dough as he pummeled and pulled.

"Aye," agreed Meron.

"Never thought to lose so many. Here am I an old man. I have had my life but the young ones are taken, leaving me to suffer," he sniffed. "And now the baby of them all lies in there wie her brains all addled."

"Angus, she'll be fine," comforted Nick. "Rest and quiet," he added, lamely feeling like one of his professors from medical school in Edinburgh.

"You're sure?" questioned Angus.

"She's strong. She'll be fine."

"Up there?" probed Angus, knocking a floury fist on his own grizzled head.

"Aye, up there too," laughed Nick. "She pulled herself out of that panic. I've seen many who couldn't and then is when you start worrying. She's too strong-willed and stubborn to lose all control," he explained, seeing the old man was genuinely concerned about Kestrel's sanity.

"How long before she's up on her feet?" asked Meron. "I would like to get some ideas of where to start looking for her sister."

"Och, Meron lad, you're not thinking of putting the poor lass through all that again!?" shouted Angus.

"Shush," warned Nick, looking toward the open bedroom door.

"Sorry," apologized the old man, continuing in a hoarse whisper as he angrily plunked the unrisen dough into several pans. "If you ask me that's what did the most damage between mother and daughter. Mind you, sparks always flew betwixt the two. Too alike they were. Butting heads," he informed as he busily stowed the pans on a warm shelf above the hearth.

"Angus, sit down and tell me what you know," urged Meron.

"I canna sit and talk on it. I have to stand and keep busy or I get too fashed up," whispered Angus, looking around for something to do.

"I'm hungry," laughed Meron. "Cook something for me and talk at the same time," he suggested.

" 'Tis no laughing matter," growled the old man.

"I ken," replied Meron softly and sadly.

"I dinna what to say. It was three years ago. No more, for it was autumn. Jemmy MacFarlane, Goliath, and Rue were coming back from meeting up wie some of Clark's wagons. Food and weapons. They were ambushed and it was thought that the bairn Kestrel saw it from the start. But no one could get a word out of her mouth."

"Why was it thought she saw it all?" probed Nick.

"She was always a little independent child. Off on her own for hours even at the age of five and six. Rowan heard the shot that killed my brother. It took him maybe half an hour to find the body and by that time the two lasses, Rue and Jemmy, were gone. Later we found signs that made us think Kess had been there. She used to play wie water-smoothed pebbles and some had been dropped. There's no brook or creek up so high."

"Who was Jemmy MacFarlane?" asked Nick.

"A red-haired lass from Glen Aucht. A wee bit younger than Cameron. Came over from Scotland wie Alexander and was like a friend and nurse to the bairns as they come along," explained Angus. "She became the daughter I never had. Och, those muckers deserved to lose their scalps, I only wish I had been the one to do it!" Angus gutted the fish he was cleaning, savagely cutting it from rectum to gill. "Where was I?" he asked after a pause.

"Pebbles you think Kestrel dropped," reminded Meron.

"Aye, well as I said it was autumn, dry and hot, nearly dusk. We got the hounds but it was nearly dawn when we found Jemmy's body up on the plain by High Tor. There were signs of about six men and horses, but no sign of Rue."

"That's where you found Kestrel?" prompted Meron.

"Aye, sitting and singing a song about puir little Jemmy lass. Jemmy would sing that song about them when they were wee and use their names. Like puir little Kessie lass or Lynx laddie. . . ." Angus trailed off, his eyes streaming. "Puir little Jemmy lass to have to die like that," he sobbed and threw the fish in the hot skillet so it hissed and spat fiercely. Nick and Meron sat silently waiting for the old man to resume. Angus blew his nose and took down the whiskey jug. "If you had seen what was done to that puir wee body by those murdering animals. Nae, not even an animal would treat their females in such a way!" he stated and drank deeply. Nick tiptoed to peer in on Kestrel as the old man's voice had raised with emotion. He nodded in answer to Meron's querying look before quietly closing the bedroom door.

"Cameron reached to take Kess in her arms but the child ran into the woods. We found her days later in the glen. She had built three cairns. How she did so I'll never know. Some of the stones weighed as much as she."

"She was missing for days after?" repeated Nick. "A child missing for days with murdering Redcoats around?"

"Aye, sounds callous, doesn't it? Well, all thought was for her sister Rue. Rowan, Cameron, and I rode out trying to pick up the murderers' trail. Each thought the other had the bairn. So the truth is we were the ones missing, not the lass."

Nick exchanged glances with Meron as they both thought of Kestrel left alone after such a traumatic experience.

"The rest I think you know. We found the bodies about thirty miles or so south but no sign of Rue. Neither Tuscarora nor Oneida was responsible and there were no other tribes about except for the other Iroquois allied wie the British."

"Could have been whites. Scalping is not just among the Indians," offered Nick.

"Taking women is, many tribes do that. Adopt them so to speak. Rue was black-haired and brown-eyed," replied Angus.

"She could have escaped and got lost in the wilderness," said Nick.

"We dinna find a trace of her. Nary a trace!" protested Angus.

"There's a lot of animals out there," replied Nick sadly.

"Then we would have found something," stated Angus vehemently. "I've been in this wilderness for nearly twenty-six years, I know these forests, plains, and valleys. Somebody took her!"

"How can Kestrel help? She wasn't where the Redcoats were killed and scalped, was she?" probed Nick.

"What if the Redcoats weren't responsible?" answered Meron.

"What do you mean? Of course the muckers were!" roared Angus. "Who else would do such a thing? My brother was shot in the back! Wee Jemmy MacFarlane's body was near rent in two! Who else?"

"Shush," warned Nick, afraid for Angus bursting a blood vessel in his indignation as well as waking Kestrel.

"Angus, did you get one word out of Kess?" whispered Meron in soothing tones.

"Nae, but there were the tracks of six shod horses where we found Jemmy, and there were six scalped Redcoats thirty miles south!" hissed the old man. "Put two and two together and what do you come up with, aye?" he added, thumping down a steaming plate of fish.

The three men ate in silence for a while.

"Angus, what did you mean when you said that's where the damage was done between mother and daughter?" asked Nick, washing down the succulent trout with fresh spring water.

"She wouldna say a word. There was Cameron out of her head wie worry. She had ridden this way and that like one possessed for days and Kess wouldna say a word. Wouldna even look at her. The wee lass was so mucky we could hardly tell who she was. Her puir hands were all cut and bleeding. Cameron tried to talk to her but the child ran. We followed her to the glen and that's where we found the three cairns. Cameron screamed and pulled down the third. She tried to take Kess back to the house but the child fought her and ran off. That night she built Rue's cairn again, and the next day Cameron took it down and so it went. Kess refused to talk about what she had seen. Cameron and Rowan rode off to every Indian village they knew, trying to find Rue, but they found nothing."

Nick stared out of the open door across the lake to the wilderness that surrounded them on every side. Out there a child had been lost for three and a half years. He shook his head in defeat.

"I find it hard to believe that she can still be living. Miracles can happen, I grant you, but even if she had been found and taken care of what would your chances be of finding her?"

"I can only try," answered Meron.

"Dinna ask Kess. If she couldna talk of it three years ago how do you expect her to now?" worried Angus. "You're a doctor, could it not hurt the lass more?"

"I dinna ken," Nick replied honestly. "Sometimes it eases to spit out certain things, sometimes it doesna. Is it possible she didna see her friend Jemmy raped but found the body after?"

Angus frowned, trying to remember.

"She used the words raped and dead but maybe she heard them from us because I dinna ken if the lass knew what rape was. But little pitchers have big ears and Kess was always listening."

"When did she use the words?" probed Meron.

"Later, much later. Nearly a year. Rowan left to join Sullivan against the Seneca. Cameron had dismantled the third cairn for the umpteenth time. The lass shouted 'Rue's raped dead.' Aye, that's how she put it. 'Raped dead'—just like that. Cameron tried to get her to tell her about it, but I really thought the lass was trying to tell her mother—''

"That she, Kestrel, was alive," supplied Nick and the old man nodded.

"They loved each other, but they had such stubborn tempers, such stubborn prideful tempers. Well, that's it. I'm worn out by the telling and the sadness of this day that has emptied out this house. Once this rambling place rang with laughter. So full of joy and love. Remember when it was just one room wie a sleeping loft?" Meron nodded.

"Then the bairns came along and we added room by room and stairs. Then come the war it slowly emptied, but we knew one day the war would be over and all the love and joy would return. . . . What happened?" he mourned, pouring himself more whiskey to drown his sorrow. "Two more cairns in the glen, and Alexander's heart as cold and hard as the stones. Wake me if you need anything," he muttered, pouring himself another generous helping of whiskey and making his way to his room at the back.

Meron looked at Nick's pensive face.

"What are you thinking about?"

"A long nap. Angus has a very good idea," he yawned, not wanting to say aloud a nagging thought. Where were the bodies of Jemmy and Goliath when twelve-year-old Kestrel was left alone?

"I suggest you sleep in there in case she takes it into her head to follow," said Meron, indicating the master bedroom where Kestrel slept. "Angus has imbibed quite a bit, and I am riding out for a few days to see what I can find out."

"Riding out?" repeated Nick in surprise.

"The trail may not be as cold as you think. The forest has many eyes," answered Meron, as he began packing a saddlebag with food.

Nick watched Meron ride out on his black and white pinto. If it wasn't for the bright green eyes, the man would appear as native to the wilderness as any Iroquois or Algonquian with his black long hair and leather clothes, he thought as he stood at the open door. It was barely noon and the day was clear and bright. He sat on the steps with his back braced against the wall thinking of the golden-haired girl who lay sleeping in the large bed. Whether he liked it or not, she was now his responsibility.

He sat lost in thought for a while before stretching and yawning. He had better sleep while he could, he decided, not knowing what he would have to face when Kestrel awakened. He shut the door and turned into the large central room. The fire was dying down in the hearth so he put on a healthy supply of wood before entering the room where Kestrel slept. Wearily he sat tugging off his boots before stretching out his long body thankfully on the large wide bed. He looked at Kestrel and then pulled her unresisting body into his arms, reasoning that if she tried to get off the bed he would be awakened. He closed his eyes and drifted off to sleep, happy with the comforting soft warmth that seemed to fit so perfectly into the hard curve of his belly.

CHAPTER SIX

Kestrel stirred and wriggled closer, pushing her bottom into the curve of Nick's belly. Half consciously he thrust against her, delighting in the warm sensations that started to build as his hands explored. Angus's lusty singing awoke him and he lay still remembering, still cupping Kestrel's soft breast. Feeling the erect nipple with his fingertip, he realized she was as aroused as he, although sound asleep. Carefully he backed away but Kestrel muttered and cuddled closer, holding his hand to her breast.

"Shush, everything's all right," soothed Nick, firmly removing his hand, determined to get out of the bed.

"No, no," protested Kestrel, turning over and flinging her arms about his chest. Nick sighed deeply and looked down at her flushed sleeping face nestled in the hollow of his shoulder. Gently he brushed some golden hair from her face and felt her brow. She was cool, he decided, trying to be a doctor and not a mere man as she curled one lithe leg around his upper thigh.

Kestrel's green eyes flew open.

"Good morning or afternoon or whatever," he said softly. Kestrel looked puzzled. She closed her eyes and burrowed her head into his shoulder. She felt safe and comfortable. She liked the musky, leathery smell of him. She opened her eyes again and smiled. Nick grinned back and kissed her nose as he sat up and gently pushed her back on the pillows. He swung his long legs over the side of the bed and stretched.

"Did you sleep with me?" questioned Kestrel. Nick nodded. "I liked it," she added.

"What?" frowned Nick, not quite sure what she meant.

"Sleeping with you. I liked sleeping with you," she explained dreamily.

"How do you feel?" asked Nick, determined to be the doctor. "Your head? Any dizziness?"

"No. Do you want to see my shoulder?" offered Kestrel, sitting up and unlacing her already open jerkin, exposing the rest of her breasts. Nick stifled a groan as she bared herself. Did she know what she was doing? he wondered.

Kestrel lay on her stomach so Nick could examine her shoulder. She pushed her breasts into the pillow, feeling her nipples tingle as his hand traced the scar on her back.

"It has healed well," Nick murmured and Kestrel rolled on her back and stared up at him. There was a long moment as their eyes met and Kestrel arched toward him, wanting to connect. Nick stood, knowing if he kissed her there would be no turning back.

"Let's see what Angus has for our supper," he suggested, determined to have a long cooling swim.

Kestrel watched him leave the room. She was confused. She slowly put on her jerkin and opened the shutters on the windows. It was sunset. The events of the day poured into her head. They had gone. Her brothers and father had left for Scotland. She sat silently for a while before going into the main room.

"How do you feel, Kessie lass?" clucked Angus.

"Confused," she answered honestly.

" 'Tis no wonder," soothed Angus.

"What happens to me now?"

"That you have to talk over wie Nick," answered the old man. "Where's he?"

"Went for a swim. I've water heating, so how about a nice hot bath? Aye, Kessie lass? Best cure in the world for the miseries," cajoled Angus.

"I don't have the miseries but I should have them, shouldn't I?" confessed Kestrel, trying to sort out what she felt.

"A good tot of whiskey'll cure most things," chuckled Angus, pouring some in a mug and some into his venison stew. "Here, my lass, I think you need this more'n me today," he added, pushing the drink toward her.

Kestrel took a long swallow and gasped. "It's horrid!"

"Gie it a minute. There now. Do you feel it?" He nodded yes to his own question and took a long pull on the jug himself. "Och, there's nothing like the glow in your belly from good Scotch whiskey."

A few minutes later Nick entered, bare-chested, rubbing his wet hair with a towel.

"Now there's another who could use a wee bit of warming up after a chilly swim," laughed Angus, pouring another mug.

"Something smells good," said Nick appreciatively, standing near the fire and sniffing the aroma of the stew.

"We are curing the megrims and miseries," chortled Angus. "A nice hot bath and dram or two of Scotch."

"I think it's a dram or two or more," laughed Nick.

Kestrel caught Nick's dark eyes smiling at her. She tilted her head to one side inquiringly at him, feeling shy. What else did she feel? she worried. She looked away.

"Where's Meron?" she asked, realizing that yet another member of her family was missing.

"He'll be back in a few days," answered Nick.

"Where did he go?" asked Angus. "And when?"

"At noon and I don't know where," evaded Nick, not wanting to mention Rue's name. He noticed a shadow cross Kestrel's face as her nostrils flared and she held out her mug to Angus, not able to drink the strong liquor.

"I'd go easy on the whiskey, you haven't eaten all day," Nick cautioned, thinking she wanted a refill.

"I can take care of myself," returned Kestrel, taking a sip. "Did he go to Scotland, too?" she challenged.

"Who?" queried Nick.

"My uncle!"

"I doubt if he could get to Scotland and back in a few days," answered Nick, sensing she was afraid. "He'd not leave you," he reassured.

"I don't care!" spat Kestrel, furious that he realized her vulnerability.

"Do you want to go to Scotland, Kess?" asked Nick softly, sitting beside her on the settle. Kestrel didn't answer. She stared down into the whiskey. "Do you?" repeated Nick. Kestrel felt tears well up within her, and not trusting her voice she drained her mug. "I asked you a question, Kestrel," pursued Nick. "Do you want to go to Scotland?" Why was the man torturing her? She seethed. "Because if you want to go, we'll go," continued Nick. Kestrel stared at him. "I don't go where I'm not wanted," she replied sharply before crossing to Angus. She held out her empty mug for a refill.

"No more before eating," ordered Nick.

Angus groaned and shook his head frantically at Nick. "Where's your sense? Now she'll drink us both under the table and eat nothing! Always contrary is Kestrel Sinclair!" roared Angus.

"I'd have to finish the jug to catch up wie you, Angus MacLeod," retorted Kestrel, snatching the jug from him.

"I said no more!"

Both Kestrel and Angus stared in astonishment at Nick whose voice was steely. Kestrel wavered. She looked at the jug in her hands and back to Nick's stern face. She felt fear and excitement. She wanted to dare him, challenge him. As she stood undecided, Nick strode over and took the jug from her. She raised her eyebrows at Angus and made a face.

"I didn't like it anyway!" she said matter-of-factly.

"I need another nap," yawned Angus. "Help yourselves to supper. *Bon appétit!*" he called as he staggered toward his back room.

Kestrel wished Angus had stayed as she felt uncomfortable alone with Nick. She sat silently watching him as he ladled out two bowls of stew and cut some bread.

"Are you angry with me?"

"And if I was?" answered Nick.

Kestrel shrugged.

"Would you mind?" he probed.

Kestrel shrugged again.

"I'd like an answer," he pursued.

"I don't know," replied Kestrel.

"I thought you rather liked to have people angry with you," said Nick, leaning back in his chair and staring intently at her.

"I don't want you angry with me," she said quietly, unable to look at him, so she didn't see his stern expression melt into a warm grin. "Well, not right now I don't," she amended and looked up in surprise at his sudden burst of laughter.

"I don't want you angry with me, either," he gasped when he could talk, noting how her eyes were flashing.

"I'm not angry. I'm worried," said Krestel after a long pause spent toying with the food on her plate, not quite knowing how to broach the subject of his promise to her mother.

"About what?"

"Me."

"There's nothing to worry about."

"How can you say that? My mother had no right to force you to take care of me!" she said savagely.

"She didn't force me."

"Just by being on her deathbed . . ."

"Don't," cautioned Nick softly, shaking his head at her bitterness.

"Don't what? Don't tell the truth?"

"Don't be so bitter and ugly, Kess," he said gently, stroking her cheek. Kestrel jerked away as if she was burned.

"Maybe I am bitter and ugly. And now you can be angry with me because I'm angry with you!"

"Why?"

"What's going to happen to me? Why won't you talk to me!" struggled Kestrel. "You don't have to feel obligated to my mother. She's dead. She won't know!"

"I don't feel obligated to your mother."

"You're lying!"

Nick's own fiery temper ignited. For several minutes there was seething silence as he glowered into Kestrel's stormy face.

"I am obligated to myself. I made a promise and have my honor," he informed her, his voice dangerously low.

"What about *my* honor? What about my *pride*?" howled the girl.

Nick nodded. "You're right," he answered. "It must feel as if you're being disposed of."

"Aye," she spat, her green eyes flashing.

"Am I such an unappealing specimen?" asked Nick dryly.

Kestrel frowned, not understanding his sudden change.

"Well, look at me." He stood holding his arms away from his tall rangy body and turning around in front of her. "Am I such a poor choice? My pride is sorely wounded!"

"Don't make fun!"

"What would you have me do? Cry and beat my breast?"

"Go back to wherever you came from and leave me be!" yelled Kestrel, heading for the door.

"No, Kess! Don't run away! You're not a coward," he cautioned and she turned, bewildered. "Come here," he said softly, opening his arms to her. "Are you afraid?" he challenged as she stood poised, one hand still reaching for the door latch.

"I'm afraid," she stated.

"You slept in these arms a short while ago," coaxed Nick.

Kestrel wavered. One part of her wanted the safety of his arms and the other part wanted the safety of the forest.

"God damn it, come here!" roared Nick forcefully and to his great surprise Kestrel obeyed. She walked toward him until she stood just out of reach of his open arms. Her eyes were wide with fear.

"Are you afraid of me, Kestrel?" he asked wonderingly. She didn't answer but stood poised for flight like some young wild animal trusting a human for the first time. Nick dropped his hands to his sides and leaned back against the wall, keeping his dark eyes on her. What a strange mixture she was. One minute a hot-blooded tigress and the next a timid faun.

Kestrel stared back at his dark handsome face, afraid and excited.

"Kess, I want your promise that you'll not disappear without telling me where you're going and how long you'll be," said Nick softly. But Kestrel made no sign she had heard. "Do you hear me?"

"*I* don't make promises," replied Kestrel cuttingly, as her temper started to rise. Nick's eyes narrowed at her mercurial change, and he grasped her wrist as she turned away from him.

"You are determined to have my anger, aren't you?"

Kestrel tried to pull away but he also grasped her other wrist, forcing her to face him. She stared into his searing dark eyes and at his firm lips, hiding her apprehension with a look of fury.

"You want anger, then be brave enough to stay and face it!"

Kestrel closed her eyes. "I don't know what I want," she said sadly. Nick looked at her drawn face and dropped her wrists. She opened her eyes and gazed at him, confused by his apparent surrender. Nick groaned at her wide-eyed, innocent look. He shook his head, not knowing how to deal with her.

"Kess, it's been a long day. A lot has happened. It's small wonder you're bewildered," he said tiredly. "We don't have to solve anything today or tomorrow. I just wish you'd give me some reassurance that you won't disappear. With or without my horse," he added with a wry smile.

Kestrel gave him a long enigmatic look and then started cleaning up the food from the table. She was tired and needed to still her worried brain. The heat of the house made her sticky and uncomfortable, seeming to aggravate her many anxieties. She needed to get out in the cool night air to clear her head.

Nick sat drowsily watching and let out an oath as she opened the door and fleetly vanished into the darkness. He stood up and went to the open door, debating whether to run after her. Instead, he slammed it shut and sat down again by the fire with the whiskey jug. Maybe it would be best for both of them if she did just disappear. It would be the answer, he decided, and wondered why he felt a dull ache at the prospect.

Kestrel dived into the icy water and swam briskly across the lake, her rhythmic strokes lulling and numbing her seething thoughts. After a while she floated on her back, staring up at the starlit sky until the cold started to cramp her muscles. Back on shore she was loath to put on her dirty clothes. Bundling them in her arms, she ran back to the house.

Nick started as the door slammed shut and Kestrel raced across the room to stand next to the fire, her golden skin goosebumped. She dropped her clothes in a heap and reached above her head for a warm towel. Nick watched the naked girl, not sure if he was awake or asleep. She was absolutely exquisite from the top of her head to the bottom of her graceful feet. The firelight played along the length of her lithe young body, the flame's reflection seeming to lick and enhance each curve. She dried her hair briskly, each movement thrusting her firm young breasts upward. There was no coyness or embarrassment: she was perfectly natural in her nakedness. Why did that surprise him? he wondered.

Kestrel stopped toweling her hair and looked at him. She frowned, puzzled at his intensity. "Are you angry because I didn't tell you where I was going?" she challenged. Nick silently shook his head and slowly stood. Kestrel suddenly felt very shy as she followed the direction of his searing gaze and her eyes dropped to her breasts. Nick walked purposefully toward her.

"You know what you want now, don't you?" he asked huskily.

Kestrel wished he would hold her instead of standing two feet away. She stared at him, unable to say anything as her body pulsated with anticipation. She arched her breasts slightly toward him but Nick stood still.

"Touch me," she whispered. "Touch me here." She stroked her nipples so they hardened. "Sleep with me again," she begged.

Nick kissed her, savoring the moment as he ran his hands down the silky length of her, but Kestrel thrust urgently against him, her body aching with passion.

"Slow down, Kess," he urged, unable to remove his clothes. "We have all night, there's no big race," he teased as she writhed against him. He pushed her back on the fur rug in front of the fire, determined to set his own pace. He wanted to slowly explore every part of her. Kestrel moaned, trying to connect to him, her mouth seeking his, her pelvis thrusting upward toward him. Nick gave up trying to undress as he cupped each buttock in his large hands and pressed her to him.

Kestrel thrust against his hardness, thinking she would go insane with the pleasure. Nick thought he would go insane with frustration as he was unable to release himself. Let her have her pleasure and then he would have his, he resolved as she strained against him in climax.

Minutes later Nick frowned at the flushed naked girl who cuddled sleepily in the crook of his arm.

"Kess?"

"Um?" she sighed contentedly. "I liked that." Nick lay back looking at the ceiling, not sure what to make of the turn of events.

"I think you should go to bed," he ventured.

"But we're sleeping together," protested Kestrel, snuggling up to him like a small child.

"Kestrel? Kestrel, sit up," he ordered, and she groggily obeyed, smiling. "Put something on or you'll get a chill," he said, distracted by her tumbled golden nakedness.

"Kestrel?" He stood and took a deep breath.

"Are you angry again?"

"Kess?" he started, again trying to avoid her wide innocent eyes. "Are you innocent?" He grabbed onto the word that popped into his mind.

"Of what?" she asked defensively.

"Have you ever been with a man before?"

"Been where?" answered Kestrel, getting very bewildered.

"Slept with a man before," struggled Nick.

Kestrel shook her head, her eyes confused and troubled.

"What's wrong?"

"Nothing," comforted Nick huskily, his groin aching.

"Don't treat me like a child!" spat Kestrel, her mood changing to anger as she became afraid. She had felt safe and at home in Nick's strong arms, her body alive and warm.

"I assure you, Kestrel, I don't think of you as a child," laughed

Nick harshly, knowing she was without doubt the most beautiful woman he had ever seen.

"Tell me what is wrong then, instead of lying!" she challenged.

"What we just did?" he began, indicating the fur rug and her. She nodded, listening intently.

"What was that?" he probed. Kestrel shrugged. "What do you call it?" he pursued.

"I don't know. What do you call it?" she answered.

"Lovemaking," he started to explain and she grinned broadly and then frowned when he didn't respond.

"Oh, because you don't love me—"

"It has nothing to do with that," interrupted Nick.

"You don't have to love me," started Kestrel. "I don't care!"

"Well, I do care," returned Nick, his voice deepening as he realized the depths of his feelings. He gazed at her standing with her hands on her hips in all her golden naked glory and grinned. "I do care. So come here, you impossible not-a-child! I am certainly not going to be bored married to you, my love," he chuckled, picking her up and swinging her around in his arms as he laughed at the top of his voice.

Kestrel wrapped her arms about his neck and laughed too, not wanting to question anything because everything felt perfectly right.

"What's all this ruckus?" growled a tipsy, gruff voice and Angus stood in the doorway, his blunderbuss in hand, frowning at the dark, bare-chested young man carrying the golden naked girl. "Where's your clothes, lass? You'll catch your death!" he fussed.

"We just made love!" stated Kestrel proudly, which sent Nick into whoops of laughter. Angus smiled seeing the two happy faces.

"Aye, it is time for the grieving to end and the living to continue," he approved before shuffling back to bed.

CHAPTER SEVEN

Kestrel awoke as bright sunlight poured through the window and across the bed. She lay with her eyes closed, feeling the golden warmth surge through her, blending with a deep joyful happiness. She had experienced a strange mixture of fear and excitement the first time she had looked into Nick's dark eyes—as though she knew her life would be woven with his. Now she opened her eyes expecting to see him beside her but the bed was empty and cold. She lay still and listened but heard no sounds except for the squabbling and chattering of the busy springtime birds as they built their nests in the eaves of the house. She swung her legs over the side of the bed and stretched, eager to start the day. It had been so long since she had been truly happy, she thought, as she fleetly raced up the stairs to her own room to dress. For a moment she felt a sharp pang as she thought of her mother, but she thrust it aside and tugged on trousers and a shirt and ran out barefoot, eager to find Nick.

It was a glorious day and every living thing seemed as happy as she was. The leaf buds had burst on the trees, and small delicate wildflowers bloomed, scenting the air. Seeing no sign of Nick by the lake, she made her way to the barn. She pushed open the door and peered into the gloom, seeing little blobs of light dancing in the dark from the bright sunshine. She heard the low rumble of voices and crept quietly in to surprise them.

"If three people couldn't find a trace then what can Meron expect to find now?" asked Nick as he raked the soiled straw into a pile.

"Meron can go where others canna. He was like Pontiac's own son. Rode on the chief's left-hand side, you know," boasted Angus.

"Pontiac is long dead," protested Nick.

"But not Meron's alliance wie the Ottawas," stated the old man. "I wouldna dare set a foot near the Maumee for fear of losing this beautiful head of grizzled locks, but Meron is welcome everywhere. If he'd been here when it all happened we'd have the lass safe."

Kestrel lost her sunny mood as she stepped out of the shadows.

"What lass safe?" she asked sharply.

"Good morning, sweetheart," grinned Nick. "Why the long face?"

"What are you two talking about?" demanded Kestrel, ignoring the fluttering of her heart at his endearment.

"Meron," answered Angus gruffly, giving Nick a warning glare.

"What about him?" snapped Kestrel, catching the look and feeling her temper rise.

"Canna we men have some talk wie out some little snippet listening in?" roared Angus, furious at her rude tone.

"Where has my uncle gone?"

"To London to visit the queen. So sheathe your claws!" growled Angus. "Go and make yourself useful. We need some fish." Nick leaned on his rake, watching the exchange between Kestrel and Angus.

"Why won't you tell me?" shouted Kestrel, furious.

"Because 'tis none of your business!" roared the old man.

"Then I'll ride after him and find out for myself!"

"Why are you just standing there letting 'your responsibility' be disrespectful to her elders and betters?" hollered Angus to Nick. "Get her out of here before I burst a blood vessel," he added.

"His responsibility? I'm not his responsibility!" howled Kestrel.

"Aye, you are, my lass," stated Nick, picking her up in his arms and striding out of the barn. Kestrel kicked and struggled, but Nick was too strong for her. He strode out into the bright sunlight.

"Put me down," she hissed.

"Let's start this morning again."

"Put me down!"

"No," replied Nick gently. "You shouldn't be so rude to Angus. He was only trying to protect you."

"Don't tell me what to do!"

"I will," stated Nick, setting her on her feet. "And you will listen," he demanded, holding her small chin in his large hand, forcing her to look up at him. "Meron has gone to look for your sister."

Kestrel paled and fear flooded in as the fateful sound of the rifle shot through her. A nightmarish panic filled her and she wanted to hit out. Nick noticed her clenched fists.

"Let me go," she whispered. Nick shook his head and she swung at him. He grabbed her fists.

"That's why Angus wouldn't tell you. He knew you'd behave like this. Now we are going to talk about it. Remember it's what you wanted. Meron has ridden out to see if he can find any news of your sister Rue."

"Let's start the morning again, please?" pleaded Kestrel, wanting to block her ears, but he held her hands.

Nick stared down into her frightened face. "Sometimes it's best to try and talk about it," he murmured.

"Talk about what?"

"About what happened to Goliath, Jemmy, and Rue."

Kestrel shook her head violently, her green eyes wide and haunted. She didn't understand the frightening feelings that coursed through her body. In her mind's eye she saw her mother's face twisted and distorted, shouting at her, Cameron's saliva spitting and pitting Kess's skin as she was shaken and shaken until her teeth rattled.

"I don't know. I don't know what you want me to say!" she shouted. Nick frowned as he realized she wasn't talking to him but was back somewhere in the past.

"It's all right," he soothed, trying to take her in his arms but she pulled free and headed toward the house. Nick made no attempt to stop her. He watched her wild flight, his eyes dark and troubled.

Kestrel reached the house and slowed to a walk, trying to unjumble her turbulent feelings.

"Kessie lass?" called Angus as he trudged from the barn toward her. She looked up and just wanted to be alone to sort herself out. She made no sign that she had heard as she skirted the house and ran into the thick forest. She walked slowly through the filtered light, lost in her thinking.

What was it that pounded her heart in fear every time her sister's name was mentioned? Each time it made her want to hit out and hurt something, someone, anything. She breathed deeply and sadly remembered the happy golden beginning of the day. Nick, she thought, and smiled softly. She would calm herself and return to his arms. Why couldn't the ghosts of the past be buried? she wondered sorrowfully. Why couldn't she just feel glad to be alive without feeling guilty about her sister? Once again she felt the torments from three years ago pound through her. She broke out of the dark woods and stared in surprise at the small sunlit glen with the two new cairns marking two more graves. She walked toward the two new mounds and sat quietly stroking the rough side of the piled stones.

"Ven?" she whispered to her older brother Raven. "Can you hear me?" Her eyes filled with tears and she started to sob. "I waited for you and you never came home to me. I waited because I knew you and Lynx would understand but you never came back and Lynx went away again." Kestrel was swept by the storm of tears that shook her small body. She had waited for her older brothers' return with every fiber of her young being; had held herself together through a lonely time knowing that they would understand and help her. "You would have been able to tell Mother," she cried and looked toward the other new cairn through streaming eyes. "Now Mother won't ever understand." She wept anew, for the first time really grieving for her mother and brother.

Angus watched Nick pace as the day wore on and there was no sign of Kestrel.

"She'll be back today, tomorrow . . . next week." He gave up trying to comfort. "I told you not to bring up the subject!" he shouted.

"Aye, so you did!"

"Dinna agree wie me, I need a good fight!" yelled Angus.

"So that's who she gets it from!" returned Nick.

"Gets what from?"

"The need for a good fight," snapped Nick, exasperated.

"Maybe she's not off in a snit but off about her business," thought Angus aloud, rubbing his stubbled chin.

"What business?"

"Like the time she took off for a couple of weeks wie yer horse," explained Angus.

"Where are the horses? They weren't stabled?" questioned Nick.

"Up in the pasture," said Angus, waving a vague hand.

"What business?" pursued Nick, determined to pin down the elusive old man. "Angus, as you so aptly put it this morning, Kestrel is *my* responsibility. Not for any other eason except I chose her to be. Do you ken?"

"Well, let's see if there are signs," relented the old man, hurrying out of the house.

"What signs," questioned Nick as he followed.

" 'Tis a lonely life out here in the wilderness for young ones," puffed Angus as they climbed through the woods up the steep side of a mountain. "Young Ven and Lynx had each other, being twins, and Rowan and Rue sort of paired off, which left Kestrel alone. She found her own friends in the Indian villages. I swear they dinna ken if she's lass or lad," he chortled. "Well, she dinna take your horse, she took mine," he mourned.

"What signs?"

"If the young braves plan a raid they leave signs."

"You can read such signs?" asked Nick.

"Aye, if she's left them. They'll be near the burial glen. The young braves don't venture too near the house."

"Raid on what?" probed Nick as they trudged through the forest toward the glen.

"British supply wagons or some such thing."

"She could get killed!" exclaimed Nick.

"Aye, but she hasn't."

"I just might kill her myself when she gets back," retorted Nick, his lean face set in uncompromising lines.

"Aye, the laddies come for her," nodded Angus as he stiffly stood and brushed the dust off his knees. Nick stared down at the sticks and pebbles.

"Well, what does it say?"

"Canna tell, she's messed it up." Angus shrugged. "Just have to wait. She'll come back when she's good and ready. Always does," he rambled, observing the angry look in Nick's dark eyes.

Kestrel forgot all her worries as she rode across the plain with the wind whirling her hair and the horse's thundering hooves exhilarating her blood. She kept pace with the five lithe young Indians as they urged their steeds competitively, laughing aloud like very small children. Kestrel was older than three of the youths, but they were all taller and stronger than she. All except Small Arm still bore their childhood names, not having earned, by good fortune or bad, a permanent one of their own. Small Arm rode side by side with her, his strong white teeth gleaming in his brown face as he grinned with the thrill of the wild race across the grassland. His arm had been broken several years before and had not grown as rapidly as the rest of his body. Kestrel grinned back at him, glad that she would have her own name for always. She looked up to the sky, hoping to see her namesake circling easily on the wind currents. Cameron had named her the Indian way, named her for the first thing she saw. A circling hawk. The six young riders slowed their pace and Kestrel felt a grim foreboding. If she had to earn her adult name, what would it be, she wondered, knowing she had been a bitter disappointment to her parents. Sister Killer, She Who Runs Away, Mother's Pain, all these shameful names flashed into her head, and she kicked her heels into her horse's heaving sides and tried to race her panic away.

A sudden shout stopped her headlong rush, and she reined the exhausted horse and looked with surprise into White Otter's worried face.

"What is it?" she asked and followed his gaze to a large black bird. Omen circled and landed heavily on Kestrel's shoulder, nearly knocking her off the horse. She forced herself to sit erect despite the large bird's weight.

"Where've you been, Omen?" she asked as the raven cocked his head to one side and looked with black beady eyes at the awed young Indians. "I haven't seen you since . . ." She trailed off, realizing she hadn't seen the bird since the night her mother died. A grim sense of foreboding increased within her and she stared around at the braves' incredulous expressions. Her mother Cameron had been a legend much as her uncle Meron still was among the native people. Much of this fame came from the presence of Omen, the giant bird of creation who guarded the green-eyed twins. Kestrel grinned proudly, enjoying the honor the bird's attendance was bestowing upon her. He had never adopted any of the children until right now, she acknowledged. For the last few years as her Tuscarora friends, younger and older, grew taller and stronger than she, they had gloated in their superiority even though she could throw a knife and shoot as straight if not straighter than most of them. Now she preened despite the sharp talons that bit into her still tender shoulder, feeling she had a definite advantage.

The pack of them galloped across the plain as the tender green leaves of grass and trees thrust lustily in the fertile spring, and at sunset they met up with three older braves whom she had never seen before and made camp, waiting for the supply train due for Fort Detroit. Kestrel felt her unease increase as she looked at the faces of the three strange braves. She shook her head, knowing she had no reason to be suspicious. She had been riding out with Short Arm and the Tuscarora for three years and this was the usual way of doing things. She sat apart, not enjoying the camaraderie around the campfire as she stared at the raven's black eyes and thought of Nick's dark gaze and hard body. As the moon rose, she snuggled down on the cold ground, wishing she had had time to properly prepare herself for the raid. She had been so relieved to have an excuse to avoid facing her own dilemma and Nick that upon hearing her Indian friend's call she had caught Angus's horse and had ridden out barefoot. Now, as she wrapped her own arms around her chilled body, she relived Nick's declaration of love as he held her high in his arms.

Nick was furious. Night had fallen, black and relentless. No moon or star pierced the dark cloud covering. He sat by the smoldering fire in the main room, listening to the nocturnal cries of the predators and Angus's rumbling snores.

What was the matter with him? he wondered as he stood and paced, unable to remain still. Why did he feel so strongly about a totally undisciplined female? He strove for sanity as he tried to understand the rapid turn of events that had brought him to his third sleepless night in a row. Good Samaritan, he cursed himself inwardly. He had escorted home a young soldier and fallen in love with the boy's even younger sister. Love? The first thing the brat had done was shoot at him! What the hell did he know of love, anyway? He poured himself a stiff drink and sat trying to remember his past loves, trying to picture all the tempting, lush bodies he had caressed and thrust into, but he could conjure up no image except a tousled golden one—and that one he hadn't been able to thrust into. For heaven's sake, he was nearly twenty-six years old, an educated man, a doctor, not some callow youth. Yet, painfully aware of every different sound in the night, he waited for Kestrel's return.

Kestrel slept very little. The night's impenetrable darkness and the presence of Omen disturbed her. As the first fingers of dawn pierced the eastern horizon, she sat shivering in the half light that made everything on earth seem grim and inhospitable. Not even a hint of the vibrant spring colors showed forth, just interminable grays, dismal and deathlike. The watery sun climbed higher, melting the cold shroud, but Kestrel still felt weighted down with foreboding. She mounted up, unable to share the excitement of her eager companions. She rode along numbly lost in her own thoughts, her usually keen senses dulled. A sudden sharp shot cracked the stillness and her horse reared, screaming in agony and throwing Kestrel clear of its thrashing hooves. For a moment she lay with the breath knocked out of her, hearing the horrible confusion of screams and shots before scrambling under the cover of some thick bushes. She peered out horrified at her poor horse who still screamed out in pain, unable to regain its legs. She had to put it out of its misery. She lay on her stomach and shimmied forward so she could get a good shot at the suffering animal. The noise of battle stopped and she froze. All that ripped through the stark silence was the panic-stricken screams of her horse. Carefully she eased back on her haunches, peering above the underbrush but not seeing anything through the morning mist and gunpowder smoke except the muted lines of the thrashing animal. She knelt, her eyes glued to the vague star on the steed's forehead. She squeezed the trigger and there was a double report. As her bullet struck true, putting the roan out of misery, another grazed a stinging path along her side. She fell forward, digging her face into the sharp blades of grass and pretending to be dead. She lay, her heart pounding painfully, her ear pressed to the ground, listening. All was still, a deathly hush; she strained, trying to hear the slightest reverberation through the firm cold earth, but nothing moved. Kestrel lay still, sensing that something—or someone—was watching and waiting. It seemed like eternity. She felt exposed and vulnerable, facedown in the dirt, unable to see. Suddenly there was another exchange of gunfire, and she felt a deadly thud reverberate and the vibrations of approaching hooves. A hoarse cawing joined the hoofbeats and Omen's heavy body landed on her back and he started pecking at her hair. The horses stopped barely short of stepping on her; she could feel and smell the heat of them. She forced her breathing to be shallow.

"Carrion's feeding on this halfbreed," snarled a voice and the horses were wheeled away. Still, Kestrel lay hearing the hooves fade into the distance. Omen's weight ached her shoulder and she wondered if the old bird was asleep. He had saved her life, she thought, as she silently thanked him. After what seemed an hour, Kestrel decided to move, hoping the raven would warn her of any danger. Very slowly she lifted her head and the bird rubbed his glossy feathers against her cheek. She pulled her aching body into a sitting position and scanned around, seeing nothing except the peaceful misty countryside. Carefully she stood and gasped as a sharp pain knifed through her waist. Blood seeped and ran a warm river down her stomach. Gingerly she felt inside her clothes and traced the path of the bullet. She sighed with relief to find the searing gouge and not a hole with the metal still lodged within her. She looked around, sadly seeing Angus's roan horse and wondered how she was ever going to explain it to the old man. She groaned as she made her way uphill, feeling that every bone in her body was bruised. Reaching the top, she gasped, horrified, as she saw the outlines of several bodies in the long grass. Dropping to her knees she felt White Otter's cheek. It was still warm but no pulse beat in his neck or wrist. Small Arm lay on his back, his brown eyes staring lifelessly at the sky. As she examined her five friends, Kestrel's tears streamed down their still faces and smeared their leather shirts.

Kestrel sat on the crest of the hill dazed as she stared down at the terrible carnage. Suddenly she froze. Not far below her and within earshot was a Redcoat patrol, and with them the three strange Indians that had met with them the night before. They were Tuscarora—she could tell from their clothing—and she wondered now what village they were from. The three Indians had rounded up the frightened horses and they and the soldiers seemed to be waiting for something. The supply wagons, she remembered, as she heard the heavy rumbling. Kestrel seethed at the cheerful laughter as the Redcoats recounted their victorious morning, and the added merriment of the traitorous Indians as they were given the ponies from their fallen brothers along with some guns. The wagons, escorted by happy soldiers, proceeded on to Fort Detroit, and the three Indians galloped back toward the Tuscarora village, leading the riderless ponies.

Kestrel stood stiffly and looked down again at her five dead friends before stoically starting her long trek home.

CHAPTER EIGHT

"Four days!"

"Aye, I can count," snapped Angus sarcastically as he watched Nick's steely expression. "There's no point worrying, she'll come back when she's good and ready and not before. Better get used to it."

"I'll not get used to it!" replied Nick, his voice dangerously low.

"Then you'll have to change it," said Angus cryptically. "Heaven be praised! Here's some relief from your dark glowering. Meron's back!" rejoiced the old man, wiping his floury hands and walking heavily down the steps into the bright sunshine.

"You're a sight for sore eyes, Meron lad," he chortled, holding the pinto's bridle as Meron lithely dismounted. "Here, Nick, take care of the horse—it'll keep your mind busy for a while," Angus added, handing Nick the reins and bustling Meron into the house.

"You'd better be hungry as I've been on a cooking spree," he chattered.

"Aye, and tired," answered Meron. "How's Kess?"

"I dinna want to hear that one's name for a while. I'm fair sick of it," grouched Angus and Meron laughed.

"She must be better and no worse for that bump on her head," he said, stretching his aching body before sitting.

"Well, what did you find out?" questioned Angus eagerly as he piled the table with cakes, breads, biscuits, and pies.

"Are you expecting company, old man?" asked Meron, raising an eyebrow at all the food and grinning at Nick who entered.

"Just keeping myself busy. Anything so I dinna have to look at that brooding black Scot!" snapped Angus.

"Any news?" asked Nick.

"Nothing to really put any hopes up. The Ottawas talk of some renegades who were killed by some French about the same time," recounted Meron as he ate.

"What has that to do wie anything?" objected Angus impatiently.

"The renegades had British guns and light scalps. European scalps. It may mean nothing at all except they were in this vicinity at the right time," mused Meron as he methodically chewed.

"The French, were they trappers, what?" questioned the old man.

"Seems it was a mixture, traders and a priest. They were attacked about forty miles southeast of here. There was a fight."

"And the French took the prisoners that the renegades held?" supplied Angus impatiently as Meron ate and drank.

"There was no specific descriptions of the prisoners except they were Indian females," choked Meron, swallowing too quickly.

"But Rue's not Indian," worried Angus, thumping Meron on the back.

"To a French priest wie her long black hair and way of dress . . ." explained Meron.

"Aye," rejoiced Angus. "Then where's the mission? Mount Royal? Quebec?"

"Apparently they were heading south not north." It was Angus's turn to choke as his whiskey went down the wrong way.

"South? There's no French-Catholic missions south!"

"There's a mission in Bethlehem, Pennsylvania, but it's neither Catholic nor French," informed Nick. " 'Tis a strange Protestant sect. Moravian, I think 'tis called."

"Well, let's think on it. I need to sleep," yawned Meron.

"Was that all you were able to find out?" fretted Angus. "What's happening wie the war? Was there talk of Alexander and the boys getting through to—" he babbled.

"Aye," laughed Meron. "Alexander and the boys had safe passage through Ottawa land thanks to Lynx's distinctive coloring so like my own." He fell silent for a moment, thinking of the youth who was as close as a son to him. "Of the war, 'tis over except for the signing of a treaty. Five young Tuscarora braves were killed by Redcoats. 'Tis said they were waiting to ambush a supply train for Fort Detroit," he recounted sadly and started when Nick stood up and his hard fist punched the table, causing the food to wobble precariously and the drinks to slop.

"What the hell?" yelled Meron, jumping up, staring first at Nick's chiseled face, then into Angus's gaping old one.

"Where?" breathed Nick, a cold knife turning in his guts.

"What is this?" demanded Meron.

"Where were they killed?"

Meron grabbed Nick's lapels and the two men stared hostilely at each other.

"Kestrel!" stated Meron, seeing the anguish deep in Nick's black eyes. Nick nodded, unable to speak. "Sit down," ordered the older man, pushing him down and prying his hands off him.

"She wasn't there," he said quietly.

"How do you know?" fretted Angus.

"Her body wasn't there," rephrased Meron, conscious of the searing black eyes pinned to him.

"When did it happen?" asked Nick quietly.

"Three days ago. I was at their village last night. Now why do you think Kess was there?"

"She rode out wie them four days ago," intoned Angus. "I should have known. A braw Scot like you doesna fret and fash for nothing," he mourned. "Have you the sight?"

Nick shook his head impatiently. "I'm not going to sit discussing the sight or whether a girl probably three years dead is in an Indian mission when a very alive one is probably screaming for help as she seems to have done for the past three years!" he roared.

"Come on," said Meron, standing. "Angus, stay here in case she comes home," he added as Nick strode out of the house and headed for the barn. Meron reached the door and turned back and looked at the old man tenderly.

"It seems my sister's faith in young MacKay was well founded," he murmured before hurrying after the impatient man.

* * *

Kestrel stood at the edge of the forest as Nick and Meron galloped off in the opposite direction. She smiled slightly before taking a deep breath in order to stagger the remaining half mile to the house. She was beyond pain; she didn't feel anything. Her purpose was to reach the wooden house she now looked upon. The smoke curled from the chimney, and the lake winked in the sunlight. She fell and the new spring grass felt cool and soft against her hot dry skin. She rubbed her burning face into the sweet greenness and breathed deeply of the rich fresh scent. In just a moment she would get up and walk some more, she decided, allowing her aching body to relax for the first time in three days. The raven roosted, his hard eyes trained on her.

Hours later as the sun set, a light rain started to fall and Kestrel curled herself into a ball, trying to stay warm. The soft grass that had caressed her burning skin like velvet now stung and cut deeply into her muscles and bones until she whimpered protestingly. The raven cawed loudly and flapped on heavy wet wings toward the house as the hounds in the barn joined in with their howling.

Angus shuddered as he stirred and tasted, unable to keep still. He swore as he heard the dogs yelping in the barn and cursed the racoon or skunk that was disturbing them.

"Early for the wolves," he muttered, a sudden fear shooting through him. He rushed to the heavy wooden door and tore it open. He stood heedless of the rain as he strained his ears. Out of the gray twilight flew the raven and Angus instantly knew that Kestrel was near. He ran as fast as his old enormous frame could go and unhooked the door of the barn releasing the dogs. He grabbed a lantern and followed their mournful baying across the wide meadow and through the shallows of the lake, not minding the drenching he was receiving.

"Where are you?" he gasped, out of breath but trying to hear beyond the pounding of his own heart. The desperate howling of animals in the distance caused adrenaline to pump through his overtired old body. "Where are you?" he lamented, unable to see as the now-fierce rain and howling wind doused his light. A hoarse cawing stilled his panic and he followed the rushing of the bird's great wet wings.

"Oh, my puir lass," he wept as he knelt in the grass and pulled Kestrel's relatively minuscule frame to his large one. Easily he picked her up and cradled her in his enormous arms, holding her close to his massive chest as he made his way blindly through the teeming rain back to the house. "Light as a feather you always was. I remember holding you in my hands fresh from the womb. No bigger than my palm, were you," he wept, terrified at the cold touch of her skin. A couple of times he tripped, staggered, and nearly fell but by some miracle regained his balance with his precious burden. He splashed thankfully through the shallow water of the lake as he saw the lights of the house through the driving storm. "Not far now, Kessie lass," he comforted, hoping his poor heart could take the strain as pain shot through his chest and arms.

Angus forced one leg after the other to mount the steps toward the open kitchen door. Reaching the top he swayed and leaned back, bracing himself against the doorway as he fought to stay conscious. He stared blearily around the kitchen, seeing the puddle on the floor, which rippled as the wind blew violent gusts. With a tremendous effort he kicked the thick wooden door shut behind him. Angus fixed his eyes on the fur rug in front of the open hearth and made his way laboriously to it. He sank to his knees, feeling the muscles in his back scream in protest as his heart pumped valiantly, sending shock waves to every corner of his being. Waves of blackness engulfed the old man as he laid Kestrel on the rug before the fire. He resisted, resting his great weight on one arm so as not to crush her inert body, and then slowly collapsed until he curled around her, cradling her with his warm girth.

Meron and Nick cursed the driving rain that washed away any trail that they could possibly have followed. Soaking and both wrapped in their own silences, they rode back to the house. As they neared they heard strange eerie howling and, both realizing it wasn't wolves, kicked their horses into frenzied gallops and raced toward the curious lamenting. The men threw themselves off their mounts, leaving them in the pouring rain as they raced splashing and slipping up the wooden steps into the house.

For a split second both men stood poised staring at the scene before their eyes. Wee Angus lay before the fire on the fur rug cradling the slight body of Kestrel.

Nick took one look at the bluish tinge on Angus's lips and immediately set to work feeling for vital signs.

"Meron, get the wet clothes off her and check her for wounds. Get her warm!" he ordered, wishing it were he tending to the bedraggled limp girl as he started to work on the old man.

Over an hour later Meron and Nick looked at each other, nodded, and sank exhausted onto the settle by the fire.

"Both alive," croaked Nick, his eyes flooding with tears.

"Aye," sighed Meron, his cheeks wet with unchecked relief. "I'll get us sustenance," he offered, getting the whiskey jug and a loaf of Angus's bread. Nick drank deeply, unable to stay away from Kestrel now that Angus was out of danger. He stood, unable to speak for a few seconds. He nodded toward the large master bedroom where a fire blazed merrily.

"Aye, she's your lass now," grinned Meron wearily, understanding the younger man's need and closing heavy eyelids that hadn't rested for over forty-eight hours.

"He has to be watched constantly," rasped Nick, looking toward Angus's room. "Any change in his breathing or heartbeat, you maun call," he explained, falling into Scottish dialect.

"I ken more than you know," reassured Meron, raising his protesting body from the comfort of the settle and walking toward the back rooms.

Nick stood at the doorway watching Kestrel sleep. She seemed so serene and unaware of the disturbance she had caused that for a moment rage coursed through him and he felt like picking her up and shaking her. His heart went out to Angus who lay critically ill, and he was filled with anger that Kestrel didn't realize that the old man had risked his life for her. He sat on the edge of the bed and stared at her beautiful face. Noticing its lack of tranquillity, however, made his fury fall away. Her mouth was slightly open, the lower lip tremulous, her nostrils flared, and under her closed eyelids was frantic movement. Beneath the blankets her body twitched, not relaxing at all. He eased himself onto the bed and took her stiff form into his arms. She gasped and went rigid. Unable to take Meron's hurried words for the extent of her injuries, he drew the covers away and stared down at the naked gold body. An ugly bullet furrow sliced her side, from belly button to waist at the right, and her body was black and blue from countless bruises. Meron was right. Her injuries, though painful, were not severe. The wounds to her already sorely abused mind might be quite another matter, he worried as he gently covered her and watched the warm firelight play across her golden features.

He dozed, starting awake every few minutes or so as Kestrel tossed and turned, reliving the horror of her friends' death. At a certain point Meron tiptoed in and, leaving the green-eyed man to watch his niece, he quietly examined the old man whose color had lost its bluish tinge.

"I think they're both very lucky," remarked Meron as they took a break and drank coffee in an attempt to keep their exhausted bodies awake.

"And so are we," rejoiced Nick, a mischievous twinkle cracking his usually enigmatic stern features as he remembered the last time he checked Kestrel and her healthy young body arched toward him, her nipples erect and demanding. He chuckled, unable to share his relief and amusement with Meron as it seemed too personal in nature and his natural reticence forbade such confidences.

"Maybe we should change patients," suggested Meron, keeping his face absolutely straight. Nick frowned at him and Meron looked him full in the face. "Well, should we change?" he asked, unable to resist Nick's incredulous expression. Meron had removed his niece's clothes, and for a moment he felt a hollow sadness as he remembered his own young love.

"I loved truly only once. Loved against reason with every fiber of myself," he confessed. "It was long ago. I wasn't even fifteen and yet I was a father for a very little time. My wife died giving birth to a son. They were buried together. With Little Fox everything was wedded. The tenderest love as one would have for a child, and the hottest passion; the protection and guidance of a father and the nurturing of a mother. Since then, there have been women, some very special, but none able to be all things like Little Fox."

"You've not loved since fifteen?" asked Nick sadly.

"I tried. Jemmy knew I tried. She loved me with all her heart, and I loved her as a small sister, much to her grief. Oh, I rut, but I've not truly loved for fifteen years." Nick nodded.

"I don't think I've loved until now," realized Nick out loud. And the two dark, usually taciturn men grinned silently, knowing a bond had been forged with their intimate confessions.

"Is Angus out of danger?" asked Meron.

" 'Tis hard to say. I think by morning I'll have a good idea."

"When he is, I'll leave you here with the two invalids and ride out to see what else I can find out about the missing lass," planned Meron. "I avoid settled areas, preferring the wilderness. What do you know of the mission in Pennsylvania?"

"Not too much," replied Nick. "Except it is for Indian girls, converting them and baptizing them."

"Turning them into Christian servants for white people?" retorted Meron savagely.

"It's hard to fathom which you detest more. Christian, servant, or white people?" remarked Nick dryly.

"All," stated Meron emphatically.

"I know of the Sinclairs by repute but nothing of your family," he said and stared into Meron's enigmatic green eyes. "I don't even know your family name," he added when the older man didn't answer.

"Cameron and I have no father's name. We were bastards. Our mother was Dolores MacLeod, half-Spanish, but not acknowledged by her grandfather the Laird MacLeod," said Meron.

"You have no knowledge who sired you?"

"Aye, but I'm not proud of it," returned Meron, refusing to say more. "I'll sleep on the floor in Angus's room," he added as he stood. Nick watched his straight broad back as he left the room. Solitary, strange man, he thought as he stood and stretched his exhausted body. He stacked wood on the fire so it would last the night, and entered the bedroom where Kestrel slept. Quietly he tended the fire in there, wanting the room as warm as possible to counteract the effects of her cold wet exposure. He returned to the main room, leaving her door ajar, and made himself comfortable on the floor. He would have preferred the comfort of the wide bed where Kestrel slept but didn't trust himself with her ardent nature. He could imagine her silky nakedness curled next to him, seducing him even in sleep.

Kestrel tossed and turned. In her dreams a horse screamed and screamed, thrashing in agony. She aimed her gun and fired, but each time one of her friends crashed to the ground dead and still the horse screamed. She took her dagger from its sheath and, avoiding the sharp kicking hooves plunged it into the suffering animal. But when she looked into its dark face, she saw Short Arm. Her hand held on tightly to the dagger that was deep in the young Indian's chest and still the horse screamed.

Nick was awakened from a deep sleep by Kestrel's strange cries. He sprang up, ignoring the stiffness caused by the hard floor, and groggily made his way to the room. He stood in the doorway watching Kestrel, who knelt and desperately pounded a pillow with a clenched fist. Unearthly cries of pain and exertion burst from her lips each time she punched. Blood ran down from the wound she had reopened. Shaking himself mentally alert, Nick reached to soothe the girl whose eyes were open and unseeing.

"Kess, wake up. 'Tis a bad dream," he crooned and then winced as her hard small fist punched him.

"No! No!" cried Kestrel as she felt her wrists held in a viselike grip. The horse was still screaming. She had to put it out of its misery but something was paralyzing her arms. "He's hurting, he's hurting. I have to kill him!"

Nick's blood froze at her anguished words, not fully understanding.

"Kess!" he said firmly.

"No! No!" she shouted, kicking and fighting so the blood ran stronger.

Nick grabbed her by the shoulders, determined to shake her awake.

"I don't know! I don't know what you want me to say!" She howled, her tortured mind back at another nightmare as her mother's face zoomed in and out, yelling at her. Nick tried to pull her into his arms but as soon as he released her wrists, she hit him with her sharp fist, causing a cut on his cheek.

"Enough!" he roared with frustration and slapped her face. Kestrel's eyes flew open and one hand went to her flushed cheek. She stared at him in confusion, her breathing labored from her exertion. Nick's breathing also was rapid. He watched her silently as she stared at him and then around the room, ascertaining where she was. She touched the welling wound on her stomach and tried to wipe the blood away.

"Kestrel, you're safe. Lie down and I'll see to cleaning you up," ordered Nick wearily. "I said lie down!" he added firmly, laying her back. "Down!" he shouted, feeling as if he was training a hound as her head popped up.

Nick's long body screamed with fatigue as he poured warm water into a bowl and tore up clean white rags. Feeling all was not right, he turned. Kestrel stood at the open door of the bedroom watching him as though to make sure she wasn't dreaming. Nick was blind to the confusion and relief on her beautiful face.

"God damn it! Do as you're told!" he shouted, too tired to be patient.

Kestrel frowned and stood, still not comprehending his anger. Nick put down the bowl and strode toward her. He picked her up in none too tender a grip and deposited her roughly on the bed.

"You are going to learn to obey me!" he snapped. Kestrel stared into his set angry face, noting the cut. She smiled tremulously, wanting to wrap her arms around him. She didn't mind his obvious anger, she was too glad to be home with him. Nick steeled himself as he saw her loving smile.

"You'll not get around me that way!" he informed her. "Lie down!"

Kestrel lay memorizing the planes of his stern face as he efficiently cleaned her wound and wrapped it with bandages. She wished he would look into her eyes but he purposefully avoided her face as he sponged the blood from her legs and dried her as if she were a baby. She felt a pang as he left the room, his tall back stiff and unrelenting. Listening, she heard him throw the water out of the door, bang the bowl down on the table, and then march up the stairs. She didn't want to be alone. She didn't want to remember. Carefully she shimmied off the bed and went into the main room, determined to follow him even if it meant his anger. With him she knew she was safe.

On his way downstairs, Nick stopped with an oath as he looked into Kestrel's pale face.

"Do you ever do as you are asked?" he clipped, holding himself in check.

"I don't want to be alone," whispered Kestrel and her eyes filled with tears, melting Nick's anger. It was the first time he had seen her cry. He shook his head with mock exasperation as he stared into the brimming green eyes.

"Put this on," he said gruffly, holding out a shirt as he walked down the remaining stairs toward her.

"Why?" questioned Kestrel.

"Just do it," growled Nick, putting it over her tousled golden head, covering her disturbing golden nakedness. Kestrel stood like an obedient child as he buttoned the buttons and rolled up the too-long sleeves. He grinned and stifled an ironic snort. He had to admit she looked as enticing in the shirt as out of it.

"Bed," he said resolutely, pointing to the bedroom, not daring to pick her up.

"I don't want to be alone," begged Kestrel.

"I'll be right here," returned Nick, pointing at the furs by the hearth and wishing he hadn't as he remembered her lying naked on the rug thrusting against him. "I'll tuck you in," he promised, trying to sound parental.

Kestrel lay under the covers looking at him sadly.

"You don't want to sleep with me," she asked dolefully.

"Angus is ill and by sleeping there I'll be able to hear both of you," replied Nick. "Do you ken?"

"Angus's sick?"

"Aye, now try and sleep. I'll be right there. The door will be open so you can see me," he comforted as he backed out of the room.

Kestrel watched him try once again to settle his long body into a comfortable position on the floor. Angus was sick, so Nick had to sleep out there. Well, why shouldn't she sleep out there too, she reasoned. She didn't want to sleep alone. There was no way she dared to close her eyes after the torment of the nightmare. She was too afraid it would recur. She waited, knowing instinctively that Nick would insist she return alone to bed. As soon as she thought him asleep, she slipped stiffly out of bed, dragging the covers with her.

Nick was dimly aware of Kestrel as she furtively snuggled up to him, but he was too tired to do more than tuck her into the curve of his body and wrap his arms around her before letting go of reality and falling into a deep contented sleep.

Kestrel lay in the safe circle of his strong arms, smelling the perfume of him. This was the haven she had fought to come home to, she mused as she relaxed in the warmth of his hard body.

Nick rose at first light and carefully carried the sleeping girl into the master bedroom and he firmly tucked her into the large bed. Kestrel sighed deeply, stretched like a feline, and then curled herself about the pillows. Nick smiled down at her apparent docility, marveling in the graceful fluid lines of her body and the glorious mane of golden hair that fanned about her. Regretfully he quietly left the room, closing the door behind him, to go see how Angus fared.

The old man opened his eyes and winked roguishly up at Nick's concerned face.

"How do you feel?"

"Like I was kicked by a mule," wheezed Angus. "I could do wie a wee dram or two or three or more," he added.

"Soon," chuckled Nick, relieved by the old-timer's healthy pink cheeks.

"How's our Kessie lass?" fretted Angus.

"Tired and bruised," reassured Nick. "And I'm sure it won't be long before she's up to more mischief," he added wryly.

"We wouldna want her any other way, would we?" chortled Angus contentedly before drifting back to sleep.

Reassured that both Kestrel and Angus were well on the way to recovery and that Nick could cope, Meron rode out to continue his search for Rue. Nick watched him go and breathed in the fragrant spring air as he stood by the lake where elegant deer peacefully drank, unafraid of his presence. He ran his brown hand through his black hair and laughed softly when he thought of the circumstances that had brought him to that particular spot in life. From the foul hell of a British prison-of-war camp to this wild Eden engaged to an untamed but exquisite hellion. Whistling happily he strode back to the house to check on his charges, who had slept the clock around.

Nick stretched himself out on the large bed in the room next to Angus's, correctly assuming it had once belonged to Angus's equally enormous brother Goliath. No matter how desirable Kestrel was to him, he decided, he would not share her bed until they worked out some of the problems between them. He tossed and turned, wondering at his sanity as he felt lonely and incomplete, his mind full of the golden beauty.

CHAPTER NINE

Nick stretched and looked around, not sure of his surroundings. He swung his long legs over the side of the bed and sniffed the air, salivating at the delicious aroma of freshly baked bread. Realizing what it meant he hastily pulled on his trousers and stormed barefoot into the main room to remonstrate with Angus.

"Och, dinna start fashing on such a beautiful spring morning," chided the old man. " 'Tis the lassie's birthday, May first," he informed him, beating batter for a cake as Nick quietly opened Kestrel's bedroom door.

"Where is she?" yawned Nick, seeing the empty tousled bed.

"Ain't she wie you?" frowned the old man. "Ain't seen hide nor hair of her."

"Not again!" lamented Nick. "What am I meant to do? Tie her down? No, no, of course not. No, I must understand that she always lands on her feet . . . or her tail," he added, cynically thinking of the bruises on her rear end. "Well, good morning, Angus. And how do you feel? Any pains in your chest? Any shortness of breath?"

"Just a wee bit tired," confessed Angus. "I think age is creeping up on me."

"Well, don't try to do too much," warned Nick. "I'll see to the animals."

Nick stroke out into the beautiful spring day. As if all nature knew it was May first, the chill was out of the air and the sun shone strong and warm. He pulled open the heavy barn door, intent on putting the horses to graze in the rolling meadow by the lake.

"I don't believe it!" he gasped as he stared at his horse's empty stall. There were only three horses left in the barn: an old black stallion who stomped impatient hooves, anxious to be out in the warm sunshine, and two wide cobs fit just to pull the plough. His own trusty steed was gone. He raked at the fetid straw, savagely swearing under his breath and thinking of the havoc he'd wreak upon Kestrel's tender young body. When he worked up a sweat, he stripped and plunged into the still icy water of the mountain-fed lake. He swam strongly, taking a perverse pleasure in slicing through the calm coldness.

Angus pulled a chair on to the veranda and sat rocking in the sunshine, watching the virile young man swim strongly back and forth across the wide lake as he smelled the aroma of the baking cake. He felt peaceful and at ease, delighting in the end of the long harsh winter. Bees buzzed excitedly among the delicate flowers.

Kestrel rode into the Tuscarora village. She had memorized landmarks so the five braves' bodies could be recovered. Omen roosted on her shoulder, and she was glad of his presence, knowing he was her passport to the elders if not the chief, Moon Elk. As she passed one of the longhouses, she heard the wailing and knew that the five bodies had been recovered, and the burial rituals had been begun. She reined Nick's horse and stared down into the hostile face of one of the traitorous older braves who immediately started shouting and drew a knife. Instantly Kestrel realized her stupidity in riding into the village alone. The man meant to kill her so she wouldn't incriminate him. She debated, digging in her heels and attempting to gallop away, but knew she would then receive the knife in her back.

She reached down to her own dagger, keeping her eyes trained on the snarling face who screamed abuse and accused her of being in league with the Redcoats who had killed their young warriors. People poured out of the longhouses, yelling and shouting while in the background the droning wail of the funeral rites continued. Omen cawed hoarsely as the knife was thrown. Kestrel ducked to one side and heard the whistle of the weapon below her ear but felt nothing. The sharp blade of the knife cut so quickly she was unaware of the blood that poured from her neck until she heard a gasp from the onlookers and felt the warmth flow down the cleavage of her breasts.

She sat tall and straight on the horse, holding her own dagger by the blade. If she threw it and killed him it would be like she was trying to silence him, she reasoned frantically, not knowing what to do but wanting to live.

"This man with two others is responsible for the death of Short Arm, White Otter, and the others," she shouted in Iroquois. "I can prove I was not the betrayer," she claimed as she remembered Angus's poor roan horse. If the Tuscarora had gone to collect the bodies they must have seen the dead animal.

The excited babbling quieted as the shaman strode upon the scene and waved one hand in an elaborate gesture. The wailing for the dead rhythmically continued.

"Small Golden Hawk, child of Little Green-Eyes and Mountain Lion," greeted the medicine man.

"Old Bear," greeted Kestrel. "I have bad things to tell you."

" 'Tis the time of the spring festival and we mourn the death of five of our young braves," intoned the old shaman.

Kestrel was ushered into the dim elders lodge by the shaman. She stared around curiously, having never been anywhere except in the longhouses. Three old men wrapped in blankets sat as Old Bear recounted what he had heard.

"Snow on the Shoulder accuses the child of Mountain Lion and Little Green-Eyes of causing the deaths of our children for whom we mourn."

"The proof is Small Golden Hawk stands living and our men are dead," snarled Snow on the Shoulder. "The puny yellow-haired one was there!"

"And so were you!" challenged Kestrel.

"I was the only survivor! I rode back to my people to fetch help knowing we were outnumbered by the white-eyed Long Knives."

Kestrel shook her head despite the sharp pain that shot through and feeling the warm blood gush. The old men looked at her and nodded, impressed by her straight erect bearing. It looked as though her throat was cut. The raven shifted his weight and looked from one old man to the other.

"Speak, child," prompted the shaman.

"I rode with Short Arm and the others as I have done many times. We met up with Snow on the Shoulder and two other older braves the evening before we were to attack the wagons from the fort," she recounted.

"What others?" jeered the traitorous youth.

"I have never seen them before. I have never seen you here before," stammered Kestrel. "They wore the garb of the Tuscarora. One was called Blue something. I was shot and my horse shot beneath me. I lay pretending to be dead and then watched this man." She pointed at the tall Indian. "He spoke and laughed with the Redcoats and then rode away with the ponies of Short Arm and the others."

"Where were you shot?" sneered the brave somewhat nervously. Without thinking twice, Kestrel tore open the lacings on the front of her leather vest. There was a slight gasp as she exposed her breasts.

"You are female!" observed the shaman in surprise.

Kestrel stood unmoving. The blood from her neck had soaked the bandage about her waist.

"Anyone can wrap themselves and say they are wounded," challenged Snow on the Shoulder.

The shaman looked to the elders who nodded. He cut through the cotton bandage and once again the old men nodded as they saw the deep furrow.

"There was a horse dead at the sight," informed Old Bear.

"Will you believe a white-faced female and not me?" challenged the badly frightened brave.

"Why did you try to silence Small Golden Hawk?" asked one of the old men.

"Anger at what she had done," answered Snow on the Shoulder.

"But that is up to the council. You know the ways of our people. You have been away for a while at a mission but you must still abide by the rules of this family of living people. She held a weapon and could have silenced you, but she chose not to and that speaks in her favor," returned the old man softly.

"I am Tuscarora. I am male. She is a paleface, a woman," spat the scared young Indian.

"She is more of a Tuscarora, more of a man, than you," spoke a quiet low voice from the back of the dark lodge. Kestrel's eyes widened as Chief Moon Elk stepped forward out of the shadows.

"I am Moon Elk, chief of this village, friend of Meron, the brother of your mother. We grieve for the passing of your mother, Little Green-Eyes, and thank you for showing us this traitor in our house," he said, turning to the brave. "Who were your two companions?"

"She lies, lies. It was her!"

"We have spies at Fort Detroit. It was strange none of our horses were found there or wandering loose near the bodies of our braves. Where are your two companions and the horses?" probed the chief, never raising his voice. Kestrel stood silently watching the tall youth incriminating himself even further as he tried to lie his way out of his dilemma.

"There were also guns he was given by the soldiers," remembered Kestrel. Moon Elk barked a sharp order and two men entered.

"Search Snow on the Shoulder's partition in the longhouse," he ordered, and at those words the terrified Indian sprang at Kestrel. She recoiled, reaching for her dagger, but Moon Elk swiftly spun the brave around.

"You'll not die swiftly," he promised, and Kestrel shuddered, knowing the kind of long, excruciating torture he had in mind. She suddenly felt sick and faint. Her neck ached and was stiff with dried blood. She swayed, wishing she could get out of the close stuffy lodge into the fresh air to clear her head. Omen's weight made her shoulder ache. She breathed deeply and tried to distract herself by lacing up her leather vest. How long would it be before she could sit? she wondered. Should she dare just do it? She was not sure of the protocol. One thing she knew for certain was that women were not allowed inside the elders lodge.

"Please." She broke the silence, knowing she didn't want to disgrace herself by fainting. Waving her hand toward the door she swayed and Moon Elk caught her as she fell.

Kestrel breathed deeply of the fresh air as Moon Elk carried her to his lodge and laid her on a pile of furs. She smiled weakly at the two Indian women who smoothed back the hair from her face, exclaiming about the color and texture. She struggled ineffectually as she was stripped and gently bathed. Dimly she could hear the rhythmic wailing for the dead. She sat up as a piercing cry joined the dirge.

"Hush," soothed one of the women, pressing her back against the furs and putting a paste of herbs on her neck and stomach.

"I feel fine now," Kestrel informed them. "I want to go home."

"Small Golden Hawk is anxious to be away from our hospitality?" asked a deep voice, and Kestrel turned her sore neck and looked into Moon Elk's enigmatic features. She followed the direction of his gaze and tried to pull the fur covers over her nakedness.

"Drink," urged the gentle Indian woman and Kestrel found her head propped up and a bittersweet liquid was put to her lips. Having no choice in the matter she drank and choked as the liquid burned her throat much like Angus's whiskey.

"Now you will sleep," said Moon Elk.

"I don't want to sleep," protested Kestrel, her limbs feeling weighted down. "Thank you for your hospitality but the brother of my mother will be concerned for my safety." She struggled, her tongue feeling strange so words were difficult to form.

"It has been taken care of," informed Moon Elk as Kestrel's eyes closed and her body relaxed into the deep pile of furs.

Kestrel opened her heavy lids and lay trying to accustom her eyes to the smoky gloom. She wrinkled her nose against the strange pungent smell that steamed from a pot hanging over the central fire in the round lodge. Hearing a strange panting she turned her stiff neck and by the red glow of the fire she saw two people writhing together, their bodies shining with the sweat of their sensuous exertions. An excitement emanated and Kestrel felt her nipples rise and push against the soft fur cover that was draped across her nakedness.

Moon Elk stared down at his second wife's serene face as he thrust into her supple body. He sensed that Kestrel was awake and it heightened his pleasure as he substituted her golden face for the one below him.

Kestrel felt a movement and turned, and her eyes met those of the older Indian woman who also watched the mating couple. Moon Elk cried out in triumph and strained against his wife for several minutes before rolling off her and barking a guttural order. The woman obediently crept to the other side of the lodge where she curled up against the older woman and went to sleep. Kestrel lay in the dimness, hearing Moon Elk's contented snores as she wondered at the position she had seen of the man on top of the woman, kneeling between her parted legs. Her body ached in two different ways. From the abuse of the last days and from what she had heard and witnessed between Moon Elk and his wife. Thinking of Nick's firm thighs and imagining herself between them, she fell asleep.

After a sleepless night worrying about Kestrel, Nick sat on the veranda watching the dawn silhouette the mountains against the sky. He frowned as he saw several horsemen break out of the edge of the forest on the far side of the meadow.

"Indians," he breathed, backing into the house intent on waking Angus, whose snores reverberated. "Well, what do you make of it?"

he asked as the old man yawned and stood scratching his belly, watching the Indians slowly approach.

"Tuscarora," growled the old man, raising a hand in greeting.

Nick watched Angus and the Indians converse, unable to understand any of the guttural language. He frowned as the Indians wheeled around their ponies and galloped off.

"Well?" he asked as Angus stood watching them ride across the sloping meadow.

"Well, Kess is safe," sighed Angus without turning. "Seems as though she took the law into her own hands and rode to the Tuscarora village to apprise them of a traitor in their midst. . . ."

"What?" ejaculated Nick and Angus chuckled as he turned and saw the young man's incredulous expression.

"And got her throat cut," added the old man wickedly.

"Throat cut?" repeated Nick, his face turning white with alarm. "You said she was safe and now her throat is cut?" he ranted.

"Just a wee *nick* so to speak," chortled Angus roguishly. "Seems our lass is the most honored guest of Chief Moon Elk in his lodge," he recounted, wondering if he should apprise Nick of all he had learned.

"What else?" probed Nick, sensing the garrulous old man was withholding information.

"It would also seem as though Chief Moon Elk would like Kestrel, or rather Small Golden Hawk, to be his third wife," he ventured, not knowing whether to laugh hysterically or cry at the expression on Nick's dark face.

"*Third* wife?" repeated Nick incredulously.

"One has to be very rich to have three wives," stated Angus seriously.

"One has to be a damnable idiot if they're all like Kestrel," rejoined Nick with a snort. "Angus? You don't think . . . he wouldn't . . . well, what are the Indians' views on . . . taking advantage . . ." he struggled, not knowing how to broach the subject.

"What are you talking about?" queried Angus, not having a clue what was making Nick so tongue-tied.

"He'd not use her as a wife, would he?"

"You mean have her wash his socks?" teased Angus.

"'Tis no laughing matter," snapped Nick.

"If she was a captive from a war party or raid, maybe. But since

Meron is close to Moon Elk, I dinna think so. They are very particular people."

"Three wives? Particular?" exclaimed Nick.

"Aye, 'tis just a different way. What about men wie one wife who whore around with twenty others?" challenged Angus. "You know what's strange?" he added thoughtfully after a long brooding silence.

"Everything," retorted Nick sarcastically.

"I dinna ken they knew our Kess was a lass," returned Angus thoughtfully. "When did Meron say he would be home?"

"He didn't. Just a few days or a week. What do you think we should do?"

Angus shook his grizzled mane of hair and sat frowning into the fire.

"There's not much we can do until he gets home. Not only has the lass rid us of our riding horses but 'tis not safe for the likes of us to go riding into the Indian villages wie all the killing that's going on."

"Once again we have to sit twiddling our thumbs while she's got herself in another mess! Gets her throat cut and is in a chief's lodge! Maybe it would set her right becoming the man's third wife!" snorted Nick.

CHAPTER TEN

"It is a great honor to be the wife of a chief," stated Moon Elk's older wife proudly.

"Yes," agreed his second wife. "And I will teach you how to please him as Morning Mist taught me," she added, smiling at the first wife. Kestrel stared at the beaming women, not knowing what to say.

"I am already promised to a man," she whispered.

"Then Moon Elk will give him seeds and horses so he will not be sad," informed Morning Mist.

"I don't think he wants seeds and horses. He wants me," replied Kestrel in a very small voice, remembering Nick's anger.

"Then Moon Elk will kill him," stated the younger woman cheerfully.

"Oh, no!" howled Kestrel. The two women watched Kestrel's agitation with alarm.

"Drink some more," coaxed one of the women, offering the bowl with the bittersweet draft.

"No, I don't want to sleep!" protested Kestrel, remembering how quickly the liquid worked. "I've been here two days! I want to go home."

The two women looked at each other, not knowing what to do as Kestrel tore open the hide curtain that hung in the doorway.

"You must stay and rest," they protested but Kestrel stormed out, only to find her way barred by Moon Elk's strong arms.

"I am going home!" she stated, staring into his stony face. "I don't want to be your third wife!" she added furiously, not heeding the warning in the tightening of his thin mouth. Without a word Moon Elk roughly pushed her back into his lodge. His two wives backed away, fear showing on their usually serene faces.

"Out!" ordered Moon Elk without looking at them and the two women scurried away.

"I am surprised that a child of Meron's household has so few manners," said Moon Elk admonishingly.

Kestrel held her ground, refusing to show the terror that she felt. "I am very sorry to abuse your hospitality," she stated, keeping her voice steady and her chin up despite the pounding of her heart. "But I am going home with or without your permission!" Her green eyes blazed into his mahogany ones in a battle of wills. His hard fingers dug into her tender forearms. "Let go of me!" she ordered, her temper rising and covering her fear. Moon Elk said nothing and did not release his grip. Kestrel tried to shrug his hands from her but he held her as if she were a tiny child. "You will let me go!" she shouted, bringing her knee up toward his groin. Moon Elk swore and evaded her parry, flinging her roughly to one side but keeping firm hold. Kestrel fought him much as she had fought Nick the night before her father left for Scotland with her brothers. She was determined to get away, to get back to Nick. Moon Elk held her easily, his anger mixed with grudging admiration. Once again Kestrel's wounds opened.

Noise of new arrivals to the village reached the chief's ears but still he stood holding the fighting, biting girl between his strong hands, his face betraying nothing.

Meron and Nick stood in the doorway and stared at the sight that met their eyes. Nick saw the blood and made a movement to stop the Indian's abuse of Kestrel. Meron stopped him.

"Greetings, Moon Elk," hailed Meron casually.

"Greetings, Green Eyes," countered Moon Elk as if there were no spitting, fighting, swearing, bloody person being held between his hands.

"Meron," breathed Kestrel thankfully, stopping her frantic fight but still unable to free herself from the chief's grip. "What took you so long," she snapped furiously.

"This is Nick MacKay," introduced Meron, ignoring his niece. Moon Elk nodded and pushed Kestrel firmly aside. She sat rubbing her arms which bore his handprints as the chief waved a hand, offering Nick and Meron a seat on the furs by the central fire.

" 'Tis good to see you, my friend," welcomed Moon Elk, clasping both Meron's hands in his. For a few silent moments the two men stared at each other. Nick watched both impassive faces, estimating they were both in their late thirties. He kept his eyes away from Kestrel, whose seething filled the smoky lodge.

"You have a look of our people," observed the chief as he turned his attention to Nick, noting the thick black hair and black eyes. Nick nodded silently, not knowing the customs.

"Stay!" snapped Meron, as out of the corner of his eyes he saw Kestrel crawling toward the door.

"Meron!" protested Kestrel.

"Silence!" said Meron, his voice steely. "And stay still."

"No!"

"God damn it, Kestrel! Sit and shut up!" roared Nick, unable to contain himself.

Both Meron and Moon Elk nodded as the sullen girl obeyed.

"I am ashamed of you, my friend," chided the chief. "The daughter of your sister runs about like a male and has no respect for her elders and even less manners." Kestrel felt stung by these words.

"I apologize for my niece, my friend, and take the responsibility upon myself," answered Meron formally. He turned to Nick and added, "The uncle is more important than the father in many tribes, as he has more perspective." He turned back to Moon Elk. "Unfortunately I was away fighting the Redcoats and protecting my twin nephews Lynx and Ravin for a long while."

"I was saddened to hear of the young Raven's death and also that of your sister Little Green-Eyes," said Moon Elk grimly. He put up a

and and stood. He shouted a few sharp orders out of the doorway and
turned to the mat.

"Go and help Morning Mist and Young Wife," ordered Meron,
looking at Kestrel. Her mouth pursed rebelliously, and she shook her
head, causing the slight but messy knife wound in her neck to bleed
again. "Nick?" queried Meron, staring at the dark young Scot and
indicating Kestrel with exasperation.

"Do as you're told," commanded Nick as she opened her mouth to
protest.

Moon Elk nodded admiringly as Kestrel sullenly left the lodge to
join the two women outside.

Nick sat listening to Meron and Moon Elk speak together in
Iroquois. He looked around at the interior of the lodge, admiring the
design and practicality of the small space. There was a heavy pungent
smell of bear grease, which he guessed was a lubricant used for
protection against the harsh elements to keep the skin smooth and free
from chafing. He marveled at the intricate artistry and design of the
weaving and embroidery on the clothes, mats, and cooking vessels
that were neatly laid out beside the central fire. Moon Elk's wives
entered and started to cook, accompanied by a sullen Kestrel. Meron
and the chief roared with laughter, causing the two gentle Indian
women to titter and Kestrel to fume. Nick relaxed despite Kestrel's
bloody neck. Except for the slight wound she seemed well and full of
spirits. A little too full of spirits, he mused, wondering what could
curb the wild rebellious nature. Meron leaned toward him, still
laughing.

"Moon Elk says he's glad that you have the taming of such a wife
and not him. He advises you to use a lot of leather."

"Leather?" questioned Nick.

"To beat her," returned Meron.

"Maybe Moon Elk would reconsider having her as his third wife,"
laughed Nick, very relaxed and enjoying the pungent liquor he was
being served. Kestrel fumed, ready to explode at his offer.

"No, I am much too old and set in my ways to deal with a rude
recalcitrant woman no matter how brave she is," sighed the chief with
relief, spreading both hands in front of him as a sign of defeat. "I
would, however, not be adverse to lending you Morning Mist and
Young Wife to teach her how to make a good wife," he offered, a
twinkle in his dark eyes showing he knew that he was inflaming
Kestrel's temper even further.

Kestrel rolled the steaming stew around in the bowl she was serving

from, debating whether to pour the mixture into one of the men's la
as they talked about her in such callous terms.

"Don't you dare," warned Nick, watching the expression on h
face and seeing the unconscious movement of her hand.

Kestrel sat and thought she would die from hunger and insult as t
men ate and she and Moon Elk's two wives docilely knelt, waiting
the men hand and foot. She resisted the impulse to just walk out, le
on the nearest horse, and ride home to Angus, knowing that if s
tried it she would be easily stopped by these three men who wou
enjoy making her behave. She absently reached for some corn brea
only to have her hand slapped away by one of Moon Elk's wives. S
curled her hand into a fist, instinctively, to punch back.

"We may not eat until our men are satisfied," preached Mornii
Mist, the older wife. Meron tried to suppress his laughter as he sa
his niece's indignant face.

"I wish you spoke Iroquois," he burst out, unable to keep t
laughter from gurgling up. "Just take a look at Kestrel's face,"
roared. Both Moon Elk and Nick looked toward Kestrel, who was to
angry and incensed to listen to them. Her small nose twitched a
flared with fury, her full sensual mouth was thrust forward in
rebellious pout, and her wide green eyes flashed. The three dark m
stared at the angry girl, struck both by her incredible beauty and t
comical side of her predicament.

Kestrel turned just in time to catch their merriment. Somethi
snapped and she knew she had to get away or she'd lose all her se
respect and pride. Their laughter rang in her aching head, and s
silently screamed before diving toward the doorway of the lodg
Nick caught her, pulling her taut lithe body close to him, stilling h
frantic movements with his strength. Kestrel relaxed, smelling t
beloved musk of him and curled into his warmth like a sleepy kitte
Moon Elk raised his dark eyebrows at the sudden docility of the wi
girl as she lay nestled against the muscular body, embraced by stro
dark arms.

"One movement and you go outside," warned Nick, knowing t
precariousness of the situation as he noted the narrowing of t
Tuscarora chief's eyes as they seemed to caress Kestrel's body. Lu
and manly pride were now coming into play, he surmised.

"My wife," he lied, indicating Kestrel and not knowing how mu
Meron had told the tall Indian, "was given into my keeping by Litt
Green-Eyes, Meron's sister," he added, putting the sticky proble
into Meron's more experienced hands.

"Aye," agreed Meron, also noticing the tightening of the chief's heek as he looked longingly at Nick's tempting golden armful.

The interminable meal was finally over and Kestrel sat upon a beautiful pinto Indian pony, anxious to leave the Tuscarora village far behind.

"For my niece, I thank you for your generosity," said Meron stiffly as he indicated the pony and the intricately decorated clothes Kestrel wore. "For my niece I also thank you for your hospitality. Our door is always open to you," he added, obviously annoyed at having to tend to what was Kestrel's responsibility.

Moon Elk looked at the exquisite young woman dressed in the soft doeskin tunic decorated with porcupine quills. Her shapely long legs clad in beaded and fringed boots drummed impatiently against the pinto's firm sides.

"Small Golden Hawk is anxious to be gone," he stated.

Kestrel inclined her head in agreement, her face closed and angry.

"Nevertheless you shall wait while I thank you for alerting us to Snow on the Shoulder's treachery. But you have still to learn how to be respectful to your elders."

Only Meron's quick reflexes as he grabbed Kestrel's bridle stopped her rude departure. She was seething with rage as she was led slowly through the Indian village. The rhythmic wailing for the dead could be heard mixed with the screams of Snow on the Shoulder as he was painfully tortured.

"What are those long structures?" asked Nick, looking around with fascination at the six buildings made of bent saplings and woven twigs.

"Longhouses. Sometimes up to ten or more families live in each, all related through the women. The oldest woman rules. As the boys marry, they move out into the longhouses of their wives. It's the women who appoint the elders and chiefs, in fact control the whole village," explained Meron.

"The structures look very sturdy. How long do they last?"

"The village lasts as long as the ground is fertile and the surrounding area has firewood and game. Sometimes ten years, sometimes more. When things are depleted the village is moved," said Meron. "Women are highly revered. They are the only owners of property, houses, and livestock. That is why Kestrel's uncontrolled behavior was so frowned upon," he added, sounding severe as they left the village and entered the forest.

Kestrel refused to acknowledge her uncle's words.

100 ALEEN MALCOLM

"Women are the source of wisdom, affection, and comfort in th Iroquois society. They have to be for the men are frequently of hunting or defending their way of life. The women are the guardian of the home, nurturing and cultivating children and crops. 'Tis n wonder Moon Elk was relieved not to have her as his third wife fo who'd want such a mother to teach her children!" stated Meron reaching out and taking the bridle of Kestrel's horse. "I have neve been angry with you until now, Kestrel Sinclair. I am ashamed of you lack of self-control. You insulted Moon Elk's hospitality and showe no sensitivity for another's way of life," he finished, dropping he bridle and turning away.

Kestrel's face burned from his censure and she stared straigh ahead, not able to look at Nick, who rode beside her. Many thing raced through her mind as she felt her uncle's unfair words and sh longed to defend herself.

It was evening when they reached home. Kestrel dismounted stiffl and Nick took her bridle.

"I'll tend to the horses. Go inside," he said curtly. Kestrel watche him lead the horses into the barn before following Meron up the step into the warm inviting house.

"Take a big sniff," urged Angus. "Go on. Guess what it is."

Meron ignored him and stood gazing into the fire. Angus looke from his straight back to Kestrel's stony face and frowned. "Well don't you look a treat," he growled, noting the ornate tunic and boots

Kestrel stormed into the bedroom and slammed the door.

"Now what?" groaned the old man. "Is my wonderful feast goin, to be spoiled by long faces and snits? You dinna mean to tell me she i to be Moon Elk's wife?" he exclaimed, thinking that the reason fo Meron's silence.

"Nay," Meron laughed harshly. "Great chiefs dinna want wive that kick them in the bollox!"

"No, I should say not," agreed Angus. "But it seems to have go the lass out of a pretty pickle," she said, striving to lighten Meron' mood. "Where's Nick?"

"Seeing to the horses," answered Meron shortly. "I'll go give hin a hand."

Angus watched Meron leave the house and frowned. "Here I'v planned a party for Kessie lass's birthday, and even though 'tis a da or so late, I'll not have it spoiled," he muttered, banging on th bedroom door. "Come out here, Kess. Quick afore they come in." H opened the door a crack and peeped in at her sitting dejectedly on th

ge bed, staring into the dead gray ashes of the fire. "Here, let's
ve no long faces on your birthday," he chided.

"My birthday's been and gone," answered Kestrel dully.

"Dinna spoil an old man's fancy," pleaded Angus. "I've baked a
aple cake and there's shortbread. And do you know what else? Take
sniff. Go on. Take a sniff and guess. It's a favorite of yours," he
axed.

"Duck," returned Kestrel, trying without much luck to join in his
ood.

"Let's see that neck, lass," said Angus, lifting her chin and looking
the long red line that welled with beads of blood. "Does it hurt?"

"Only when I move it," laughed Kestrel bitterly. "Oh, Angus, I
ake everyone angry with me. Even Meron. He's never shouted at me
fore. And now you're going to be angry, too."

"Nay, not on your birthday," protested the old man.

"I took your horse and he's dead," she confessed.

"Aye, Nick told me," nodded Angus, his rheumy old eyes filling
th tears. "He dinna suffer, did he?" he croaked.

"Oh, no," lied Kestrel as the memory of the animal's screams
ooded her mind. "I have another horse for you. Moon Elk gave him
me, so he's yours."

"Let's have no more sadness. Tonight will be jolly and happy,"
ated Angus, blowing his nose and hugging Kestrel's thin shoulders.
Nick watched the old man and the girl through the open door. He
iffed appreciatively the assorted aromas and peeked into one of the
errily boiling pots.

"What do you think of those smells?" chortled Angus, catching
ick in the act of sneaking a taste.

"Not only smells, but tastes delicious," returned Nick, looking at
estrel who stood held by the old man's powerful arm. Kestrel was
nbarrassed and avoided his eyes.

Angus sensed her discomfort. "You should take a look at that neck
hers before it stains her beautiful new birthday clothes more," he
ggested. "You know it's the first time I've seen our lass in a dress."

Kestrel stood silently as Nick sat in front of her looking at her neck.
e stood between his long legs and flushed as she remembered the
ief lying between his wife's limbs.

"Don't pull away," chided Nick softly as she unconsciously drew
ck from the warmth of him. "Keep your chin up," he ordered as he
plied a soothing balm. "There," and he held her by the waist,
eping her between his muscular thighs as he stared into her small

unhappy face. He didn't know what to say to her. He knew she stu
and smarted from her uncle's censure, and he had to admit it was
tongue-lashing she should have got many times as a child, but ev
though it was less than he had wanted to do to discipline her, he ach
and hurt for her unhappiness. He longed to pull her down onto his l
and kiss her into a sparkling sunny mood.

Kestrel stared down into Nick's dark eyes not knowing what he w
feeling. The sharp planes of his face seemed severe and censurin
and she supposed he was as angry as Meron.

"How's your belly?" questioned Nick, feeling her taut narro
waist between his large hands. Not trusting herself to speak, Kest
tried to smile to let him know it was all right.

Meron entered and Kestrel, head down, moved toward him.

"I'm sorry you are ashamed of me, too," she whispered.

Meron frowned at her, not liking the defeated attitude she ha

"I am not ashamed of *you*. I was only ashamed of your behavior
was also angry about other things and unfortunately you receiv
more than your share."

"What other things?" questioned Angus.

"A few weeks ago a mission south of here was attacked by Briti
militia, under a Colonel David Williamson. They killed and scalp
ninety-six young Indians," recounted Meron sadly.

"Not the mission in Pennsylvania?" asked Nick.

"No, but coincidentally it was the same religious sect. Moravia
This mission was in a place called Gnadenhutten. Ninety-six your
Indians!" repeated Meron savagely.

"Male or female?" questioned Angus.

"Young males."

"What of the young females?" whispered Kestrel.

Meron didn't answer. He had seen the hollow eyes of ravage
children.

"They opened their arms to the soldiers, invited them for food ar
worship, not having any interest in the war. The soldiers played wi
the children, broke bread with them, and that night lay down to sle
side by side with them. It was as the boys slept that they were kille
and scalped," continued Meron, trying to rid himself of the anger ar
frustration. He had ridden south on his search for Rue to find a sce
of senseless tragedy. Each girl had been beaten and raped, b
thankfully none had been his niece. He had felt callous asking all h
questions and rode away gratefully, knowing his niece had not bee
part of such abuse.

"Any young girls that could have been my sister?" asked Kestrel, ...ing a breath to give her courage as the panic started pounding her ...art and the crack of a rifle echoed in her head.

"No," returned Meron.

"You'll never find her because she's dead," stated Kestrel, her face ...athly white. ·

"How do you know?" asked Meron, walking slowly toward her, ...s green eyes pinned to hers.

"I shot her."

"What?" gasped Angus as all three men stiffened in surprise. ...estrel stood in the middle of the room, hearing the horse scream.

"I killed my sister," she intoned. "I didn't mean to. I was trying to ...oot them," she continued as her sister's and Jemmy's screams ...ined the horse's.

"Oh, my Lor'! You puir wee bairn," choked Angus.

"Hush up, Angus," whispered Meron. "You shot Rue?"

"Aye," she answered as though in a hypnotic state.

"Tell me what happened," urged her uncle.

"It was dusk and the soldiers were hurting Jemmy and Rue. Jemmy ...as screaming and screaming but I couldn't see her for the Redcoats ...ere all around her. One soldier had Rue. I tried to shoot him but my ...ster fell and stopped screaming."

"What else?" probed Meron, holding her shoulders and stooping ... he could look her in the eye.

"I don't know. I don't know what you want me to say!" she ...reamed and Nick, recognizing those words, caught her as she tried ... race from the room.

"I don't know what you want me to say, Mother! I don't know what ...u want me to say, Mother!" she screamed.

"It's all right Kess, it's Nick," he soothed as she fought to be free. "No need to struggle, I'll not let you go." Kestrel stared at him in ...nazement and rubbed her hands against his cheeks before wrapping ...r arms about his neck and bursting into tears.

"Well, there's another first," choked Angus, tears pouring down ...s face. "I've not seen her cry since she was a wee baby." Nick ...rried Kestrel into the privacy of the bedroom, somehow sensing her ...ride would be hurt by her display of emotion.

"I've not had a dram since my funny spell," sniffed Angus, taking ...own the whiskey jug and pouring a healthy tot for Meron and ...mself. "Well, what do you think of Kess's story?" he probed after a ...ng burning swallow.

"If Kess had killed Rue, the body would've been left wi
Jemmy's," pronounced Meron.

"Aye," agreed Angus. "But to a young child to think she's kill
her own sister and keep it locked inside her all this time!"

Meron nodded, unable to speak for several minutes.

"Well, it just might help us in our search. Now that we know R
was wounded, we have something to aid us."

"So you visited one mission south of here, and then there's the o
you mentioned in Bethlehem," mused Angus. "But why would
French priest be going to a Protestant mission? It doesna make a
sense," he grumbled.

"You're right, but I've not heard of any Catholic ones south in t
Colonies. Further east in the Huron's area and north in what was Ne
France. Unless 'tis way, way down, which I dinna think wie the w
and all going on complicating things," brooded Meron. "No
where's all this food you keep promising?"

"Hold your horses, let the lass pull herself together. 'Tis h
birthday we're meant to be celebrating," chided Angus.

Kestrel sighed deeply and hiccuped. She lay back against t
pillows, watching Nick set and light a fire in the hearth. She wasr
sure how she felt. There was a relief and yet a numb emptiness. Ni
smiled down at her.

"Want to talk about it? Or better yet, let's not disappoint Angus.
he said softly, somehow sensing she needed time to get her feelings
order. Kestrel nodded even though eating was the furthest thing fro
her mind. She would have much preferred to be alone, feelir
strangely vulnerable and confused and not knowing how to act.

"There they are," rejoiced Angus, rubbing his hands together wi
excitement.

"Kess, come here," said Meron, holding out his arms to her as I
noticed her shy embarrassment. She walked to him, keeping her hea
lowered, and stopped a few paces in front of him. Meron pulled h
into his arms. "I am proud of you. Very, very proud of you and so w
your mother." He held her tightly as she tried to pull away. "Kes
you didn't kill your sister. You may have wounded her but you didn
kill her or her body would have been with Jemmy's."

Kestrel stared up at him in surprise, hearing the logic of his word
It had been so long that she didn't know what was one of her recurrir
nightmares or what really happened.

"No more talk. Let's eat!" shouted Angus, proud of his lade

table. Meron squeezed Kestrel to him, feeling for her the same aching tenderness he had felt for her mother, his twin.

"Dinna change her too much, MacKay," he said huskily, releasing her so she fleetly returned to Nick's side.

"My turn," growled Angus, opening his arms. "Even us old-timers need a hug."

Nick gave Kestrel a little encouraging push and she walked into Angus's bearlike clasp. Confused and afraid of the love that emanated from the three men who surrounded her, she toyed with the food on her plate, finding it hard to swallow. Then suddenly unable to bear her feelings of unworthiness any longer, she dropped her fork loudly on her plate so it clattered sharply.

"I killed my sister and . . . and . . . " She strove to explain her guilt.

"And what, lass?" returned Angus innocently.

"And . . . all of this," she struggled, waving her hands at the laden table. "And this and this," she continued pointing her finger at each one as she parodied his fond expression. "I cannot bear it!" she yelled, pushing the chair back from the table. She saw Angus's stricken expression and her shoulders slumped. "I'm sorry," she said, remembering Meron's chastising words about her defiant display in front of Moon Elk. She resolutely pulled her chair back to the table and picked up her fork.

Nick winced, knowing what Kestrel was experiencing. As a doctor he had seen people forced to behave a certain way because of a certain set of circumstances; as a soldier, imprisoned for six months, he also knew the strange feelings that accompanied being suddenly released. He guessed Kestrel felt disorganized and disoriented after spending three years holding everyone at bay because of the terrible secret she held inside. He watched her valiant effort to eat for Angus's sake; he wished there was some way he could let her know he had empathy for her pain and confusion.

Meron watched his niece, whose usually fluid graceful movements had become stiff and stilted. Only Angus seemed to enjoy the meal as he ate his cooking with noisy gusto—probably because of the amount of whiskey he had consumed, surmised Meron. The large old man cut the maple cake, putting generous slabs on each plate, before staggering to his feet with his mug held high.

"Up, up," urged the old man, feeling as though the success of the meal depended solely on him. "We shall toast our own Kessie lass," he declared.

Finally the painful meal was over and Kestrel sat hugging her knees beside the roaring fire, not heeding the three men who cleared the table as she tried to put her teeming thoughts in order.

"Do you really think I didn't kill her?" she earnestly asked, turning impulsively to the men at the table.

"Kess, you didna kill Rue, or we'd have found her body," reassured Meron, wishing she had been able to voice her fears to her mother.

"I want to come with you to find her," said Kestrel, excitedly jumping to her feet and rushing to her uncle.

Meron regretfully shook his head.

"Why?" protested Kestrel.

"You ken I always travel alone," he reproved gently.

"You dinna wie Lynx and Raven," she contradicted, lapsing into the dialect he had.

"That was to watch over them. You're needed here wie Angus and your man, Nick," informed Meron as Nick's arms encircled the girl.

"But I hurt her," insisted Kestrel.

"You were trying to help," comforted Nick, pulling her down on to his lap as he seated himself beside the fire. "Now when do we get married?"

Kestrel frowned, not understanding.

"I think you are already," laughed Meron. "Or rather, you would be if we were in Scotland. By declaration," he added as Nick's usually noncommittal features looked puzzled.

"In the awesome suroundings of Chief Moon Elk's lodge and undenied by either of you," he explained.

"Now I'm hungry," declared Kestrel, her mouth watering as she thought of the rich maple cake that Angus had made.

"You go jump into bed and I'll bring some in," promised Nick, wanting to talk to Meron alone. But Kestrel curled into his lap, loath to leave his safe warmth. He laughed and stood carrying her easily into the large bedroom where a cheerful fire blazed.

"Here," he said, throwing her a freshly laundered shirt.

"Why?" she frowned.

"Now we are wed you better start obeying some of the time," he chided gently, kissing her nose and leaving the room.

Kestrel stretched out, staring at the blazing fire and thinking over the strange events of the day. She absentmindedly unlaced the front of the ornate tunic, feeling physically and emotionally exhausted.

Nick entered the bedroom ten minutes later brandishing a large

hunk of maple cake, only to find Kestrel sound asleep. He caught his
breath at the beautiful picture she made. His shirt was still where he'd
thrown it, her new clothes cast to one side, and she lay naked, her
golden hair like a halo catching the warmth of the firelight, her
creamy supple body curled, and one slim graceful arm outstretched
like an archer. He longed to wake her up slowly and sensuously by
running his exploring hands over the whole of her, but regretfully he
covered her, knowing what she needed most now was sleep. He
quietly left the room. They had a whole life ahead of them to explore
one another, he comforted himself as he stretched out on the large bed
in Goliath's old room.

CHAPTER ELEVEN

Late the following afternoon Nick floated in the lake, feeling at peace
and in harmony with every living thing. All vestiges of the long cold
winter had gone and although it was still spring, the feel and smell of
summer was in the air. The trees were full and the tender green had
intensified to a deep lushness. He thought of Kestrel as he floated in
the water, staring up at the sky that was streaked with gold and red. He
had waited all day for her to awaken and his disappointment and
impatience had driven him to seek a refreshing swim. He heard a
small splash and looked about expecting to see an otter, dog, or water
fowl but saw nothing.

Kestrel swam underwater toward Nick, silently surfacing just
behind him. Mischievously she put her hands to his shiny black head
and dunked him. Two strong arms came underneath grasping her slim
hips, and she was pulled down with him. They looked into each
other's eyes underwater, then joined in a kiss. Gasping for breath they
broke to the surface and burst into laughter, each knowing neither had
wanted the kiss to stop, and both refusing to be the first to give up.

Kestrel faced Nick, holding onto his broad brown shoulders and
treading water. Nick looked down, seeing their two bodies fore-
shortened and shimmering in the crystal clearness. Kestrel's eyes
followed his gaze, then grinning wickedly she neatly duck-dived.

Nick smiled at the pert bottom as it popped out of the water followed by the long slim legs and arched pointed feet. His eyes widened and he choked swallowing some water as he felt Kestrel's curious hands examine his manhood. Pleasure coursed through him and despite the frigidity of the water, he pulsed and grew in her small hands. He exploded with laughter as Kestrel's incredulous face broke the surface of the water again, and she stared at him in astonishment and then back down at the object of her exploration.

Nick drew her up into his arms, delighting in the cool silky feel of her, and he kissed her tremulous mouth. She pressed her breasts against his broad chest and wound her legs about his waist, trusting his strength to keep them both afloat as she returned his kisses. She felt a deep aching need in the core of her. She arched her back trying to get closer and Nick loosened her legs, lowering her until she was touching his man-root. Her eyes flew open, and putting her small hands on his chest and keeping her legs wound closely around him, she stared into his unfathomable black eyes.

"Let's swim to shore," suggested Nick huskily, preferring to expend all his energy in making love rather than in keeping both of them afloat. Kestrel was loath to change her exciting position so Nick swam strongly to shore carrying her.

"I don't want to go to the house," begged Kestrel, spreading the two towels under the trees on a soft carpet of pine needles and lying down. Nick stared down at her, lost in the wonder of her beauty; Kestrel looked up at him, mesmerized, then held out her arms. Slowly Nick sank to his knees and Kestrel pulled his wet head down to her breasts where he kissed the tight-budded nipples. Her soft, curious hands busily explored, imitating Nick's larger ones as the sun set in a blaze of red.

Kestrel felt ablaze as Nick parted her lean thighs and knelt between them gently rubbing his man-root at the burning entrance. She arched toward him as little cries burst from her mouth.

"It will hurt for a little moment, my love," he whispered huskily, entering her tightness. Kestrel bucked toward him, driving him in to the hilt. She gasped at the tearing sharpness, and Nick held her closely.

"Do you want to stop?" he asked and he felt her violently shake her head as she started to gyrate her hips, urging him to continue. Nick paced himself, not wanting to make her sore, but Kestrel impatiently ground herself to him until he lost all sense of time and place. As he felt the spasms of her climax squeeze, he let go and they strained together, feeling each other's hearts rapidly pounding. Next time would be long and lingering, Nick promised himself, holding her close and rolling onto his back, still joined. Kestrel stared down at him and he wished he could see the expression on her face but it was too dark.

"I love you so much I could burst with it," she whispered and Nick felt and tasted the salt of her tears before capturing her soft warm mouth.

"We should get back to the warm of the house before Angus sends the hounds out after us," suggested Nick regretfully, feeling her skin goosebump as a chill breeze swept over the lake.

Kestrel sighed as he withdrew from her and she sat back on her haunches and gently took his manhood in her hand. Nick laughed, understanding her confusion. She stood and whirled away into the near-darkness. Nick, hearing a splash, got up and followed her into the lake.

"About time," admonished Angus as the two ran dripping into the house. He threw dry towels at them and they disappeared into the bedroom and closed the door. "There's good food here going to waste!" he protested, pouring himself a stiff drink.

"We'll not be long," laughed Nick. He turned to Kestrel, who knelt on the bed drying her hair. The fire roared in the hearth and Nick felt a different kind of heat once more surge through him. "Well, not too long," he amended, wanting to see all of her as he gently took her in his arms and kissed her.

Kestrel lay still, her eyes half closed, concentrating on the sensations that Nick was arousing in her body as he examined every inch of her with his hands and mouth.

"No more today," he said, seeing she still bled as she bucked against him, very aroused. Kestrel's eyes flew wide with indignation; she frowned and looked down at his rearing member. "You'll be too sore and then tomorrow we'll have nothing to look forward to," he explained gently. Kestrel's green eyes narrowed and she lay down putting her head on Nick's upper thigh as she idly stroked his manhood.

"Witch," groaned Nick, staring down at the gold head in his lap. Kestrel softly kissed him and he thrust toward her and sighed deeply as she captured him in her warm soft mouth. Nick extricated himself, pushed her back, parted her legs, and drove himself into her. Kestrel purred with pleasure.

"We'll both be sorry tomorrow," promised Nick, knowing he could never have enough of her.

"Dinna blame me if it tastes like shoe leather," grumbled Angus when Nick appeared ruefully several hours later.

"Fell asleep," protested Nick, only a half truth as they had slept between making love twice.

"Well, I'm for bed, myself," returned Angus. "Help yourselves." He poured himself a final drink and staggered to his back room.

"Well, madam, what do you feel like eating?" asked Nick as Kestrel stood at the bedroom door, dressed in his shirt. She walked stiffly toward him, feeling very sore. Nick frowned and shook his head.

"I feel like I've been riding for a week nonstop," she groaned.

"Well, in a way you have." Nick grinned.

"You did most of the riding. I was the saddle," laughed Kestrel.

"Get back into bed and I'll serve you supper," offered Nick. "What do you want?"

"What is there?" called Kestrel, taking his advice and scrambling back into the large comfortable bed.

"Lots of things," said Nick, looking into the array of pots.

"A bit of everything."

"I couldn't eat another bite," gasped Kestrel, lying back on the pillows and holding her stomach. She watched Nick who still ate, delighting in his strong lean body. The firelight played along the planes of his face, the flames reflecting in his black eyes. She caressed his broad brown chest with her eyes and frowned when she saw he was wearing his tight buckskin trousers.

"Why are your pants on?" she challenged.

"To protect myself," he answered, chewing stolidly.

"From what?" asked Kestrel indignantly.

"Guess," returned Nick.

"Me?"

"No, what makes you say that?" mocked Nick, still eating, pretending to ignore her caressing hands as she felt the outline underneath his tight trousers.

"Hah!" said Kestrel triumphantly, feeling him stir and harden. "Nick?"

"Um?"

"Did you ever make love before?"

Nick choked and took a long drink of spring water.

"Your mind can switch from one thing to another very quickly," he stated, playing for time and biting into some pie.

"Have you?"

Nick nodded.

"Oh. What was it like?"

Nick chewed and shrugged.

"Is it the same?" probed Kestrel.

"The same as what?"

"The same with everyone?"

"No," answered Nick shortly.

"How many times?" asked Kestrel and Nick wondered how to go about telling her there was no way of counting.

"It doesn't matter. 'Tis not important," he stated, putting the tray of food aside and kissing her. "You are who is important for me to make love to. The others don't exist."

"How many others?" queried Kestrel.

"A man is entitled to some secrets from a nosy wife," protested Nick humorously.

"Any of them fat?"

"What?" laughed Nick, staring down into her innocent face.

"Fat? You know, fat?" She blew out her cheeks and pushed out her stomach.

"Why?"

"There's a fat woman at the trading post who I think makes love with lots of men. I didn't understand it until today. Angus goes there sometimes. He once got very angry when I asked him about it. Have you ever made love to the fat woman at the trading post?" asked Kestrel earnestly.

"What if I had?" returned Nick, wanting to know her reaction.

"Have you?" cried Kestrel, very distressed.

"No, of course not. But if I had?"

"I wouldn't like it. I don't like any of those other women, either!" shouted Kestrel in a jealous rage.

"And I wouldna like it if there were any other men in your life. But I'm a lot older than you and a man," explained Nick.

"So?"

"I was jealous of Moon Elk," returned Nick, not having the energy to explain the different neeus of men.

"I saw him make love to Young Wife while Morning Mist watched. I don't think I'd like anyone to watch us," yawned Kestrel as Nick stacked the tray and stood to take it into the other room. "I'll help," she offered.

"No, you stay still. I can manage," said Nick. Kestrel lay drowsily in bed, watching Nick through the open door. She felt very happy and peaceful despite the ache between her legs.

"Did Meron leave?" she asked, trying to keep her eyes open until Nick came to bed and she could cuddle into his warm hardness.

"Aye, yesterday," answered Nick, throwing the dirty water from washing the dishes out of the door and drying his hands.

"Hurry up to bed," yawned Kestrel. "Before I fall asleep. I want to fall asleep with you."

Nick climbed into bed and Kestrel sighed contentedly and burrowed into him.

"Nick?" she murmured.

"Aye," he answered, holding her close, but there was only the rhythmic sound of her breathing.

Nick lay staring at the flame's pattern on the wooden rafters of the ceiling, cradling Kestrel in his arms and feeling very complete. A tender smile softened the normally hard lines of his face.

Meron entered the mission, his dark face revealing none of the distaste he felt for the almost prisonlike atmosphere. Everything was set in rigid rows; sterile with no individuality, he observed, his keen green eyes taking in the overorderly appearance of everything from tables and chairs to clothes to the lines of dull-eyed Indians.

"It would have been about October 1778," he informed the stern-faced, thin old man.

"Three and a half years ago."

"Three and a half years ago," repeated Meron, trying to keep his patience. "A girl of thirteen. Black hair, amber eyes."

"Amber?"

"A golden color."

"Brown," stated the lined old man.

"Aye, but light. She could have been wounded. A bullet wound."

"Where?"

"I don't know. She was dressed in leather like a native, and with her dark hair and tan skin could pass for one except for her light eyes," explained Meron, for about the tenth time. It seemed everything had to be repeated and repeated. The old man stared at him, not saying a word as he nodded and cleared his throat. Meron forced himself to be still as the old man got up and paced around the room.

"Brought here you think by some French? One a Catholic priest? With some other Indian females?" The old man broke the silence. Meron nodded wearily.

"Gold eyes and a bullet wound?"

Meron nodded.

"Mute?"

"Mute?" repeated Meron, sounding like the old man.

"We have a mute halfbreed that answers your description. Was your niece mute?" asked the old man impatiently.

Meron shook his head.

"Then I cannot help you."

"I'd like to see the girl. Maybe shock and terror caused her silence," suggested Meron.

The old man shrugged and stood.

"Are you a Christian, Mr. Meron?"

"Why?"

"That does not answer my question. Are you a Christian."

"Of course," lied Meron. "But not of your religion."

"Catholic?"

Meron nodded. The old man nodded back and left the room, returning several minutes later with a petite black-haired girl dressed in a gray smock and white apron. Meron caught his breath.

"Rue?" he called to her softly, but the girl stared down at her small bare feet.

"We call her Martha."

Meron lifted his hand to raise the small chin and the girl ducked as though to avoid being hit.

"Who has abused her?" he asked harshly, feeling tremors of fear shake the undernourished little body. He gently lifted the heart-shaped face and gazed down into the wide amber eyes.

"Rue!" he rejoiced, his voice cracking with emotion. But the upturned face showed no recognition, just terror.

"Wait outside, Martha," snapped the old man and the girl docilely obeyed.

"There is no doubt. That is my niece, Rue Sinclair," stated Meron as the door closed behind her.

"Are you positive?"

"Aye," returned Meron, for though three years and obvious

hardship had left a dreadful mark, there was no mistaking his niece's delicate features.

"The girl was brought to us, not only wounded but sorely abused. She gave birth to a child six months later. Mercifully the child died. We have tried to place Martha with several good Christian families but even though she is dumb and appears docile, she has a stubborn streak," complained the dry old man.

"It runs in our family," murmured Meron, rejoicing that his niece hadn't been totally bowed and wanting to be gone from the rigid gray place.

"Perhaps a wanton, immoral streak," added the man spitefully.

Rue stood in the long corridor, her thin back pressed against the hard cold wall, trying to still the terror that beat through her. Once again she was to be hired out to one of the neighboring farms. She wanted to scream, but there were no tears and no sound. Other times she had held on tightly to the door so they had to pry her hands open to carry her kicking and biting to be beaten for disobedience. She heard the muffled rumble of male voices but couldn't understand what was being discussed. She shrank back as the door was thrust open and clawed, trying to find a handhold on the smooth wall to prevent herself being dragged off. As cold and cheerless as the mission was, it was better than being at the mercy of brutal men who used her any way they wanted to.

Meron held out his hands to the small dark girl who crouched against the wall, her teeth bared like a cornered wild animal.

"Martha," warned the old man with a vicious note in his voice.

"Rue," said Meron gently. "Your name is Rue. Rue Sinclair," he added, bending down so his face was level with hers. "We are going home."

Rue's thin chest heaved as she tried to still her panic. She heard what the dark man said and it struck a painful place deep inside. She allowed him to lift her in his arms and carry her to his horse.

Meron's craggy face was set on stern lines as he strode carrying the skeletal frame of his niece. The girl was rigid, her face blank, showing nothing of the tumult that roared inside her. He lifted her onto the high back of his horse, mounting behind her, and they rode out of the oppressive, orderly mission into the surrounding farmland. As they left the signs of civilization behind, Meron noted Rue's bowed shoulders straighten and her too thin body stiffen until she at last sat with dignity, her lithe legs instinctively gripping the horse's girth.

"We're going home," he informed her, reining his horse and

dismounting. He held his hands out to lift her down and she winced. 'Do you ken your name is Rue Sinclair?" he asked softly, keeping his hands out to her. Amber eyes stared into his green ones and slowly she nodded, heavy tears sliding down her cheeks, before she reached out her own thin arms and fell off the horse into his. Meron held her tightly to his heart feeling a terrible ache well inside as he thought of his dead twin. "I have her safe, Cameron," he whispered, and he sat upon the ground cradling her to him, his tears mingling with hers. " 'Tis all over, Rue. 'Tis home we go," he crooned, lifting her back onto his horse.

Rue kept her eyes straight ahead as she listened to her uncle's low voice tell her of Angus and Kestrel. A feeling of impending doom gnawed within her at the avoidance of other members of her family. She concentrated on the hypnotic rhythm of the horse, not daring to feel anything as she waited to awaken back at the mission. She dozed, sagging against the muscular body of the man who rode behind her.

Meron tightened his hold on Rue as he felt her slight frame relax against him in sleep. As he did so, she stiffened in terror and tried to leap from the horse, causing it to rear in panic.

"Whoa," crooned Meron, to both the animal and the frightened girl. "Rue, what is it?" he asked, trying to control the horse and his niece.

Rue fought, forcing Meron to dismount, holding her easily in his arms. She stiffened, waiting for the assault upon her body. Waiting to be thrown down on the ground, her legs to be cruelly yanked apart. Waiting for the searing pain to thrust tearing into the center of her, grinding her into the dirt.

"Look at me, Rue," directed Meron softly. "Look at me," he coaxed as he stroked her cheek. "Your mother never gave up hope. She knew I'd find you and bring you home."

Slowly Rue unthawed and started listening to her uncle's words. She turned her head and looked up at him. She reached out and traced the contours of his aquiline face and smiled wonderingly. It wasn't a dream. It was real. She was going home.

Meron saw her amber eyes light up as though a fire burned within and she nodded excitedly, pointing to the horse. Meron grinned. 'Aye, we're going home."

The following evening Kestrel stretched like a cat and turned, rubbing her body against Nick's long hard one.

"Kess, can you not let a puir man reserve his strength and get a wee bit of rest?" he protested mockingly as he surrendered his relaxed body to her ardent nature. He lay in a delicious half-waking state feeling her nibble and kiss his ears and eyes. He opened his mouth at the insistence of her probing tongue and sighed deeply as if sorely put upon as he anticipated her slow descent along the length of his quite willing body.

It had been six days since making love under the fir trees by the lake and he doubted they had been out of bed more than an hour at any one time. Poor Angus felt abandoned and he made his displeasure known as he banged the pots around.

Kestrel hungrily kissed and nuzzled, making circles with her pert tongue on his belly, getting lower and lower until Nick arched and groaned with pleasure. He rearranged their positions and started a sweet, tortuously slow assault upon her willing body.

"Rue!" rejoiced Angus's gravelly voice from the other room and Kestrel sat up. She and Nick looked at each other and scrambled around for their clothes.

Rue stood looking up at the enormous old man, her eyes full of tears. Impulsively she hugged him and he wrapped his thick arms about her.

"She's nothing but skin and bone," he exclaimed to Meron who nodded. "What did those fanatics feed you, Rue lass?"

"She canna talk," explained Meron and Angus frowned with alarm. Rue pointed toward the bedroom door, her mouth moving up and down as though to say "mama."

"She doesna know? I wouldna let her in there. I doubt they're decent," fretted Angus. The bedroom door opened and Kestrel ran out barefoot, dressed in trews and a shirt. She stopped in amazement as she looked at her sister in her gray smock.

"Rue? Is it really you?" she asked, not seeing the Rue she knew three and a half years ago.

Nick watched the reunion from the bedroom door. The two girls were the same height and build, with similarly shaped faces and features. All that was different were the contrasting colorings. Rue was painfully thin, he also noted. She turned, bewildered, and looked at Nick.

"This is my husband, Nick MacKay," introduced Kestrel, confused by the solemn girl.

"Rue cannot talk," repeated Meron, noticing Rue's thin shoulders shaking.

Rue stared around the large warm room. She felt she was in a dream, at the end of a long, long tunnel. Angus's, Kestrel's, and Meron's faces zoomed in and out of a strange reality. She felt disconnected. She needed Mother. Where was Mother? She walked to the door of the master bedroom feeling strangely disjointed, knowing everyone was looking at her. The room was empty and the familiar bed tousled. A fire roared in the hearth and there was a musky intimacy that she recoiled from.

"Rue, sit down," urged Meron, guiding her to the settle. She allowed him to lead her and she sat staring at her bare feet, unable to look at her vibrant golden sister or the tall dark man. She was home, she told herself, not quite able to grasp the enormity of the fact. She was back in the warmth away from the cold gray of the mission, and yet nothing seemed real. Many things were missing. Where was Mother? She stood up suddenly and crossed the room to the carving on the wall that proclaimed her birth and those of her siblings. She traced her name with her finger, then she traced Rowan's name. She banged the wall and pointed to his name.

"Rowan is on his way to Scotland with Lynx and your father," said Meron gently.

Rue pointed to the name Cameron and banged the wall.

"Your mother is dead and so is your brother, Raven," her uncle told her.

Kestrel's blood ran cold at the terrible animal scream that issued from Rue's mouth as she pounded her small fists against the wood. Kestrel clutched at Nick, wanting his strong arms about her, but he gently put her aside and went to help Meron. She and Angus watched helplessly as Rue fought both men.

"Not another one," gasped Nick as a small fist caught him in the stomach. Rue's strange cries continued rhythmically.

"Don't touch her! Let go of her!" screamed Kestrel, suddenly understanding the panic on Rue's face as screams from three years ago tore into her mind. "Let go!" she shouted, pushing Meron to one side and taking her sister in her arms. "Rue, oh Rue, it's all right, my sister, it's all right," she wept. Rue looked into Kestrel's face and, wonderingly, traced the tears with her fingers.

Kestrel and Rue wept together as they held each other close.

"Supper's ready," proclaimed Angus, as Kestrel led her sister to the fire, both of them still wet-cheeked.

"Are you hungry?" asked Kestrel and Rue smiled blearily and nodded.

"It's all right to eat, Rue," urged Meron, who saw her tentative movements. Kestrel gasped as her sister ducked to shield her head when Nick raised his arm to hand Rue some bread.

"Nick is a doctor," said Angus, "I think you need a lot of doctoring, and love, Rue lass."

Rue's eyelids drooped and she tried to keep them all in focus but the effort was too much. She couldn't eat. She couldn't cope with any more. She put her head down on the table and fell asleep. Nick picked her up and carried her to the settle by the fire.

"She doesn't weigh a thing," he remarked as he reseated himself at the table. "What did you find out?"

"Nothing much," evaded Meron, not wanting to talk in front of Kestrel.

"Well, what?" probed Kestrel, her keen senses knowing her uncle was avoiding the issue. "What did you find out? What was the place like where you found her? Aren't you going to tell us anything?" she demanded hotly.

"She was at a mission. A comfortless, strict, bare, gray place," struggled Meron. "She has had no love, just religion and sweeping and scrubbing for three and a half years, so we have to bring spring and summer to her after such a long winter."

"Where did I shoot her?" whispered Kestrel.

"I don't know," replied Meron.

Kestrel turned and stared at her sister who was curled on the settle. She looked so young and small.

"I feel like the older sister," she said softly.

"Aye, she doesna look like she'll be seventeen in August, does she?" remarked Angus.

"Good food and rest and she'll fill out," informed Nick. "Maybe I should examine her. Kestrel can help me as it seems she has a fear of men."

"Can you blame her?" Meron questioned and the three looked at him in surprise. "There was a bairn, died at birth. Born early," he replied in a clipped staccato fashion as anger and sadness restricted his throat.

"What?" roared Angus.

"Shush!" cautioned Nick, indicating the sleeping girl. "When?"

"Six months after she arrived at the mission. She got there in mid-November, so the following March."

"She had a baby?" asked Kestrel, trying to sort out what was being said.

"Aye."

"How?" persisted Kestrel.

"Had to be from the rape," mused Angus.

"From a rape?" echoed Kestrel.

"I'll explain later, my love," said Nick softly, wishing he didn't ave to as it seemed somehow to sully their lovemaking. "Right now t's get a fire lit in her room and tuck her into bed."

Kestrel stared down in shock at her sister's emaciated body that was risscrossed with welts from numerous whippings.

"Oh, Nick, how could anyone do such a thing?" she whispered. ue crossed her thin arms across her tiny breasts and looked at them ith haunted eyes. Nick smiled down at her.

"You're going to be fine, Rue," he reassured her as he handed estrel a nightshirt and left the room.

"You're going to be fine," repeated Kestrel as she pulled the shirt ver Rue's head. She tucked the blankets around her sister and kissed er softly on the cheek. Rue's arms reached up and held her. "It's oing to be fine," she soothed, holding her close and thinking of the oincidence of the bullet wound scar that they had found. A straight hite scar from the belly button to the waist just like the one Kestrel ad received at the ambush, except Rue's ran to the left.

Kestrel held her sister until she slept and then tiptoed from the oom, leaving the door open. She walked into the central room, where e men spoke in hushed voices, and crossed to the front door. She tood staring out over the tranquil lake, listening to the night noises. lick came up behind her and put his arms around her waist and pulled er back up against him.

"When I look out there it's hard to think of anything horrible appening," said Kestrel softly.

"Aye," agreed Nick, thinking of Rue's abused little body.

"I shot her right where I was shot," she said wonderingly, turning face him.

"You were shot where you shot her," corrected Nick. "Aye, that's e strangest coincidence."

"Who beat her like that?"

Nick shrugged and shook his head.

"Who beat her like that?" repeated Kestrel, pushing past him into he house.

"I dinna ken," responded Meron wearily. "The dried-up old man the mission said something about her being stubborn and not ooperating with the families she was supposed to work for," he

added, wishing he had checked her before leaving so he could have
avenged such abuse.

"She's home wie us now and we'll see she mends and gets fattened
up," growled Angus, pouring himself a large drink.

Kestrel turned and burrowed into Nick's chest and he wrapped his
arms around her.

CHAPTER TWELVE

Rue awoke and frowned, seeing the warmth of the fire reflected on the
rich brown wood. She lay still, expecting the pleasant dream to fade
to the dismal cold gray of the mission. Her body was cosy and warm
and she waited for the usual chills to grip her, aching her joints. She
sat up and looked out at the dawn sky, hearing the chorus of birds
greet the day. She was home. Really home, she realized, cuddling
down under the covers again. She didn't have to get up and dress in
the freezing bare room and empty the slop pails of the elders. She
didn't have to get on her knees and scrub until her arm felt it would
fall off. She could sleep more, she told herself, closing her eyes.

But sleep eluded her as sadness welled and she thought of her
fragmented family. All that seemed to be left was her uncle, her sister
and Angus. Mother and Raven were dead, she thought and tears
welled. Just like Goliath and Jemmy, and as she remembered, the
tears stopped and terror took over. She sat up suddenly, trying to think
of something different, something so she didn't have to remember.
She got out of bed and walked to the window. She smiled seeing the
lake and recalling her carefree childhood, laughing and tumbling
about in the water with her brothers and sister. She looked at the
sloping meadow, remembering rolling down the verdant green, and
hide-and-seek in the forest. She looked around for her clothes, and
seeing the gray smock, her rage boiled up and she threw it into the fire
before opening the cedar chest in the corner.

She sighed deeply and was filled with nostalgic sadness at seeing
her doll, made out of a corn husk and dressed in fur and leather. She

hugged it to herself as the tears fell. All her treasures had been saved, she realized as she unfurled and read the letter her mother had left her.

> My darling daughter Rue,
>
>   I never doubted that you were alive. These last three years without you have been without sunshine. Each day you were in my thoughts and I know if you are reading this you are at last safely home. Sadly I will not be there to hold you and that breaks my heart. But be happy, my little daughter. Put sadness behind you, and I will live on through you.
>
>   All my love,
>   Mother

Rue threw herself facedown on the bed and wept.

"What is it, Rue?" whispered Kestrel entering the room, sitting beside her and stroking her head. Seeing the letter in her sister's hand she gently extricated it and read. Her own eyes and nose ached with the need to cry but something froze the tears. Nick stood in the doorway and he frowned as he saw Kestrel's concerned face harden. Her nostrils flared and her cheeks hollowed as though she were bitten from within. Kestrel looked up and saw him, her green eyes blazed with a violent emotion, and then she fleetly raced from the room.

Rue sat up, bewildered at her sister's sudden departure. Nick picked up the crumpled letter, smoothed it, and read. He swore under his breath, knowing the hurt Kestrel had received. Rue shrank away from him, cowering, and he groaned at the terror he saw in her wide gold eyes.

" 'Tis all right, Rue," he comforted, making sure his movements were unhurried, as she seemed to shy from sharp movements as if expecting a beating. Rue waved toward the door and then ran to the window. Nick stood beside her and they both watched Kestrel race into the forest.

"She'll be all right," he reassured her. "Now, how are you?"

Rue nodded solemnly and then pointed out of the window and then at herself.

"You want to go outside?"

Rue nodded and Nick smiled and nodded. The poor girl had been a virtual prisoner for three and a half years, having to ask permission for every little thing, he reflected sadly as he left Rue's room, determined to find Kestrel.

He found her in the small burial glen. She stood glowering at her mother's cairn, her face as stony and cold as the rocks. She wheeled around as she sensed his presence. She stood poised to run. Nick silently opened his arms and without hesitation she ran to him. He smiled contentedly and enfolded her in his strong arms.

"You're my sunshine," he said softly after a long pause.

Kestrel looked up at him, her brow creased in a frown. She was confused, not understanding the nature of her own turbulent emotions on reading Cameron's letter to Rue. "Let's talk about it," added Nick, sitting down on the lush grass and pulling her onto his lap. "You know I find out something new about you every day."

Kestrel stared into his dark eyes, not knowing what she felt or what to say.

"Today I found out that you could read," Nick continued. "Who taught you?"

"My mother," replied Kestrel, the words sticking in her throat. "Nick, am I a bad person?"

"Why do you ask such a silly question?"

"I have to go back to the house," she stated, trying to stand but Nick held her firmly.

"Whoa," he murmured. "Why?"

"Poor Rue, I just ran away and she was crying and needed me. I'm always doing such cruel things and I don't mean to," confessed Kestrel in frustration.

"Angus is wie Rue," soothed Nick. " 'Tis better you talk about the letter."

"All my love!" mocked Kestrel bitterly. "All my love!"

"Aye, 'tis a way a lot of people have of signing letters—'tis not to be taken literally," explained Nick. "Not to be taken at the very meaning of the words," he added, seeing her puzzlement.

"Sometimes it is," retorted Kestrel.

"Your mother loved you."

Kestrel shrugged. "I'm lucky. I always wished I was Rue, but I wouldn't have liked to be beaten like she has been," she stated, pulling herself free of Nick's arms and standing. She walked slowly to one of the cairns and started lifting off the stones.

"What are you doing?"

"This is Rue's cairn, but she's not dead after all," Kestrel informed him and Nick stood and helped her dismantle the monument. "Nick, why can't Rue talk?" she asked as they stacked the heavy stones on top of the stone wall that encircled the glen.

"I dinna ken. Maybe fear has locked her voice away. She can hear well, so unless she's had a sickness or injury to her throat or mouth . . ." Nick trailed off as he saw Rue's slight figure enter the glen.

"Rue, I'm sorry," apologized Kestrel, walking to her sister and stroking her cheek softly.

Rue stared wide-eyed at the cairns. She pointed to the one nearest. "That's Mother," answered Kestrel. "Raven. Goliath. Jemmy . . ." Rue pointed to the half-dismantled one and when her sister wouldn't answer, stared challengingly at Nick. Rue nodded in the silence and pointed to herself. Nick nodded and she smiled sadly. Tears poured down Kestrel's face and Rue wiped them away, trying to reassure her sister that she understood.

"When you have rested and healed, I think we should go to Scotland to your father and brothers. You'll be a great comfort to Alex," said Nick as they walked back to the house for breakfast.

"May I go, too?" asked Kestrel, a bit panic-stricken, thinking she might once again be left behind. Nick caught her up in his strong arms and nuzzled the fragrant warmth of her neck.

"Do you honestly think I'd leave you behind wie all the mischief you get up to?" he laughed. Kestrel wrapped her arms about his neck and rubbed her soft cheek against his rough one.

Rue watched and smiled wistfully as she remembered her mother and father, who demonstrated their love for each other in similar ways. She sat under the fir trees, hugging her knees, and she wondered if she would ever find love.

Kestrel and Nick lay entwined in bed. Nick drowsed, sated from the long, busy day, the large supper, and the hectic lovemaking.

"Nick?"

"Um?" he murmured, not really wanting to waken.

"Nick?" insisted Kestrel, shaking him.

"Shush up," he protested, holding her tightly.

"When can we go to Scotland?"

"We'll talk tomorrow."

"No, now!"

"No!"

Kestrel lay quiet, sulkily resenting Nick's deep even breaths as her mind raced, full of a million things. His heart beat strongly under her ear as her head rested on his broad chest. Deep inside of her she felt a panicky fear that destroyed her golden happiness. She twisted around so she faced him and stared into his face. To her surprise a pair of black eyes stared back and Nick sighed resignedly.

"There's nothing to be afraid of," he said softly, his rich voice warmly comforting her.

"How do you know?"

"I can read you like a book, Kestrel Sinclair MacKay," Nick smiled. "You've been afraid since Meron brought Rue back."

"Why?" worried Kestrel. "I'm happy she's home. I'm happy she's alive, but—"

"You're afraid," prompted Nick. Kestrel nodded. "You tell me why," he insisted. "Go on, be brave."

"That you'll love her more than me," whispered Kestrel.

"What? I canna hear."

"That you'll love her more than me," she repeated, her low voice trembling.

"Do you hear how silly that is?" chuckled Nick, cradling her in his arms.

"Everybody always did."

"Nay, you just thought they did. Now 'tis time to sleep. Night at the end of a long day is no time to try to sort things out. I love you and as I told you this morn, you are my sunshine," he told her lovingly, closing his eyes once more, hoping to drift off to sleep.

"I love you," professed Kestrel, ardently wiggling around so her naked warm stomach and breasts pressed urgently against him as she captured his mouth, hungrily prying his firm lips apart for her tongue to feel the satiny warmth within.

"Och, there's no rest for the wicked," bemoaned Nick, running his hands up and down her silky back as she undulated her hips and pried his long legs apart with her small sharp knee. "Careful," he warned, lifting her so she lay atop the length of him. He stretched and yawned, pretending a nonchalance as she busily writhed against him.

"Ouch!" he complained as she painfully nipped his ear.

"You have to help," she panted.

"Nay, I want to sleep," he teased, smiling up at her as she sat straddling his waist. "You'll have to manage all by yourself." He gasped as she firmly lowered herself and guided him into the heat of her. He ran his strong hands up her firm belly to caress her straining breasts as she rode him. He smiled at her serious concentration before closing his eyes and losing himself in the incredible sensations as her rhythm increased and they raced faster and faster until they strained to each other. They fell asleep still coupled together.

Kestrel awoke at the first light and lay still embraced by Nick's strong arms, listening to the dawn chorus. They were going to go to Scotland, she mused and shivered with excitement at the prospect. From her earliest recollections she remembered the stories her parents told. She couldn't imagine the houses and castles and purple moors but now she was going to see them. She quietly slipped from the bed, not knowing that Nick's black eyes watched her. She pulled on a shirt and bundled her buckskin trews and jerkin in her arms and tiptoed out.

From the window Nick watched her dive into the tranquil lake. Then he got back into bed and closed his eyes for another few hours' sleep.

Rue watched Kestrel swimming cleanly across the lake. She longed to plunge into the cleansing clearness but was somehow afraid. As children they had all bathed naked together, but at the mission Rue had learned it was a sin. What was a sin? she brooded, not understanding the logic but feeling the fear of punishment.

"Come and swim, Rue," hailed Kestrel and she shook her head. "Why not? It's not cold," cried Kestrel. "Come on," she insisted, seeing her sister waver.

Rue slowly pulled the shirt over her head and stood cowed and ashamed, her arms crossed over her breasts. Kestrel frowned with concern, not understanding her sister's obvious shameful expression. Rue's eyes widened and she backed away from Kestrel's disapproving look.

"What's the matter?" Kestrel asked, walking out of the water.

Meron watched his two nieces. One so golden straight and proud in all her naked glory and the other beaten and cowed. His eyes filled with tears and he lifted the deer's carcass off his shoulders and laid it in the grass.

"Rue?" he called and his heart constricted as he saw her pitifully thin and bruised body shudder with fear. " 'Tis all right, lass, there's no one here that'll beat you. You maun remember times before," he urged, not knowing how to undo the terrible harm.

"Come in for a swim," pleaded Kestrel, knowing that once in, Rue would relax. Rue looked to her uncle for permission and Meron nodded.

Rue walked slowly into the water and then dived under. Meron held his breath waiting for her to resurface. His brown face broke into a wide grin as she appeared fifty yards out and then duck-dived again. Kestrel swam after her and soon the two girls were smiling and playing.

Meron watched for a while and then picked up the venison. He walked toward the house whistling tunelessly, his brow creased with worry. Angus rocked on the porch, his face stern and sad.

" 'Tis good Cameron dinna live to see her bairn cringe like a beaten cur," he mourned.

"Time will heal," stated Meron, trying to convince himself as he carried the meat behind the house to butcher it.

Angus stood and stretched before entering the house to cook breakfast.

Kestrel and Rue ran back to the house. Rue's lips and fingernails were blue-tinged and she shivered violently. Kestrel rubbed her briskly with the towel and pulled the shirt over her wet head.

"Get near the fire, Rue lass," ordered Angus, worried at the chill the girl was obviously feeling despite the warmth of the day.

"Nick? Nick?" shouted Kestrel, urgently running across the main room toward their bedroom.

Nick groaned as he was shaken from his warm sleep by wet arms and cold water dripped on his face and chest. He sleepily tried to pull his cool, silky wife into bed with him.

"Nick, it's Rue. She's all blue and shaking!" Kestrel yelled and he opened his protesting eyes, sat, shook his head and pulled on his trousers. "Hurry, quick," she added impatiently, feeling guilty for having forced her sister into the water and dragging him out.

Nick smiled at the small shivering girl by the fire in the main room.

"You've not enough flesh on your bones for a long swim. Gie her a hot drink, Angus," he ordered, wrapping Rue in a thick blanket. As he enfolded her, his heart ached for the violent shudders that tore her tiny frame. He pulled her onto his lap and cradled her like a baby as he tried to still the tremors and get the circulation moving to warm her chilled body.

Kestrel's green eyes narrowed as she watched. Angus, noting the closed hard look, handed her a steaming mug.

"No time for jealousy, Kessie lass," he whispered gruffly. "Go help warm her."

Kestrel stood, feeling pain, unable to move toward the fire. Nick looked up and understood.

"Come help me, my love," he said softly and she moved toward him, her eyes pinned to his so she didn't see the girl in his arms. "Hold her, too," he coaxed and Kestrel stared down into Rue's poignant face. She knelt and wrapped her arms around her sister, feeling Nick's hands embrace her, too. She shivered as she felt the painful tremors that shook Rue.

"I'm sorry, Rue, I didn't know you shouldn't swim."

" 'Tis not that she shouldn't, but a little at a time," corrected Nick, aching for both of Cameron's daughters.

Rue slept peacefully, curled on the settle by the fire, her face relaxed and rosy, as Meron, Nick, and Kestrel ate at the long rough-hewn table. Angus, unable to sit, fussed with his pots and checked every few minutes to see if the raven-haired girl was breathing.

"I've not had occasion to examine her throat or tongue as yet," informed Nick in answer to Angus's query about Rue's muteness, "but I dinna think I'll find anything. I think fear has locked her voice away."

"She arrived at the mission unable to speak," recounted Meron. "So 'twas probably the abuse at the hands of the Redcoats."

"When can we go to Scotland?" asked Kestrel.

"Not for a while. Rue's going to need a lot of building up if she's to survive the traveling," answered Nick.

"What's a while?" insisted Kestrel.

"At least a month or two."

Angus beamed, not wanting them to leave at all.

"Then I'll have some help stocking up for the winter," he growled.

"Will you come with us, Meron?" asked Kestrel.

"Nay," responded her uncle. "This is my home now. When the time comes I'll lead you to the coast and send you on your way."

"And we'll be here for when you return," chorused Angus. "You do mean to return, do you not?" he added, alarmed.

"Aye," laughed Nick. "But not so far into the wilderness as I'll not have many patients. The natives have their shamans and have no need of me. I'd like to learn their natural ways of healing," he mused aloud.

"And so you shall," returned Meron. "I think the meeting of Indian and Scottish shamans might make for good medicine," he laughed.

CHAPTER THIRTEEN

May turned to June; the sparkling crystal days turned rich and hot as the blossom blew away like confetti and the fruits swelled. Rue filled out, her skin bronzing until her body turned the warm whiskey color of her eyes. But still she remained silent. Still she winced if someone raised their hand too quickly. But despite the terror that often beat through her, she kept her back straight and her head proudly lifted. Meron nodded his approval, fanning her confidence whenever he could.

Moon Elk, hearing of Rue's return, came with both a beautiful jet-black pony, the very color of her hair, and some intricately embroidered clothes. He arrived with several of his braves one hot noon in mid-June as Kestrel and Rue played in the lake. Meron and Nick were off hunting and Angus rocked and dozed on the porch, surrounded by sleepy hounds. The Tuscarora chief reined his horse and raised his hand to halt his braves when he saw the two lithe girls playing in the clear water.

Angus awoke suddenly and nearly fell out of his chair as the hounds barked menacingly, and he opened his eyes to the spectacle of the proud colorful chief and his braves. He pulled his enormous girth to his feet and staggered down the steps, his hand outstretched in a sign of welcome, but the Tuscarora were too captivated by the sight of the golden- and ebony-haired maidens swimming like young otters in the serene lake. He frowned and scratched his grizzled head, not knowing the protocol of telling an Indian chief to take his lustful eyes off his young charges. He knew Kestrel could take care of herself but worried about Rue's precarious recovery.

Kestrel's green eyes widened in surprise at seeing Moon Elk looking so dignified as he sat upon his horse watching her and her sister. She stuck her tongue out at him and did a saucy duck-dive, exhibiting a cheeky bottom before disappearing under the rippling waters. Angus choked and beat his massive chest, pretending to have a coughing fit. Rue frowned, looking toward the horsemen who posed like statues on the rolling green meadow. She stared around trying to locate her sister, and not seeing her, swam toward Moon Elk and his men. Angus stopped in his tracks as Rue walked proudly and uninhibitedly out of the lake.

"Small Sadness, it does my heart much happiness to see you after so long," greeted Moon Elk formally as though she were dressed in finery. Rue nodded respectfully, forgetting she was naked and gracefully arched her arm indicating the house. Angus puffed up.

"Please accept our hospitality, Chief Moon Elk, sir," he panted. The tall Tuscarora leader barked an order to one of his men and dismounted in one lithe movement. His keen eyes noted the scars on Rue's young body but his enigmatic face showed nothing as he accepted Angus and Rue's invitation.

Rue watched the men walk to the house and turned back to the lake, looking for a sign of her sister. There wasn't even a ripple on the clear calm water. She stretched in the sunlight before picking up her clothes and climbing into them. Dressed in a thin blouse and buckskin-fringed trousers, she ran barefoot to the house, eager to help Angus serve their guests.

"Small Sadness," hailed Moon Elk and she stopped and looked up at the glistening black pony he held. "I remember when you were born," he reminisced as he cupped his large brown hands and lifted her effortlessly onto the bare back of the beautiful horse. "Ride out the bad times, daughter of my friends."

Rue felt the wind sing through her long wet hair. She felt the warmth of the animal's muscular sides as she pressed her long lean legs against him. Strange little noises of satisfaction burst out of her mouth as she galloped over the rolling green meadow.

Meron and Nick reined their horses as the slight ebony-haired rider streaked across the green. They grinned as they saw the wide happy smile on the pixielike face.

"Where did she get that magnificent horse?" exclaimed Nick.

"Moon Elk, it seems," replied Meron, his keen eyes seeing several Indians clustered on the porch of the wooden house. They kneed their mounts and raced home where they found Angus in his element, piling the table high with his home-cooked cakes and pies.

"Where's Kestrel?" asked Nick after checking their bedroom.

"I think she did not trust her manners," responded Moon Elk with a twinkle in his eye.

"If those were manners that popped out of the lake when she saw you, then I'm a monkey's uncle," chuckled Angus. Meron and Nick looked inquiringly at him, but the old man and the chief just laughed together.

"It is good you found Small Sadness, but it appears she's received many beatings," stated Moon Elk. "Who marked her so?"

"If I knew I would mark them in a similar fashion," retorted Meron.

"I thought you felt women should be beaten, Moon Elk?" challenged Kestrel, staring down at him from the top of the stairs.

"No, not women, they should never be beaten," replied the chief after a long silence. "But rude mannerless children should be taught to behave," he added, staring at her long and hard before turning back to the table. Nick noted the angry flush that burned Kestrel's face at the censure and wondered what she would do to retaliate. He turned back to the conversation at the table after shaking his head in silent warning to her.

Kestrel looked down at the four men as they ate and conversed, feeling left out and ignored. Her stomach growled with hunger and she resolutely descended the stairs, determined to sit and eat also despite Moon Elk. To her surprise no one objected. Angus even pulled a chair out for her and cut her a wedge of savory pie. She stared victoriously at Moon Elk.

"Kess?" warned Nick, knowing she was about to do or say something goading. Kestrel frowned as it seemed Nick could read her mind as she was about to comment scathingly on the Iroquois tradition of women eating after the men.

"What?" she said innocently.

"Behave yourself," replied Nick sternly. "I mean it!"

Kestrel flushed and chewed stolidly, keeping her chin high despite the instinct to lower her head in shame and embarrassment.

Rue ran into the room, her eyes shining with excitement and her berry-brown skin glowing from her exhilarating ride. Meron, Nick, and Angus beamed at her happiness as she motioned toward the door and pulled at their hands, trying to get them to stand.

"All right, Rue lass," chuckled Angus as the petite girl herded them to the door and pointed to her new horse whose ebony coat shone in the sun. "Aye, he's a beauty."

Kestrel stared at the picture her sister made with the horse and at the cluster of men who admired them both. One of the Indian braves threw Rue up onto the horse's high back and she sat back digging in her small bare heels, causing the magnificent animal to rear up on his back legs. She laughed, her white even teeth like pearls against her brown skin that was haloed by her raven hair. Kestrel stared up into Nick's face as he was transfixed by the horse and rider. Fear raced through her and she fought the temptation to rush away. She looked down at Nick's broad brown hand and tentatively put her small hand in his. Without looking down at her Nick wrapped his arms around her and they both watched Rue proudly showing off her new possession and her riding skills.

"Why don't you ride your new horse, too?" suggested Meron, knowing Moon Elk would appreciate seeing his gifts were welcomed.

" 'Tis not mine," replied Kestrel. "I gave it to Angus because I shot his," she added in answer to the query.

"Nay, lass," protested Angus. " 'Tis a generous gesture but I canna take him."

" 'Tis not a gesture!" retorted Kestrel angrily. "I killed your horse so I gave you mine." She pulled herself free of Nick's arms and stalked into the house, not sure why she was so furious.

Nick sighed but did not follow her. He had a pretty good idea why Kestrel was in a foul mood but didn't know quite how to deal with it.

"Small Golden Hawk is angry again?" remarked Moon Elk.

"Afraid," corrected Nick and the chief nodded, a wry smile twisting his usually noncommittal features.

"Of what?" probed Angus.

"I think of her sister," ventured the chief. "Why does Small Sadness not talk?"

"I think because of fear," replied Nick.

"Strange that the two fearless daughters of Cameron should be so afraid," remarked Angus. "Except for their mother I've never seen or heard of two females who could ride better, shoot straighter, swim stronger, and show so much courage."

"It will be very strange for them in Scotland," remarked Meron. "I canna for the life of me see them dressed in fancy corsetted gowns wie wigs and the like. Glad I am that you have the keeping of them and not me, Nicholas MacKay. For I'd not be in your shoes."

Nick scowled. "I had not thought of that," he confessed with a snort of ironic laughter as he imagined Kestrel powdered and painted. "It should prove very interesting."

"Aye, you'll not be bored," chortled Angus.

Moon Elk made his farewells and rode off with his band, promising to return for another of Angus's sumptuous meals. Kestrel watched them leave before rejoining the men. Rue led her horse into the dim cool interior of the stable.

"Feeling better?" asked Nick, and Kestrel shrugged. "Do you want to go for a ride?"

"I have no horse except my mother's Torquod and he's too old."

"Kess lass, I dinna want your horse," protested Angus, getting angry at her stubborn persistence.

"That's very insulting of you!" retorted Kestrel.

"We'll ride my Rufus. He's strong enough for both of us," laughed Nick, swinging her up and over his shoulder, knowing she was spoiling for a fight. He strode to the stables, ignoring her struggles to get down.

Rue looked up from currying her horse as Nick entered carrying Kestrel. She watched as she saw her sister slide down the front of the tall dark man to be held tightly against him, her bare feet off the ground as their mouths joined and Nick's strong hands cupped Kestrel's firm buttocks. Rue shrank back into the shadows and crept from the dark stable into the bright sunshine, her heart beating frantically.

Nick heard the slight scuffling and looked around, seeing the currying combs and brushes lying near Rue's black horse. He threw Kestrel up onto his chestnut's high back and mounted behind her. He had been ready to take his golden-haired wife in the hay but now he kneed the large horse out into the sunlight, wanting privacy with no surprises.

Kestrel wiggled back so her bottom was pressed between Nick's firm muscular thighs as they galloped over the meadow toward the dense cool forest with its soft mattress of pine needles. Rue watched them go, bewildered by her fear. It wasn't always, she thought. She had witnessed Nick and Kestrel's kisses and embraces without fear. It was a certain indefinable thing that happened. A narrowing of Nick's eyes, a sudden tension, a crackling intimacy, an intensity; she strove to understand what caused her such alarm.

She slowly walked back to the stable, lost in her own whirling thoughts. She knew only too well what happened between men and women but she didn't understand how Kestrel could possibly like it. Each time it had happened to her it felt like she was being rent in two. She shuddered as the painful memories sliced through her. There had been so many of them. Once, in the beginning, she had fought and fought, bitten and clawed but each had plunged into her, his hot panting breath blowing in her face, his narrowed eyes not seeing her below them. Once, in the beginning, she had screamed and pummeled the man who thrust into her but to no avail. She had screamed until she couldn't scream any more as one by one they used her raw young body again and again and again.

Rue methodically brushed her new horse, her chest heaving as she remembered. Everything after had been a dim dream, not quite real. She had watched the soldiers killed and scalped, feeling nothing. Unable to sit a horse she had been laid in a wagon where she lost all sense of time in the rhythmic trundling of the wheels until she awoke at the gray cold mission.

"Och, there you are," hailed Angus and she jumped, looking at him in bewilderment. "Dinna mean to gie you a start," he frowned, seeing the tearstains on her cheeks. "Are you all right, Rue lass?" Rue nodded and wiped her cheeks with the back of her small brown hand.

"Now doesn't he look a treat," proclaimed the old man admiringly, walking around the high-spirited black horse. "What are you going to call him?"

Rue knelt on the floor and with her index finger wrote in the chaff, "Sin."

"Sin?" exclaimed Angus and Rue resolutely nodded and underlined her emphatic word. "Sure you dinna mean Sun?"

Rue shook her head and wrote the word again.

"Well, it's your horse." Angus looked at Rue's bowed head as she wrote another word, "Shame." He frowned, not understanding what she was trying to convey. "You are going to call the horse Sin or Shame?"

Rue pointed to one of the words and then the other as if to ask him which.

"Well, I canna say I like either," replied Angus. "What about a nice normal name like . . . Bessy, Beauty, or Blackie?"

Rue raised an eyebrow and gave him a look of complete disgust before sitting on her haunches and looking at the two words. She erased "Shame" and drew a circle around "Sin" and nodded. She pointed at the horse and then to the word.

"Sin," grumbled Angus. "Hah!" He left the stable and made his way back to the house.

June turned to July and the days were golden and productive as the crops ripened. Rue gained weight and confidence.

" 'Tis nearly time to leave," said Nick, wanting to be traveling in the summer and autumn rather than in winter. "Do you think it's best to leave from Boston or New York?"

"Neither," returned Meron. "From the St. Lawrence River. Many vessels leave from Quebec."

"Is that where Alexander left from?"

"Aye," answered Meron. "I wouldna trust being in waters farther south until a treaty has been signed. Who knows what sea battles are still raging."

"Will you be taking the horses? Or will Meron bring them back?" inquired Angus.

"I had not thought that far ahead," confessed Nick. "It will depend on the vessel, I suppose. I'd hate to sell Rufus and yet I'm loath to subject him to a stuffy ocean voyage."

Rue thumped her small fist on the table, demanding attention.

" 'Tis surprising how alike are Cameron's daughters," chuckled Angus, and Nick nodded his agreement as he stared from Kestrel to Rue. Now that Rue was healthy, she looked even more like her younger sister with their identical features, stature, and wild manner.

"What is it?" asked Meron, staring fondly at Rue's determined little face.

She thumped the table again so that everyone's eyes looked down to her hand before she traced the word "Sin." Then she shook her head and placed her hands on her breast bone as her body undulated. Everyone frowned, not understanding, and Rue grew frustrated, shaking her head. She traced the word again and embraced her own arms, rocking.

"You'll not leave Sin behind?" questioned Kestrel and Rue laughed, nodding as she jumped up and down excitedly.

"Do you have money for passage?" asked Meron.

"There's no problem there," returned Nick.

"There's money needed for clothes for Kess and Rue as they canna travel looking as they do now unless they're to travel as lads," informed Angus.

"I dinna think they'd pass for laddies," laughed Nick, staring from one beautiful sister to the other. "I'm going to have my hands full chaperoning them. But dinna fash Angus, I have plenty to outfit them both."

"A rich man, are you, lad?" chuckled Angus.

"Nay but not puir," returned Nick. "My brother is the rich one, being the older. I have a small holding. A medium-sized manor house wie seven farms."

"Will we go there?" asked Kestrel excitedly.

"Of course, I have to set my house and lands to order, not having been there for the past two years. I have also to introduce my people to my wife," he explained.

Rue watched her sister's radiant face as she excitedly talked about the coming adventure. She was afraid and wished she could stay hidden in the wilderness with Meron and Angus. What was the point in her going to Scotland, she wondered. She wanted to see her father and brothers and the places her parents had told her about as she grew up. But to go with Kestrel and Nick, who were totally involved in each other, she wasn't sure about. She had tried to explain how she felt but everyone had been adamant that she should go.

Meron watched Rue's expressive little face, understanding much that ran through her mind. At first he had wavered, feeling it better that Rue remain with him in the tranquil solitude of the wilderness. But then he realized his own selfish investment for wanting her near. To travel, to have new experiences, was how Rue would grow and hopefully eventually regain her speech. Hiding was too easy a solution. Rue had to get out into the world and start living and loving so the abuses of the past could be healed.

Rue crept away from the cheerful table, wanting to be alone. She walked quietly around the lake, listening to the crickets' chirpings in the hot heavy night. The air was oppressive and she knew the charged atmosphere would soon explode into a cleansing storm. She rocked in anticipation, sweating in the stillness and yearning for the release nature would provide. A silent streak of lightning cleaved the darkness and Rue strained her ears for the answering clap of thunder, but nothing sounded or stirred. Then suddenly the thunderheads rolled and clashed together and she froze, feeling the vibrations build in the core of her until they burst, rending the dark sky and bending the tall firs as a roaring wind whistled down from the north. Tears poured down Rue's cheeks as large beads fell to the earth, one by one, making individual circles in the smooth lake. Rue howled with the wind, not hearing the sound as she became one with the raging tempest; cleansing herself, purging herself of what she did not know.

Meron watched his niece silhouetted by the lightning, stretching her lithe body and shaking her fists at the firmament. He quietly approached and heard the strange mournful cry that issued from her open mouth. Her face was pure emotion, pure pain, as she grieved with the elements. He silently left her, knowing her need for solitude.

Kestrel and Nick watched the storm from their bedroom window. Kestrel stood in the circle of Nick's arms feeling the electricity run through her. Storms elated and excited her, charging her blood with countless primitive emotions until she writhed against Nick's hardness, wishing the heavy rain was pouring down her naked body, mingling with the sweat of their loving exertions.

Only Angus shuddered with the mighty crashes, knowing the dampness would ache his old joints. He poured himself a mugful of whiskey and wished there was a fire despite the oppressive humidity.

"Puts it all in perspective," he muttered, hoping the corn wasn't going to be battered down.

The storm raged all night, but Rue, exhausted and soaked, numbly returned to the dry house. Meron put his arms about her but she didn't acknowledge him. It was as though she was in a trance. He toweled her raven hair and gently wiped her smooth brown cheeks. She stared blindly at him, standing still like a docile child.

"Och, you're worn out, Rue lass," he groaned lovingly, knowing how much energy she had just spent. Rue blinked and stepped back from her uncle, frowning as she concentrated on getting him into focus. She opened her mouth and tried to make the sound of the wind, but nothing happened.

"I heard. I listened to you," said Meron gruffly, and Rue smiled tremulously, nodding her head and pointing to her mouth. "You'll speak and sing again, my little one," he comforted.

Rue mouthed the word "sing." It had been so long since she had even thought of the word. She rubbed her slender throat, remembering the vibrations as she tried to hum, but nothing happened. She groaned in frustration and immediately opened her eyes with surprise upon hearing herself. Meron smiled tenderly, reminded by her attempts of a very small infant who desperately wanted to talk.

Rue pursed her lips and started whistling a cheerful Scottish tune. Meron laughed and clapped his hands in time as Rue started gracefully to dance. Angus staggered in, not wanting to miss anything and took his bagpipes from the wall. After a few false starts the pipes and the old man warmed up and joined Rue's lilting reel. Kestrel and Nick, awakened by the music and laughter, opened their bedroom door and watched the petite dark-haired girl whistle as she whirled gracefully around the room.

CHAPTER FOURTEEN

They set off for Quebec at sunrise on July tenth after a tearful farewell to Angus who stood on the porch waving and yelling long after they were out of sight and earshot.

"It still seems to me we'd have been better off traveling by water through the lakes and up the St. Lawrence," observed Nick.

"You're right, but you'd have a mutiny on your hands," replied Meron, watching Rue streak ahead on her spirited black horse. "You and Kestrel have each other. Rue has her horse. 'Tis going to be strange and frightening for her in an alien country, unable to speak," he added, urging his horse into a gallop to follow his older niece as they traveled along the southern bank of Lake Erie toward the giant waterfalls at Niagara.

Rue was impervious to the beauty of the fertile countryside. She was afraid and she tried to mask the terror by racing her horse across the plain. She was dressed in buckskin-fringed pants and a vest, her arms and feet bare in the hot sun. A beaded thong was tied about her forehead, keeping her heavy thick hair away from her face. Nick watched Meron closing in on Rue's wild gallop before turning to the golden girl who rode at his side. Kestrel was dressed in a fashion similar to her sister.

"Come on," he laughed, digging in his own heels. They raced side by side, feeling a heady, giddy joy.

They made camp that night within earshot of the thunderous falls. Rue lay unable to sleep as anxiety over the journey mingled with the irritating buzz and picking of the mosquitoes that swarmed in the heavy night air. She was conscious of Nick and Kestrel wrapped in each other's arms despite the sticky humidity. She quietly arose and walked down the moonlit shore of the lake where she sat with her feet dipped in the gently lapping water. She thought about Meron's and Nick's explanations and descriptions as they tried to prepare both sisters for what lay ahead. Kestrel had become excited by the prospect of encountering a more sophisticated society but Rue, on the contrary, shrank inside, afraid of people as she remembered the many houses and farms that clustered around the mission.

She hugged herself protectively as she recalled being sent as a servant to work in the farms and houses. She had fought off the advances of the pious men who came to the Sunday services with prim wives and daughters. The times she had successfully escaped she had returned to the mission only to be beaten for running away from gainful employment. Other times she had been flung down in the hay and taken brutally as the soft-eyed cows placidly chewed. At first she had tried to scream, but when no sound was forthcoming she just ground her teeth tightly together, knowing that when the straitlaced men had had their fill, she would still be whipped for tempting them. They were secure in the knowledge that she couldn't tell.

" 'Tis a peaceful night," breathed Meron appreciatively, staring across the wide lake, seeing nothing but endless water. "The ocean will appear so," he explained, stretching his hand out to where the horizon blended with the sky. Rue and Meron sat side by side in companionable silence, looking out over the gently rippling water, listening to the distant roar of the waterfalls meld with the night noises.

"You are afraid?" he whispered as he felt her weight sag against him and he wrapped an arm parentally about her. Rue nodded.

"It will be all right," he comforted as he leaned back against a tree and cradled her. Rue sighed deeply and snuggled closer. Meron stared down at his drowsy niece, wishing there were some way he could take her fear away but knowing it was impossible. No one could live another's life for them or feel another's pain. He stroked her glossy hair.

"You're a strong one," he whispered. "You'll find your voice and your love, I know." Meron drifted off to sleep lulled by Rue's even breathing. It seemed his eyes had barely closed when the bright morning sun pried his lids open. After a quick refreshing swim and a breakfast of fish they were once more on their way.

Kestrel and Rue raced side by side by the twinkling blue water as Nick and Meron rode deep in conversation.

"I dinna think she was abused just the once," informed Meron.

"You think after the child was born?" questioned Nick.

"Aye. I'm almost positive that she's been raped many times. You maun be careful for I have seen terror written across her face at any sign of passion between you and Kestrel. Affection she can handle, but with a sense or smell of lust, she canna," strove Meron, wanting to protect Rue. Nick nodded thoughtfully.

"Aye, I think you're right. I shall guard her like my sister," he reassured the older man.

"It is hard to tell if she will ever heal enough to trust a man," mused Meron sadly. "She has been abused so sorely that I doubt she could dare to love and be loved as a woman should be."

"Maybe the right man," returned Nick.

"Are there any more like you at home?" laughed Meron, trying to lighten the mood.

"My older brother, but I dinna think he's the one for Rue. Dour stony man. He doesna trust women. Too many of them have been trying to snare him and he uses them in much the same way."

"Sounds as though you have no liking for your own brother," remarked Meron.

"I like him well enough, but I'm a man," laughed Nick. "I think I'd gie him a very wide berth if I were female."

"There's a trading post that rents out rooms where we can spend the night. It'll gie the lassies a taste of what's to come. Maybe we should buy them their first dresses so it'll not be too much of a shock later as we near Mount Royal," suggested Meron, changing the subject.

At sunset they rode into a small town. Rue kept her eyes focused straight ahead, but Kestrel looked all around, delighting in everything. She grinned broadly at the curious people who gawked at the four riders who were dressed in fringed Indian clothes and waved at little children.

"Meron!" hailed a hearty voice and a large-boned, jovial woman picked up her skirts and rushed across the dusty road toward them. Meron laughed and dismounted in one lithe movement.

"Chastity!" he laughed, swinging the woman around despite her size. "We were on our way to find you. We need beds, one of your wonderful dinners, and some provisions. This is Nick MacKay," he introduced and Nick nodded and grinned down at the cheerful painted face. "My niece Kestrel, married to Nick," added Meron, seeing the air of speculation Chastity was bestowing on Nick's dark handsomeness.

"That's a pity," mourned the woman with a bark of laughter. "Well, you are a little beauty and no mistake," she purred as she assessed Kestrel's golden looks. "And who's the little dark Injun there?" she asked, frowning at Rue's straight back as the girl stared straight ahead, not acknowledging her.

"My niece, Rue Sinclair."

"Is that paint on your face?" exclaimed Kestrel with delight, leaning down from her horse and examining Chastity's makeup.

"Kess?" warned Nick with a groan but Meron roared with laughter.

"This, young lady, is my natural complexion," lied the large woman indignantly, as she tucked her chubby dimpled hand through Meron's arm and walked him down the street toward a noisy, cheerful house where people spilled out and sprawled onto the road. A large sign proclaimed it as "Chastity's" and from what Nick could fathom she just ran everything except the church. There was a tavern, boardinghouse, trading post, and livery stable all under the garish sign.

Kestrel and Nick dismounted and tied their horses to the rail as the buxom woman directed. Kestrel grinned and preened as whistles and catcalls showed the leering bystanders' appreciation for her charms. Nick scowled, wishing he had lectured his bride on modest deportment.

"Rue?" called Kestrel, not liking the warning look Nick had bestowed, and he turned to see the raven-haired girl still sitting on her black steed.

"Rue?" he said softly, sensing her panic at all the people and noise. She dismounted and walked her horse to the rail, her small face closed and set. They entered the rowdy house shepherded by Chastity. Kestrel gasped at the array of merchandise and she moved around eagerly examining and touching everything she saw as if she were a small child in a toy store. Nick smiled, appreciating his wife's enthusiasm. Meron frowned at Rue's strange withdrawn expression.

"For tonight, Nick, you and I should share a room. Kestrel and Rue another," he stated, not wanting Rue alone for fear she might run away. Nick nodded and sniffed the air as his mouth watered.

"What is cooking, Chastity?" he asked.

"There's a whole steer roasting on a spit out back," she informed them and Nick and Meron rubbed their hands together with anticipation.

"Nick, look," shouted Kestrel, holding a red dress up against her and spinning around.

"No, not that one!" declared Nick firmly, noting the plunging neckline.

"Why not?" protested Kestrel, delighting in the feel of the satiny fabric.

"Because I say not," replied Nick, not knowing how to explain to Kestrel.

"But she has one," pouted Kestrel, pointing to a scantily clad, painted girl who was flirting with several men.

"And that's why not," insisted Nick, conscious of Meron's barely suppressed mirth.

"And a hat like that, and what are those things on her legs?" chattered Kestrel, staring at the garters and stockings that the woman exhibited proudly. Nick ushered her briskly into the yard at the back where a succulent steer slowly cooked over an open pit.

Rue followed, numbly unaware of Meron's hand in the small of her back guiding her.

"Injuns!" yelled a voice, and Kestrel stared around, frowning when she realized the person referred to Meron, Nick, and Rue. Low angry buzzing started, accompanied by threatening gestures.

"They're not Indians, just folks from the backwoods!" screamed Chastity.

"What's wrong if we were Indians?" asked Kestrel, not understanding the animosity.

"Not allowed to be served drinks or the like," answered Meron tersely.

"Why?" she probed.

"Ignorance!"

Rue ate silently, sitting in the shadows while Kestrel sat on the table, her leg swinging, trying to imitate the painted young women who entertained the men. Nick slapped her leg and glared a warning down at her as she thrust her chest out and pouted earnestly, attempting to appear sophisticated despite her leather clothes.

"Why can't I have a dress like that? It's pretty, Nick," she begged. Nick groaned and Meron laughed.

"I warned you that your hands would be full," he chuckled.

"It seems to me that you have fallen down in your duties, Meron," returned Nick. "What was it Moon Elk said about the mother's brother?" he reminded, mischievously referring to the Indian tradition of the maternal uncle raising his sister's children. "I think you should explain. . . ."

"They're whores!" stated Nick after a long silence.

"Like the fat lady that Angus used to visit?" asked Kestrel with delight, clapping her hands together with excitement.

"How do you know?" Nick shrugged and wished he hadn't said anything.

Kestrel gasped and turned to him in alarm. "You're not going to sleep with them, are you?" she asked in a loud voice. "Not make love to them?" she added when he couldn't answer.

"Kess?" hissed Nick with exasperation.

"You wouldn't, would you?" she said in a very small voice. Nick took a deep breath and closed his eyes as he silently asked for help from any quarter.

"Aye, I think it's appalling for an uncle to raise his niece in such ignorance!" he repeated savagely to Meron, who choked on his beer. "No," he snapped curtly to Kestrel, who stared at him wide-eyed. "Of course, I'm not," he reassured as he attacked his meat ferociously.

"Will you buy me a dress?" persisted Kestrel. "Not a whore's one," she amended quickly, seeing the danger lights in his dark eyes.

"Tomorrow, if you behave yourself tonight," he answered.

"Oh, listen, let's go and see," cried Kestrel as the sounds of a fight were heard, and before Nick could register her request, she whirled away into the mob of people who clustered around the tavern door. He groaned, put down his unfinished supper, and followed, not trusting her to stay out of trouble.

"Oh, you golden-haired li'l honey bunny," growled a whiskey voice and Kestrel was grabbed by a leathery old man. She had no time to scream before his slack lips and toothless mouth sucked at her.

"I found her first!" complained the old man as Nick picked Kestrel up and pushed his way outside through the throng of lonely, drinking men. He put her firmly on her feet and was about to give her a stern reprimand when he noticed how scared she was. He said nothing, just pinned her with his black eyes. Kestrel looked up into his hard forbidding face.

"That was horrid," she whispered, rubbing at her lips furiously. "I think I'm going to be sick." Nick still said nothing as fury beat through him. Up until the last few minutes he had been the only one to kiss Kestrel's soft mouth, but now some toothless old man had violated and trespassed. "Are you angry?" she asked after a long throbbing silence.

"Aye," he snapped. "Very!" he added, hoping to subdue her a little.

"Why? The smelly old man didn't kiss you."

Nick herded the two girls up the narrow wooden stairs to the bedrooms he had rented for the night.

"You will slide the bolt and lock yourselves in," he ordered, heartened by Rue's determined nod.

"Why?" asked his bothersome wife.

"Because you'll not get a dress if you disobey me!" he answered coldly.

"Where will you be?"

"Next door. Just knock on the wall that side. Meron and I will be there," he said, gentling his tone as he looked into her woebegone little face.

"I want to sleep with you."

"We've been all through that," he said, firmly kissing her softly and shutting the door. "Slide the bolt," he ordered as he stood in the hall listening. Rue slid the large bolt before sitting on the wide bed and looking sorrowfully at her pouting sister.

"It sounds like such fun downstairs," sighed Kestrel, hearing the laughter and singing. "Maybe we can go down in a little while when Meron and Nick are asleep," she planned excitedly. Rue shook her head violently and barred the door.

"Just for a little while. Wouldn't you like to look at all those beautiful clothes, Rue?" she pleaded, but her dark sister shook her head.

Kestrel and Rue lay in the big bed, listening to the revelry shake the windows. Every few minutes Kestrel furtively leaned on one arm and bent over to see if Rue was awake, only to face an alert pair of eyes. Rue knew what her willful sister was planning and she forced herself to keep watch. She jerked herself awake as she felt her eyelids closing and softly wound a tendril of her sister's long golden hair about her finger.

"Ouch!" shrieked Kestrel, pulling away, but Rue held firm. "Let go!" But Rue determinedly shook her head. Kestrel wanted to smack Rue's small solemn face and she raised her hand threateningly, but Rue didn't even wince, just stared at her with tears running down her face. Kestrel dropped her hand, feeling ashamed of herself. "Sorry," she whispered. "I'll not hit you. Please don't cry."

Rue wished she could tell Kestrel why she was crying. It was not for being threatened but for not being able to protect her younger sister by telling her the dangers. What would she tell her? she mused sadly, knowing she'd not want to rob Kestrel of her romantic dreams by telling about the pain and degradation of rape. The sisters fell asleep holding each other, but Rue still had Kestrel's golden hair wound around her finger.

They were awakened the following morning by a hearty thumping on the wall, and Kestrel sprang up and screamed as her hair was nearly torn out of her head.

"You all right in there?" asked Nick, his deep voice sounding worried at the sharp cry of pain.

"Aye," laughed Kestrel as Rue sleepily released her so she could leap off the bed and unbolt the door, wanting Nick's arms around her. She had not been away from him so long since they had come together, she realized, running into the corridor without any thought of propriety.

Nick gasped as Kestrel burst into his room stark naked and threw herself in his arms. Meron raised an eyebrow as he pulled on his boots and left the room. Kestrel snuggled into Nick's warmth.

"I missed you," she murmured. "Why are you dressed?" she complained, pulling impatiently at his clothes.

"Why aren't you?" he returned, trying to be severe.

"I was asleep," she answered, puzzled at his question.

"Kess, you mustn't run around wie no clothes on. Not in strange places wie strange people around," he informed her.

"But I'm here with you," she protested.

"No arguing, Kess! Put this around you and go and get dressed," he ordered, wrapping her in the bedspread. "Ha, not a word! Do as I say or there'll be no dress!" he added as her mouth opened to speak. "Go!" he insisted, slapping her rump and pushing her out of the door.

After a hearty breakfast of eggs and beef, Rue and Kestrel sat in Chastity's private rooms. Kestrel paced back and forth in front of a long mirror, studying herself critically as she impatiently waited for Nick, who had gone to select some dresses for them to try on. Rue was dejected. She did not want a dress as they reminded her of the gray mission smock that had afforded her no protection from rape. The flimsy material had been pushed up, allowing men easy access.

Nick entered with his arms full of clothes and laughed when he was virtually pounced on by his over-eager wife.

"Whoa," he cautioned as he draped several gowns over a screen. "You may choose one each, as we'll buy more in Quebec and have only saddlebags for now." He sat back and watched Kestrel feel the material and rub her face against the softness.

"Where's the red one?" she asked, disappointed in the drab colors.

"The red one is not suitable," stated Nick firmly. "Look at this green one." Kestrel picked up the full dress and held it against her.

She smiled, as she liked the contrast of her golden head against the cool mint. "Try it on," he urged. "Behind the screen," he ordered as she started to pull off her clothes. With a disgusted look Kestrel obeyed him. Nick looked at Rue, who watched him, her face showing nothing of what she felt.

"You'll not try on a dress?" he asked softly and was shocked at her vehement rejection. Her eyes blazed and she shook her head wildly. "All right, 'tis all right. You dinna have to," he comforted, determined to buy a dusky salmon-pink dress for her which he'd hide away until they reached Quebec.

"Look at me!" rejoiced Kestrel, whirling around so the full skirts lifted in the breeze displaying her long lithe legs and bare bottom. Nick made a mental note of the underclothes he had to purchase as he grinned his appreciation. Rue followed his gaze and her eyes blazed in fury. She sprang up, wrapping the skirts tightly around her sister and hiding Kestrel's legs from Nick's sight. Kestrel looked down in amazement at Rue crouching on the floor.

"What's the matter?" she asked as Rue's arms encompassed her knees as though protecting her. She looked at Nick whose black eyes were narrowed as he understood the dark-haired girl's fear of dresses. He swore savagely under his breath as he realized how she had been used and he felt unable to undo the terrible harm. "What is it?" demanded Kestrel, alarmed by Rue's intense reaction.

" 'Tis all right, Rue." Nick spoke soothingly as he bent so his face was on a level with hers. "You have my promise that I will never harm Kestrel. I love her. She is my wife," he said as he unwrapped her slim brown arms from Kestrel's legs. "Do you understand?"

Rue nodded.

"What is it? What's wrong?" repeated Kestrel. "Why did Rue think you would hurt me?"

"Because she has been very hurt," answered Nick huskily, still keeping his eyes pinned to Rue's.

"I don't understand."

"I'm glad you don't," replied Nick and he was rewarded by a tremulous smile from Rue, who tearfully nodded her approval at his words before quietly leaving the room.

Kestrel was confused, not understanding anything. She stared at Nick's broad back as he stood turned away from her, his eyes fixed on the softly closing door.

"Don't treat me like a child," she said in a small voice, feeling rejected by him. "Explain to me," she begged. Nick turned and drew her into his arms and kissed her upturned face.

"One day, but not now. Now we have to hurry or Meron will lose patience and take off wie out us. Now climb out of the dress and back into your riding clothes," he said absently as he left the room, first to find Rue and then to purchase undergarments before he forgot.

"But . . ." protested Kestrel as the door swung shut behind him. She hastily undressed, frightened at being left alone. The numerous buttons and hooks caught in her hair. She cried out in frustration as she became hopelessly entangled, unable to get the gown off.

"Nick? Nick?" she yelled, furiously tugging and tearing at the offending garment and becoming more ensnarled. "Nick?" she screamed, clutching at the door and rushing into the corridor toward the main trading room.

Nick heard his name and gasped in astonishment at the vision of Kestrel half in and half out of the green gown. Her golden breasts were displayed as were her long legs as the material was bunched tightly around her slim waist.

"Oh, Nick, it won't come off! It's stuck!" she wailed, oblivious to the spectators who grinned appreciatively. He groaned loudly and quickly pushed her behind a counter piled high with bolts of cloth.

"Och, Kestrel," he sighed. "Where are your clothes?" Kestrel waved her hands toward Chastity's private rooms and Nick grabbed the nearest bolt of cloth and draped it over her before propelling her back the way she had come, with the material unwinding behind them.

"My good brocade!" shrieked Chastity, chasing them and trying to wind up the spilling yards.

"I'll pay for it," roared Nick and the buxom woman shrugged, dropping the rich fabric as she grinned with satisfaction, and the door to her private parlor tried to slam but got caught in the mess of yardage.

"Behind the screen!" ordered Nick as the male spectators clustered trying to peek through the doorway.

"But I'm stuck," wept Kestrel, not ever wanting to see a gown again. Nick calmed himself and pushed her behind the screen where he played a very inept lady's maid as his too large hands fumbled with the tiny buttons and hooks. Finally in exasperation he ripped the dress to shreds and Kestrel thankfully climbed out of it.

"Oh, I never thought I'd breathe again," she rejoiced, reaching exuberantly for him and knocking the flimsy screen down in the process so she stood completely naked, much to the rowdy pleasure of the spectators at the half-open doorway.

Nick closed his eyes and groaned loudly, wondering what he had done to deserve such aggravation as Kestrel pulled on her trews, not fazed at all by her admiring audience.

"Come again!" chorused a multitude of voices as they mounted up and rode away from Chastity's. Kestrel waved merrily and Nick stared stolidly ahead as he wondered what else was in store for him on the long journey.

CHAPTER FIFTEEN

Thankfully the foursome reached the city of Mount Royal without further incident as Meron wisely steered them around most forts and settlements, not trusting Kestrel's exuberant, uninhibited disposition. Rue welcomed her uncle's decision, preferring the quiet solitude of the magnificent countryside to the noisy, grasping clamor of the Colonial towns and forts.

Kestrel loved sleeping beneath the stars, pressed against Nick's hard, safe body. Her wide green eyes hungrily absorbed each new sight and experience. Although she had been a wild independent person from the age of four or five by the very nature of her upbringing in the protection of the wilderness, with each new exciting day she felt she had been shielded for most of her life. Each morning she attacked the day with a certain inexplicable zest that had Nick in awe despite his noncommittal, enigmatic face.

Rue rode on numbly, knowing soon civilization would burst in and there would be nowhere to hide from people. Many times a day she leaned over her horse's handsomely arched neck and hugged him, feeling almost a part of him. As they neared Mount Royal, the river widened and the mountain soared into the summer sky. Rue tried to avert her eyes from the numerous houses and other travelers on the dry dusty road heading east. She tried desperately to lose herself in the plodding rhythm of her horse as panic surged within her and she longed to dig in her heels and race back to the verdant green forests.

Soon instead of the dusty road beneath the horses' hooves softening the tread, a staccato rhythm developed as the hard cobblestones reverberated. Stone houses loomed on either side and the windows of roadside houses lit up the dark night sky with warm tones.

"Are we going to sleep inside?" asked Kestrel guardedly, not wanting to share a room with her sister, let alone a bed.

Meron didn't bother to answer.

Kestrel stared around, her eyes widening at the beauty of the houses and the boats as they skirted the harbor.

"Maybe on board?" asked Nick as he scanned the vessels that rode the waves, creaking their protests at the chains that tied them, prohibiting them from surging along the river to the wide freedom of the ocean.

"Maybe," evaded Meron, looking for a familiar ship.

"We need clothes, trunks, medicine, and I canna begin to tell you what else," protested Nick but Meron laughed and held up a brown hand, signifying he understood.

"If the vessel I suspect is in harbor you'll have berths tonight and time to spend all your money," he reassured.

Rue breathed deeply of the rich harbor smells. Fish swirled with the fresh and salt water; lingering odors of exotic cargoes mingled and entwined. Saffron, sandalwood, herbs, and spices blended and assailed the nostrils, filling the imagination with thoughts of distant magical lands. Kestrel beamed and Nick groaned, knowing well his turbulent bride's fertile mind was afire with romantic adventure.

"I've read about pirates capturing females and carrying them off . . ." she burst out.

"No!" protested Nick before turning and staring at her in amazement. "Where on earth did you read such things?" he roared, genuinely perplexed, never having heard of any such literature.

"Angus brought these novels back from Boston once," she informed him happily. "Do you think . . . ?"

"NO!" repeated Nick, thinking if she voiced such a fantasy aloud it would probably happen. "No pirate is going to carry *you* off!"

"Why?" pouted Kestrel, bitterly disappointed.

"He'd not value himself or his vessel if he did," he answered under his breath, not wanting a fight. Meron barked out his laughter. Rue remained self-contained, not trusting herself to think, feel, or see as the gulls swooped and complained, their clamoring cries breaking the still sunset and touching a lamenting sadness deep within her.

"There's an inn where the food is very good and I can find what ship is docked and what vessel sails where," informed Meron.

"How can I take them into a public place dressed as they are?" asked Nick.

"Through the back door to a private room," smiled Meron triumphantly. "I might look like a backwoodsman, but I have my sophisticated ploys when civilization demands."

Nick nodded cynically, enjoying the banter and Kestrel's perturbance.

"Lead on, MacDuff," he laughed.

"Shakespeare?" stated Meron, raising an eyebrow in mock appreciation.

"None other," replied Nick seriously.

Rue started out of her numb haze and stared sharply at her uncle.

"Aye, lass, you remember?" said Meron softly. Rue nodded. "'When I consider everything that grows /Holds in perfection but a little moment.'"

"'That this huge stage presenteth nought but shows,'" continued Nick.

"'Whereon the stars in secret influence comment; /When I perceive that men as plants increase, cheered and checked by the self-same sky,'" quoted Kestrel and giggled as she saw Nick's startled look.

"There's a lot to learn about my two beautiful nieces," said Meron softly. "They have been raised with nature, away from a lot of civilization's cruelty. Though not far enough it seems," he amended, looking sadly at Rue's proud straight back. "Rue?" he called and she looked around startled. "What is your favorite sonnet?" he asked.

Rue smiled sadly as she recalled being romantic and young.

"'Shall I compare thee to a summer's day?'" whispered Meron softly as he read her silent lips.

"I know John Donne and Robert Herrick," giggled Kestrel, for the first time feeling Nick in awe of her. "Nick, 'tis so strange. I've felt like a child with you as you know so much and are so much older. Yet just now seeing your face when we quoted William Shakespeare, it was like you had not really seen me before," she struggled to explain.

"We know so little of each other," replied Nick, "that each day you surprise me. Sometimes more pleasantly than others," he added, thinking of her golden breasts spilling out of the mint green dress at Chastity's bawdy trading post.

"There's Cowley, Lovelace, Carew, and Suckling, too," recited Kestrel, loving to be appreciated. "'Why so pale and wan, fond lover?'" she quoted with great spirit, sending Nick into whoops of laughter. Rue tried to dull her thoughts and feelings as the words of Robert Herrick paced through her brain. Meron frowned, reading her lips, and Nick ached, also understanding the bitter words that droned in Rue's head. "'The hag is astride/this night for to ride,/the devil and she together;/Through thick and through thin,/Now out and now in,/Though ne'er so foul be the weather.

"'The storm will arise/and trouble the skies/this night; and, more for the wonder,/The ghost from the tomb/affrighted shall come,/called out by the clap of the thunder,'" recited Kestrel somberly.

"Here's the place," stated Meron, welcoming the diversion from the gloomy verse.

"The Bones from the Sea!" read Nick with irony. "Cheerful," he added sarcastically.

"Around the back past the stables," directed Meron with a wry grin.

Kestrel excitedly bounced in the back door of the tavern called the Bones from the Sea. She sniffed appreciatively, delicious smells wafting up the back stairs from the basement kitchens, as she followed Meron and a small bubbly woman along a carpeted corridor.

"A bath?" she exclaimed as Nick unwrapped a crumpled emerald silk dress for the housekeeper to iron. "Is that for me?" she cried, picking up the gown and dancing in front of the mirror. Nick laughed at Kestrel's untrammeled joy as he shook out the lacy underwear and stockings.

Rue sat quietly watching Kestrel's happiness as servants carried in two enameled hip baths decorated with tiny flowers and filled them both with hot scented water.

"Rue, these are for you," said Nick softly, unwrapping a dress of dusky salmon pink complete with stockings and pantalets. Rue tentatively touched the filmy fabric, loving the warmth of the subtle color but afraid.

"Wear it for me, little niece, for soon you'll be gone," urged Meron, seeing her fear.

Rue sat in the scented water, allowing a chattering maid to scrub her back and wash her thick luxuriant hair. Kestrel lay back in a similar bath, excitedly talking in French to the bubbly maids, as her green eyes caressed the graceful green gown that was pressed and hung expectantly awaiting her.

Rue didn't know how she felt as the excited chattering swirled around, and she sat at the dressing table as her hair was styled and perfume softly dabbed.

"Isn't this wonderful?" breathed Kestrel. " 'Tis just like one of Angus's books," she rejoiced as she watched her golden hair curled and piled high on her proud head. Rue stared in the mirror as though in a dream, not believing her eyes as her own glossy hair cascaded, gracefully framing her small pointed face with ringlets. She stood like a doll as the little French maids giggled and fussed, lacing her into countless frothy undergarments. She obediently lifted her arms as the lighter than air, almost gossamer dress was thrown over her head and descended gracefully in billows around her fluid lithe figure.

"I wish we had some paint for our faces like Chastity had," sighed Kestrel, turning this way and that, in awe of the vision of herself in the glass. "That must be Nick," she added as there was a firm rapping at the door. One of the maids opened the door and Nick stood transfixed at the vision of the two sisters. He whistled soundlessly through pursed lips, unable to say a word. He knew they were beautiful but to just what extent he hadn't conceived. He closed the door behind him and leaned back appreciatively as the two little French maids giggled. It was a sin for any two women to be so stunning, he mused, thinking maybe he should lock them up away from leering lustiness.

"Nick, will you buy us some paint?" asked Kestrel, enjoying the satisfaction she saw in Nick's smoldering eyes. Nick silently shook his head as he stared mesmerized, looking from one girl to the other. Kestrel was radiant, her golden hair and skin vibrantly alive against the emerald silk that matched her eyes completely. Rue's dark beauty was perfectly offset by the sultry dusky pink. He bowed gravely, offering each girl an arm.

"*Merci,*" Kestrel called gaily over her shoulder to the beaming little maids.

"You speak French?" exclaimed Nick.

"*Mais oui, monsieur,*" laughed Kestrel pertly, "both my mother and my uncle spoke French to us." They walked along the wide carpeted corridor, her face glowing with anticipation, hearing the laughter and chatter of many voices. Nick felt Rue's hesitancy as her small hand clutched his arm tightly. He stared down at her set little face and was glad they were to eat in a private dining room.

"Where is everyone?" exclaimed Kestrel, indignantly looking around the small but handsome room.

"Meron will be back shortly," replied Nick as Rue stood at a bay window staring out over the dark harbor. "There is a vessel that needs a ship's doctor sailing for Quebec tomorrow before going on to France."

"But we're the only ones in here," protested Kestrel. "Why can't we go where everyone else is?"

"This is better for Rue," whispered Nick, not wishing Rue to hear for fear she might think she was an imposition.

"But Rue won't mind," blurted Kestrel thoughtlessly. "Will you?" Nick breathed angrily, exasperated, wanting to slap his reckless wife as Rue turned, distress marking her exquisite little face. Her small nostrils flared as she agreed with her sister, not wanting to spoil her happiness.

"See, she doesn't mind!" rejoiced Kestrel gaily.

"Well I do!" stated Nick coldly. "There'll be many days and nights when we'll not be able to get away from noisy people cooped up on the ship. Tonight we shall have a tranquil supper," he added, seeing the rebellious glint in his wife's green eyes. "Come in," he called in answer to a discreet rapping. A manservant dressed in livery entered and Kestrel's eyes lit up as she saw the gold braid on his uniform.

"Do you wish for any refreshments before your meal, sir?"

"Are you a butler?" inquired Kestrel excitedly. The servant shook his head, his expression showing nothing. "A valet?"

"Kess!" warned Nick.

"Would you like your dinner served now, sir?"

"We are expecting another person," replied Nick, wondering what was taking Meron so long. The manservant inclined his head to show he understood and silently left the room.

"Can't we just have a little peek at what everyone else is doing?" pleaded Kestrel. "I've never been dressed like this before and there's no one to see me."

"Am I no one?"

"Of course not. That isn't what I meant," corrected Kestrel hastily, running to him and nuzzling his neck.

"What's on your feet?" frowned Nick and Kestrel looked down and pulled up her full long skirt.

"Stockings, of course," she informed him. Nick shook his head and grinned wryly.

"I forgot shoes!"

There was a brief knock and a manservant opened the door to admit Meron, deep in conversation with another man. He stopped in mid-sentence at the beautiful picture of his two nieces.

"*Excusez-moi, Jacques,*" he apologized and laughed as he saw his guest was similarly entranced.

"You did not prepare me, *mon ami*," exclaimed the stocky weather-beaten man. "I am Captain Jacques Gillette of the *Étoile* and you must be the young doctor Meron has been speaking of," he said, introducing himself and holding out a square work-worn hand. Nick nodded and his dark eyes assessed the white-haired sea captain.

"My nieces, Rue and Kestrel."

"Enchanted," murmured Jacques, holding Rue's slim brown hand and bowing gravely.

She smiled tremulously into his deep blue eyes, instinctively trusting and liking him.

"Mademoiselle Kestrel." He bowed.

"Madame," corrected Nick. "She is my wife."

"If you look out there you can see my *l'Étoile*. There she rides," proclaimed the captain, proudly pointing out to the misty dark sea. "I am not sure about having two such beautiful sirens on board my *l'Étoile*, she might get very jealous."

"Jacques was a very successful *corsaire,*" recounted Meron, accepting a drink from the discreet servant.

"Rapparée," explained Jacques, seeing the frown on Kestrel's face. "Privateer, buccaneer," he added.

"A pirate!" exclaimed Kestrel and Nick groaned as he saw her wide green eyes sparkle dangerously. "Do you have many battles and carry maidens off to tropical isles?"

"*Non*, not for many years, *ma petite,*" laughed the captain. "I am too old for such romance," he chuckled as they sat down to a sumptuous meal.

"What is that?" cried Kestrel in alarm, staring at the enormous lobster that seemed to look back menacingly at her.

" 'Tis much like our freshwater crayfish," explained Meron, cracking one of the large claws and placing the delectable pink flesh on Kestrel's plate where she looked at it distrustfully.

"You look more courageous, little one," said the old captain, offering Rue some lobster. She smiled and opened her mouth and he popped the delicious morsel between her softly parted lips. "It's good?" She nodded enthusiastically in agreement.

Rue and Kestrel ate many things they had never seen before, all fruits from the sea—oysters, mussels, prawns, crabs—delighting in the taste and texture until they couldn't eat another bite. Rue stared in dismay at the large roast suckling pig and rack of lamb that was ceremoniously carried in. Kestrel groaned.

"This would last us half the winter, " she exclaimed, clutching her full tummy in a very unladylike way. "Nick, can you undo something before I burst."

"Don't mind me," chortled the French captain, totally captivated by the two young beauties and catching Nick's look of exasperation as he tucked into the tender pink lamb and savory appled pork.

"Kess, just take deep breaths and sit quietly," suggested Nick.

"I cannot take deep breaths," gasped Kestrel. "This stiff, laced thing under here is stopping me," she informed him, banging on her midriff so the baleen on the corset resounded. Meron and Jacques exploded with mirth at Nick's look of total helplessness.

" 'Tis not funny! Can you imagine such behavior in a public place?" mourned Nick. "Why are you wearing a corset?" he added.

"You bought it!" returned Kestrel with spirit, her breasts heaving.

"I wouldna buy such a thing! They do more damage to a female's body than . . . the rack!" roared Nick. "Those silly twittering maids must have supplied them. Are you wearing one, too?" he added, looking angrily at Rue. Rue grinned and shook her head and Meron roared with laughter.

"Och, Rue, my . . . my . . . och, you precious jewel," he cried, his throat constricted and at a loss for words as he saw the mischief in her amber eyes. "You'd never know it, MacKay, but that wee silent lass there had more devilment in her little finger than Cameron and Kestrel put together." Tears of sadness and mirth poured down Meron's lean dark features. " 'Tis still there! Och, gie thanks to the Great Spirits," he sighed, kissing her smooth glowing cheek that was the same dusky pink of her gown.

"You have no voice?" said Jacques softly, staring down into Rue's radiantly piquant face. He ran a broad finger across her smooth lips. "Why?" he asked, bewildered, knowing she could hear.

"Why don't you two girls get into more comfortable clothes and leave us to our after-dinner drinks and smoking," suggested Meron, not wanting to talk about Rue in her presence.

"Oh, it is a shame for us to lose such exquisite company. I will be very bored just in the company of you two men," complained Jacques. "I think it is a very stupid custom."

"*Custom? What custom?*" demanded Kestrel.

"It is the custom after dinner for the females to retire so men can smoke and converse freely," stated Nick, knowing as each word came out of his mouth he was making a mistake.

"Converse freely about what?" she insisted.

"Of things that would put your tender ears to the blush," chuckled Jacques, causing Meron to explode with merriment.

"Kestrel is more likely to have you blushing," he roared as he remembered the performance she had put on for Chastity's clients. "No, I'll let you find out for yourself, my friend," he added, refusing to explain despite Jacques's bewildered look.

"What is it, *ma petite*?" asked Jacques as Rue's small hand shook his arm in a bid for attention.

Rue instinctively felt safe as she stared into the wrinkled face with the piercing blue eyes. Rue shook salt onto the tablecloth and taking up a knife she wrote the word "Sin."

"Sin?" read the old sea captain in surprise.

" 'Tis the name of her horse," explained Meron. "It is all right, there is room," he reassured.

"*Oui, trois*. Three 'orses," laughed Jacques, holding up three thick fingers.

"No, two! *Deux*!" disagreed Kestrel. "Meron, you promised. It is Angus's horse I borrowed. You promised to return her." Meron nodded.

"Sin? *Sacrebleu*, that is a strange name for a 'orse," remarked Jacques, shaking his head and looking down at his silent dinner companion. "Did you give such a name to your *cheval*?" he asked and when she nodded, he frowned. "*Mais pourquoi*?"

Rue stared straight into his inquiring blue eyes before shrugging and looking down at her plate but not before Jacques had seen a bitterness harden her amber eyes.

"When shall we board your vessel?" asked Nick.

"I would very much like you to sleep on board the *Étoile* this night," answered the captain. "As tomorrow at first light we sail to Quebec and then to France."

"But we have to buy lots of clothes and shoes and paint—" protested Kestrel.

"Paint?" interrupted Nick.

"In Quebec, I 'ave a very good friend. *Une chère amie* who 'as the clothes fit for a queen," chortled Jacques. "She owes me many favors and will enjoy dressing two such beautiful young women," he added.

"My niece Kestrel has a penchant for very low cut, red gowns," offered Meron roguishly, before roaring with laughter at Nick's indignant expression. "Och, where's your humor, laddie?" he asked, seeing the angry tic in the lean dark cheek.

"Yes, I really would love a red dress," agreed Kestrel earnestly, causing her uncle to howl out loud and slap his firm thigh and wish he hadn't eaten so much, as his stomach ached. Kestrel frowned as Nick shook his head in disbelief.

"You are bound for France?" he asked, turning to Jacques and trying to change the subject.

"How will we get to Scotland then?" inquired Kestrel, stung, as she sensed she was being laughed at.

"There's plenty of smugglers crossing the channel," informed the old sea captain and Nick groaned aloud as Kestrel's eyes lit up with excitement.

"Smugglers," she breathed with pleasure. "Brandy and lace in the thick swirling mists. The creaking of oars . . ." she recited with relish as Meron collapsed back in his chair, unable to control his mirth.

"Where the hell did Wee-Angus find such literature?" lamented Nick.

CHAPTER SIXTEEN

Rue looked around the small compact cabin and then out of the porthole at the dark ocean, seeing a light from the ship reflected on the rippling waves. She examined the narrow bunk that was securely built into the wall and the washbasin that was ingeniously held down by a plank with a hole in it. She struggled to understand what she felt as she looked around at the simple barrenness. Loneliness, she realized, stark bare loneliness. She wished there were a way for her horse to be with her as she felt the need for another warm living thing.

"Are you all right?" Meron asked.

Rue looked into Meron's concerned face and nodded. His green eyes narrowed as though looking right through her.

"I'll be back soon," he promised and fleetly turned, exiting out of the narrow cabin door. She needed something, he knew, as he hurried across the listing deck and quickly strode down the bouncy gangplank into the close darkness of the harbor city.

Rue watched her uncle's tall lithe shape disappear on shore but still she stood staring out into the darkness, straining her eyes.

"Rue? Rue?" called Kestrel, standing in the doorway watching her dark sister. Something clutched inside as she noted the solitariness of her older sibling. Rue turned, startled. "Do you want to see our cabin? We are really to get married. Though I dinna ken what is real or no. The captain, Jacques, will do the ceremony when we are out to sea," chattered Kestrel excitedly, afraid and nervous at Rue's silent aloneness. "Rue?" she repeated and opened her arms, wanting the comfort as much as giving it.

Nick watched Rue walk into Kestrel's open arms, knowing the fear and apprehension both vulnerable women felt. Without thought he entered the cabin and wrapped his long strong arms about both of them, giving his strength.

"I love you both," he murmured and was rewarded by Kestrel's radiant smile as she beamed up at him more golden than he had ever seen her. He ached, knowing that at last there was a trust and she understood where she was in his heart. He loved them both. One as a lover, one as a brother.

Rue looked with surprise at her sister as she felt strong arms about her and Kestrel smiled tenderly into her eyes.

"Aren't we lucky?" she cried huskily.

Rue sat on the bed as the door softly closed behind Kestrel and Nick. Would there ever be such love for her? she wondered. And would she be able to accept it? she thought cynically.

Meron returned an hour or so later with a large gangly puppy whose glossy baby coat was the color of Rue's own hair. He had wrapped the rambunctious hound in two burlap sacks, trying to disguise his gift. He thumped awkwardly at the cabin door, scarcely able to hold his wriggly bundle.

"Rue?" he called, not knowing if the rest of the vessel slept and not wanting to disturb anyone.

Rue opened the door dressed in a nightshirt. Her face was sad and apprehensive as though she had been sitting waiting to be abandoned, thought Meron, sidling by her through the narrow doorway and plunking his boisterous burden on the narrow bed.

"Rue?" he called, pointing at the wildly moving bundle. She stood with her face serious and set to one side. A small woof penetrated the sacking and her face lit up as she scrambled to the bed and tore at the burlap. The most adorable, large-footed pup leaped out, his long pink tongue and cold black nose wetting Rue's delighted face.

"What'll you call him?" laughed Meron after watching them play for half an hour or more.

Rue licked her finger and wrote the letter "S" on the dry wood that surrounded the anchored basin. She licked her dried finger and wrote "h" and laboriously followed with the letters "a," "m," and "e."

"Shame," recounted Meron sadly, wishing she could have found more positive optimistic titles. "Seamus?" he added hopefully.

Rue shook her finger and smiled at him as she wrote "not he;" when her uncle frowned, not understanding, she turned the wriggling hound onto its back and lifted the tail.

"A she," understood Meron. "Well, there'll be no lifting of legs in this confined space," he laughed.

Rue wished she could express in words her thanks to her uncle for understanding what she herself had not known. Her horse Sin was on board but way below her in the hold. In the adjoining cabin, thankfully with thick wooden walls, her sister Kestrel and Nick were able to hold each other as tightly as they wished. Now she, Rue, would not be so alone. She tried to express her joy and surprise to her uncle as she wondered how he could read her heart before she could even interpret it.

"You look so much like my twin," he said, his low voice vibrating, causing a ghost to tread her spine so she shuddered violently.

"My mother?" she mouthed mutely and he nodded, ruffling her glossy ebony head and quietly leaving for the solitude of his own cabin.

Rue sat on the bed, delighting in her puppy's long warm wet tongue as she tried to get her new mistress to play.

Nick and Kestrel lay on their broad double bunk, softly kissing as they delighted in the rolling rhythm of the lapping waves that rocked the vessel.

"Are you afraid?" asked Nick softly as he nipped a velvety earlobe. Kestrel sat up and puffed out her bare breasts proudly as she pointed comically to herself as if to say "Me?" and then she nodded, grinning wildly. She put up her index finger into the air begging for silence as she listened. From the cabin next door she heard a wild scratching, followed by sharp thuds. Nick leaped from the bed.

"What's wrong?" gasped Kestrel, landing on top of him as they both scrambled for the door. The sight that met their eyes so relieved them that they fell across Rue's narrow bunk screaming with laughter, much to the exuberant joy of the rambunctious puppy Shame.

Captain Jacques, having reports of strange happenings on his most virtuous vessel *Étoile*, stood at Rue's cabin door wishing the bunk was wider and he knew the occupants better as he observed three virile handsome people plus a dog gamboling in innocent abandon.

"Where did you get her?" gasped Kestrel, very observant of sex.

"From me," professed Meron at the door, his arm about his old friend Jacques's shoulders as they stood appreciating the scene as the female pup lifted her leg and made a warm yellow puddle on the cabin floor. "She doesna know what she is?" roared Meron, his lean taut stomach aching.

"Like others I know," teased Nick, rewarded by Kestrel diving into him, and insinuating her lithe, very female body close to his. Rue froze as the timbre of the tomfoolery changed in a way she couldn't fathom, and suddenly she needed to be alone. Jacques nudged Meron as he saw Rue's eyes widen in fear and his own laughter at Nick and Kestrel's lusty antics dried on his lined lips.

"Who has abused *la petite enfante*?" he swore, recognizing the veiled passionate looks that the lovers exchanged as Rue flattened herself against the wooden wall.

"Come, my lass," beckoned Meron. "Let's gie the pup a stroll upon the deck so she doesna make more mistakes this night."

And Rue was escorted topside by both these caring men.

"You know I would do anything for you, Meron," sighed Jacques with mock sadness. "But a dog with so much water in it!" he complained as the large-pawed puppy skittered across the rolling deck leaving little puddles. "You must tell me what happened to your silent niece," he added seriously as Rue walked ahead to the gunwales and stared across the dark water seeing the moon reflected and fragmented in the waves.

"When she sleeps," promised Meron, determined to have a blasting talk with Nick. "I have asked MacKay to curb his lust for Kestrel when Rue is present," he hissed.

"*Mon cher ami*, that is not possible when love is so new and young," protested Jacques.

Rue heard Jacques's words and winced knowing she dampened the ardor that Nick and Kestrel had for each other.

"We will talk later," whispered Meron, knowing Rue listened.

"There," stated Jacques with great satisfaction as he tucked soft rags into a basket for the puppy. He patted the soft inside but Shame ignored him and stared expectantly up at her new mistress who sat in bed leaning against the pillow.

"Tomorrow will be a very big day," smiled Jacques, kissing the solemn girl on her clear brow. "Sleep well, *ma petite,*" he added before quietly leaving the cabin.

Rue lay awake, unable to sleep despite her fatigue and the gentle rocking of the ship. Shame leaped onto the narrow bunk and cuddled down next to her new mistress who mercifully was petite, otherwise there would not have been room for them both. Rue watched the night sky through the porthole, seeing the stars winking down and thinking of one of the Indian legends that told how each bright spot was a loved one who had left the land of the living. She thought sadly of her mother, Cameron, wishing she could have been with her before she died and remembering the stories of her voyage from Scotland. Rue drifted off to sleep in the wee hours of the morning when the sky had already begun to lighten.

She awoke to bright sunlight and a strange sensation. She got out of the narrow bunk and crossed the tilting floor to look out of the porthole. They were on their way, sailing up the St. Lawrence river toward Quebec. Seagulls wheeled and wailed overhead as winches, needing oil, creaked and screeched and the wind billowed and beat the canvas like taut drums. Rue quickly pulled on trews and a jerkin, eager to be topside in the fresh breeze. She agilely ran up the steep stairway and onto the deck. The sunshine was blinding against the clean, white wood. Shame immediately marred the freshly scrubbed deck with several puddles, but Rue was oblivious to her hound's indiscretions as the wind sang in her ears and blew her hair, invigorating her blood. There was an incredible feeling of freedom as the clean lines of the vessel cut through the water. She breathed deeply, looking up at the sky, seeing the white fluffy clouds scudding and felt she was flying.

Jacques stared down from the bridge at Rue's upturned little face and nodded his satisfaction at the exhilaration he saw mirrored. The little silent one had salt in her veins, he noted, knowing the long voyage, that could be so painful for some, was going to be a joyful experience for her.

"*Bonjour, ma petite,*" he called and he laughed aloud as she grinned, waved, and scampered fleetly up the steps toward him.

"There is Three Rivers, the sight of a bloody battle," informed the captain as they approached quite a large settlement on the north bank. "You slept a long time. We have been under way for several hours.

Are you hungry?" he asked and laughed when she nodded. "Then you shall eat, my beauty. Pierre, take the wheel," he directed and a large burly man with an eye patch obeyed. Rue stared at him with interest and when Pierre winked, she smiled shyly.

"He's too pretty for a *garçon*," he chuckled, looking at Rue's trim figure in her boyish attire. "This is our new cabin boy?"

"Rue Sinclair, this is my brother Pierre Gillette," he introduced, pronouncing Sinclair with a French accent, "*San*clair." "Now my little barefoot one," he bowed, offering his arm and leading her to the galley where Meron, Nick, and Kestrel sat eating an enormous lunch of fresh bread and fish.

"How long before we reach Quebec?" asked Kestrel excitedly.

"Oh, not until this evening," returned Meron, enjoying the carefree happiness they exuded. "Rue, how is your hound behaving?" he added, not wanting to use the name Shame and spoil the sunny atmosphere. Rue nodded and carefully boned a portion of fish for her ravenous dog.

"Tonight, my friends, we will eat courtesy of Jacques Gillette in Quebec," pronounced the captain, pouring glasses of white wine for all at the table.

Kestrel and Rue both sniffed the sparkling liquid, never having seen or smelled wine before, except for Angus's homemade brews from dandelions and elderberries.

"Sip it," directed Nick, enchanted by the girls' refreshing innocence. "Slowly," he laughed as Kestrel sipped and then drank thirstily.

"More," she asked, holding the drained glass out to Jacques who filled it once again to the rim.

"Careful, Kess," cautioned Nick, not wanting to be too autocratic, knowing how she rebelled, but also not wanting her sick.

"Why?" she replied.

"Well maybe 'tis one of those things you must find out for yourself," he sighed as she drained the second glass.

Rue ate and drank quickly, eager to be back in the sunshine with the wind in her hair.

"She's a sailor, that one," boasted Jacques as Rue and the hound raced out of the galley. Meron grinned and followed his dark niece after seeing the younger golden one turn slightly green from her fourth glass of wine.

"Nick?" wailed Kestrel.

"It seems she has found out for herself. That was a very quick

lesson," remarked the captain, hastily leaving Nick to deal with the
suffering Kestrel.

"Nick?"

Nick groaned, seeing the sweat bead on the wan little face. Maybe
he should be more autocratic, he mused, it would save both of them a
lot of discomfort.

While Kestrel leaned over the side wishing the boat would stop
moving, Rue leaned over the other side, loving the fluid motion. She
longed to dive into the swirling water and she mimed her desire.

"When you have left Quebec far behind and you are near
Tadoussac, then you shall swim. Here there is too much trafficking.
When the river broadens on its way to the ocean, she is cleaner,"
answered Pierre Gillette, fixing her with his one good eye, which was
twice as blue as his brother's.

"It's a pity your sister has *malaise*. But let us pray it is just *le vin*
and not *le mal de mer*," said Jacques thoughtfully as he saw the
golden head hanging over the side.

Nick found himself praying the very same thing as he heaved
Kestrel's inert but thankfully light body over one shoulder and carried
her down to their cabin. He would hate to play nursemaid the whole
voyage, he thought as he laid her on the wide bunk and placed a
cooling cloth across her brow.

"Don't leave me!" cried Kestrel weakly as she clutched him
strongly when he stood to quit the cabin. "I think I'm dying!" she
added dramatically.

"Next time you drink wine like water, I'll leave you to take care of
yourself," threatened Nick, relenting and sitting beside her. "Now try
to sleep."

"I can't! Every time I close my eyes I get dizzy," she complained.

"Put one hand on the wall," he told her tersely, wishing he was out
in the bracing breeze instead of the confined closeness of the airless
cabin.

"Am I drunk like Angus gets?" asked Kestrel after a long pause.

"Unfortunately, no. When Angus gets drunk he is happy and
mellow. He does not turn green and vomit," returned Nick, coldly
wishing she would fall asleep.

Soon Kestrel was fast asleep and Nick thankfully extricated her
hand from his sleeve and crept silently from the cabin up into the fresh
air. It was late afternoon and the river reflected the hot molten sky. He
strode across the deck to where Rue sat up on the gunwales watching
everything with wide-eyed fascination. He smiled at her happy

flushed face. What an incredible change from the emaciated terrorized child of a few months before, he noted, delighting in the vibrant joy that emanated from her amber eyes. She sparkled, he realized, radiating a giddy elation.

"You are happy, little Rue?" he laughed and she grinned impishly and stretched her slim brown arms wide as though to show him the whole world.

Meron watched his niece from the bridge where he stood talking to Pierre and Jacques.

"How do you define that?" he murmured, entranced by the vitality that glowed from the small dark girl. The two Frenchmen shook their heads, at a loss for words. There was something about Rue that could not be described but which caused aching lumps of tenderness in their throats.

"Do you think she will always be silent?" asked the captain after a long pause.

"I hope not," returned Meron.

"I would like to meet the animals who used her so," snarled Pierre, his one eye flashing dangerously.

" 'Tis in the past and must remain so," answered Meron. "She is healing."

As the sun set, they reached Quebec, and Nick stared down at Kestrel's sleeping face and decided not to wake her. He doubted that her stomach could entertain the thought of eating, and not wanting to mar Jacques's plans for the evening, he left her on board in charge of Pierre and accompanied Meron, Rue, and Jacques to shore.

Rue wore her buckskin fringed trousers and vest, not wanting to be hampered by the long skirt of the salmon-pink gown. She was loath to leave her new puppy, but Pierre found a large meaty bone and the young hound was curled at the burly man's feet, happily gnawing away.

"Well, I hope we are going somewhere that will accept Rue's unconventional mode of dress," laughed Meron, himself dressed in fringed buckskins.

"We go to a very unconventional place," responded Jacques, enigmatically refusing to divulge their destination. "Smile, my friend," he urged Nick, who strode lost in his own thoughts. "Your golden wife will be quite safe with Pierre."

Rue's expressive amber eyes widened as they entered the dim smoky room.

"Your Kestrel will not be talking to you when she hears where we've gone without her," chuckled Jacques. "A pirates' meeting place, but one where there is a chef who has the magic from the Orient."

"It will teach her to heed her husband," answered Nick tersely, looking around as his eyes accustomed to the candlelight and he saw all sorts of colorful characters and animals.

"Now you see why Jacques said no dogs," laughed Meron as a parrot and a monkey had a screaming fight with a rainbow of feathers and fur flying.

Rue sat hearing every language and dialect under the sun chattered, murmured, and sung. Her eyes could not hold on to all the bright images of people, things, animals, colors, actions, and countless other visions as Gypsies danced and whirled; and at jugglers, swordsmen, acrobats, and a multitude of other new and exciting events her eyes had never witnessed before.

On the table before them were a dozen or more dishes that steamed curls of strange but delicious odors.

"The soup of the bird's nest," Jacques announced with relish and as the meal progressed, he regaled them with impossible stories of some of the ingredients being buried for many hundreds of years.

Rue had been raised on Angus's wonderful cooking but nothing had prepared her for the subtle tastes of Chinese cuisine. She ate paper-thin pancakes stuffed with exotic-sounding things like lotus and ginger, mushrooms and bamboo, oysters and black beans, and many other previously unheard-of delicacies like peanuts, anise, soy, and pineapple. Rue ate and ate, listened and listened, watched and watched, unable to absorb everything.

"You like the lemon? It is very good. I make you eat very many lemons and these, the limes, as we sail for Europe," informed Jacques, enjoying every second of the evening. "I have never, never . . . had so good a time giving," he added, trying to explain how rewarding it was with such an appreciative guest as he looked at Rue's glowing face. Nick had never experienced so many different taste sensations. He had no words, he just used his mouth to eat the tender steamed dumplings and crisp wonton, the crisp duck and the pork in the sweet pungent sauce. Finally they all pushed their chairs back from the still-laden table, unable, although wanting to, to eat another bite.

A light summer rain was falling as they left the noisy smoky den.

Rue held her hot face up to the cooling mist and then removed her soft leather moccasins, wanting to feel the moisture between her toes.

"No," cautioned Nick, kneeling and replacing her shoes. "In large towns like this 'tis not advisable. There are parasites that dig their way through the flesh and can cause harm to you." Rue stood still, allowing Nick to gently replace her shoes. There was a split second when fear surged in at feeling the warmth of his strong hands on the sensitive flesh of her foot, but she relaxed and the fear receded.

They walked through the narrow, cobbled streets of the Quebec waterfront, hearing the cheery raucous Gallic voices spill out of the taverns and echo through the wet summer night.

Kestrel heard Jacques's deep French voice recounting a bawdy story a full five minutes before her keen eyes saw the four figures loom out of the misty darkness. She leaned over the side of the ship, fuming. She had awakened about an hour after Nick had left and on being informed that she couldn't leave the boat to find him, had thrown a furious tantrum that had sent Pierre into howls of laughter. When she had imperiously demanded that he inform her where her husband was, the one-eyed man had pretended not to speak English and when she had resorted to fluent French, he had given way to more mirth and then spoke Spanish, of which she had no knowledge. Three times she had tried to sneak off the boat only to be intercepted by numerous French seamen.

Kestrel longed to shout out to the returning group but anger and pride got in her way. She stood in the shadows and watched them board, noting furiously the laughing, happy faces. Rue's young puppy bounded up to her mistress, barking and affectionately leaping to lick everyone in welcome.

Kestrel felt miserable, wanting to fling herself into Nick's strong arms, but she was so angry at being abandoned she hid, hoping he would get very worried when he couldn't find her. She sat, as the light rain turned to a heavier fall, getting drenched to the skin, hearing the happy voices drift out onto the deck. Unfortunately she was not near enough to hear specifics of the conversation, especially when Nick got up to go to their cabin to check on her, only to be stopped by Pierre.

"She is sleeping and does not want to be awakened," lied the large French seaman glibly, feeling the haughty golden beauty needed a lesson.

"How is she?" worried Nick.

"So-so," prevaricated Pierre. "*Mal de mer.* So, my friend, sleep is the best remedy." Nick nodded, relieved that he did not have a tantrum on his hands.

Kestrel finally could not stand the humiliation. She sat dripping wet on the deck listening to the men happily laughing and singing as they drank liberally. She debated crawling into the bunk in her cabin but she was too furious.

Nick lay back listening to Jacques's incredible adventures, a tankard of rum in his hand. Rue was happily curled half-asleep with her dog next to Meron, who was thoroughly enjoying the French captain's exaggerations. Pierre added spicy tidbits here and there coloring the already dangerous stories. Finally Kestrel burst in and stood dripping in the doorway, too angry to say a word.

"Kess, come and sit with me," offered Nick after a few seconds in which he accurately summed up her mood. "Jacques is telling some very entertaining stories about his pirate days."

Kestrel felt like a fool as Nick patronizingly patted the cushion beside him and then ignored her. Unable to say a word she just turned around and left, hoping Nick would follow. She rushed down to their cabin and stripped off her wet clothes. She sat on the bunk drying her long hair, her ears straining to hear Nick's even tread.

Nick was in no rush to face Kestrel's obvious fury. He leisurely finished his rum and then stood and stretched.

"You need much good luck," laughed Jacques.

"I very much doubt that she sleeps," chuckled Pierre. "She has a very, very bad temper."

Nick smiled wryly and left. He walked slowly across the wet deck breathing deeply of the refreshing night air before descending to the cabin and Kestrel.

Kestrel sat fuming on their bunk lit by the warm glow of the gently swinging oil lamp. Her hair was tousled from the vigorous toweling she had given it, and her breasts heaved with suppressed anger. Nick stood in the doorway appreciating the beautiful golden picture she made.

"Fury becomes you, my love," he remarked, and his usually lightning-quick instincts were dulled by the enormous meal and the rum so he was not in time to duck the missiles that Kestrel let fly. A soap dish cracked his brow, breaking the skin so that blood spurted and ran freely down his lean cheek, followed by a hairbrush, comb, book, pillow, and a boot. The hairbrush gave a sharp blow to his jaw and the boot bounced off his chin as he braved the onslaught. Kestrel saw him coming nearer and she reached in vain for more objects to hurl. Not finding any, she slapped his face hard and he slapped her back. There was a moment as she stared at him in shock, unable to believe that he had actually hit her. She slapped him again, and again he slapped her back. Kestrel's green eyes flashed dangerously, her usually soft mouth was contorted into a hard line with her intense rage. She clenched her fists and swung, but Nick caught them in a steely grip. He looked down at her silently, his face stern and uncompromising. She stared defiantly into his dark fathomless eyes, hiding the apprehension she felt as she noted the blood that ran from his brow and felt the air crackle with his cold anger.

Nick fought to control himself, not trusting himself to speak as he stared down at the rebellious little face, seeing the marks of his hands on her soft golden skin. He dropped her hands and turned away to the open porthole where he breathed deeply, trying to calm himself. He absently rubbed his jaw and winced at the painful bruise. He stared into the mirror and noting the havoc Kestrel had wreaked upon his face, he did not feel so bad for the two handprints he had left on her. He turned and stared at her. She sat on the edge of the bunk trying to look pugnacious but managed only to seem a small mutinous waif.

"I do not like to be hit, Kestrel," informed Nick in cold measured tones, refusing to be softened. "This time you are lucky. Next time I shall return your blows in kind. Do you understand?"

Kestrel refused to answer as her anger overcame her fear. She had been abandoned while he had gone out and enjoyed himself. She fumed.

"Is that understood, Kestrel?" repeated Nick, advancing, his own fury rekindled by her defiance. "Or would you like the thrashing that your behavior warrants?"

Kestrel stood firm, resisting the urge to back away. She had seen Nick angry before but not like this. His black eyes seemed to blaze out of his chiseled face. She kept her own eyes pinned to his, as her chest heaved.

Nick grabbed her by the shoulders and lifted her so their faces were level.

"Do you understand?" he repeated, but Kestrel pursed her lips together, refusing to give him the satisfaction of an answer. They glared at each other and suddenly Nick brutally kissed the mutinous mouth. Kestrel bit him but he increased the pressure, forcing her lips open so she tasted the saltiness of his blood. Her tongue warred with his as she writhed against him angrily, her fury igniting into frenzied passion.

Nick violently threw her onto the bunk, spread her legs, and plunged into her, taking a savage delight. His thrusts were like blows and she arched upward, accepting, wanting more as they hammered at each other. Kestrel clawed at his back, tearing the shirt and his skin, sobbing her frustration at not feeling the warmth of the whole of his body. She wrapped her legs around his hips and thrust upward, fiercely matching him in ferocious intensity, her face as seriously set as his. They came together, their breathing harsh and gasping, and lay entwined, feeling the ache of their bruised pelvic bones.

"Is that the thrashing you promised me?" asked Kestrel huskily when she could speak and Nick rolled over, taking her with him so she lay on top of him. He stared up at her tousled face, her eyes still veiled and half-closed with passion. Kestrel looked down, seeing his cut brow, bitten lip, and swollen jaw. She winced and gently touched each place and then her face hardened.

"You deserved everything you got," she stated. "Next time don't go anywhere without me."

Nick sighed deeply and looked thoughtfully up at her pouting face.

"I mean what I say, Kestrel. You'll not hit me again or you will be very sorry," he threatened softly, his eyes seeming hooded and ruthless. Kestrel frowned, feeling fear even though they lay still joined together intimately. "Do you understand?"

Kestrel nodded silently and put her head on his broad strong chest as his arms held her close.

CHAPTER SEVENTEEN

It seemed that Rue had barely closed her eyes before she was awakened by an excited pounding on her door and Kestrel burst in.

"Come on, up, up!" she chattered. "We're going shopping for shoes, and clothes and books, trunks and hats. Everything we can possibly think of."

Rue smiled wearily at her golden sister's joyful mood, wishing she hadn't heard the violent lovemaking through the cabin wall. She had blocked her ears and rushed up to the dark wet deck unable to cope with the fear it aroused in her. She had crept back at daybreak and thankfully the neighboring cabin had been peacefully quiet.

"Come on, lazybones! Breakfast is ready. Meron and Nick are nearly finished," urged Kestrel, pulling the covers off Rue.

In the galley Nick ate stolidly, despite the hilarity his battered face caused. Meron tactfully just raised an eyebrow but Jacques fell back in his chair with tears of mirth flooding the wrinkles on his leathery old face.

"*Sacrebleu!*" he wheezed. "'ow does she look? Eh? Pierre? Pierre? *Viens ici,*" he shouted and his large one-eyed brother entered and joined in with laughter and comments.

Rue and Kestrel entered, smiling at the laughter.

"Come here, *ma petite,*" beckoned Jacques and Kestrel obeyed. She stood still as Pierre and Jacques examined her unblemished face.

"What is it?" she asked, frowning in bewilderment as the two rascally old Frenchmen clucked like broody hens and waved fingers of shame at Nick.

"Maybe it is where we may not look?" suggested Pierre, wickedly patting his own behind.

"What is?" questioned Kestrel. "Nick?" she added as she saw the two men look to the dark man, who ate with no amusement on his stern face.

"The beating for marking such an 'andsome face," supplied Pierre. Kestrel scowled and blushed, not knowing what to say but wanting to deny having anything to do with the bruised cut brow, the bitten lip, the grazed chin or the purple jaw.

Nick looked up and met Rue's concerned expression. He frowned, noting she looked tired and heavy-eyed.

"Do you feel all right?" asked Meron before the young doctor could make comment.

Rue nodded and grinned before sitting down to a huge breakfast of ham and eggs.

"*Mal de mer?*" worried Jacques, thinking his star sailor was about to let him down.

"Definitely not seasickness," laughed Pierre as the petite dark girl consumed the enormous meal.

"Trouble sleeping?" asked Nick, concerned for the dark smudges beneath her eyes. Rue blushed and looked uncomfortable, and avoided looking at him. Meron raised his customary eyebrow at Nick, whose lean face tightened.

"Jacques, I think Rue should have my cabin when I leave today. It is larger and with that hefty hound of hers she'll need the room," suggested Meron.

Rue stared at her uncle with dismay as she heard that he would be leaving.

"You don't want to leave your cabin?" asked Jacques, not understanding the cause of her troubled expression.

Rue nodded and then shook her head, not knowing how to say yes she wanted to change cabins and finally gave up and leaned her head on her uncle's shoulder. He wrapped his arms tightly around her, feeling the frantic beating of her heart.

"I have to go. We canna leave Angus all alone now, can we?" he said softly, understanding her concern and fear. Rue resolutely shook her head and smiled tremulously. "That's a braw lass. Now are we nearly ready for our expedition?" he laughed, trying to lighten the mood.

Rue faced the shopping expedition with great trepidation, and Kestrel with great glee. Nick felt he was traveling with night and day when he looked from the dark beauty's brooding silence to his own wife's golden excitement.

"Mme. Charbonnière, she knows . . . everything about everything for *le bon ton,* for *le beau monde,*" boasted Jacques, directing the coachman with a great flourish. "She is a very good friend," he bragged with a wink and a wicked leer.

Rue stared silently out of the window at the many, many houses they passed. She had never seen so many people at one time, or ever in her life. The narrow cobbled streets were jammed, leaving very little room for the horse and carriage, as wares were sold and customers haggled and screamed. Soon the streets widened and the houses were more spread out with trees and gardens around, and Rue relaxed. Kestrel hung out of the other window, enthralled with everything as she regaled everyone with reports of what people were wearing, doing, and saying.

The carriage stopped at a large well-appointed house. A footman opened the door and a shocked expression flitted across his stony features as the two girls dressed in Indian leather clothes leaped out without his assistance. Rue batted his white-gloved hand aside indignantly, causing Jacques to roar with laughter as Kestrel examined the footman's shiny buttons and braid.

"Well, Meester Smeeth, what you think of these two beauties?" asked Jacques impishly of the haughty footman as they were led into the ornate, ostentatious house.

Kestrel's eyes were as big as saucers as she stood in the central hall. Nick had a hard time not laughing at the incongruous marble busts that stared at them from all sides.

"Mme. Charbonnière's taste has me a bit worried," Nick confessed quietly to the irrepressible sea captain. "This place looks like a Roman mausoleum." Meron hooted with laughter.

"Do not worry. Her clothes are very chic," pronounced Jacques as he struck a gallant pose and bowed elaborately toward the sweeping marble staircase. Kestrel's mouth hung agape at the vision that slowly descended. Dressed in about ten shades of purple from royal to violet, with an enormous intricate hairdo bedecked with ostrich feathers, a tiny plump woman appoached very solemnly. Nick breathed hard and concentrated seriously on unfocusing his eyes so he didn't disgrace himself by going into gales of merriment. Meron looked at the tip of his right moccasin, not wanting to see anything, especially his younger niece's rapt expression.

"*Mon petit chou*," purred Jacques, lovingly clasping one lilac-gloved hand in his and kissing it.

Rue could not believe her eyes as she examined the tiny round woman from her fuchsia shoes to the puce plumes that were balanced precariously atop the powdered lavender wig that was nearly as tall as the woman herself.

"Oooooh!" breathed Kestrel, in awe that the hair hadn't fallen off on the long descent down the sweeping staircase. Nick choked and hurriedly buried his face in a large handkerchief. Meron thumped him on the back, preferring to divert his attention from Kestrel's unabashed appraisal of Mme. Charbonnière's painted face.

"This is my dear dear friend, Ghislaine Charbonnière," introduced Jacques.

"Madame," stated Nick soberly.

"Nick, can I have my hair like that? How does it stay up?" chattered Kestrel, never at a loss for words for very long.

"Madame," bowed Meron.

The tiny purple-clad woman led them into a salon that was decorated in every conceivable shade of green where she sat looking like the only flower in the garden, her layers of gauzy gown seeming like petals as she posed upon her satin leafy pillows.

Rue sat quietly watching as Kestrel eagerly examined and touched everything in the room. A footman entered with a silver tray of cut-glass goblets of still another shade of green. Nick judged Mme.

Charbonnière's age to be in her late sixties. He was aware of her sharp eyes regarding him seriously.

"So you are a doctor?" She finally spoke, without any trace of a French accent. Nick nodded assent to her question. "Child, stop fiddling and come here," she ordered imperiously and Kestrel, after her first startled acknowledgment, slowly obeyed. "Nearer," beckoned the madam. Kestrel stood silently as the old woman turned her from side to side, and then she rang a little green ceramic bell.

"Michelle, take this young lady and fit her in an undertunic," she directed the uniformed maid who answered the bell. Kestrel followed the woman from the room with a backward awkward look at Nick.

Mme. Charbonnière regarded Rue silently and then beckoned her with one curled finger. Rue gracefully stood and crossed, wanting to see the old woman's face closely. It was like a doll's, she mused, remembering a cold china face devoid of expression that Angus had once brought from Boston. Once again the little green ceramic bell was rung and a maid entered. Rue silently followed the servant from the room and up the sweeping marble stairs.

Kestrel stood in an entirely white room with long mirrors, dressed in a simple white tunic. She grinned at herself in the mirror and laughed delightedly as she noted that only her face, arms, and feet seemed to exist as the white tunic blended into the white walls and floor. She dug her bare toes into the soft pile of the carpet and spun around, seeing herself reflected from every mirror. She threw back her golden mane of hair and grinned mischievously at herself mirrored on the ceiling.

"She can't see or hear us!" exclaimed Nick after trying to get Kestrel's attention as she stood looking right at him, assessing herself wonderingly.

"They are magic mirrors," informed Jacques proudly.

"God, she's beautiful," breathed Nick, entranced. "But it seems somehow dishonest," he added.

"If she knew she was being watched she would not be so natural and graceful. In another room Mme. Charbonnière watches. She is an artiste and this is her canvas," exclaimed Jacques, indicating the room and Kestrel. "When Madame is inspired and knows 'ow she will dress *la petite,* we shall be entertained. It is a small service for the gentlemen who pay the big bills."

Nick, not understanding, raised a questioning eyebrow at Meron, who grinned expectantly.

Kestrel was led from the room and Rue entered, her eyes wide with apprehension. Whereas her sister had spun about delightedly, Rue slowly examined the sterile room, noting the mirrors on the walls and ceiling. She stood still, somberly staring at herself, seeming to find no joy but a profound sadness in her reflected image.

"*Ma pauvre petite mademoiselle*," whispered Jacques, seeing stark loneliness haunt Rue's large amber eyes. "Now we shall have our treat," he declared, banishing the moroseness of several seconds before as Rue was led from the room.

"Treat?" questioned Nick as Meron and Jacques settled back in their chairs and sighed with anticipation, their eyes glued eagerly to the empty white room.

"Aah," sighed the old captain with rapture as three tall women entered in flowing diaphanous robes. Nick didn't know what to expect as the air was suddenly highly charged. He sipped his potent drink and looked at Meron, but the man's attention was riveted on the unfolding scene as the three statuesque women approached the mirror, their movements sinuous and unhurried, their hands stroking and molding the sheer fabric across their ripe breasts.

"Which one takes your fancy, my friend?" asked Jacques, and he chuckled heartily when Meron spread his broad hands in a gesture that illustrated his dilemma. He reached out to stroke the round, tempting bodies and just connected with the cold, one-dimensional glass as the three sultry beauties let their robes float seductively to the floor. Nick breathed deeply as the women pressed themselves against the cool surface of the mirror, their parted, moist lips misting in little spurts.

"Well, Nick, which one do you choose?" probed Jacques, his blue eyes twinkling as he saw the two younger men sit forward in their chairs watching the three naked women make love to their own images. Nick shook his head in disbelief, fascinated by the voluptuousness displayed to him. "You want to pass the time while Mme. Charbonnière turns your Kestrel into a sophisticated woman?" he added. His words swept over Nick like a bucket of cold water and his eyes narrowed as he observed the subtly applied makeup that the women wore. Kestrel's fresh, open young face was superimposed in his mind's eye and suddenly the three women looked garish and tawdry in comparison.

"Which one is for you?" laughed Meron.

"Me? Do I look loco? *Stupide*?" exclaimed Jacques indignantly. "I am a tired old man. You think I would perform in the same room with young bulls like you two? I have my pride," he blustered.

The door burst open and Kestrel fleetly ran in, bubbling with excitement about the materials and designs. She stopped in mid-sentence, aware she wasn't getting the amount of attention she expected. She followed their gaze and her green eyes widened with shocked amazement at the sight of three very voluptuous naked women writhing against the windows.

"That's the room I was in!" she exclaimed, unable to put into words what she thought about the erotic spectacle. She frowned as she looked down at her much smaller breasts and pouted speculatively at Nick, who tried to hide his amusement at her very transparent expression. "Don't look!" she shouted as he pulled her into his lap. "Ooooh!" she hissed, feeling his arousal through the fabric of his tight trousers and knowing what had possibly caused it. She ground her firm buttocks into his lap as jealousy coursed through her.

"Careful," warned Nick, shifting her to one side.

"Excuse me," said Meron huskily, standing stiffly and exiting.

"Oh!" gasped Kestrel as she saw her uncle enter the white room and the three naked sirens surrounded him. Her mouth dropped open as he embraced each one.

"There must be French in him," chuckled Jacques with appreciation. "Only a Frenchman could satisfy three women at one time." Kestrel groaned with disappointment as curtains were dropped, shielding the scene of her uncle's romantic endeavors from her eyes. Nick sighed with relief, his hands unconsciously caressing Kestrel's firm young body as he was fully aroused both by what he had witnessed and by Kestrel's closeness.

"Mme. Charbonnière is a very civilized couturiere, not only does she have treats for the . . . er, senses, but also the stomach," Jacques announced, standing and patting his own as he felt the sexual tension emanate from the young couple. He quietly left the room.

Nick and Kestrel were unaware of Jacques's departure as they stared into each other's eyes. Kestrel felt every nerve end tingling as her breathing seemed difficult.

"You wanted to mate with those other women, didn't you?" she challenged hoarsely, the pain of that thought shooting through her and fusing her with the passion she felt.

"No," whispered Nick, pulling her golden head toward him as he closed his eyes, wanting to melt into her kiss. Kestrel resisted but his strength overpowered her and she drowned in his kiss, her body thrilling to his possessive mastery.

Rue sat in the beautiful gardens admiring the profusion of flowers and multicolored birds in Mme. Charbonnière's aviary, blissfully unaware of the sensual delights being enjoyed within the ostentatious house as Jacques regaled her with stories of the land where each treasure had been found.

"In the jungles of Africa the colors of the birds could blind your eyes and the cries deafen your ears. The flowers have magical powers that could bring passion from a stone, love to the most cynical, and sleep of every kind," he recounted. "And yet it is a dark, exotic continent with many mysteries and here there are but a few of them," he boasted, spreading his hands to encompass the trees, flowers, and shrubs. Magic, love, mystery, thought Rue, as she breathed deeply of the fragrant perfumes of the countless blossoms.

Later they all sat in a little arbor, being served by several liveried manservants. Nick stared into Kestrel's glowing face as they ate and conversed politely, as if they had just attended a church service and not coupled lustily on the floor of Mme. Charbonnière's waiting room. Meron ate ravenously, ignoring Kestrel's rapt staring as she thought with awe of him with three women.

"Meron?" ventured Kestrel.

"Not now, Kestrel," said Nick hastily, with barely suppressed amusement when he guessed correctly what she was about to ask.

"But how—" she continued.

"Not now!" reiterated Meron as Nick howled with laughter. Kestrel stared angrily from one man to the other as she remembered Nick's arousal from watching the three women.

Rue frowned as she stared around the table, sensing something had been shared that she was not a part of. She felt a mingling of fear and sadness as she realized what they all shared as she saw Jacques and Mme. Charbonnière stroking each other's hands as they popped grapes into each other's mouths.

"You are all welcome to spend the night," proclaimed the small round woman expansively. "The gowns will be ready tomorrow."

"I thank you but think not," answered Meron cordially.

"Did you not enjoy the diversions at your disposal?" laughed Jacques wickedly. Meron inclined his head gravely in acknowledgment.

"You mean those three naked women?" pounced Kestrel triumphantly and Nick spread his arms wide in a gesture of defeat before howling with laughter.

"She is your niece, Meron," he gurgled.

"If I hadn't come into the room you would have been with them too, wouldn't you?" accused Kestrel.

"Of course, he is a healthy young male," offered Jacques before Nick could defend himself.

"And I am a healthy young female," spat Kestrel. "Mme. Charbonnière, have you any naked men for me? Maybe five or six?" she added as an afterthought. Jacques choked and thumped the table with his fists, unable to release the roars of merriment.

Rue sat quietly, wishing she could leave the perfumed, cloying atmosphere of the ostentatious house and too colorful gardens. Suddenly the paradisial birds and flowers hurt her eyes and ears.

"Rue, you look very tired," observed Nick, not anxious to meet Kestrel's rebellious face, knowing she was spoiling for a battle. "I think we should take our leave."

"But what about our gowns?" protested Kestrel.

"They will be delivered to the *Étoile* tomorrow. I shall have my seamstresses working all night," comforted Mme. Charbonnière. "Are you sure you will not pass the night with me, Jacques?" she purred, popping another grape into his mouth.

"*Non, mon petit chou,*" he murmured, seductively rolling a grape between her painted lips.

"But what about shoes and everything?" complained Kestrel petulantly.

"The shoes and lingerie will accompany the gowns," informed Mme. Charbonnière, suddenly dropping her enticement of Jacques and clapping her puce-gloved hands together in a very businesslike way to summon several footmen to usher her guests out.

"Well, *mes amis,* was I not correct? Did you not have a marvelous time?" chortled Jacques with a sideways look at Meron, who kept his eyes fixed to the passing scenery as they rode back to the harbor in an open carriage.

"No!" pronounced Kestrel as she thought of Nick and the three women. She was afraid and suddenly wished she was back in the house by the lake with Angus.

"Why don't Rue and I shop for the trunks?" suggested Meron, feeling the undercurrents and wanting Rue to himself for the little time they had left together. Rue's face lit up as she was anxious to be away from the sexual innuendos that were being bantered about. Meron called out to the coachman, who halted the horses, and he leaped down and Rue lithely jumped and was caught in his strong arms. Nick watched the tall dark man with the slight dark girl until they were swallowed up by the noisy throng of people on the narrow dock streets.

The rest of the ride back to the ship was silent as Jacques dozed and Kestrel refused to talk and kept her eyes pinned to the passing scenery as disturbing thoughts stung her brain. She felt like an unformed, ignorant child in comparison to the worldly lushness of the women at Mme. Charbonnière's. From the carriage she saw many more sophisticated, elegant women and she closed her eyes, unable to bear the thought of so much competition. In the wilderness Nick had only her to choose from, but out in the world there were thousands of females with much more to offer him than she.

Silently Nick and Kestrel boarded the *Étoile* and entered their cabin. Nick sat and watched her pace back and forward, her face troubled and her small hands clenched.

"Kess, come here," he said quietly, opening his arms wide. Kestrel stood poised, her vulnerability and fear very apparent, before thrusting out her small firm breasts and tossing back her golden mane as voluptuously as the three women had.

Later Nick held her closely, her hair fanned across his naked chest, thinking of the passion with which Kestrel had just made love. What a wonder she was. She stirred and he caressed her gently.

"Nick, have you ever made love to three women at the same time?" she whispered.

"No," answered Nick honestly, without a tinge of regret in his voice.

Rue kept tight hold of Meron as they were jostled and squashed by the crowds of people. Seeing her nervousness, Meron led her to the quieter side streets where she excitedly stared into the windows of dim dusty shops. Meron bought her a beautiful dagger, the handle made of intricately carved ebony and the blade etched with pastoral scenes that belied its lethal purpose.

"It is small enough to be hidden anywhere on your body, and sharp enough to protect you," he told her. "I know you can use it accurately if you have to."

Meron also bought two large steamer trunks and had them sent to the *Étoile* as he and Rue preferred to spend their remaining time together browsing through the maze of shops. Rue felt her mind would burst from all she saw and experienced. Paintings of palaces, elephants, castles, cities, and many things she didn't know existed.

At sunset they sat staring over the river, hand in hand.

"Rue, I know it is hard for you to leave, but you must. You have grown and it is time to fly. You have been hurt and abused by lust. No, listen," he insisted as she tried to pull her hand away, not wanting to hear. "You are brave, Rue, so listen. You have been hurt by men's lust but dinna let them steal something wonderful from you. Only if you let them can they steal love from you. You will fall in love and want to give your body . . ." He struggled to explain as Rue shook her head, emphatically disagreeing and covering her ears. Meron sadly nodded.

"All right, no more," he said, recapturing her hand, and holding them tight. "It's back to the ship before we have everyone worrying about us."

Rue held her uncle's hand tightly, knowing soon she would have to let go and stand alone as she sailed across the wide ocean to the unknown.

"Your father and brothers will be on the other side," comforted Meron, knowing her trepidation as they walked along the jetty toward the moored dories.

Rue trailed her hand in the cool water as Meron rhythmically rowed to the *Étoile*.

"Before I leave I'll help you to get settled in your new cabin," he said as he moored the small boat to the larger vessel. Rue sat in the bobbing dinghy, staring up at the tall side of the *Étoile* and the rope ladder.

"Come on, up you go," directed Meron, standing with his feet apart to steady the light craft. Rue stood and agilely climbed the rope, knowing her uncle climbed behind. She stopped halfway up and smiled back at him as his concern seemed to weigh her down. She wanted to reassure him that she would be all right. Meron threw back his head and laughed out loud, comforted by her mischievous grin.

Pierre looked over the side and beamed down at the saucy expression on Rue's face.

" 'Tis the cabin boy!" he proclaimed, scooping her up as though she were a feather and putting her on one of his massive shoulders. "We thought you two had been shanghaied," he chuckled as he carried Rue to the galley so she had to keep ducking her head to avoid the low clearance.

Rue found it hard to enjoy the large festive dinner, knowing soon her uncle would be gone. Pierre noticed her anxious looks toward Meron.

"You will have not one but two *oncles, ma petite,*" laughed Jacques, exchanging winks with his one-eyed brother.

"Meron, when are you leaving?" asked Kestrel in a small voice, feeling as afraid and bereft as her older sister.

"Not until first light so let's not talk on it," Meron answered. Kestrel stared sadly and absentmindedly drained her wineglass as though it were water.

"Careful," warned Nick, but Kestrel didn't hear as she thoughtfully toyed with the food on her plate.

"When do we sail?" she asked.

"Tomorrow afternoon," informed Pierre. Kestrel felt torn; one part of her wanted to sail away with Nick to new adventures and experiences, but another part wanted to go back to the house in the woods, to Angus and all that was familiar.

Rue saw her own feelings mirrored in her sister's face and she reached out and took her hand. They grinned weepily at each other, sniffed, and both drained their wineglasses.

Rue and Meron stood on the deck, looking over the dark water to the warm lights on shore. Her few possessions were in her new cabin with her hound and sparkling new empty trunk.

"I wish I could stay and see you dressed in all your new finery, but I've stayed longer than I planned. Wee-Angus will be having a snit thinking something is wrong," said Meron, smiling down at her. Rue nodded bravely. "Now you write care of the trading post and Angus or I will get it. Will take a few months but you know all that." Rue flung her arms about his waist and buried her face into his stomach, trying to commit his leathery fragrance to memory.

"To bed now," he said gruffly, but she stubbornly shook her head, knowing she would wake to find him gone. They sat together until the first fingers of dawn crept into the eastern horizon.

Rue watched her uncle row himself to shore. He waved once and strode out of eyeshot. Jacques and Pierre stood on the bridge, looking down at the small valiant figure who wiped her wet cheeks with the backs of her hands. She gave a resolute sniff, threw her shoulders back, and followed by her gangly pup, made her way down to her cabin.

CHAPTER EIGHTEEN

Jacques and Nick surveyed the two woebegone faces at the breakfast table.

"Women!" teased Jacques. "Nevair 'appy! Today they get a wardrobe fit for the queen and 'ere they sit with the long face!"

Rue managed a watery smile and Kestrel dropped her fork in surprise.

"I can't believe that I forgot!" she exclaimed.

"It sounds like maybe your new finery 'ave arrived," rejoiced the captain as a great commotion was heard. Kestrel leaped up clapping her hands as Pierre entered looking very harassed.

"Your new passenger 'as arrived, *mon frère*," he hissed, rolling his one eye back into his head as he was unceremoniously shoved aside by an enormous woman dressed in tiers and layers of stiff shiny black.

"What new passenger?" mouthed Jacques, stunned by the apparition.

"Are you the captain?" demanded the large female.

Jacques nodded with his mouth agape and Kestrel started giggling.

" 'Scuse me, ducky," she said to Nick as her voluminous hooped skirts bounced and brushed his head as he sat trying to finish his breakfast. Kestrel's giggles turned to outright laughter at the look on Nick's face.

"Whoops!" And the woman tottered as the boat listed and put out a hand to steady herself right into Nick's half-eaten breakfast. Kestrel howled, her eyes streaming and her stomach aching. She desperately tried to get her breath to say something but caught Pierre's one eye as he wept with hilarity and renewed her merriment. Jacques thumped the table, impotently unable to let his own laughter out, and Nick sat with his shoulders shaking, silently ready to burst. As Nick and Jacques let loose with their roars, they were joined by the fruity chuckle of the enormous lady. For a full five minutes everyone was bent double holding their aching sides. Rue leaned weakly against her sister as the laughter died down only to burst out again as the woman slapped the side of her face with her mucky hand, leaving sticky yellow egg yolk on her rouged cheek.

"*Mon Dieu,*" gasped Jacques, panting for breath and wiping his streaming eyes.

"Bless my soul," hiccuped the fat woman. "Oh, it's good to 'ave an 'ealthy chuckle now and then, ain't it? Mind if I 'ave a sit down?" And she sat without waiting for an answer and her skirts flipped over her head, exposing bright red voluminous underwear the sight of which stunned the witnesses to silence as the poor woman fought to see, her fists punching against the offending black bombazine.

"Oh, no," screamed Kestrel, her stomach aching from so much laughter as it bubbled up again, and she collapsed against Rue who leaned her head on the table, thinking she would die if she didn't stop shaking with hilarity.

The fat woman fought her offending skirts and finally captured and tucked them down under her large anchoring legs. She surveyed her mirth-filled audience with a satisfied smile, waiting for the laughter to die down.

"Now where was we?" she asked, rubbing her dimpled fat hands together in a very businesslike way. "You're the captain?" she said, pointing at Jacques, who blew his nose like a trumpet to rid himself of the last vestiges of his amusement.

"*Excusez-moi,*" interrupted a timid voice. "*Mais, Mme. Charbonnière—*"

"The gowns!" declared Kestrel, jumping to her feet.

"From Charbonnière's?" the large woman said, pursing her painted red lips to show how impressed she was.

"Excuse us," bowed Nick, tucking Kestrel's hand through one of his arms and Rue's through the other, leaving Jacques to deal with the enormous painted woman.

The wily old French captain stared with speculation at the woman as she excitedly stood as though to follow Nick and his two charges.

"Madam? You wish to sail with me?" he asked, detaining her.

"I'd love to take a gander at some Charbonnière togs," she said, licking her greedy lips.

"Your name, madam?"

"Gladys Mackintosh."

"Profession?" probed Jacques, his usual gentle warmth honed to a razor-sharp edge.

"You and yer like enjoyed my charms many times when I was younger. Promised me the moon just to get yer ways and then leave me 'igh and dry with a couple of brats ter raise. Then get all 'igh and mighty when a girl 'as ter make a living one of the few ways she can."

"Profession?" repeated Jacques.

"Courtesan once, then prostitute, then just a common 'ore," stated Gladys Mackintosh. "Now? Just a lonely, fat lady."

"How you get thees side, Mees Mackintosh?"

"Bonded servant," she replied simply. "I was thirteen years old and pregnant. I stole and got caught. Luckily the ship went down and some luverly 'andsome sailor saved me 'ide. So I changed me monicker and made me way."

"And now? *Maintenant*?"

"You're worse than the bloody Inquisition!" complained Gladys.

"*Pourquoi* . . . why do you want to go 'ome to *l'Angleterre*?"

"Porky? Porky?" mimicked the fat woman. "Oh wee-wee, I parley froggy. I go 'ome because 'ome is 'ome. England is my 'ome and I wanta die there."

"*Pourquoi?*" asked Jacques, astounded that she would want to return to a country that virtually enslaved her at thirteen.

"Porky? Porky?" sniffed Gladys, covering her vulnerability. "Paska . . . I dunno. 'Omesick, I suppose. I've bin 'omesick fer forty years!" she confessed, blowing her nose.

"*Café?*" offered Jacques, lifting the coffee pot.

"Wee-wee, mercy," Gladys said, nodding.

"You 'ave money for the passage?" asked the captain idly as he poured the strong brew.

"Some," she said, patting an ample thigh. "The rest I thought I might work off?" she ended lamely.

"Doing what?"

Gladys dimpled and puffed out her bosom. Jacques sadly shook his head; Gladys sadly shook hers.

"No?" she said softly.

"*Non!*" repeated the captain firmly.

"Oh," murmured Gladys.

"Can you do anything else?"

"Anything else?" repeated Gladys.

"*Oui. Faire autre chose?*"

"Otro shows?" repeated the woman at a loss.

"*Oui.*"

Gladys sadly shook her head.

"Cook?" asked Jacques hopefully.

Gladys shook her head.

"Sew?"

"Oh wee-wee, I can sew. Take care of clothes. Iron, mend, wash," babbled the woman excitedly.

"*Les enfants?*" asked the captain, liking the woman's honesty and admiring her cunningly quick mind. "Children?" he added as she frowned.

"What are children doing on this vessel?" she asked. "Oh, do you mean them two little girls dressed like Injuns?"

"*Oui*," replied Jacques, feeling Gladys Mackintosh would make a formidable protector of Rue.

"Well they ain't exactly children."

"An abigail. A lady's maid. *La petite* with the black 'air," pronounced the captain. "Come," he ordered, taking her soft forearm and liking the warm bounciness. Gladys, very aware of the nuances of men, gave him a veiled, come-hither look, and then stuck her nose in the air. Jacques playfully slapped her ample bottom and nearly broke his knuckle on the metal hoop.

"*La petite* with the black hair?" asked Gladys. "What's she called?"

"Rue Sinclair."

"Strange name. French, too?"

"*Non*, Scottish," answered Jacques, handing her up the steep companionway and standing underneath to better admire her red underwear.

"And the gorgeous dark man?"

"With or without the eye?" chuckled Jacques.

"With or without the what?" asked Gladys and gave a squeal of merriment as the captain covered one of his twinkling blue eyes. "The one with the two nearly black eyes. The young one?"

"The ship's doctor, Nicholas MacKay."

"Doctor? I shall be ailing the 'ole bloody voyage!" rejoiced Gladys.

"He is married to the little sister of Rue. The beautiful young girl with hair golden like the sunshine."

Gladys sighed, then grinned at him. "Ah well, between you and yer one-eyed brother I shouldn't get into too much mischief," she gurgled.

Kestrel tried to twirl around in her new bronzed dress and nearly fell flat on her face as the material caught between her legs. Until that unfortunate moment she had taken Nick's, Jacques's, and Gladys's breath away as the metallic material seemed molten around her like a second skin, the deep rich color an unexpected but brilliant foil for her golden complexion and coloring.

"Oh that girl would make a wonderful 'arlot," mourned Gladys, shaking her bright hennaed locks and lumbering to her feet. "You ain't no donkey girl, yer a lady, so walk like one. Sashay, sashay, feel yer 'ips. That's the way," she directed and Nick's jaw dropped as he mentally shook a fist at the beaming Jacques. Kestrel loved the attention as she exaggerated Gladys's movements and sashayed across the listing deck.

"What's on your feet?" asked the large woman, hiking up Kestrel's skirts and exposing her long lean tan legs and bare feet. "Where's your shoes?"

"They weren't very comfortable," confessed Kestrel.

"And no undergarments!" screeched the indignant woman. "If I'm to teach these young ladies, there 'as ter be some decorum!"

"Teach?" repeated Nick in his dangerous low voice.

"Gladys?" warned Jacques. "We 'ave not set sail yet. *Mes petites*, I would like for you to meet your new *maid. Connaissez-vous, madame?* MAID!"

"Wee! Wee! I conny *bien*," surrendered the irrepressible large woman. "'Ow d'ye do, I'm Gladys Mackintosh." She bobbed a curtsy that was slyly copied by Kestrel.

"Mackintosh?" echoed Nick. "You're no Scot!"

"Never said I were!" retorted Gladys. "I'd not be one of you cold lot!"

"Where did you get your name then?" probed Nick.

"Off some poor drowned 'arlot!" replied Gladys candidly. "Afore that me monicker was Annie Wiggins but that ain't ter bandy abroad. I ain't bin called that since I was fourteen."

"Annie Wiggins?" repeated Nick, wondering which sounded better, Gladys Mackintosh or Annie Wiggins.

"Where's me young lady?" asked Gladys, looking around for Rue.

"*Où est Rue?*" asked Jacques.

"She went to her cabin to see to the hound," offered a young seaman, enthralled by the fashion show he had been allowed to witness.

"Come, I will take you there," offered Jacques.

"Jacques, a moment. Excuse me." Nick bowed slightly to the large woman before ushering the captain out of earshot of the inquisitive ex-courtesan. "What are you doing? I am responsible for Kestrel and Rue, not you!"

"You are responsible to your young bride but not for *la petite Rue*! No man 'ave the energy for both. You keep making the love to the golden one so she not fight so," he said, pointing to Nick's cut, bruised, and bitten face. *"Comprenez-vous?"*

"No, my friend. I dinna think you understand," retorted Nick angrily. "That Madam Mackintosh or Wiggins is not fit company for my wife or her sister, *comprenez-vous*?"

"Why ain't I? Aye?" interrupted Gladys, her gray eyes flashing, her dimpled hands on her ample hips. Nick breathed furiously, unable to answer as Kestrel's curious little face grinned enticingly at him, waiting for his answer. "Why not? 'Cos I was an 'ore? An 'arlot?"

"What's an 'arlot and an 'ore?" asked Kestrel eagerly.

"Remember Wee-Angus's fat woman at the trading post?" answered Nick, deciding to take the bull by the horns.

"Are you really?" gasped Kestrel, not at all fazed.

"And the three women in the white room at Mme. Charbonnière's," added Nick, hoping to dampen her enthusiasm.

"No, they weren't as old and fat," contradicted Kestrel, shaking her golden head. Gladys roared with laughter and hugged the girl.

"Nothing like an honest woman. Just like me," she rejoiced and Nick groaned and buried his head in his hands.

"Miss Mackintosh, we must talk," he interjected after a pause in which he was aware of every eye. Kestrel smiled happily, truly liking the funny fat woman in her black bombazine. "Privately," he added as his bubbling wife hugged her new funny friend.

"Of course," agreed Gladys, trying to look very grown-up and respectable despite her flowsy-blowsiness and fifty-three years.

Nick and Gladys walked away from Jacques and Kestrel. Nick stopped and turned to the woman, assessing her, trying to fathom what it was that caused Kestrel and Jacques to trust her so quickly. He wished Meron were there.

"Well?" prompted Gladys, aware of him evaluating her. " 'Ow am I doin' so far?"

"All right," grinned Nick, nodding his head. "I have charge of two very different females," he started awkwardly. "One is Kestrel, my wife, who has been raised in the wilderness so everything is new and exciting."

"Going to lead you a fine dance," remarked Gladys sagely.

"The other, Rue, has been . . . hurt," struggled Nick, not

knowing how much to divulge. "She cannot speak because of the abuse. She was also raised in the wilds but for the last three years has been in a mission."

"The poor little tyke. 'Ow old is she?"

"Nearly seventeen," answered Nick. "My wife is sixteen."

"Ain't used ter wearin' women's clothes, are they?" remarked Gladys and at Nick's acknowledgment she patted his arm in a motherly way. "Never mind. It's a good thing we 'ave the time on board to teach them a thing or two or they'll be embarrassin' your family somethin' awful," she reassured. "Don't you worry yerself, I'll 'ave them be'avin' like little princesses time I'm done with 'em."

"Little princesses!" muttered Nick, shaking his head with disbelief at the imagined vision of Gladys Mackintosh performing such a feat.

"Little princesses," purred the large lady. "Now where's the poor little black lamb?"

Rue opened the door of her cabin and stared at Jacques and Gladys. Her puppy leaped up trying to lick the merry painted face and got caught in the shiny black bombazine. Gladys staggered backward from the boisterous onslaught, slid down the wall, and sat unfortunately on one of her hoops again, flipping the voluminous skirts over her head and exposing her garish red underwear.

"This is getting to be a bit of a bother!" she panted as Jacques hauled her to her feet with much difficulty.

"I 'ave to be captain of my ship. So I leave you ladies to . . . er"— he waved his hands, searching for the right word— "make acquaintance. Rue, thees is your new maid, Gladys Coat," he introduced.

"Mackintosh, sonny. Mackintosh!" she corrected.

Rue frowned in puzzlement.

"Something wrong, ducky?" asked Gladys, noting Rue's amazement.

Rue pointed to herself and then to the large woman and mouthed the word "Maid?" and furrowed her brow.

"Well, not really a maid, ducks. More of a friend. Have you got a mother?" and when Rue shook her head sadly, Gladys added, "Well, that's what I'll be, sort of like yer mum. Now let's see all yer pretty frocks." She bustled over to the bunk to look at the pile of clothes. "Oh, don't let the doggy bite them. Oh look, they're gettin' 'air all over them. We 'ave to 'ang 'em up."

Rue sat on the floor stroking her dog as Gladys bustled about hanging up the gowns and lovingly folding and smoothing the lacy underthings before putting them away in the shiny new chest.

"There, everything in its place," pronounced Gladys proudly, sitting heavily on the bunk and looking down at the girl. "Sit!" she firmly cautioned the puppy as it tensed to spring onto her wide inviting lap. "You are a pretty little thing, ain't you?" she said, leaning forward and brushing a tress of ebony hair from Rue's face. Rue didn't know what to make of the enormous, flamboyant woman. She had never experienced anything like her except for Chastity.

"Can't talk?"

Rue shook her head.

"Well, never mind, ducky, there's a lot of men who'd give their right arms for a wife who'd lost 'er tongue," comforted Gladys. "Now let's go find that captain so I know where I'm to sleep."

Rue and Shame led Gladys up on the deck where Jacques supervised the loading of cargo and supplies.

"Pierre, show *la madame* to her chamber!" he yelled and the one-eyed man leered suggestively at Gladys as he picked up her shabby trunk. Gladys preened under the attention and puffed out her ample bosom as she followed him back into the depth of the ship.

Rue thoughtfully swung herself down to the cargo hold and made her way to where the horses were stabled. Sin blew through his lips and whinnied in welcome as she picked up brushes and started to groom his glossy black coat. Shame barked and leaped around, trying to get the stallion to play with him, and the horse lowered his head and gently butted the boisterous puppy. Rue smiled, feeling at ease with her two animal companions in the dark hold with the sunlight filtering from the open hatch above.

"Rue?" hailed a voice and she looked up to see Nick silhouetted against the sunshine. He agilely swung down and stood beside her, nodding his appreciation of the horses' glossy coats. "You shouldn't have done Rufus, I was going to," he said, rubbing his steed's nose. Rue smiled, happy that she had been useful.

"Rue? About this Gladys Mackintosh?" started Nick thoughtfully. Rue nodded attentively. "What do you think?" he probed.

Rue shrugged and grinned mischievously.

"Well, do you like her?" he asked, trying to pose yes and no questions to make Rue's answering easier to understand.

Rue splayed her small lean hands and moved them from side to side to signify she wasn't sure, and then smiled and nodded.

"I know how you feel," laughed Nick. "I like her despite my better judgment."

Rue laughed, agreeing with him, and Nick heard the sound she made. It wasn't harsh or awkward as a mute's laughter sometimes was. It was infectious and bubbly like a mountain stream in springtime after the thaw. Rue frowned as she saw his intensity and put her dark head to one side questioningly.

"We set sail the day after tomorrow. I must check out the infirmary," said Nick, taking his leave.

That day and the next were spent in a frenzy of last-minute shopping. On one such hurried excursion Kestrel insisted on dressing up in all her finery, carrying a parasol, and imitating Gladys Mackintosh's every move. Nick stifled a sigh that was a mixture of impatience and amusement as he rowed to shore. Rue watched enthralled as the large woman, looking like an enormous black shiny tent under a black umbrella, was showing Kestrel how to be a coquette.

"Miss Mackintosh, sit still!" roared Nick, losing all feeling of amusement, as the dinghy rocked precariously. Reaching shore, Rue in buckskins agilely leaped out with the mooring rope in hand. Kestrel cursed under her breath as her gown hampered her legs, making her awkward and clumsy. She finally kicked off her pinching shoes, picked up her skirts, and exhibiting her long stockinged legs to all and sundry, jumped off the boat with her parasol in hand. The boat rocked dangerously and Gladys screamed, reaching out to Nick for balance. There was a loud cursing and an almighty splash as the boat capsized and Nick and Gladys were pitched into the water.

Rue collapsed with laughter, her infectious giggles causing Kestrel to give up on her attempt at haughty composure as she posed in her new finery.

"Oh, Nick, look," howled Kestrel, pointing at Gladys, who bobbed about in the dirty water like a beached whale as her voluminous bombazine skirts had filled with air, making her very buoyant. Nick pulled himself up onto the dock and sat dripping, watching Gladys using her umbrella much like an oar as she tried to scoop herself to shore.

" 'Ere, 'ere, Doctor, don't make me laugh 'cos I 'ate swallerin' water," choked Gladys as she saw Nick's shoulders start shaking with mirth. "I must look a proper sight!" she wheezed, unable to be serious as she saw Rue, helplessly bent double, clutching her elegantly attired sister. Gladys leaned back on her air-filled skirts and howled. The howl of laughter turned to a bubbling gurgle as the air-filled bombazine collapsed and Gladys Mackintosh sank. Nick reached out, managing to get a firm hold on the strong fabric and hauled the flailing woman to shore. Still choking, the valiant wet woman managed a soggy curtsy to the watching sailors who gave a rousing cheer.

Kestrel smiled at the admiring audience of French Canadians as they walked up the cobbled harbor street. She stumbled, hobbled by her chic skirts, so she hiked them up again and was greeted by whistles and shouts of appreciation.

"Kestrel," warned Nick, indicating that she cover her long legs.

"But I can't walk," she complained, stamping her foot and immediately crying out as blood spurted from a deep gash caused by a piece of sharp glass.

Nick groaned out loud and herded his charges back to the dinghy, aborting the shopping spree.

As the *Étoile* was laden and stocked for the long voyage, Rue's anxiety grew. The hive of activity was nearly to fever pitch and their departure was imminent. She stood on the bridge with Jacques and Pierre as orders were barked and the anchor raised. Slowly the sails filled out and they glided up the St. Lawrence River. She stared behind, wishing it were night so she could see just the lights of the receding city of Quebec. At seven in the evening in July the sun was still high in the sky and her departure didn't feel as it should. She was leaving the continent of her birth to go to her parents' native land of Scotland. She was taking an enormous step and yet the sun shone as though it was any other day. Nothing was ominous, nothing spectacular, nothing thrilling, nerve-shattering or dramatic, she thought and frowned at the realization.

A hoarse cawing broke into her introspection, and she gazed up at the cumbersome large bird who circled. Pierre and Jacques stood with mouths agape, unable to make a sound as the old raven landed on Rue's outstretched arm. They shook their heads mutely, having seen many unusual sights in their over fifty years but none like the one they now witnessed.

Rue, followed by her puppy Shame and with Omen on her shoulder, eagerly raced to Kestrel's cabin, knowing her sister chafed at her confinement, unable to walk about with the several stitches that closed the ugly gash in her foot. She raised her hand to knock at the cabin door and then hesitated. What if they were . . . what? Fear clawed into her mind before she could even think of the word for the activity

Nick and her sister might be engaged in. Rue shook her head, trying
to control the intense terror, and the door was flung open by Nick.

"Omen!" rejoiced Kestrel, leaping up and hopping toward the
door. Nick opened his mouth to tell her to lie down but closed it
silently as the large bird cawed a welcome.

Rue helped Kestrel hop up on the deck, unaware of the consternation that bubbled around as the superstitious seamen stared with awe
at the ominous bird. Gladys Mackintosh, in yet another black dress,
this time of watered silk that made dizzying patterns in the sunlight,
tottered about not knowing if she was dreaming or not.

"I ain't used to all this nature, yer know. Water and now big black
birds," she complained to Pierre and Jacques, who watched the two
sisters. "It's a raven, ain't it? Anyone'd think we were at the bloody
Tower of London!"

Quebec faded into the distance and the sun slowly set, turning the
light blue sky to soft pink and then blood-red. The two girls stood
with their arms wrapped about each other as the St. Lawrence River
widened and the ship seemed to fly, inexplicably drawn to the open
sea. Omen, the raven, circled above their heads, silhouetted against
the fiery sky, before flapping heavy wings and catching the wind to be
hurtled back to the shore.

"Take our love to Wee-Angus and Meron," called Kestrel huskily,
straining her eyes until the bird was a faint dot among the angry red
striations on the sky. The girls clung together, feeling the loss, feeling
lonely and very small against the enormous expanse of heaven and
ocean as the *Étoile* broke free of the American continent and sailed
toward the Old World.

PART II

She shall be sportive as the fawn
That wild with glee across the lawn
Or up the mountain springs;
And hers shall be the breathing balm
And hers the silence and the calm
Of mute insensate things.

WILLIAM WORDSWORTH
"Three Years She Grew
in Sun and Shower"

CHAPTER NINETEEN

Rue's favorite pastime on the voyage was to climb the rigging and hang on with her fingers and toes, her lithe body arched like a sail in the wind. She glorified in the vibrations of the taut ropes and canvas, the thunderous roar of the full sail and the wheeling, wailing lament of the circling kittiwakes. Her cheeks tingled and every inch of her was exhilarated as the graceful vessel cut cleanly through the deep mysterious water.

Shame, her gangly hound, sat faithfully on the deck below staring up with mournful puppy eyes, her long tongue dangling and dripping on the scrubbed-white wood.

Gladys Mackintosh shook her frizzled red head and stared dolefully at her gray roots, wishing she had the foresight to stock up with henna so she could have maintained her crowning glory. She shook her head again as she thought of her "dark little lamb" high up in the rigging still dressed in "Injun clothes." She smiled fondly as she thought of her "golden joy," Kestrel, who was eager to learn every single artful female ploy in Gladys's repertoire.

Nick MacKay really questioned his sanity in allowing a woman such as Gladys Mackintosh, or Annie Wiggins as the case may be, to be an influence on Kestrel and Rue. He applauded Rue, high in the rigging, feeling free and proud. Sometimes he caught a sadness as he noticed her hunched little shoulders and would realize the silence she was wrapped in, but he preferred it to the constant acting and simpering imitations that Kestrel subjected him to of late. Although he realized Kestrel was very young and everything was new and unknown, each day he found his patience sorely tried, as her usually attractive voice took on artificial, grating tones that demanded constant praise and attention.

Jacques and Pierre clicked their tongues against their teeth, showing their concern and displeasure at the rift that grew between Kestrel and Nick.

"You must make the wedding before the young doctor, he change his mind," announced Pierre to his brother as he watched Kestrel promenade about the deck dressed to the nines.

Every crew member seemed to ogle her lustily, and she appreciated their admiration with fluttering eyelashes and saucy wiggles. Yet despite her coquettish, flirtatious manner, Kestrel was miserable as each day Nick seemed more and more unapproachable, refusing to react with admiration, jealousy, or anger, just seeming to ignore and avoid her by locking himself up in the ship's infirmary to read medical books or tend to petty injuries of the crew. Didn't he realize she was learning as much as she could just for him? she fumed as she sashayed. She wanted to be a credit to him in every situation. She didn't want to lose him to a more sophisticated, knowledgeable woman. Her sashaying stopped and she stood staring morosely over the enormous expanse of water, not seeing land anywhere. It was awesome, frightening, and she shivered, allowing her dread to seep in. She was terrified of meeting Nick's family: his grandfather and older brother. What if she disgraced herself by her ignorance of social graces? she worried.

Nick left the hot stuffy infirmary to take a walk around the deck. He blinked in the blinding sunlight and shaded his eyes. Kestrel stood dejectedly, her very glum face resting on her hand that was propped on the gunwale. As he watched her, he acknowledged she seemed more natural than he'd seen her in the last two weeks. There was no artifice, no falseness. Kestrel turned and saw him and he groaned as she smiled, twirled her parasol and paraded toward him, waving flirtatiously at several crew members. Nick shook his head and scowled, stopping Kestrel's eager approach. She frowned and for a second was the old Kestrel, but then she covered her fury with a coquettish toss of her head. Nick turned away and wearily rubbed his forehead, not wanting to lose his temper in public. Kestrel stamped her foot.

"Nick?" she called angrily. "How dare you turn your back on me!" she yelled as he strode quickly toward the other end of the deck. "Nick?" screeched Kestrel, forgetting her sedate sashaying and racing after him. Her tight stylish shoes, however, skidded, nearly breaking her ankles. She angrily wrenched them off and threw them at his retreating back, cracking the side of his head.

Nick's temper erupted and he turned sharply, surprising Kestrel, who froze at the intense fury that flashed. Holding her parasol out in front of her like a rapier she backed away as he approached.

"I have had quite enough!" he roared, wrenching the parasol out of her hand, snapping it in two and throwing it overboard before picking her up and turning her over his knee.

"*Mon Dieu!*" exclaimed Jacques, watching Nick and Kestrel through his telescope.

"That is good!" approved Pierre.

Rue heard Kestrel's screams of fury from her perch high up in the rigging. She fleetly shinnied down, not knowing what was happening. She landed on the gunwale and frowned, hearing the cheers of the crew as Nick held Kestrel across his thighs with her voluminous skirts over her head muffling the stream of colorful curses.

Nick fought to control his temper as he became aware of his admiring audience. He quelled the desire to slap her enticing round buttocks and turned Kestrel off his lap. She landed with a thump on the hard deck all tangled up in her Charbonnière finery.

"It is all right, Rue," he comforted stiffly, seeing her white worried face. "Your sister very nearly got the spanking she deserves."

Kestrel managed to stand, and she glared haughtily, trying to cover her embarrassment from the audience of booing French sailors who loudly expressed their disappointment at Nick's deference. Rue looked questioningly at Kestrel, who stared right past her as she glowered at her husband. Nick glowered back and Rue felt trapped between the two, whose eyes were locked in a battle of wills.

"Go down to the cabin!" ordered Nick coldly and Kestrel refused to move. "I would prefer to solve our differences in private but obviously you enjoy an audience," he added cuttingly, nodding politely to the clustering seamen. Kestrel gave a snort of rage before rushing belowdeck. Nick followed her to their cabin at a slower, more deliberate pace. Rue unhappily watched them go.

Nick closed their cabin door and leaned back on it, watching his wife who, refusing to look at him, stared out of the porthole.

"I don't like losing my temper, Kestrel. But I dislike being hit even more," he pronounced after a long pregnant pause. "I won't tolerate it."

"I don't care if you lose your temper, it's better than your silence!" spat Kestrel, turning on him. "I don't care if you beat me, but I will not be punished when I don't know what I've done."

"If you behave like a child with your tantrums I will treat you accordingly," replied Nick with measured tones.

"That's not what I mean. It feels like you don't love me anymore.

Every day I'm trying to be a proper wife, learning to wear clothes properly and have society manners, and you pretend I'm not here," struggled Kestrel, trying to explain herself. "Ever since we sailed you have been different. It's been three days since we've made love even. I go to bed alone every night 'cause you're locked up in the infirmary, and I know no one is sick in there," babbled Kestrel, trying not to cry.

Nick had to acknowledge that there was some truth in what Kestrel said. He stared at her sadly as she continued.

"I don't like sleeping alone and I want to go home to Angus and Meron. I feel all cooped up. I cannot swim or ride, but none of that would matter if you were like you were before. But you're not and I'm afraid," and on that note Kestrel burst into tears. Nick picked her up and wrapped his arms around her.

"You don't love me anymore. You love Rue more, just like everyone else," hiccuped Kestrel.

"Dinna be so silly," returned Nick gruffly, as he admitted to himself that lately he did prefer the dark girl's unpretentious company.

"Then why?" wailed Kestrel, placing her hands on his chest and pushing herself back so she could see his face.

"I canna find you, Kestrel," replied Nick quietly.

"I'm right here."

"Right now you are but for the last weeks there's been someone else. Not my Kestrel but a stranger. False and playing flirtatious games that I dinna like. Dressed in so many layers of clothes that I canna find my own golden love. If I close my eyes I'd think I was wie Gladys. It's you I want, not Miss Mackintosh," explained Nick.

Kestrel sniffed and looked at him thoughtfully. "But Gladys said we canna wear boys' clothes when we get to France or Scotland and that we have to learn to be ladies."

"Kess, do you trust me?"

Kestrel nodded silently.

"Then I'll teach you what you should know. Aye, 'tis good to learn how to wear clothes and shoes, but not the simpering, sickening tricks that you've been doing with parasols and fans. Be yourself, Kess, that's who I love best," urged Nick.

"But that made you angry, too," replied Kestrel, her brow furrowed with her dilemma. Nick kissed her soft mouth, tasting the salt of her tears.

"No time for buts. We have three days to make up for, so let's get you out of those layers of clothes," he said huskily, starting to unfasten the tiny little hooks.

"So you can find me?" whispered Kestrel.

"Aye, so I can find you," replied Nick, shaking his head as he estimated there had to be at least fifty of the fussy little fasteners. "I dinna think I'll find you for a fortnight," he teased, losing patience and ripping the gown.

"Nick?" protested Kestrel.

" 'Tis all right, my love," murmured Nick, nuzzling between her warm breasts. "It will gie Miss Mackintosh something to do other than teaching you a lot of nonsense."

Kestrel gaily skipped up into the bright warm sunshine on the deck and Jacques and Pierre chuckled seeing her face alive and happy. They watched her nimbly shin up the rigging and join her sister high up where the wind blew their hair and colored their smooth cheeks.

Gladys frowned and shook her head disapprovingly as she saw her star pupil's hoydenish clothes.

"Dressed like a savage again, oh deary me!" she clucked, hating the heat that caused her clothes to stick uncomfortably to her body and her hair to droop limply around her paint- and sweat-streaked face. She mopped herself with a large hanky and plopped heavily in a canvas chair that groaned protestingly. She panted like the large puppy that sat beside her as they both stared enviously up in the rigging where the two girls enjoyed the cooling wind.

"You know, if I 'ad less of me to 'ide, I might take off a few of these clothes," she confided to the hound.

"You would be much cooler if you didn't wear black," suggested Nick, overhearing.

"I 'ave ter wear black," replied Gladys defensively.

"Why? Are you in mourning?"

"Oh, yeah, fer me misspent youth," cackled the large woman. "It's what's proper at my time of life being an old maid and all. Anyways it makes me look thinner," she added. Nick laughed at her candor and looked up at Kestrel.

Gladys followed his gaze.

"All my 'ard work out the winder!" she remarked, shaking her head.

"You know how I feel about what you're teaching my wife," replied Nick icily.

"Never know when they might come in 'andy," returned Gladys pertly.

"When?" probed Nick, intrigued.

"Never know," repeated Miss Mackintosh. "Never know what could 'appen tomorrer," she added sagely.

"What could happen?" insisted Nick.

"You ain't goin' ter live ferever. Then what's a poor abandoned girl to do, aye?"

Nick shook his head.

"If I 'ad 'ad a few of them feminine wiles I might've made a better life for meself," stated Gladys Mackintosh with conviction.

"I would prefer that you leave the teaching to me and I'll leave care of our clothes and the sewing to you," returned Nick coldly before striding away.

"Oh, 'oity-toity!" sulked Gladys, sticking her nose in the air and heaving her girth with difficulty out of the frail chair.

"Madame Pelisse?" hailed Pierre.

"Mackintosh, you one-eyed scoundrel, Miss Mackintosh," corrected Gladys irritably.

Pierre frowned. "You are not 'appy this day?" he said softly. "It is the weather that make you have bad temper," he added sagely. "Soon we 'ave beeg storm and you be funny Mees Coat again," he added, wickedly pinching her bottom.

"Take yer 'ands off!" cried Gladys, indignantly slapping his hand.

"Oh *mon pauvre petit chou*," purred the rascally Frenchman.

"I ain't no poor little cabbage, you soppy bloke," giggled the large woman, flattered, regaining her sense of humor.

"That is good. You smile. Now you are my 'appy Mackintosh!" declared Pierre. "We go to bed? *Oui*?" he suggested slyly.

"We go to bed? *Non*! It's too 'ot, you lusty one-eyed frog!" teased Gladys, not removing his hand from her breast as they left the brightness of the deck for the intimate darkness below.

Rue watched them go. Kestrel laughed.

"I cannot imagine it, can you? Gladys with no clothes on? It must take a long time," giggled Kestrel. Rue looked away, not wanting to think about or imagine it.

"Rue?" said Kestrel, her face getting serious as she saw her sister's discomfort. "What's the matter?"

Rue shrugged and tried to smile as she stared across the endless ocean. She frowned and squinted her eyes before pointing excitedly. Kestrel looked and waved.

"There's another ship. Jacques!" she screamed over the thunderous beating of the wind in the sails.

Jacques had been aware of the other vessel for some time. His usually cheerful face was grave as he barked orders.

Rue and Kestrel watched the sailors racing around.

"They're manning the guns!" gasped Kestrel, unaware of Nick calling to them from below. "It must be an enemy ship. Ooh, maybe it's pirates!" she declared gleefully. Rue shook her arm and pointed below to Nick who beckoned them down.

"Pretend you didn't see him," urged Kestrel, knowing they would be tucked safely belowdeck and unable to see anything of what might be an exciting sea battle. The other boat puffed out smoke and there was a deep resounding boom. Kestrel squealed as the water splashed near the side of the ship.

"They missed us!" she rejoiced. Rue shook her arm indicating they should climb lower as the *Étoile*'s guns answered and the air was filled with the sulfured fumes of the gunpowder. "Rue, we'll miss everything," she complained, watching the other boat approach.

The sail suddenly slackened as the wind stopped. It was as if both vessels froze in the molten sea as the heavy hot air was deathly still.

"The calm before the storm," whispered Kestrel and Rue shivered. It was as though everything in existence held its breath as both ships sat in the sea out of reach of each other.

"Get down here!" roared Nick and the two girls agilely swung down to the deck. "Now go down into our cabin," he ordered tersely and Kestrel's eyes widened as she saw the sword he had buckled on. She stood on her tiptoes and kissed his lean somber face before clasping Rue's hand and complying.

"What's 'appening?" gasped Gladys as Pierre swore and leaped into his trousers and rushed out of her cabin, bare-chested. She stared at the closed cabin door and collapsed back on the bunk, still dressed in several layers of undergarments. "Well, it's too 'ot anyways," she sighed.

Kestrel knocked on Gladys's door.

"Come in, you one-eyed French monster!" she yelled, heaving herself upright and attacking her buttons and hooks. Kestrel popped her head around the door with one hand over one of her laughing green eyes.

"*Oui, mon petit* cabbage," she giggled. "How can you just lie about, Gladys?"

"It's too bloody 'ot ter do anything else," answered Miss Mackintosh, lying back down and fanning herself.

"But there's pirates attacking the ship!" declared Kestrel with relish.

"What?" she shrieked, struggling to sit up and waving her fat dimpled hands at the two girls, hoping for assistance.

Rue and Kestrel pulled the large woman to a sitting position as an almighty boom echoed throughout the ship. Gladys clutched her heart and fell back.

"Hear that?" rejoiced Kestrel. "I wonder if it was them or us."

"Come back 'ere!" fussed Gladys as Kestrel ran out fleetly, followed by her sister. "It ain't safe fer females ter be left alone when there's pirates about!" she gasped, struggling to her feet and trotting out of the cabin after her two charges.

Rue drew out her dagger and showed it to Kestrel in an attempt to see if she were armed. Kestrel grinned and pulled her sister into her cabin where she emptied out her saddlebag on the bunk and found her own dirk.

"Don't go up there!" shrieked Gladys as the two girls climbed the stairs to the upper deck. "We're on fire!" she screamed, wrinkling her nose up at the sulfur fumes.

Rue and Kestrel crept onto the smoky deck, unable to see anything. There was the sound of confusion and clashing steel, shouts and cries of victory and pain. The deck shook with the vibrations of booted feet and the two girls dived under the protection of the gunwales as several large shapes loomed out of the smoke.

Rue carefully stood and looked over the side of the *Étoile* and gasped as she saw the attacking vessel lying alongside. She ducked back down next to her sister, her heart pounding fearfully. She pulled Kestrel's arm and indicated she should also look. Kestrel stood, gasped, and ducked back down.

"What shall we do?" she hissed and Rue pointed to the rigging high above their heads. From up there they would be able to better see what was happening. Kestrel nodded and nimbly both girls climbed under the cover of the belching smoke.

Kestrel climbed, as the cold rasping of steel against steel cut into her mind and she thought of Nick. What if he were killed? What if he were lying injured and needed her? Rue nudged her sister as she stopped, urging her to climb higher.

"Nick," whispered Kestrel and Rue nodded, understanding her concern. The two sisters clung to the rigging, watching the battle rage below them.

Gladys Mackintosh pulled herself together and systematically searched the cabins until she found and armed herself with a broadsword that was so heavy she had to use the strength of both arms to lift it. She staggered up the steep stairway in search of her two lost lambs, determined to protect them. On deck she stood in a patch of smoke, hardly able to see or breathe as her eyes teared and she choked, the acrid smell burning her nose and throat.

There was a shout of derisive laughter as the smoke lifted and Gladys found herself ringed by a colorful band of armed men. She held the broadsword threateningly in both hands and struck a fiercesome pose. She circled as the jeering mirth came from all sides.

Kestrel and Rue watched Gladys Mackintosh, clothed in her layers of underwear, her warlike stance defiant. They saw no humor in the scene, however, just someone they had grown to love in terrible straits.

On the bridge Pierre, Jacques, and Nick, each with a rapier pricking his Adam's apple, also watched.

Gladys used the earthiest language she knew as she turned this way and that, feeling the sharp points of rapiers nick and slap. There was a strange cry from above and two lithe, slight forms lightly landed on small bare feet and stood protecting the buxom lady, each with a drawn dagger.

"Hold," ordered a deep masterful voice as the colorful pirates closed in on the two girls who stood back to back.

"It is the Hawk," hissed Jacques, receiving a nicked chin for speaking. "He pays me back for stealing his last cargo!"

Kestrel and Rue held their ground, taking comfort in the feel of each other's lean back. Rue grinned, feeling closer to her sister than ever before as they circled, their hearts beating as one.

A very tall dark masked man strode into the circle. He stood still and appraised the two crouched alert girls, nodding his appreciation.

"Go, take an inventory but harm no one!" he dismissed. "Take the fat one belowdeck," he added, waving a careless hand at Gladys, who stood proudly despite her underwear.

"My poor little cabbage," groaned Pierre, his one remaining eye flooding with uncharacteristic tears as he watched Miss Gladys Mackintosh, haughtily still holding her broadsword.

"I ain't goin' nowheres!" stated the valiant lady. "And you 'arm one 'air of my little . . . er ones," she stammered, not wanting to give away their sex, "you'll get this 'ere sword on yer thick 'ead!"

The colorful pirates roared with laughter, but their dark masked

leader impatiently waved his hands and Gladys was easily disarmed
and carried kicking and screaming belowdeck.

"If they 'arm one leetle 'air on my leetle cabbage they will die!"
threatened Pierre, pushing the rapier held at his throat away so it
sliced his bare hand. Blood spurted and he howled with pain. The tall
masked man turned toward the sound and made a sign. Jacques,
Pierre, and Nick were herded down until they stood side by side with
the masked man called the Hawk.

Rue felt the ache in her back and legs as she and Kestrel still
crouched, ready to pounce, their daggers drawn.

"Who are these children?" asked the deep cultured voice, and Nick
frowned as it rang a familiar chord. The dark pirate seemed startled as
he assessed the young doctor.

"One is my wife and the other her sister," Nick answered.

"Which is which?" probed the Hawk, recovering his presence.
Nick didn't know what to answer.

"They are both under my protection," he answered tersely. "I hope
you're a man of honor. As you observed, they are both very young,"
he added, his dark eyes narrowed as he tried to fathom why the tall
pirate was so familiar.

"Which is which?" repeated the Hawk.

Kestrel wanted proudly to state that she was his wife but somehow
sensed it would leave Rue unprotected. She transferred her dagger to
her other hand and pressed her back firmly against her sister as they
both dared the tall pirate to make a first move.

Rue stared up at the masked face, her amber eyes open and curious,
yet every nerve prepared to attack at the least provocation. The Hawk
casually removed his cloak and wound it around his arm as he also
drew a lethal dirk from its sheath. Nick leaped forward as he
understood the man's intent and was solidly punched in the jaw.
Kestrel gave a scream of fury and attacked as her husband fell
backward, his head sharply cracking against a metal winch.

"So you are the wife," remarked the Hawk, quickly disarming
Kestrel and allowing her to fall sobbing on Nick's prone body. He
nodded silently, unprepared for Rue's swift attack as her sharp blade
sliced his left forearm. Without a cry of pain he spun around as she
sprang back on the balls of her bare feet. He didn't touch his wound or
in any way acknowledge it as he stood tall and dignified, assessing the
crouched dark-haired figure dressed in the fringed leather clothes of
the native Americans. A low snarling threatened from his left and a
sleek dark hound crouched also ready to pounce. He smiled slightly

and made a movement toward the pup, anticipating the dark child's instinct as she hurled herself forward to protect her pet.

The Hawk scooped Rue into his strong arms as the young dog attacked to save his mistress.

"Call her off or she shall die," he whispered in her ear so she felt the heat of his breath.

"She cannot speak," cried Kestrel as he imprisoned Rue's arm as she tried to make a movement to her hound.

Rue stared up, noting the cruel lines of the masked man's face and knowing he must be hurting from Shame's teeth that were buried deep in his left arm. Jet-black, obsidian eyes looked deeply into hers and she was confused. She clicked her fingers and Shame reluctantly released the Hawk, who silently strode, still carrying his light burden.

"Put my sister down!" screamed Kestrel as she lay across Nick's inert body.

"*Monsieur le 'Awk.* I surrender. You 'ave the victory. But *la petite,*" stated Jacques, indicating Rue, "she has harmed no person, yet she has been very much hurt. That is why she does not talk."

The Hawk stared down at the dark-haired girl in his arms. A pair of the warmest amber eyes stared back at him without blinking. One of the most perfect faces he had ever seen bravely looked at him, showing no fear except for the slight flaring of the nostrils of her little straight nose.

"You cannot speak?" he asked in his low resonant voice.

Rue slowly shook her head.

"You will bind my wounds," he ordered.

"There is a ship's doctor," spat Pierre.

"It seems he is no use to any," observed the Hawk, staring down at Nick's inert body. He glanced down at Rue, who sucked in her breath with surprise, wondering how he knew who was the doctor without being told.

"You have a very quick mind," he remarked. "Now where is your cabin?"

"No!" screamed Kestrel. "Nobody shall rape my sister again!" she yelled, wrenching a sword from the scabbard of a stunned pirate. She was quickly disarmed.

"I have never found it necessary to rape," remarked the Hawk idly, setting Rue on her feet so she reached out to steady herself on the large head of her dog. She frowned, knowing she should be afraid and wondering why she wasn't as she led the way to her cabin.

CHAPTER TWENTY

Nick sat up and gingerly felt his pounding jaw. He groaned as the pain radiated into his head.

"Are you all right?" wept a voice and he stared into Kestrel's tear-stained face. He looked beyond her at the foggy blue sky crisscrossed with rigging and frowned.

"Where the devil am I?" he ejaculated and winced as his words reverberated through his sore head.

"On the *Étoile* going to France," whispered Kestrel, fear clutching at her heart as he seemed to look right through her.

"Who the hell are you?" he said softly. Kestrel couldn't answer. She stared down at him in horror and swallowed with difficulty. Nick lifted his head from where it rested on her thighs as she knelt on the deck, and groaned as sharp pain shot through.

"Well?" he repeated impatiently. "Who are you?"

"Your wife," whispered Kestrel in a very small voice.

"Wife?" retorted Nick and immediately regretted his loud tone and laid his head back on her lap with a groan.

"*Oui*, your wife," insisted Pierre and Nick opened his eyes to the vision of the dark unshaven visage of the black-patched Frenchman.

"Who are you?" he asked belligerently.

"And you, monsieur? Who are you?"

Nick frowned and rubbed his eyes before looking at the concerned faces above him.

"I don't know. Who am I?" he answered slowly and the beautiful golden angel burst into tears and hot salty drops fell on his face and chest.

"*Non, ne pleures pas* . . . don't cry, Kestrel," comforted Jacques. "It sometimes 'appen but the memory, she come back *comme ça!*" he proclaimed, clicking his fingers to illustrate.

"Kestrel?" repeated Nick, staring with wonder up at the beautiful face above him. "What the hell sort of name is that?"

"Mine!" stated the gorgeous golden apparition.

"Whoops, draw in your talons, my little eagle," laughed Nick. So this was his wife, he mused. This breathtakingly winsome, attractive, enchanting female. He inwardly rejoiced as he ran out of superlative adjectives. "So you are my wife?" he murmured, unable to believe his luck.

"You can walk, *mon ami*?" questioned Jacques roughly, not waiting for an answer as he and his one-eyed brother pulled Nick to his feet where he stood weaving slightly as he looked around, not recognizing anything. He gritted his teeth as panic clawed in and he stared down into the tear-filled, bright-green eyes of the one called his wife.

"Do you mind me asking my own name?" he asked as he grinned mischievously to cover his intense fear.

"Nicholas MacKay," sobbed Kestrel. "Dr. Nicholas MacKay," she added after a big sniff as she tried to control herself.

"Take me to my bed, dear wife," he directed as he stared around trying to find one familiar thing to anchor himself to.

A wild howl made him stop in his tracks and he turned and stood in stunned amazement at the strange sight of a very large woman with orange and gray stiff straight hair who pranced toward him wearing strange, shiny red undergarments.

"Who's that?" he asked.

"*Votre mère!*" spat Pierre cruelly and Kestrel burst into hysterical laughter.

"My mother?" wailed Nick, shaking his head in alarm.

"No," soothed Kestrel, trying to control herself and be strong for him. "It's Gladys Mackintosh," she informed him as she led him to their cabin.

"Gladys what?" he echoed.

"Jackette, Pelisse, Coat, Redingote," spat Pierre. "My little cabbage. Come 'ere, *mon petit chou*," he cried and the large woman ran sobbing into his outstretched arms. Nick shook his aching head in disbelief, thankful that he wasn't married to or spawned by the strange Mackintosh woman as he turned to follow the golden-haired apparition.

Rue stood in her cabin, looking from the bunk where the tall dark masked man lay to the open door where two armed men stood. She chewed her lip thoughtfully, glancing once again from one to the other before closing the door. No sooner had the door closed than it was thrust open with a crash that made her jump.

The Hawk sat up and looked at her. Rue drew herself up to her full height, standing straight and proud, feeling as though she were several feet tall.

"Get bandages and alcohol," he ordered tersely. Rue nodded, thinking he spoke to her, and turned to leave the cabin only to find herself caught up in a very strong grip by the tall dark man who moved quickly and silently. She gasped as she was pulled beside him onto the bunk. Her amber eyes widened in terror as she felt the warmth of his breath and body as he lay next to her.

"You fight valiantly, showing no fear, and yet here I lie next to you bleeding from two wounds and you are white with terror," he remarked.

Rue fought to control her panic and his eyes narrowed behind his mask as he remembered her golden sister's words, "Nobody shall rape my sister again." He gently brushed the glossy raven hair back from her beautiful face.

"What a terrible injustice," he murmured, seeing her try to cover her terror. "Get up and see to my wounds," he demanded roughly, wanting to kiss her well-shaped mouth.

Rue suppressed the urge to scramble up and rush out, as she arose with measured dignity and crossed the cabin with her nose and chin held high. The Hawk nodded his appreciation of her control and silently shook his head as his henchmen tried to stop her exit. He lay back and closed his eyes, confident that she would return.

"Rue, are you all right?" asked Kestrel as her sister entered the crowded infirmary in search of salve and bandages. "Nick can't remember anything except doctoring," she added bitterly as the tall dark man efficiently tended to the wounded of both sides. Rue helped herself to what she needed, then went to the galley for hot water where she found Gladys, still in her underwear, serving food to demanding pirates as Pierre scowled and batted free-roaming hands away from his little cabbage's cleavage and buttocks.

Rue entered her cabin, carrying the steaming bowl of water with the bandages, alcohol, and salve tucked under her arms. Her hound growled threateningly at the two armed guards as they opened the door to admit her. Rue put the bowl down and stood looking at the very tall lean man asleep on her bed. The blood from his wounds had seeped through, caking the material of his sleeve. Rue took a breath, unsheathed her dagger, and cut through the sleeve, ignoring the eyes that opened and watched her alertly through the slits of his mask. Shame seemed to nod as he watched his young mistress examine the puncture wounds made by her strong pointed teeth, and Rue chewed the inside of her lip when she saw the damage done by her sharp knife. The Hawk didn't wince even when she poured the boiling water to sterilize. He made no movement when the alcohol saturated the painful lacerations. Thoughtfully she bandaged after liberally applying the salve and then sat not knowing what to do.

There was a knock at the door and Rue started, not realizing that she had been dozing. She sat up and looked around in alarm as food was carried in and set up on an improvised table, supervised by the Hawk, who strode around no worse for wear.

"Good, you're awake. Come over here. Sit," he ordered, pulling out a chair for her. Rue sat silently, her eyes not leaving him as he sat opposite her and served her and then himself. She ate and obediently drank the wine he poured. The air was still and humid as the earth waited for the storm that built.

Thunder rolled ominously and Rue's eyes flashed as she recklessly held out her empty goblet for more wine.

"You enjoy the tempests," remarked the Hawk, throwing a bone to the hound and refilling her proffered glass. Rue nodded, wanting to go on deck to feel the full fury of the elements. She sipped the wine and raised her eyes to the heavens, listening intently for the first heavy drops of rain.

"Come," laughed the tall dark man, reaching and taking her small brown hand.

Rue and the Hawk stood on the heaving deck, their faces raised to the cooling rain as it fell in sheets amid the flashing and crashing of thunder and lightning. Shame barked and raced back and forth before winding down and curling exhausted inside a coil of hemp. Below-deck the horses stamped and complained in the close darkness and Rue forgot her fear of the tall masked man and made her way down to the bowels of the vessel where her horse Sin champed and tossed his noble head.

"He is a beauty," appreciated the Hawk, softly running an experienced hand along the fine bones of the splendid animal. "He's yours?" When Rue nodded he asked the horse's name.

The dark man frowned as she savagely wrote in the fetid straw the word "Sin."

"'Sin,' interesting name for a young lady to call her horse," he remarked. "What is your poor dog named? Evil? Rape?" he asked harshly. His face tightened as he read the word "Shame."

Rue felt emotionally drained as it seemed that the day had gone on forever with so much happening even before the battle with the pirates. She fought to stay awake as she wondered what was to happen. She went back on deck, knowing the tall masked man followed her, and she stood not knowing what to do as the rain misted down until she was drenched. She sat on the coil of hemp, stroking her soaked dog who whimpered as she curled her body around it and cuddled close, smelling the warm sweet puppy odor.

The Hawk stared down at the two dark heads, knowing the fear the girl had. He bent and picked her up, surprised at her lightness for the second time that day. He sighed as he felt her lithe gracefulness stiffen in his arms but he ignored her struggles to be released, determined that she should learn to trust. He entered her cabin and gently set her on her feet. Both of them dripped pools of water and the dog shook furiously, drenching them further. He grabbed a towel and threw it over Rue's head but she stood frozen with fear. He resisted the temptation just to quit the cabin, leaving her to her own devices as his eyes narrowed at the sight of her set little face. The girl expected to be raped, he realized, acknowledging the fact that she was both desirable and beautiful. Who had brutalized her so before? he wondered. He watched her, not really knowing what to do, before deciding that if he had a child who had been so hurt he would nurture and comfort her.

Gently he toweled her hair and then as she shuddered, he quickly undressed her and rubbed her chilled wet body as he would have a small child. She stood before him and despite his paternal resolve he had to admit she was absolutely perfect from the top of her head to the bottoms of her feet. Not the perfection of a society miss, all pallid and wan, but the glowing, glorious perfection of a sun-kissed beauty. He quickly pulled a soft nightgown over her wet little head, pulled back the covers of her bed and, picking her up as he would a baby, he tucked her tenderly between the sheets as she wondered at the aching feeling he felt. He stood looking down at her, knowing what she now expected. He stroked her cheek and turned the lantern down so there was just a faint glimmer of warm light. He wondered whether he should leave as he felt an indefinable loneliness. Was it emanating from her or from him? he mused as he stared down at the terrified Rue.

Rue lay rigidly waiting for the assault upon her body. She was bewildered at being so gently undressed and dried as no cruel fingers had pinched and pried, defiling the most intimate parts of her body. She shivered in the unbearable suspense, waiting to be hurt as the lantern was turned down to a dim warmth, and to her surprise she heard the creak of a chair as the Hawk stretched out resignedly to try to sleep. Some victorious pirate captain, he thought cynically as his heavy eyelids drooped behind his mask.

Rue lay rigidly waiting for the attack and slowly relaxed until she fell fast asleep. But the eventful day had taken its toll and she tossed and turned, reliving the terrors of more than three years before. She gasped in horror as Goliath thudded to the ground, his wonderful loving face smashing into the dry dirt as the blood spurted from his vast back. She leaped from her horse at the same moment as Jemmy and they knelt over the large man who had been like a grandfather to them. She screamed as hard hands grabbed her, tearing her away from the beloved man.

The Hawk sat up, rudely awakened by the scream. He stared at the small thrashing body on the bed and his blood ran cold as he heard the mute girl speak.

"You are hurting her. Dinna hurt her. Please dinna hurt my Jemmy," pleaded Rue, tears streaming down her smooth brown cheeks. He stood staring down, not knowing how to comfort as Rue's body arched in agony with her legs spread wide so he knew exactly what she was reliving. Her small face was contorted and the eerie screaming started.

He reached down to waken her from the nightmare and her body jerked once and then she was still, her amber eyes wide and unseeing. He lifted her in his arms and held her close, feeling her trembling. He cradled her like a tiny baby as he slid into the bunk tucking the covers about both of them and crooning a Scottish lullaby. He smiled in the darkness, feeling her racing heart calm near his own until it beat a steady rhythm, and she relaxed and curled into him, trusting his warmth and strength.

The nightmare burst in again and Rue opened her mouth to scream but no sound came out. She felt she was suffocating and she thrashed, trying to summon help, but her throat was constricted as though she were being strangled. She felt that her lungs would burst as she strained to release the scream.

"Hush, 'tis all right. Nothing will harm you," crooned a deep reassuring voice, and a gentle hand smoothed the hair from her hot forehead while another hand held her close.

Rue opened her eyes as she heard the steady secure beat beneath her ear and stared across the expanse of a broad chest where her head was pillowed.

"Sleep, little one, sleep."

And she obediently closed her eyes, feeling safe. The Hawk felt the hot tears soak his shirt and he tenderly ran large fingers over her wet cheeks, and felt her sweet breath as she sighed deeply in her sleep.

CHAPTER TWENTY-ONE

Kestrel awoke the next morning and stared at Nick, willing him to rouse but also afraid that when he did he would still not know who she was. What were they going to do if Nick never regained his memory, she worried. How would they reach their destination? She sat up and hugged her knees as she remembered they had been captured by pirates.

"Oh, Nick," she whispered gratefully as she saw his dark eyes watching her. "I'm glad you're awake. I've been so worried." She slid down under the covers and cuddled up to him. Nick grinned appreciatively as he felt the length of warm silky skin.

"Good morning," he murmured huskily, as he remembered a very passionate previous night, and was fully aroused and ready for an equally fervent morning.

"You remember?" asked Kestrel hopefully.

"How could I forget?" growled Nick lustily, nuzzling her neck and running his eager hands down the length of her.

"Stop it a minute!" protested Kestrel as he caressed her most intimate places until she writhed against his hardness.

"Stop what?" teased Nick, turning her over and parting her legs. "Stop what?" he repeated against her lips as he slowly inserted himself. Kestrel bucked against him trying to drive him in deeper but he wickedly held back, chuckling at the intense look on her determined little face as she arched, pressing her firm breasts against his broad chest.

"Stop what?" he taunted huskily, holding his hips back so he was barely inside her. Kestrel raked his muscular buttocks trying to press them to her, as she thought she would go mad with frustration. She opened her eyes and seeing the roguish amusement on his handsome face, decided on some mischief of her own. She stopped all movement and lay still. Nick opened his eyes and looked down at her in surprise. Kestrel yawned and scratched, pretending to be totally bored. Nick stared thoughtfully at her rigid nipples and feeling the hot moisture of her knew she was as ready as he was. A deep infectious chuckle shook him and Kestrel opened her eyes suspiciously.

"I don't know who you are, sweetheart, but you are certainly amusing," he laughed and Kestrel's quick temper was ignited. She tried to roll him off her but he plunged to the depth of her and she melted with a deep sound of pleasure, and arched to meet him.

"I don't know who I am, but whoever I am, I have excellent taste in women," sighed Nick much later as they lay still intimately joined together, exhausted and satisfied.

"You really don't remember?" probed Kestrel with a very small voice as all the very real terrors poured in. "But that's terrible! Only you know where we're going to meet your family and mine. And we've just been captured by pirates so we'll probably be killed before we ever get there. And you've lost your memory and don't know who I am. And my sister who can't even scream for help has probably been ravaged for the hundredth time by the pirate captain!"

"Whoa!" gasped Nick, in awe of his bedmate's dramatic dialogue. He rolled her over, taking care to stay joined, so she lay atop his long lean body. Kestrel propped herself on her pointy elbows and surveyed him sadly.

"Ouch," protested Nick, firmly unfolding her arms so his chest wasn't abused. "Now what was that about a sister who can't even scream for help being ravaged for the hundredth time?" he laughed.

"It's not funny!" spat Kestrel. "And I don't even know what has happened to poor Gladys Mackintosh!"

Nick chuckled and then roared with laughter, tears of mirth pouring down his face. Kestrel was so angry she slapped him hard across one cheek and then swallowed hard, expecting to be hit back. Nick's laughter stopped abruptly and he frowned at her.

"Don't do that again," he warned with his old familiar cold tones.

"Why?" challenged Kestrel impishly.

"I'll hit you back," threatened Nick, and Kestrel beamed happily.

"You like to be hit?" exclaimed Nick with surprise.

"No, I hit back, too," replied Kestrel. "It's just it gets a bit lonely with you not knowing who I am."

"This is lonely?" laughed Nick, bucking his hips against hers.

"Never mind," surrendered Kestrel, pulling his dark head down and rubbing her face against his black hair as she smelled his

fragrance. "You don't know who you or I am but *you* are still *you*,"
she struggled to explain as she felt him grow and stiffen within her.

Rue opened her eyes and lay still, wondering where she was as she
heard a steady beating pulse beneath her ear and a profoundly warm
security encasing her. She inhaled, smelling a fragrant smell of pine
and leather as strange sensations churned within. She ran her hand
over a hard unyielding expanse and pushed herself back to better look
at her environment.

"Good morning," said a low voice that reverberated through her,
quivering her spine, and she stared into a masked face.

Rue nodded, not knowing what to say or how to react as she felt the
length of her body curled intimately against the stranger's warmth.
She closed her eyes, willing herself back to the rosy sleepy suspension
as her leg pressed against the hard muscles and her toes rubbed
familiarly. She yawned and stretched, suspecting she was hallucinat-
ing and cuddled closer, delighting in the firm heat of the embracing
arms. She didn't want to think or even to waken as she ran her leg
down the length of this man and then recurled herself, cuddling
closely to the enticing warmth.

The Hawk looked down at the glossy hair that lay across his chest
and waited, knowing her breathing was shallow and she was really
about to waken this time. Something about this petite dark female
intrigued him greatly, he mused. He watched her closed eyes, seeing
the movement beneath the lids, very conscious of her lithe limbs that
tensed as she slowly became conscious of where she was and whom
she laid against.

Rue froze as the ominous pounding of the male heart under her ear
quickened. She instinctively reached to her thigh feeling for her
dagger but nothing was there save her smooth leg. She lay still as her
fertile mind tried to decide what to do, her senses taking in the scent
of maleness. Her muscles tightened, aware of and inhibited by the
Hawk's proximity.

The Hawk felt the tightening of her muscles and the quickening of
her breathing against his chest as well as the rapid beating of her
heart. A brittle, angular, uncomfortable person now lay where the
conforming, yielding, trusting child had slept. His arms, which had
willingly held, now rebelled against the tight, rejecting burden. His
hands dropped to his sides freeing the small tense girl.

Rue felt her freedom and was filled with a painful feeling of loss as
what seemed like iron bars dropped away and she was naked and

unprotected. She jerked, making small mourning whimpers before she re-collected herself and breathed deeply, strengthening herself against anything she was likely to encounter.

"Good morning," the Hawk murmured a second time as Rue dared open her amber eyes and stare with steeled bravery into the shielded dark apertures of the masked man. Rue nodded slightly, wishing her skin wasn't tingling from the contact with his coarser flesh, setting her pulses pounding with fear and excitement.

"You are very beautiful," stated the dark man, brushing her hair back from her clear forehead, and for the first time in his life he was surveyed by a female without artifice. There was no coyness or simpering. He stared back at Rue and was inexplicably drawn into the mysterious allure of her wide bewildered eyes.

Rue didn't know what to do. She shook her head, trying to clear her thoughts and then firmly closed her eyes, willing herself back to sleep so she didn't have to cope. Who do I pray to? she wondered as she tried to fathom her mixture of fear and excitement. Every part of her tingled uncharacteristically. Every nerve ending and pore was aware of the hard muscular body that she lay against in the wide double bunk.

"What is your name?" he asked softly as he gently stroked the warm cheek that lay on his chest. He was loath to break the silence and yet somehow he wanted to claim the silent dark girl. Rue shook her head and pointed to her mouth.

"You spoke last night," stated the dark masked man and Rue frowned. "You awoke me with a dream!" Rue froze with her cheek still pillowed on his bare chest. A pulse beat in her temple joining the steady beating of his strong heart.

"You spoke clearly," repeated the Hawk. Rue felt a shiver of pure joy race through her. She sat up, slapped her own chest with an open splayed hand as she raised her eyebrows comically and mimed "Me?"

The Hawk nodded and she frowned dubiously.

"Please dinna hurt my Jemmy," quoted the dark man and his eyes narrowed at Rue's reaction. Her face contorted as she tried to scream but there was no sound. He reached out to embrace her but she cowered and backed away, her eyes searching for something to grab, anything to protect herself. The Hawk leaped up in time and wrested the dagger from her as her hand closed around it. He then held her against him as she struggled to get free. Rue fought, making strange mewing sounds of exertion; her hair was stuck in strands to her sticky

face as she battled to be free from the unyielding arms that held her.
Finally she lay still, panting and exhausted. The Hawk turned her to
face him.

"Now speak," he ordered.

Rue's chest heaved from her long struggle and she blew through her
dry lips to cool her hot flushed face. She stared up at his firm jaw and
shook her head. "You can speak, little one," he said gently.

Rue was confused. The dark eyes behind the mask seemed to burn
into her and she wearily closed her eyes and leaned her hot aching
head on his broad chest. She fought to catch her breath as terror
pounded through her.

The Hawk felt the furious pounding of her heart reverberate
through him. He tenderly cupped her head in his strong brown hands
and lifted it so he looked into her frightened face.

"Who hurt you so, little one?" he whispered huskily, seeing the
haunted amber eyes. Rue pursed her lips, trying to speak, but her
breath became constricted and she turned red as she desperately
struggled to make a sound.

"Whisper," directed the pirate captain softly. "Don't try to make a
big noise." Rue blew silently through her lips, calming herself. "Try
to tell me your name."

Rue mouthed her name but there was no sound. She wrenched
herself free of the Hawk's strong arms and angrily shook her head as
she glanced around looking for her clothes. Her damp buckskins were
in a heap on the floor so she lifted the lid on the shiny new trunk,
ignoring the masked man as if he were not there as she looked for
something else to wear.

The hound Shame whined and scratched at the door. There was a
sharp knocking and the Hawk strode across the small cabin and
admitted two of his men. The puppy bounded out and Rue debated
following him as she was stared at curiously.

"Tell Jacques Gillette I will see him shortly," stated the pirate
captain, motioning the men out and shutting the door. Rue climbed
into her trews and laced up a beaded leather vest. She looked around
for her dagger and seeing it by the bunk where the Hawk had placed
it, she crossed to retrieve it. As she reached for it, her hand was
caught in a painful grip and she stared up into the masked face. Her
eyes flashed furiously, showing no fear.

"You may have it with the condition that it not be used on me
again," stated the Hawk. Rue's eyes narrowed as she refused to
acknowledge his words. She didn't make promises she couldn't keep.

She stared at him steadily, her hand around her sheathed knife and his larger hand on top. "If you try to use it on me, you'll be sorry," he threatened, releasing her hand. Rue nodded as she saw the ruthless line of his firm mouth, knowing he meant what he said before she tied her dagger to her thigh.

Dressed and hungry, Rue opened the door to her cabin intent on going to the galley for breakfast. Two large armed men barred her way, and she turned back inquiringly to the Hawk, who was examining the contents of her trunk and wardrobe. Rue flushed with anger at his presumption as he raised appreciative eyebrows at the beautiful gowns and lacy underwear.

"I would much prefer you dressed as befits your sex," he remarked, laughing at her indignant expression. "Put this on!" he added, holding out the salmon-pink dress. Fortunately they were interrupted by loud squeals of protest and a man's bellowing oath as Kestrel arrived to visit her sister. Finding her way past the two large, armed pirates didn't daunt her in the least as she kicked one's shins and tried to elbow her way through.

"Let me go, you bloody bastard!" she swore, using Gladys Mackintosh's colorful vocabulary. Rue rushed through the open door and attacked, coming to her sister's aid. The Hawk lithely caught the dark girl's arm before one of his men was stabbed by the raised knife.

"You are too free with this little toy," he stated, forcing it from her clenched hand so it dropped to the floor. He covered it with his booted foot and held her tightly.

"Let my sister go, you thieving murdering mucker!" snarled Kestrel, kicking and struggling as she was held by two burly men. The Hawk stared at the raging golden beauty and then down at Rue's belligerent yet exquisite face. He silently looked from one to the other, unable to choose which girl was the most perfect. He made a movement and the two men let go of Kestrel and silently left the cabin, closing the door behind them. He kept tight hold of Rue's wrist as he drew her close until she was pressed against him, his arm encircling her.

Kestrel frowned up at the masked face, confused by the cold ruthlessness she felt. She looked down at the arm that held Rue, noticing a certain tenderness.

"What is your name?" he demanded.

"Why should I tell you?" returned Kestrel feistily. The Hawk nodded as he realized the stubbornness in both sisters.

"It would be more comfortable for you," he replied.

"What are you going to do with us?" asked Kestrel, wishing she could see Rue's face. She took a breath and dared approach the tall man. "Are you all right, Rue?" she whispered, tentatively touching her sister's cheek.

Rue nodded.

"You didn't hurt her, did you?" she asked quietly.

"Who is Jemmy?" probed the masked man, holding tightly to Rue, who jerked with shock.

"How did you know?" exclaimed Kestrel, her face paling.

"Who is Jemmy?" he insisted, putting both arms around the struggling Rue.

"Who *was* Jemmy," corrected Kestrel bitterly. "Let her go. Look what you're doing to her," she cried, seeing Rue's contorted face.

"What is your name?" asked the Hawk ruthlessly, not releasing the terrified girl.

"Kestrel Sinclair MacKay," obeyed Kestrel, her eyes pinned to her sister.

"And her name?" probed the pirate after a pause.

"Rue Sinclair," replied Kestrel.

"Rue Sinclair," repeated the masked man. "Rue—such sadness. Rue who names her horse Sin and her dog Shame. Who named her so?"

"She is named for the plant herb-of-grace, not for sorrow!" stated Kestrel. "How did you know of Jemmy?"

"Rue told me."

"Rue told you? But she canna talk," exclaimed Kestrel.

"Apparently not when she's awake," replied the Hawk, looking down at the ebony head he held close to his heart. "How long since she spoke?"

"I think maybe since it happened," whispered Kestrel as terror pulsed into her. "More than three years."

The Hawk's dark eyes narrowed behind the mask as he saw the distress mirrored on both exquisite faces and wondered what tragedy had befallen the two.

"I'm hungry," he proclaimed, changing the subject as he realized he wouldn't get very far as both beauties had their hackles up.

"What are you going to do with all of us?" asked Kestrel as he released Rue and herded them toward the door. Rue reached for her dagger but he kicked it out of the way with an exasperated sigh.

"Where are you bound for?" he asked as they walked along the passageway toward the galley, followed by his two armed henchmen.

"Breakfast," replied Kestrel, deliberately misunderstanding. The masked man caught the mischievousness of her expression and didn't rise to the bait.

They entered the galley and Gladys lumbered to her feet and rushed toward them, enfolding them into her voluminous black bombazine.

"Are you all right, my little lambs?" she gushed. "Did they 'urt you? If you've 'armed one little 'air on their 'eads . . ." she threatened.

"You'll what?" asked the Hawk.

"You'll wish you 'adn't, that's what!" warned Gladys lamely.

"Who are you to these girls?"

"Governess," lied Miss Mackintosh, sucking in her cheeks and standing as imperiously as she could.

The Hawk roared with laughter.

"That accounts for their lack of manners," he quipped as he motioned his two men to keep the women in the galley before leaving to go up on the top deck.

Rue watched him leave with a frown on her face, not knowing why she felt bereft.

"Did he hurt you?" asked Kestrel and Rue shook her head. "Was he with you all night?" she added. Rue nodded and Gladys and Kestrel exchanged worried looks. "Oh, Gladys, what's going to happen? Nick's lost his memory."

"That's terrible!"

"He doesn't even know who I am!" cried Kestrel and Rue reached out and held her.

"That's 'orrible!" gasped Miss Mackintosh.

"What's going to happen to us?"

"Me Pierre says the 'Awk ain't such a bad sort," comforted the large woman.

"What does that mean?" asked Kestrel.

"Well, that 'e don't go around killin' like some other pirates he knows."

Kestrel and Rue ate glumly, tasting nothing.

"Where's Shame?" questioned Kestrel, looking around for the dog that was never very far from her sister. Rue also looked around and then leaped to her feet to go and look for her but was stopped by one of the armed men. She reached down instinctively for her dagger but the sheath was empty. Gladys gave a bloodcurdling scream and launched her enormous shape at the pirate that barred Rue's way. As the two men struggled, getting tangled up in the yards of black dress,

Rue and Kestrel fled out of the galley and up the companionway to the deck. Keeping themselves hidden they looked desperately around trying to find the hound and see what was going on. Unable to see much crouched low, Rue pointed above her head to the rigging and Kestrel nodded. Fleetly the two girls jumped up onto the high gunwales, Rue nimbly swung herself up a taut rope but looked down when she heard her sister's furious shout of protest as she was grabbed by one foot. Kestrel hung suspended, desperately kicking out with her free foot as she clung to the ropes above her head.

"*Mon Dieu!*" swore Jacques as he saw Kestrel's dilemma. "Idiot!" he roared at the pirate who tugged at Kestrel's foot. The Hawk followed Jacques's eyes.

"Let her go!" he shouted, but was too late as Kestrel's hands gave way and she went crashing down onto the hard deck where her head smashed sickeningly. The rash young pirate was torn between the furious roar of his captain and the inert shape at his feet. A spine-chilling howl from above his head stopped him cold as Rue sprang to avenge her sister. She dropped down and hung on his back as she reached down for his rapier. She withdrew it but it was slapped out of her hand as she was plucked off the spinning young pirate. The Hawk set her on her feet and swiftly knelt by Kestrel.

"Do nothing rash, Rue. Your sister's life depends on it," he hissed as Nick and Pierre raced up.

Nick stared down into Kestrel's still face. For a moment he was filled with dread at her strange bent position as he thought her neck had been broken. Carefully he felt her neck and then her spine and sighed with relief.

"Broken clavicle," he said softly as he ran a practiced hand along her collarbone. "Probable cracked skull also," he added tersely as blood covered his probing hand and the golden hair was drenched and darkened. "I don't want to move her without support. I need a board or something," he explained, glowering at the cowering young pirate whose face had been raked by Rue's nails.

"You heard, young man. Go find a board!" ordered the Hawk, his dark eyes burning into the embarrassed scratched young man's. "If your wife obeyed, she would not be lying there now," he added to Nick. Nick didn't bother to answer as he looked at the still young face.

"She is so beautiful," he said softly. "Hard to think I would ever forget being married to such a one."

"Forget being married?" repeated the masked man.

"I don't even know who I am or what I'm doing on this vessel," returned Nick wryly.

"Yesterday you said both Rue and Kestrel Sinclair were under your protection," probed the Hawk after a sudden snort of laughter.

"What else did I say?"

"That Kestrel was your wife," supplied the taller dark man. "Let me correct that, you did not say which was your wife but she's the one who leaped to your defense. I, unfortunately, had occasion to hit you and you struck your head, which seems to have robbed you of your memory. I find that very unfortunate as I would like to know exactly what has been going on with these two."

"I don't wish to sound impertinent, but why would you, a conquering pirate captain, want to know about these two backwoods girls?" questioned Nick.

"I'm intrigued. This one is mute, except when she's asleep, and is terrified of male attention," recounted the Hawk, catching Rue to him as she tensed to escape, not liking to be spoken of so.

Nick frowned at the ruthlessness of the man's tone.

"And the golden one, though certainly not mute or averse to male attention, has shadows in her past."

The Hawk left Kestrel to Nick's tender ministrations and led Rue toward the bridge. She fought against him, wanting to stay with her sister, but was no match for his strength.

"Don't be such a bother. There is nothing you can do for your sister except get in the way," he said coldly as he wondered why he was so taken with the two half-grown wenches. They weren't even ripe women, he chided himself.

Shame barked with joy and threw herself toward her young mistress, but a short rope prevented contact. Rue howled with rage when she saw her dog tied. She grabbed at the Hawk's belt to obtain his knife to cut her pet free. The masked man allowed her to take the blade, lifting his strong arms in mock surrender.

"It's amazing what noises you can make when you don't try too hard," he remarked as she sawed through the strong rope. Pierre and Jacques Gillette watched the exchange and frowned, noticing a current that ran deeply beneath the looks that were exchanged by the very tall dark masked man and the petite dark girl.

"What do you know of this infant?" demanded the Hawk, waving a careless hand at the crouching Rue, whose face mirrored her feelings at his insults.

"What is it you want to know, monsieur," pronounced Pierre a Jacques looked apoplectic and unable to speak.

"Who are they? Where are they going? What happened to strik that one mute? What do you know about the young doctor?" rattle the impatient man.

"Why you want for to know?" blustered Jacques. "*Oui*, I stea your cargo but that is for you and me to fight about, yes? Not *le enfants*. No more hurt for *la petite mademoiselle*," he begge indicating the dark girl who hugged her dog.

"I have no wish to hurt anyone," snapped the Hawk. "Just answe my questions. Who are they?"

"*Je ne connais pas*," lied Jacques, shrugging. "Payin passengers."

"Going where?"

"France."

"France?" queried the masked man.

"Where else would I, Jacques Gillette, go?"

"And the ship's doctor? Nicholas MacKay?"

"The husband of Kestrel with the hair of gold," supplied th captain.

"Why would a Scottish doctor with two Scottish lassies go t France?"

"Because the ship, she does not go any farther," laughed Pierre flexing his bandaged hand.

"You are most particular about who travels with you. Usually ther are no passengers to witness your dirty dealings," insisted the dar man.

"Monsieur, we cannot be so particular as you are aboard ou vessel," insulted Jacques. Rue sucked in her breath as she felt th shaft go home, but the masked man laughed.

"*Touché*."

"Why have you interest in *la petite*?" asked Pierre seriously indicating the crouched girl.

"The doctor has no memory. The golden one is very hurt and i seems I am the cause of the newest misfortunes. So there is a *pauvr petite* with no protector," answered the man lightly.

"I will protect her with my life," pronounced Jacques.

"*Moi aussi*," joined in Pierre.

"Bravo," applauded the Hawk. He stared down at Rue, marvelin in the expressive poignant face as she sat with her dog, listenin intently to all that was said and all the undercurrents that flowed. "

will make a deal with you. I will forget the cargo that you stole, the seven lives you took, and let you have your *l'Étoile*."

Jacques and Pierre frowned suspiciously at the lounging dark man.

"Go on," they insisted, rolling their hands to illustrate.

"You are Captain Jacques Gillette, and you have the authority to sanctify a marriage?"

"*Oui*," agreed Jacques very suspiciously.

"Then you will bind Rue Sinclair and myself in holy matrimony."

"*Sacrebleu!*" ejaculated Pierre.

"*Mon Dieu!*" gasped Jacques, slapping his face with his hand and staring down at Rue who sat with her amber eyes as big as saucers.

"Rue?" questioned Pierre but she couldn't react.

"If you do not do as I say, I shall take her aboard the *Dolphin* as my woman without the sanctity of marriage and you'll never see her again," threatened the lean dark man. Pierre looked at Jacques whose eyes were fastened on Rue's drawn white face.

"Meron, my dear, dear friend, forgive me," mourned the old captain. "I promised to protect *la petite*. Forgive me! I promised to marry Nick *et* Kestrel and I have not," he lamented.

"They are not married?" questioned the Hawk sharply.

"Meron say by declaration," offered Jacques morosely.

"Meron?" queried the masked man.

"*L'oncle des petites*," supplied Pierre wearily.

"And if you harm one hair on their heads, he will find you and cut your heart out, Monsieur le Hawk," promised Jacques with relish. "But why you want to marry such a one? She is not even a woman and too skinny," he added, changing his tone to a wheedling whine in a last-ditch effort to change the pirate's mind.

"So she'll not be hurt by anyone else," stated the Hawk harshly, not understanding why he was so concerned with the strange mute girl.

Pierre and Jacques froze at the unexpected enigmatic words and looked at Rue, who stared up at the tall masked man.

"Kestrel? Can you hear me?" whispered Nick.

Kestrel lay as the waves of pain washed over her as she fought to recall everything that had happened. She remembered that Nick had forgotten who he was and even in her discomfort a plan formed in her throbbing head. Her eyes flew open and she stared vacantly into the concerned face that hovered above her.

"Who are you?" she said huskily and groaned with pain. Nick

frowned down into the limpid green eyes as the full portent of her words broke into his head.

"What?" he asked, not wanting to hear what she had said.

"Who are you?" repeated Kestrel, wanting his arms about her so she could bury her face in the soft warmth of his firm neck.

"Nick," he said, clearing his throat.

"Nick?" answered Kestrel, puzzled. "Who am I?" she added and Nick groaned.

"Gladys, take care of her. Dinna let her move about too much," he directed, unable to deal with the new turn of events. Kestrel's heart thumped painfully as she heard the cabin door close behind him.

"Aw what's the matter, lovey ducks?" crooned Miss Mackintosh, seeing the large tears fall down Kestrel's smooth cheeks.

"He doesn't know who I am," sobbed the golden girl.

"You know who he is?" exclaimed the fat lady. Kestrel sniffed and tried to nod but howled with pain due to the broken collarbone.

Nick, pacing the narrow passageway outside their cabin, leaped through the door at Kestrel's anguished scream.

"What happened?" he asked and Miss Mackintosh beamed with satisfaction and glanced down at her charges' wet cheeks. Nick didn't remember who Kestrel was, but there was a clutching at his heart seeing her pathetic little face as he remembered their passionate lovemaking earlier that day.

"Where's Rue?" sniffed Kestrel, melting into the dark eyes that showed their concern for her.

"She's fine. You just worry about yourself and try and sleep," comforted Nick, drowning in her liquid green eyes and wishing she wasn't hurt so he could climb into bed with her and make her forget all her worries.

"Who are you?" asked Kestrel wickedly, knowing how much she was desired as his eyes seemed to spark. "Whoever you are, don't leave me alone," she begged, and smiled with satisfaction as he sat next to her on the bunk as he motioned to Miss Mackintosh to leave.

Kestrel lay with her eyes shut, knowing she had done something wrong as Gladys left with an exasperated shaking of her head, feeling Nick's dark eyes burn into her. She peeked out of one eye and he grinned down at her.

"Kestrel? I know you have your memory," he confessed.

"How?" she challenged and he marveled at her resilience.

"You asked after Rue," he said softly and bent and kissed her smooth cheek. Kestrel reached to hug him and screamed in agony.

"My darling, you've broken your collarbone," he explained, stroking the sling to show her.

"Do you remember me?" she whispered, tears pouring down her face and Nick couldn't lie to her even though he wanted to. He softly shook his head.

"Nae," he murmured gently.

"But what about our bairn?" sobbed Kestrel.

"Bairn?" questioned Nick. Kestrel nodded. "What bairn?" he probed at a loss.

"I have na bled for two months and Angus said I maun tell you when the second month passed," she informed him.

"Angus?" queried Nick. "Second month?"

"Aye. I didna bleed in June before we set off and now 'tis nearly August and Angus said I maun tell you for it meant I was wie child," explained Kestrel, getting afraid by Nick's intense look.

"When did we join together?" asked Nick awkwardly.

"Which time?"

"The first," replied Nick. Kestrel refused to answer as danger seemed to pound through her. "Kestrel, did you hear me?" But she knew not to try and shake or nod her head as suddenly she felt too tired and achy to care about anything. She looked sadly at him and closed her deep green eyes.

Nick lay back on the bunk watching her sleep, confused by the many things that ran through his mind as he surveyed and committed to memory each of her flawless features. He filled with impotent rage at his inability to remember any details about his personal life beyond the last twelve hours. Luckily his medical knowledge seemed intact. All else had to be taken on trust: that he was in the middle of an ocean between the American continent and Europe on his way to Scotland via France, with his golden-haired wife and her dark mute sister; that the vessel he had passage on called the *Étoile* captained by Jacques Gillette aided by his one-eyed brother Pierre had been taken over by pirates, the captain of whom was called the Hawk. It was a miracle that he remembered all he apparently had been taught as a doctor.

Unable to absorb the enormity of his predicament, Nick closed his eyes and stretched out next to his supposed wife and closed his mind, willing himself to sleep and hopefully some dreams that would clarify many things.

CHAPTER TWENTY-TWO

Rue sat high in the *Étoile*'s rigging as she sailed side by side with the Hawk's *Dolphin*. The dark girl felt free and joyous as the wind blew her hair and brightened her cheeks. Down below, cooped in a stuffy humid cabin, Kestrel lay restless, nursed by Gladys Mackintosh who had confined herself again in corsets and heavy black mourning fabric no matter how many yards of gay yellows and reds Pierre wooed her with.

Rue felt the Hawk's eyes on her as he stared from the bridge of his vessel. She smiled victoriously, feeling so far above him, racing with the clouds. Nothing could touch her, nothing could harm her. She didn't examine the exhilarating emotion as she sensed it was fleeting and not destined to last. When she was near the Hawk, she was afraid, cowed by his tall shadow, and yet when he left she felt bereft. She was relieved that there had been no more mention of a wedding. Below on the deck Shame kept his adoring eyes pinned to his reckless young mistress as each morning they rose with the sun, gulped a brief breakfast, and raced to the fresh upper deck.

The Hawk watched his young bride-to-be as he questioned his sanity. Yet each morning he waited for her appearance as she raced onto the deck and nimbly shinned up the ropes until she stood silhouetted against the bright sky. At first he had tensed as she climbed, but now he was confident and admiring of her agility. He rejoiced as he saw her lithe body arch with the wind as though she were a sail, and he felt her competitive spirit as the *Étoile* and the *Dolphin* sliced neck and neck through the deep waters. As he questioned his rash proposal of marriage, he debated turning the wheel and disappearing over the horizon, never to be seen again. It would be easy, he had stayed a bachelor for over thirty years, he told himself, and yet the thought of leaving the mute wild girl was inconceivable. But why? he strove to understand. His eyes narrowed as he thought of Nick, and he wondered how long the fortuitous amnesia would last.

Each day he boarded the *Étoile* and made a duty visit to Kestrel, who lay furious over her confinement. Each day he silently watched Rue lovingly tend the horses and hound, wishing he was one of her beloved animals for she was free and relaxed about them. With him she froze, her usually graceful movements inhibited and sharp. It made him angry and he wished he could wreak vengeance on those who had hurt her so.

Each night he reluctantly swam back to the *Dolphin* wishing he could lie with Rue and once again undress her and observe the perfection of her sun-kissed body, and hear her voice even though it was in the fearful throes of a dream. There was a husky, honeyed tone to her voice, he recalled, remembering the nightmare and how he'd held her in his arms until morning.

"Do you still intend to be married?" pressed Pierre as several weeks passed since his announcement and the French brothers hoped he'd changed his mind.

"When Kestrel is better," the Hawk improvised, knowing he didn't know how to approach Rue.

"What happened to Rue?" he asked.

"Rape," informed Pierre.

"That's obvious," he snapped. "But who? When? Why?" he probed, and to his frustration both brothers shrugged.

"Ask my little cabbage," suggested Pierre. "*Peut-être,* she know something."

"Ask Kess," suggested Miss Mackintosh, and so the Hawk found himself staring into the bright green hostile eyes of Kestrel.

"What happened to Rue?" he asked, trying to gentle his tone despite all the signs of battle laid down by the golden lass.

"None of your business," returned Rue's sister, promising nothing.

"I'm making it my business!" he stated forcefully, and Kestrel snorted irreverently. She was unused to inactivity and her temper suffered. She also wished she had not told Nick about having his baby as he had withdrawn, moving to another cabin.

"You know what happened," attacked Kestrel.

"Aye, she was raped," returned the Hawk.

"Doesna your face get hot and sweaty under that stupid mask?" challenged the girl, longing for a fight to stop the endless confining boredom. She didn't want to think about what happened so long ago. It made her feel guilty and uncomfortable.

"What do you know?" demanded the Hawk impatiently, cupping her chin. Kestrel's face paled and her green eyes widened.

"I don't know. I don't know what you want me to say," she intoned.

"The truth," he replied, frowning at her haunted look.

"I shot her. I shot my sister. She has a scar just like mine but it goes the other way," volunteered Kestrel, obviously very disturbed and fumbling with her nightshirt and pulling it up to show the smooth white line on her stomach. The Hawk's eyes narrowed as he pictured Rue's naked body and remembered the similar scar.

"Why did you shoot her?" he asked softly, seeing the pain he was asking her to recall.

"I tried to shoot them because they were raping her dead. She screamed and screamed like Jemmy. I tried to shoot them but I shot my sister," wept Kestrel. "My mother never knew. I couldn't tell my mother. I thought she would love me because I was the only daughter left but I couldn't let her love me, could I? That wouldn't have been fair. Now Meron found Rue and everyone will love her more again but that's right, isn't it? She was born first. They loved her first anyway, didn't they?"

The Hawk stared down at Kestrel who was caught back in childhood. A noise behind him caused him to turn and he stared into Nick's concerned face. He motioned for him to remain quiet, somehow knowing Kestrel would stop talking if there were any interruptions. The two men stood silently listening and Nick frowned as he felt a familiar comfort in the pirate's presence.

"Now Nick will love Rue more and that's right, isn't it, because she's good. She doesn't do bad things and hurt people, does she?" asked Kestrel, her face open and inquiring like a tiny child's.

The Hawk quietly left Kestrel's cabin, leaving Nick to sit with the girl. He strode across the deck, feeling the wind scour his cheeks as he tried to piece together what he had learned. Shame barked a welcome and leaped up to lick his face. The Hawk stared above and shaded his eyes against the bright sun as he watched the tiny figure high in the sails. On an impulse he grinned and started to climb the rigging, wanting to be arched beside her above everyone else.

Rue frowned as she saw the dark masked man below climbing toward her. She debated climbing higher, but knew he would just follow so she waited, growing angry at the intrusion. He stood level with her and stared out in appreciation at the vast vista of the ocean, feeling the wind blow through every pore, cleansing and revitalizing. Rue stared at him and his broad grin caused her to smile. His hearty free laugh caused her to throw back her head and join her voice with his.

Belowdeck Nick stared into Kestrel's furious face, not knowing how to reach her. Usually her loving looks made him feel uncomfortable and guilty because he couldn't remember their past and the coarse presence of Gladys Mackintosh made him feel a giant hoax was being played on him. There was no loving look that day, but even her fury made him uncomfortable as he remembered the anguished words he had been privy to.

"You shot your sister?" he said softly.

"Get out of here before I shoot you!" she threatened, unable to be near him without wanting to be held. Her pride would not allow her to throw herself into his strong arms and cuddle into his strength when he had so obviously rejected her. "I mean it!" she screamed and Nick left, not wanting to aggravate her more and have her do further damage to herself.

Kestrel felt miserable. She had no one. She lay back in the bunk in the confining cabin feeling full of self-pity and hating herself for it. She ran her hands across her stomach, feeling the firmness and wondered at the child that grew inside. If only she could see it, she wouldn't feel so alone, she mused angrily and then sat up, determined not to be an invalid any longer. She clumsily inched out of the hard bunk, her one bound arm making the exit difficult. She stood and, propping herself against the constantly shifting wall, climbed into a pair of buckskin pants. She shoved most of the nightshirt into the waistband and deliberately opened the door. She felt a bit giddy and leaned for a moment, clearing her head before staggering up the reeling corridor. She stood staring up the steep metal ladder to the sunshine above as she questioned her sanity, attempting such a thing with one bound arm.

"I will do it," she promised herself out loud, knowing she couldn't languish one more day cooped up in the stuffy cabin. She swung herself agilely up the metal rungs and stepped into the fresh sunny air for the first time in weeks. She breathed deeply and laughed, stretching her unhurt arm out to embrace the open space as her bare feet tried to dig into the bleached wood boards.

Nick stood on the bridge with Jacques, Pierre, and Gladys watching the Hawk and Rue arch with the sails, their identical ebony hair flying with the wind. Pierre had a claiming arm flung carelessly across Gladys's generous black shiny bosom and she glowed, refusing to acknowledge the large hand that tweaked impudently.

"Sacrebleu!" exclaimed Jacques as his keen eyes spotted Kestrel poised on the high bulwark, her lean legs braced apart as she reached above her head with her only free arm.

"She's mad!" hissed Nick, swinging out of the high bridge and leaping to the deck. He raced across the bleached wood and craned his neck, watching her awkwardly climb the rigging. "What the hell do you think you're doing?" he screamed, most of the violent volume of his words lost in the sharp wind.

Kestrel stared down impassively, wanting to poke out her tongue but feeling that would show concern. She felt like a bird with one wing as she ignored Nick and concentrated on climbing to freedom where her sister hung on the cobwebbed ropes against the white clouds that scudded across the deep blue sky.

Rue spotted her sister and all joy faded as she deflated like a sail deprived of wind. The Hawk followed her concerned gaze and he stiffened. Rue and the masked man held their breaths, their young bodies cramping in the tense moments as Kestrel climbed the rigging with one bound arm. Several times everything stood still as she wavered and fought to keep her balance, but at last she stood on a level with them, grinning her triumph in the wind. Kestrel turned to her sister and smiled hesitantly and Rue beamed. Both girls turned as they heard the deep infectious laughter and their faces opened even more as they both joined the Hawk in the exultant joy.

Nick stood below, smoldering with rage as he wondered how the maimed one was going to descend from her high perch. He rubbed his head as many worries poured in.

"Are you all right, *mon ami?*" asked Jacques, seeing Nick's stark fear imprinted.

"No," he answered shortly. "Tell me what you know of me and those up there," he added shortly, pointing above to the three silhouetted against the bright sky.

"No memory yet?" asked Jacques sympathetically and at Nick's impatient shake of the head, shrugged unhappily. "I know very little, my friend, except that you are married to . . ." He twirled a thick finger in the air indicating Kestrel.

"You are very certain of that fact?" insisted Nick harshly.

"*Oui*, Meron would never lie. It is by declaration and I am supposed to perform a wedding ceremony, myself being a captain," he added morosely.

"Declaration?" probed Nick.

"*Oui*, it is a barbaric custom in your country of Scotland," stammered Jacques, not understanding the young man's intensity.

"You are saying that I am not married to Kestrel Sinclair?" he roared.

"*Oui et non*," procrastinated the French sea captain.

"In English," hissed Nick.

"Yes and no," unhappily complied Jacques.

"I am either married or not married," insisted the doctor.

"Yes, you are married and no you are not married," supplied the captain unhappily. "If you want to be, you are. If you do not want to be, you are not."

Nick breathed heavily through his nostrils as he stared above his head, unable to tell which shape was which.

"Just wait a minute," protested Gladys, disengaging herself from her paramour's claiming greedy hands. "Kess is pregnant and you are now trying to say you ain't married? You put a bun in 'er oven, got 'er in the family way, and now wanta wash yer 'ands of the poor little tyke?" she screamed gracelessly.

Jacques and Pierre stiffened and looked at Nick expectantly, trusting him to answer. The young doctor sighed, not wanting to get a long harangue. He shook his head wearily and unfolded his lanky shape from against the wall where he leaned.

"*Non!*" growled Pierre, his only eye glowing alarmingly. "You'll not go until you give us an answer!"

"I have no answer," replied Nick simply. "I have no idea who I am, who you are, or who they are," he added savagely, indicating wildly the threesome above his head. Jacques nodded sadly, understanding his dilemma. "Yet you would have me trust all you say and marry?"

"You bet your britches!" shrieked Gladys, furious with the males who nodded sympathetically with the young doctor. "The poor little thing! No mum! No dad! No family 'ceptin' for a dumb sister and now just 'cause she's expectin' she's gonna get dumped?" she yelled, so angry she jerked around not able to keep still. "Well, 'oo needs you lot? Aye? We're women and can do a lot better without yer!" she added impotently as she marched out of the bridge and nearly broke her neck on the steep steps to the deck. Poor Gladys Mackintosh tore furiously at the offending black material that tripped and impeded her dignified exit. She strode over the heaving deck with her nose held high and fell flat on her face. She lay stunned, trying to pull her wits together to finish her sedate departure, but everything suddenly felt so sad that she buried her hennaed head in her soft forearms and cried.

Pierre's one eye nearly popped out of his Gallic face as he saw his lady love lie defeated on the listing deck. He stared with complete bewilderment at Nick, his brother, and then back at the heaving mound of shiny black bombazine

"My little cabbage!" he exclaimed before choosing to rush to her groaning form.

"Well, my friend?" said Jacques, sympathetic to Nick's confusion, and yet aching for Kestrel. Nick shrugged, unable to commit himself either way. He left the bridge and avoided the tender scene between Pierre and Gladys by striding to the back of the boat and staring over the side at the churning, troubled waters that spewed out behind the graceful vessels.

Nick was hypnotized by the turbid water that so aptly illustrated his thoughts and emotions. What sort of person was he? he wondered. Who was Kestrel with her obvious sexuality and whorelike companion by the name of Gladys Mackintosh? His head ached as he thought on the rest of the rascally characters. One-eyed Pierre, Captain Jacques, and a pirate called the Hawk. Was he meant to trust them totally? Place his life in their hands? Marry the pregnant girl? The questions whirled and tortured as there seemed to be no answer. He turned and stared up into the rigging that crisscrossed the sky at the three dark figures. Who was the masked pirate? Was knowledge of the man locked away in his lost memory?

Kestrel felt purged by the bracing wind that swirled, blowing her shirt out like a sail. She shrugged her arm free of the confining sling and hesitantly stretched her arm. There was an aching weakness but no sharp pain. She moved her head from side to side and flexed her hand, feeling the strength return. She grinned at Rue and waved her hurt arm to show how she had healed. Rue smiled back with a tiny frown to warn her reckless sister to be careful, but Kestrel threw back her head so her golden hair streamed with the air currents. She had been cooped up too long, now she was free.

"Look over there," directed the Hawk and Rue and Kestrel turned to see porpoises leaping and playing together. "Soon we'll be in sight of land," he added as he swung himself down toward the deck.

"Land?" repeated Kestrel, and she and Rue exchanged glances as they followed the masked man.

Kestrel leaped down the remaining few feet to the deck and felt the jarring ache her shoulder. She rubbed it as she moved her neck from side to side.

"Let me see," clipped Nick coldly, hiding the fear he had felt watching her perilous descent from the high rigging. Kestrel glared at him and moved away, refusing to allow him to touch her.

"Rue?" She called her sister and the two girls went below to Kestrel's cabin.

Nick and the Hawk watched them leave.

"I hear the golden one is with child," remarked the masked man.

"I hear the same," replied Nick.

"You claimed her as your wife before you lost your memory," stated the Hawk.

"You said she claimed me, but that I didn't specify which," corrected the young doctor.

"We will be in sight of Spain by morning. What do you propose to do?"

Nick shrugged and wearily rubbed his eyes. "I don't have much choice it seems, except to take everyone's word for it. I'll marry her but in name only. She'll not truly be my wife until I find out who the hell I am!" he promised vehemently.

"You must have papers among your possessions that tell you something about yourself?" probed the Hawk.

"Aye, I am Nicholas MacKay of Tain and Edinburgh, it seems. I have two addresses and a certificate from the University of Edinburgh but I have nothing that states I am responsible for the three females or who the hell they are and where I came across them. One pregnant girl who's little more than a child herself, another wild one who is a mute, and the third a member of an old profession if I'm not mistaken. So I marry the pregnant one and turn up on the doorstep of a strange house in Edinburgh to be met by another wife, maybe?" spouted Nick recklessly, laughing cynically. "And you, my masked friend? I hear that you are to marry the mute? Why? There is no way she can be pregnant as she seems petrified of men!"

"I don' know why. Maybe she is a challenge," murmured the tall man softly. "Tonight you are invited aboard the *Dolphin*. I want Kestrel and Rue dressed in the gowns I have seen hanging in their cabins."

"I am a doctor, not a lady's maid," returned Nick.

"I don't care how you manage it, but I want them dressed for their weddings. I'm sure Miss Mackintosh, the leetle cabbage, will help

when she hears you are to make an honest woman of her little lamb,"
insisted the Hawk sardonically, before gracefully diving off the high
bulwark into the sea. Nick watched him swim strongly toward the
Dolphin.

CHAPTER TWENTY-THREE

Rue moved all her things into Kestrel's cabin with Gladys's help.

"There we are," puffed the large woman after single-handedly
carrying Rue's large trunk. "Now let's see what pretty frocks you're
going to wear for the 'Awk's little party."

"Gladys, we aren't going!" stated Kestrel firmly.

"Don't talk stuff 'n' nonsense! You ain't in any condition to
refuse!" blustered Miss Mackintosh. "You're going to 'ave a baby!"

"What has that to do with anything?" demanded Kestrel.

"Everything! Didn't yer mum tell you nothin'?" bemoaned the
large woman.

"About what?"

"About 'avin' babies when you ain't married?" sighed Gladys
impatiently.

"Well, I *was* married," returned Kestrel belligerently.

"Don't count!"

"Why?"

"Prove it," crowed Miss Mackintosh triumphantly, staring into
Kestrel's frowning face. "Well, go on, prove it! Yer 'usband's lost 'is
memory."

"Who wants a husband?" snapped Kestrel.

"You do."

Rue listened and watched the battle of wills, thinking of her own
baby. She remembered the terrible pain that racked her body and the
tiny blue, hardly formed fetus. The people at the mission had buried
the dead child and looked upon her as a fallen woman, a bad influence
to be kept away from the virginal girls.

"Your baby won't 'ave a name save fer bastard," continued
Gladys, determined to come out the victor.

"My baby shall be named anything I want," declared Kestrel.

"Your last name is Sinclair because your mum and dad were married. Your poor baby won't 'ave no last name."

"It'll have Sinclair."

"Then everyone'll know it's a bastard," crowed Gladys.

"It's all silly!" shouted Kestrel. "I'm not marrying someone who doesn't want to marry me!"

"Marry 'im for the baby and then you can do what you want. First things first, I always say." Kestrel looked unhappily to Rue, who smiled sadly and nodded that she agreed with Miss Mackintosh.

"What about you, Rue? You can't marry that masked pirate?" cried Kestrel.

"There's only one thing to be done and that's to do as the 'Awk says, for now anyway. But you trust yer old Gladys, she's going to 'elp 'er little lambs, don't you worry. That one-eyed darling can be twisted around my little finger. So put smiles on yer little faces and let old Gladys 'ere get you all prettied up."

Kestrel was undecided, but as she watched Rue docilely allowing Gladys to help her dress, she sighed and started undoing her own shirt.

"When you two are gussied up, their jaws are goin' ter drop ter their knees," babbled Gladys excitedly as she turned from one to the other, pulling laces and hooking hooks.

Rue and Kestrel grinned appreciatively at each other as they stood in their frilly undergarments.

"Now which gowns?" fussed Gladys as she critically rifled through their wardrobe trying to find just the right frames for her little works of art. "Hah!" she exclaimed gleefully, finding the bronze metallic dress that fitted Kestrel like a second skin. "This'll make their eyes pop out of their 'eads," she chuckled, laying it on the wide bunk. "Now for my little black lamb," she muttered, pulling out the long skirts and sucking the air through her teeth as she ruminated. "Hahah!" she proclaimed as she surveyed a dress of burnt orange. Rue shook her head determinedly and took down a simple black dress. "Ain't a funeral, lovey, it's a weddin'!" protested Gladys.

"You're right, Rue!" laughed Kestrel, rummaging through her gowns until she also found an identical black one. "We shall be dressed properly as we've been ordered," she giggled, stepping into the soft crepe dress as Gladys clucked her disappointment and disapproval.

"Ain't right for youngsters to wear mourning rags whether they wants to be married or not. Me, I'm an old maid, it's proper!" she grumbled as she buttoned them into the black crepe dresses. "Oh, my!" she exclaimed as she stepped back. "Oh, my!" she repeated as her eyes popped out of her head and she sat heavily on the bunk. "That Mme. Charbonnière certainly knows 'er business!"

Kestrel frowned and looked at Rue, not knowing why Gladys Mackintosh was so affected. Rue frowned back at Kestrel and then their mouths hung open in surprise. The black crepe dresses were molded to their young lithe bodies, the necklines cut artfully low so the orbs of their firm breasts gently swelled.

"Oh you two do look a treat!" gasped Gladys, clapping her dimpled hands together. "I ain't ever seen such perfection!" she gushed, waxing poetic. "Visions!" she added, fanning herself furiously. "You don't need nothing else 'cepting maybe a little scent."

Kestrel twirled around, delighting in the soft flowing fabric.

"Shoes and stockings!" exclaimed Gladys.

"No!" shouted Kestrel. "We don't need them." There was a sharp rapping at the door.

"Yes?" yelled Miss Mackintosh, hurriedly powdering her nose and dabbing rouge on her already ruddy cheeks.

"It is time, my petite cabbage," called Pierre.

"No, no, don't open the door yet. Put on these wraps, loveys. You 'ave ter make an entrance. Make their eyes pop out of their 'eads when you get unwrapped!" she giggled as Rue and Kestrel slipped on the hooded capes. "And you don't get unwrapped till I gives the signal!"

Rue and Kestrel sat in the rowboat holding each other's hands, knowing they shared the same feelings of trepidation. Nick and Gladys sat facing them as Pierre and Jacques expertly propelled the light craft through the dark water toward the dark hulk of the *Dolphin*.

Rue shivered and squeezed Kestrel's hand as they came alongside the other vessel.

"Glad we didn't wear shoes," hissed Kestrel as she stood and hitched her long skirts up before climbing the ladder.

"I ain't climbing up there!" protested Gladys as she watched Rue fleetly follow her sister. "Don't look!" she admonished Pierre as he stared up at the lithe bare legs of the two girls.

"Nick, he go first and I will help you from the behind," urged Pierre as the small boat rocked furiously.

Rue and Kestrel stood on the deck of the *Dolphin*, listening to Gladys's agonized complaints as she slowly made her way up the swinging rope ladder. The Hawk, dressed in a white full-sleeved shirt and tight black trousers and boots, offered his arms and led them to a luxurious stateroom followed by Nick.

Kestrel's eyes widened as she stared around at the rich red and gold fabric on the walls, and the thick deep red carpet on the floor. She and Rue sank their bare feet into the lush pile and looked at the handsome carved furniture.

"Your capes?" said the Hawk, holding out a hand. Kestrel and Rue shook their heads silently as they waited for Gladys, whose strident voice could be heard shattering the calm night.

"I would not have let you fall, my petite cabbage. I would 'ave caught you in these strong arms," soothed Pierre as they entered the beautiful room. Jacques chuckled as he pictured his one-eyed brother catching the vast woman and Kestrel giggled.

"Oh, my," exclaimed Gladys as she stared around at the opulent surroundings. "Stand straight," she hissed at her young charges as she swept by them into the room. She turned, posed dramatically, and winked.

Nick stood apart watching the two sisters as they undid the ribbons of their capes. He caught his breath as the silky coverings floated to the floor, revealing the identical seductive black dresses with their plunging necklines. Kestrel caught his burning dark eyes, and her heart pounded in her chest. She looked to her sister and to her surprise Rue walked proudly across the room, so she steeled herself, raised her chin, and followed.

The Hawk's ruthless mouth tightened.

"Rue, come here," he ordered, sounding harsh and displeased. He felt fury pound through him. The dark beauty looked at him, her amber eyes flashing before slowly obeying. She stared up at him, trying to see his eyes behind the black mask. "You are in mourning?" he asked, and she nodded and infuriated him with a mysterious half smile. "If this is a joke, I should like you to share its meaning," he added harshly and Rue lowered her eyes. "Dr. MacKay, it seems our brides feel that they have come to a funeral," he announced, signaling a servant to pick up the discarded capes and another to serve wine.

Nick grinned sardonically as if he felt he was at his own funeral.

"Very apt, my dear Kestrel," he said coldly, letting his eyes run hotly across her breasts that thrust daringly out of her dress. Kestrel flushed as she looked into his face and saw his lust. She turned away, but he gripped her forearm, stopping her. "You will stay near me," he ordered arrogantly, handing her a glass of wine, and taking one for himself.

Kestrel longed to throw the sparkling contents into his face as he stared down at her breasts, knowing it was enraging her. She tried to turn away from him but he held her firmly.

"What is it? I am not to look? Then why wear such a gown?" he said cruelly. Kestrel's self-control snapped and she flung the wine in his dark sardonic face. Nick slowly and deliberately poured his wine down her cleavage. Kestrel stood still with her hands clenched into sharp fists, fighting the desire to attack.

Rue froze, watching the exchange as every eye was pinned to Nick and Kestrel. Rue stared up at the Hawk's harsh face and back to Nick's, seeing the dark ruthlessness in both tall black-haired men. She started to walk toward Kestrel to comfort her, but the masked man's hard hand stopped her. She shrugged, trying to remove it, but his grip tightened. She glared up at him but the Hawk didn't look down at her as he watched the altercation between the golden-haired girl and the young doctor. Rue struggled, determined to get free.

"Stop!" hissed the Hawk, holding her with two hands. Rue wanted to break the cruel spell that kept everyone looking at Kestrel, who stood shamed and mortified, not knowing what to do. She kicked back and hurt her bare foot on the shiny leather boots.

"You are a bunch of animals!" screeched Gladys, wishing she had brought her umbrella so she could break some skulls.

"Dinner is served," announced a very proper voice and Kestrel burst into laughter. Rue stopped struggling and listened, not knowing if her sister was hysterical. Nick's laughter joined Kestrel's and Rue frowned.

"Your sister has to learn to work things out with her husband," remarked the Hawk in a low voice. Rue's amber eyes stared up, trying to pierce the black mask as the word husband sent shivers down her spine. What was she about? she wondered as she allowed him to lead her into a large dining room. She allowed herself to be seated and sat looking down at her place setting, feeling very conscious of his presence. She was about to be married to a man whose face she had never seen, whose name she didn't know. She recklessly drained her glass of wine.

The Hawk watched with wry amusement as he signaled a servant to refill the glass. He knew she was terrified as her slim brown hands unsteadily held the fork, and she toyed with the food on her plate.

"Jacques, I thought you told me that Rue liked lobster?" he laughed down the table to the old sea captain, who ate and drank with gusto to ease his guilty pangs. Rue straightened her back and put down her fork as she reached for her wineglass, refusing to be pressured into eating. There was no way she could chew with the Hawk's pervasive presence beside her. She watched Kestrel, who seemed to have a similar problem as she sat next to Nick, a mocking grimace on his dark handsome face. Kestrel drank her fourth glass of wine and sarcastically raised her glass to the rest of the table.

"What long faces! This is a happy occasion!" she proclaimed and giggled infectiously.

Rue reached for her glass but it was moved out of her way. She frowned furiously up at the Hawk.

"I don't like drunk women," he said with a small smile.

Kestrel exchanged a look of sympathy with her sister, raised her glass, and drained it.

Rue felt the meal was interminable as course after course was served and she watched Kestrel drinking more and more. Gladys and Kestrel chattered and giggled happily and the men grew more and more silent. Rue refused to eat and she sat imagining pulling off the damask tablecloth and spilling all the hot dishes into the laps of the somber, smug men. Several servants carried in a parade of rich desserts. Rue's eyes locked with her sister's and a ripple of pure devilment ran between them as they eyed the mounds of creamy pudding and pies. Kestrel giggled mischievously as she reached for a rich custard.

Rue eyed a foamy syllabub made with thick cream and Madeira.

"Don't!" commanded the masked man who had caught the impish exchange. Rue stared up at him with surprise, wondering how he knew, as Nick bellowed with anger.

Kestrel sat smiling sweetly, looking very innocent next to the infuriated young doctor with custard in his lap.

"What's the matter?" asked Gladys, who had been too busy eating and could not see over the laden table to the cause of Nick's discomfort.

"Oh, dear," giggled Kestrel, dagging at the incredible mess with her napkin. Nick slapped her hand away, wanting to strangle her as he wondered how he was to make a dignified exit.

Rue's eyes streamed as she choked with laughter, and her small fists beat helplessly on her lap. The Hawk's lean cheek twitched with suppressed amusement as he pushed his chair back.

"Ladies, why don't you adjourn to the other room and allow us privacy for our pipes," he offered in tones that brooked no differing, as he beckoned to servants to lead Rue, Kestrel, and Gladys back into the salon.

"But I 'aven't finished," mourned Gladys, eyeing the rich cakes and desserts as she tottered out of the dining room behind the two shaking girls. As the door closed between them and the men, Kestrel and Rue flung themselves onto the couches and roared with laughter as Miss Mackintosh stared bewildered from one to the other, not understanding the reason for such amusement but collapsing into snorting giggles nevertheless.

Nick swore as the peals of laughter issued from the other room.

"What 'appened 'ere?" asked Jacques, very confused. Nick stood sheepishly with his hands held out in mock surrender.

"*Sacrebleu!*" exclaimed Pierre. "How? Oh, *la petite*?" he chuckled, pointing at the closed door.

"*Mon Dieu!*" laughed Jacques. "What a beeg mess!"

Nick stood impatiently as several of the Hawk's servants got most of the custard off his lap and then he retired to change into borrowed clothes.

The Hawk threw open the connecting doors between the two rooms and surveyed Kestrel and Rue, who had helped themselves to brandy, much to Gladys's consternation.

Kestrel and Rue recklessly lifted their glasses saucily at him before drinking. Rue looked away, keeping her chin up so she wouldn't see his anger as he strode toward her.

"Are you nearly ready?" he clipped. Rue still refused to look at him and he took her chin between his thumb and forefinger, forcing her to. She steeled herself and glowered, her amber eyes sparking red and orange lights similar to the brandy she swirled in the glass. She drank and handed the snifter to him.

The Hawk looked down at her, touched by her display of bravery and absently placed his own lips to the place where her lips had been and finished the last dregs of the brandy. Kestrel watched him with a frown on her face. He seemed so large and overpowering next to her white-faced sister. As her green eyes met his, she flushed at the harsh expression on his swarthy face.

"Are you ready?" he asked curtly.

"The question is, is he?" she snapped, nodding her head to indicate the dining room and Nick, hiding her own apprehension. The masked man looked down at the two sisters as they unconsciously reached out to each other and clasped hands.

"Come on, lovey duckies," cooed Gladys, herding her charges toward Jacques who cleared his throat and opened a large impressive Bible.

Rue looked at the large black book and shivered as she thought of the mission.

"What book is this?" asked Kestrel, touching the gold-edged, tissue pages curiously. Nick entered in time to hear her question and see the surprise on the other faces.

"Don't you know a Bible when you see one," he replied cuttingly.

"Interesting that you know what to call the book and not yourself!" she returned angrily, noticing other people's surprise at her ignorance. "This is ridiculous! I'm marrying a man who doesn't know who I am, and my sister is marrying a man called the Hawk who keeps his face hidden!"

" 'Ave a little decorum, lovey," begged Gladys, dabbing her eyes as she always did at weddings.

Rue and Kestrel hardly heard the droning voice of Jacques's pidgin English as he married them to the two tall dark men.

"What?" asked Kestrel as Gladys nudged her and everyone looked at her expectantly.

"Say 'I do'," whispered Gladys.

"Why?"

"Just do it!" ordered the irate woman.

"I do," said Kestrel with a frown as Jacques turned to Nick.

"Do you take this woman to be your wife?" improvised Jacques.

Kestrel looked expectantly up at Nick, who stared silently down at her. Gladys nudged him and he nodded quietly.

"I now pronounce you 'usband and wife," quoted Jacques with relish, relieved that he had performed one ceremony. "Now," he sighed, turning to the Hawk and Rue. He stared up at the masked face with mute appeal as he remembered his promise to Meron to protect Rue, but he received no comfort from the hard glittering eyes.

Rue felt dwarfed by the tall man at her side as once more Jacques droned through the wedding ceremony. She frowned, hearing the words honor, love, cherish, and obey and looked up in confusion at the dark masked face. Gladys nudged her and she nodded.

"Do you, Monsieur Hawk, take Rue Sinclair as your lawful wedded wife, to 'ave and to 'old from this day forth, in sickness and in 'ealth, to *love* and to *cherish* as long as you both shall live?" recited Jacques, desperately accenting the positive words.

"I do," stated the Hawk, softly staring down into the bewildered amber eyes.

"*Enfin!* There! I make you 'usband and wife!" sighed Jacques, shutting the Bible with a thump and drinking thirstily from a brandy snifter as guilt gnawed, knotting his stomach.

Kestrel frowned as she repeated the words to herself, realizing and hearing for the first time what she had promised and what Nick had silently agreed to.

"Love, honor, cherish, obey?" she whispered.

"Particularly the last," replied Nick harshly, accepting a glass of sparkling wine from a servant.

"Let us toast the brides!" rejoiced Gladys, unaware of the seething friction as she wished there had been a third ceremony joining her with her one-eyed man Pierre.

Rue felt frozen to the spot as she was imprisoned by the Hawk's heavy hand on her shoulder and he civilly bade his guests good night.

"Aren't you coming back to the *Étoile*?" questioned Kestrel.

"A wife's place is with her husband," stated a deep voice. "Her rightful place is now by my side wherever I choose to go."

"But . . ." protested Kestrel, startled and afraid for her tense white-faced sister.

"Don't be a nuisance. Thank our host for his generous hospitality," ordered Nick. "I never expected to have to teach manners," he groaned, firmly taking Kestrel's elbow and marching her across the deck.

Rue's heart thudded in her chest as Kestrel's bright head disappeared over the side, and she heard the rhythmic pulling of the oars as the French brothers rowed the people back to the *Étoile*. This was something she hadn't thought about. What had she thought? Did she and Kestrel really think they would be married and everything stay the same? Her small hands hung clenched at her side as she was steered back into the opulent salon.

"Would you like some more brandy?" he asked and Rue nodded, needing as much courage as she could muster. He handed it to her and stretched out in a comfortable chair. "Why don't you sit?" Rue shook her head. The Hawk watched her, wondering how he could put her at ease as she drained the glass and choked as the fiery contents burned her nose and throat.

"It has been a long evening, maybe you should go to bed," he said softly, taking the empty glass from her hand and leading her to a large bedroom. Rue swallowed painfully as she stared around wide-eyed at the lush furnishings and at the exquisite lace gown tossed intimately across the wide bed. "If we were on dry land there would be a maid to help you undress. If you need assistance I shall be quite happy to oblige," he offered, keeping his tone light and casual. Rue waited stiffly for him to leave before picking up the nightgown and examining it. She dropped it dismally before cautiously opening the doors to find a means of escape. She gasped at the array of clothes that met her eyes in one of the wardrobes. About fifty dresses of all different sizes and colors with matching shoes. She hastily closed the door and opened another that led to a long corridor.

"Do you need help?" murmured the Hawk, and she turned guiltily. He stared down at her flushed face and softly stroked her cheek. "I shall teach you not to be afraid of me, Rue. There is nothing to be afraid of," he soothed and her eyes instinctively fell to the front of his trousers as she remembered.

"Making love has nothing to do with rape, little one," he murmured, following her eyes and seeing her recoil. "I promise that is one way I shall never hurt you."

Rue looked up at him, wishing she could see behind the mask.

"Sleep, I shall not disturb you," he reassured and Rue smiled timorously, hoping to soften the hard line of his cheek, and then motioned to the long row of buttons on the back of her gown. He silently nodded and Rue shivered as the warmth of his hands touched the bare skin of her neck as he fumbled with the tiny fastenings.

"Anything else?" he asked softly as she stood clutching the dress so it didn't fall to the floor. Rue shook her head as she stood with her eyes as big as saucers.

"You are very beautiful," he whispered huskily, putting two fingers under her little chin and lifting her face. He bent and kissed her lips lightly before leaving the room. Rue let the gown drop to the floor as she touched her lips. She had never been kissed before other than by her family. Raped many times but never kissed, she mused as her mouth tingled. She crept into the large bed still dressed in her tight lacy underthings, not wanting to ask for further help in getting them off. She pulled the heavy coverings over herself, somehow needing their protection even though it was a humid August night.

CHAPTER TWENTY-FOUR

Kestrel stood silently as Gladys Mackintosh undid the long line of buttons on the back of her gown.

"There you are," stated the woman impatiently, giving Kestrel a shove as she seemed to be dreaming. "Step out!" Absently Kestrel obeyed and didn't protest while Gladys yanked her this way and that as she unlaced and unhooked the lacy undergarments. "You can manage the rest yourself," she said, hanging up the gown and bustling to the door eager to be with her one-eyed paramour. Her natural caring stopped her rushing right out as she stood at the open door and looked back at the pensive naked girl. "You all right, lovey ducks?"

Kestrel looked at her, startled.

"What did you say?"

"You all right?" fussed the large woman.

Kestrel nodded.

"Well, toodleloo, 'ave a good night sleep!" And Gladys scurried off to Pierre's cabin, undoing her own clothing as she went.

Kestrel stood looking out the porthole toward the *Dolphin* and wondered how Rue was. What if the *Dolphin* sailed away in the middle of the night and she never saw her sister again, she worried. Thinking of the Hawk's claiming words, she paced back and forth. There was only one thing to do, she decided, she had to get back on board the other vessel. She looked out the porthole again. It wasn't very far, she could swim it easily. She rummaged through her chest looking for light trews and a jerkin that wouldn't weigh her down.

There was a cursory knock and Nick walked into the cabin and watched Kestrel throwing clothes left and right as she impatiently searched through her trunk. He leaned nonchalantly against the wall, admiring her golden nakedness as he waited to be noticed.

Kestrel found what she was looking for and spun around as she shrugged into a dark shirt. She stopped dressing and scowled at him.

"Don't mind me," offered Nick, curious as to what she was planning.

"What do you want?" she asked shyly, remembering the words of the marriage ceremony. Maybe he wanted to love and cherish her, she thought, breathlessly clutching the dark trews into a ball in her nervous hands.

"To talk, but it seems you're about something," returned Nick.

"I want to talk," whispered Kestrel, sitting on the bunk and curling her legs beneath her. She stared up at him, her green eyes sparkling with hope. Nick turned away, not wanting to be seduced.

"Finish getting dressed," he ordered shortly. Kestrel frowned at his back and obediently stepped into the dark trews and buttoned them. She waited for him to turn back to her but he started to talk as he stared out of the porthole.

"We are married, but it will be in name only," he informed her harshly.

"What does that mean?"

"Precisely what I said. In name only. Nothing else," he explained, not wanting to mention out loud the intimacies he was depriving them both of.

"I don't understand."

"We will not sleep together! You have my name and my protection. I shall support you and the child when it is born—"

"Bastard!" interrupted Kestrel, flinging anything she could find at his rejecting back.

Nick turned with an oath and imprisoned her flailing hands in his.

"I have not finished!"

"You have! Get out! I don't want to see you! Get out!" screamed Kestrel, trying to bite as she kicked and struggled to be free of his iron hold. Nick's face hardened as he saw the tears streaming down her cheeks. He moved quickly aside as her knee aimed at his groin, and he flung her onto the bunk where he pinned her down.

"You will hear me out!" he insisted.

"I won't!" yelled Kestrel, fighting with every ounce of her strength till it was impossible for Nick to do anything except struggle with her. He didn't want to hurt her, but she fought savagely, landing painful punches and kicks anywhere she could.

"Stop it!" roared Nick, but she increased her battling if it were possible. "Kestrel, stop before I have to hurt you!" But it only served to add oil to the fire. He exerted more energy, leaning his full weight to pin her down, holding her arms on each side of her head as his legs held hers in a bone-crushing way. "Now you will listen to what I have to say, Kestrel!" he panted, glaring down at the flashing green eyes. Kestrel spat full in his face. There was a still, tense moment and Nick deliberately slapped her flushed cheek. Kestrel froze at the sharp shock. Nick let her go and silently walked out, slamming the door.

"Everything all right?" queried Jacques, who hovered in the corridor drawn by the violent screaming and crashes. Nick breathed deeply, calming himself as the heartrending sobs started. Both men looked at the door, knowing raw human pain when they heard it. Nick rubbed his head, not knowing what to do.

"You no walk away from that, my friend," stated Jacques softly.

Nick quietly reentered Kestrel's cabin and sat beside her, stroking her hot head as she sobbed. He pulled her into his arms and she tried to struggle but was emotionally and physically depleted. He rocked her until she calmed and lay looking up at him numbly. The imprint of his hand stood out angrily on her face.

"I wanted to say that until I remember who I am, I feel incomplete and cannot be a whole man," he said softly. "It's not because of you. . . ." His words trailed off as he saw her eyes close and she relaxed and slept, her breathing ragged and uneven from the emotional storm.

Nick stared down at the tousled golden armful and reluctantly laid her back against the pillow, steeling himself against her protesting murmurs as she tried to cuddle back into the warmth and safety of his arms. He covered her with a sheet and turned down the lamp. He stood for a moment gazing down at her and frowned as he saw her eyes shine in the dim light as she looked back at him.

" 'Tis for the best, Kestrel," he whispered hoarsely as he left her cabin for a long walk around the top deck.

Kestrel heard the door close quietly behind him, and she wanted to howl out her hurt and anguish and break the silence of the night. She lay feeling her hot eyes flood with aching tears, and she wrapped her thin arms about her stomach as though to cradle her own baby.

"I hate weeping!" she sniffed furiously, angry at herself as she threw the sheet back and got out of the bed. She looked out the porthole toward the *Dolphin* and she remembered Rue's dilemma.

The Hawk quietly entered his bedroom and stared down at the slight mound under the heavy covers. His eyebrows raised as he thought she must be excessively hot in such humid weather. He stripped himself and turned down the lamp before removing his mask.

Rue stirred in her sleep as she felt the mattress sag under the Hawk's weight, and she kicked at the heavy covers that seemed to suffocate her.

"Hot," she muttered. "Too hot."

The Hawk smiled in the darkness as he heard her speak and he tenderly pulled back the heavy covers. He frowned, seeing her still constricted by the confining undergarments. Rue tossed and turned as the offending clothes pinched and pulled unnaturally. She was used to sleeping unfettered and it felt like she was being tied.

"Dinna do that," she admonished. "I don't like it."

"Dinna do what?" dared the Hawk, wondering if her sleeping mind would let him into the conversation.

"Dinna tie me up," she stated strongly, tugging at the lacings.

"I'll untie them for you?" he asked. He felt her nod in the darkness, but wanting to hear her voice he repeated. "Do you want me to untie you?"

"Don't tie me up. I won't run away. Please don't tie me up," begged Rue, her voice rising with panic.

"No, I'll not tie you up," soothed the Hawk, feeling for the laces in the darkness. He swore softly as he was unable to make head or tail of the mass of strings and hooks. He swung his long legs out of the bed and lit the lamp, which he placed on the bedside table.

"Please, I promise, I won't run away," cried Rue as she thrashed from side to side. The Hawk pulled on his trousers, not wanting to terrify her more if she awoke, and leaned over to try to fathom how to loosen and remove the torturous undergarments. Why did women have to bind themselves so? he raged, as his large hands found the tiny strings and fastenings aggravating.

He was so intent on his task he didn't see Rue's amber eyes fly open. He felt her body stiffen and looked to her face.

"You'll be more comfortable without all these lacings," he reassured her. Whoever had hurt, abused, and terrorized the girl had certainly done a very thorough job, he cursed inwardly as finally he loosed the tight ribbons.

"There," he soothed, wanting to remove the offending garments but sensing she would panic even more.

Rue stared up into the Hawk's face. It was the first time she had seen him without his mask. She reached up, mesmerized by his deep-set dark eyes, and touched the high bones of his prominent cheeks. He held his breath as the small brown hand softly felt his face. As her light fingers traced the firm line of his mouth, he gently kissed her little fingertips and watched the expression cross her poignant face. Feeling choked with tenderness, he stroked her soft cheek, running a large finger down her tiny straight nose and tracing her well-shaped mouth.

"All tied up in those silly wrappings," he teased huskily, and Rue pulled and tugged, trying to rid herself of the uncomfortable clothes. The Hawk undressed her for the second time and marveled at her perfection. She lay without embarrassment, staring up at him as he caressed every inch of her body with his eyes, not daring to touch for fear of breaking what seemed like a magical moment.

Rue didn't know what she felt. There was a magnetism about the dark eyes above her that seemed to burn and tingle every part of her body. She remembered another time waking up pressed against his hard muscles and she wished that she could curl up to him, but was afraid of what else might happen.

The Hawk gently covered her with a light sheet and blew out the lamp. He sighed deeply, the space between them seeming infinite, and he lay back with his head on his arms, staring at the beamed ceiling. Rue shivered, feeling cold despite the hot summer air. She, too, was conscious of how very large the bed was and how far away her husband seemed to be. She closed her eyes trying to sleep, but she was tense and rigid feeling his proximity. She couldn't sleep and sat up suddenly hugging her knees, unable to deal with all the confusion that churned her mind.

"Come here," said the Hawk gruffly, reaching strong arms for her and pulling her down so her head rested on his strong chest. He lay feeling her slowly relax as her frantic heartbeat slowed, and she slept with one slim arm flung possessively across him. He smiled in the darkness, feeling a bittersweetness as he acknowledged he desired her and wondered how long he would have the control to sleep just holding her.

Kestrel crept up on the deck and stood looking over the dark water toward the *Dolphin*, wondering what she would do when she found Rue.

"Kess, what are you doing now!" exclaimed Nick, reaching up and grabbing her as she prepared to dive over the steep side into the ocean below. His heart beat furiously as he assumed she was trying to hurt herself.

"Let me go!" hissed Kestrel, struggling against him, knowing she hadn't much energy left.

"It is much too late at night for a swim," snapped Nick, turning her to face him. His smoldering eyes raked her face, looking for some clue to her state of mind.

"I shall do as I want!" she spat.

"No, you shall not!"

"What is it to you?" questioned Kestrel.

"I'll not have you deliberately hurting yourself."

"Hurting myself? How?" probed Kestrel, confused.

"By diving from that height at this time of night."

"You couldn't get hurt diving from here unless you canna dive," returned Kestrel.

"What about the baby?" pursued Nick.

"What about the baby?"

"You could hurt it."

"What is that to you?" challenged Kestrel, hearing the wisdom of his words but wanting to hit out at him and hurt him.

"According to you it is my child."

"Aye, according to me it is your child," she taunted, furious at his choice of words. "Well, maybe it is and maybe it isn't. And maybe there's no baby at all!" she added, pulling herself out of his hands and jumping onto the high bulwark. She leaped out into the dark black space and welcomed the cool water that closed over her head as she plummeted down into the depths.

Nick strained his eyes, waiting for her head to break the surface.

"Kess?" he bellowed, fear clutching him when he could hear or see nothing. "Kess?" he roared before wrenching off his boots and leaping into the ocean after her.

Kestrel heard the splash as Nick's body hit the water but she dived under the surface like a seal and swam strongly under the water toward the *Dolphin*.

"Kess?"

The Hawk opened his eyes hearing Nick's anguished shouting. He gently disentangled himself from Rue and laid her back on the pillows before putting on his mask and quietly quitting the stateroom.

Rue watched him go and then sat bolt upright as she heard Nick call for her sister. She jumped out of bed and looked around for something to wear.

"What is it, MacKay?" called the Hawk as he stared down into the dark water toward the splashing.

"Kestrel went over the side," choked Nick, swallowing some water.

"How well does she swim?"

"I have no idea," returned Nick.

Kestrel grinned to herself as she listened to the exchange and quietly shinned up the anchor chain. The metal was rusty and painful to her hands and legs but she was determined to find Rue. She thankfully clambered aboard the *Dolphin* and made her way toward the lush apartment of the Hawk. She quickly ducked behind a longboat as she saw a pale shape approaching. She gasped as she recognized her sister wrapped in a sheet.

"Rue?" she hissed, grabbing her arm and pulling her down into her hiding place. "Are you all right?" she whispered, hugging her sister in her wet arms and bursting into tears. Rue put her cheek against her sister's and held her tight, feeling a hollow sorrow, knowing how much Kestrel loved Nick and the complications caused by his loss of memory.

"Come on," sniffed Kestrel, pulling herself together. "We have to go."

Rue frowned at her sister and hung back. "We have to go around this way so they won't see us."

Rue shook her head, not understanding what Kestrel meant to accomplish.

"Take off that white sheet or we'll be seen," and before Rue could object, her only covering was whisked off and tucked into the long-boat. "Now if we jumped together they'll only be one splash," directed Kestrel as Rue resignedly stood on the high carved side of the *Dolphin* holding her impetuous sister's hand.

The Hawk turned as he heard the splash and swiftly moved to the opposite side of his vessel, surveying the lightening of the dark water as millions of bubbles rose to the surface from Kestrel and Rue's descent.

"See anything?" panted Nick, dripping water. The Hawk pointed as two heads broke the surface.

"I don't think you've anything to worry about. They both swim like fish," remarked the masked man as he watched them keep to the shadow of the hull and swim toward the prow.

"They're swimming the long way around," remarked Nick. "If we just cross the deck and dive in we could be on the *Étoile* to meet them."

"What do you suppose this is all about?" sighed the Hawk as they strode across the deck. Nick shrugged and the two dark men dived over the side.

Rue and Kestrel swam wearily around the endless prow of the *Dolphin* and tiredly stared across the dark expanse of water toward the *Étoile*. Rue tapped Kestrel on the arm and pointed back to the *Dolphin* and the ladder that hung invitingly, but her sister stubbornly kicked her legs and struck out toward the other boat.

Kestrel's legs felt like lead and her arms even heavier. Rue sensed her fatigue and swam behind, taking care of her drained sister.

"We're there," sighed Kestrel as she hit the side of the *Étoile* hurting her already scraped hands. She pulled herself onto the first rung of the ladder and achingly swung herself up. Rue trod water watching her go before hauling her nakedness out of the water. Despite the warm night, both girls were shivering uncontrollably as they climbed the endless steep ladder.

Kestrel reached the top and straddled the bulwark waiting for Rue. As Rue's head topped the side the Hawk stepped out of the shadows and lifted her down. He frowned at her nakedness and she stared up at his dark masked face before turning to her sister, who battled Nick.

"Leave me be," hissed Kestrel, so tired she thought she would fall down but struggling against his hard grip. Rue tentatively touched Nick's arm and shook her head, silently begging him to be loving. But Nick gave her a long hard look before swinging Kestrel into his arms as though she were a bundle of wet clothes and striding away, his face set in stern lines.

Rue shivered and looked up into the dark shadowy face above her, wondering if her reception was going to be as cold and censuring as her sister's. The Hawk grew angrier at her shivering as she stood wet and naked.

"Go and find some clothes!" he barked and she whirled away into the darkness as he stood regretting his harsh tone.

Rue knocked on the door of the cabin she shared with Kestrel and Nick stormed out. Rue poked her head in and watched her sister standing sorrowfully in her wet clothes. She ran to her and they hugged each other.

"What are we going to do?" asked Kestrel listlessly. "You're married to a pirate whose name you don't even know. Have you seen his face?" Rue nodded. "Is he handsome?" Rue nodded. "As handsome as Nick?" And Rue frowned at the question. There was something very similar about both men, she realized. They were of the same height and breadth, the same hair color and eyes, the same bony, chiseled faces.

"What is it?" queried Kestrel, stripping off her wet clothes. Rue absently toweled her hair and her chilled body. "Rue? What is it?" demanded Kestrel. Rue shook her head and shrugged to indicate there was nothing wrong.

"We have to do something. We have to get away. Go home to Angus and Meron. I won't let you be taken away from me on a pirate ship and I won't go anywhere with a man who doesn't want to touch me or sleep with me!" pronounced Kestrel hotly and Rue smiled sheepishly. It was as if everything was the wrong way around. Her hot-blooded, sexual sister married to a man who didn't want to touch her, and she married to hot-blooded man and she didn't want to be touched. Or did she? Rue frowned in wonder, knowing the pleasurable tingling she felt as her cheek rested on his strong chest and her leg curled around his. She rubbed her face tiredly and sighed before rummaging through her trunk to find some comfortable clothing. She clutched a shirt and sat on the bunk feeling confused and fatigued.

There was a sharp rap at the door that jarred through Rue's spine and she turned startled eyes toward the sound. The knock was repeated and the door opened. The Hawk stared at the two girls who sat on the wide bunk. He was silently surveyed by a pair of amber and a pair of green sad eyes.

"You look like two drowned rats," he remarked, sucking in his lean cheeks as he appreciated their naked beauty. He lounged in the doorway sipping a mug of rum, watching Kestrel's golden proportions. She was every shade of gold imaginable from the top of her streaked head to the bottom of her tan toes, he observed as if he were looking at a rare painting. He turned his eyes to Rue's less flamboyant gracefulness and smiled wryly at the sultry lights that glowed in her nearly blue-black hair and amber eyes that glittered. Beneath her sunbrowned skin a warm pink radiated, making her seem a sexually passionate woman. He drained his mug as he felt a tightening in his groin and admitted he wanted his wife in every way.

"I shall send a boat for you and your possessions tomorrow," he said tersely before quitting the cabin and shutting the door firmly behind him.

The sound of the door shuddered through Rue as her stricken eyes filled with tears.

"We have to have a plan," worried Kestrel, staring out of the porthole toward the *Dolphin*. "Maybe we can get Jacques to turn the boat around so we can go home to Meron," she said excitedly, trying

THE DAUGHTERS OF CAMERON 251

to get her morose sister to smile as she quickly pulled on trews and slipped into a shirt. "Quick, get dressed," she urged Rue, who sat twisting her clothing in her lap as waves of dejection washed in, bowing her spirit, as she admitted she loved the tall masked pirate.

CHAPTER TWENTY-FIVE

Nick lay on his narrow bunk trying to sleep as a series of images flashed through his mind. Images of Kestrel riding a horse across a sloping green meadow; dressed in a beaded Indian dress; swimming in a clear lake surrounded by lush green fir trees. He sat up with an exclamation as he remembered making love on a carpet of soft pine needles by the crystal-clear lake. Piece by piece the images merged and he remembered clearly.

"Pirates!" he gasped as the sea battle exploded into his mind and he swung his long legs over the side of the bed and started to get dressed. Where was Kestrel? He stared around, seeing none of her clothing. It wasn't even the same cabin, he realized as he noted the extremely narrow bunk. He frowned as he examined his head for injury to find his hair still damp and sticky with seawater.

Kestrel tenderly covered Rue with a thin muslin sheet and patted the large hound that cuddled close to her sleeping mistress before leaving the cabin in search of either Pierre or Jacques. She listened outside the one-eyed man's room for a minute, and hearing the unmistakable sounds of rollicking lust, decided against knocking and made her way up to the bridge. Finding no sign of Jacques there she made her way to his cabin.

"Go away! There is no one at 'ome!" shouted the old captain, putting a pillow over his head at the urgent knocking. "*Vas-t'en!*" he roared as the noise persisted, and the door was thrust open and Kestrel rushed in.

"Jacques, get up. We have to get away before the Hawk takes Rue away," she chattered, pulling the pillow from his head.

"I am so sorry, but I had to marry *la petite* to that pirate," mourned

Jacques. "He would have taken her away anyway," he babbled drunkenly, having imbibed a great deal to drown his guilt.

"Jacques, sit up and listen to me. It's very important," urged Kestrel, and with a groan the Frenchman sat up rubbing his watery eyes. "Rue is on the *Étoile*," she informed him slowly, catching a whiff of Jacques's brandy breath.

"*Non, non,* Rue, she is with the 'Awk," contradicted the captain.

"No, she swam back. She's in my cabin. That's why we must get away," insisted Kestrel, trying to keep patient. "Pull up the anchor or do whatever you have to do so we can get away and go back to Meron."

"*Ce n'est pas possible.* We 'ave not enough food and water," lamented Jacques, closing his eyes as his cabin spun alarmingly.

"No, you mustn't go to sleep again!" shouted Kestrel.

"Again? Again? I have not had sleep yet this night," replied Jacques indignantly. "I worry too much about *la petite* and what your *oncle* Meron do to me when he hears of all this."

"Then get us away from here. Pull up the sails and get us to our father and brothers in Scotland," begged Kestrel.

There was another furious knocking at the door.

"What is this? A party? I am a captain. Where is my respect? It is the middle of the night," groaned Jacques, lying back on his pillow.

"Who is it?" yelled Kestrel and the door was violently opened.

"Kess, thank God you're safe," sighed Nick, pulling her into his arms oblivious to her look of total amazement. Kestrel put her hands flat on his broad chest and pushed herself backward so she could see his face.

"Who did that?" asked Nick with a dangerous note in his voice as he softly touched the bruise on her scowling, beautiful face. "The pirates?"

"You!" snapped Kestrel.

"Me?"

"Nick, tell your wife why we cannot just pull up the anchor and sail away," pleaded Jacques, trying desperately to sober up. Kestrel stood with her hands on her hips glaring at Nick whose face was creased with bewilderment.

"What is going on? Why is Kestrel in here? Why aren't we sharing a cabin?" questioned Nick. "I just came from our cabin and it's full of Rue's clothes and she's asleep there with her dog."

"You remember?" whispered Kestrel, her face lighting up like a beacon. "You remember?" she rejoiced, reaching up and holding his craggy face between her slim brown hands. "Oh, Nick, you remember," she sighed, wrapping her arms about his hard muscular body and burying her nose into his chest.

"How long was I unconscious?" puzzled Nick with great suspicion, not able to understand her elation.

"Unconscious?" frowned Kestrel. "When?"

"You lost your memory," supplied Jacques.

"You don't remember that you lost your memory?" intoned Kestrel.

"I lost my memory?" repeated Nick, astounded. "For how long?"

"More than five weeks, my friend," replied the old sea captain. Nick shook his head in disbelief.

"Who am I?" challenged Kestrel belligerently.

"Kestrel Sinclair MacKay, my wife," he answered in a daze, pulling her to him and resting his cheek on her golden head.

"What is the last thing you remember?" murmured Kestrel.

"The battle with the pirates. I was hit," he recalled. "What happened? I've been all over the ship looking for you and there's no sign of any pirates."

"Look out there," said Kestrel, pointing at the porthole.

"And there's none on board?" snorted Nick with disbelief after staring across the dark sea at the *Dolphin*.

"*He* made a deal with the pirate captain," accused Kestrel, turning angrily on Jacques, who sat with his mouth agape, surprised at the sudden attack. "The Hawk wanted Rue. That's why we have to get away. He's coming for her in the morning."

"Why?" asked Nick, sitting on the end of Jacques's bunk and rubbing his aching head.

"Don't you remember anything of the last weeks?" cried Kestrel with frustration. Nick shook his head slowly as strange bizarre images zoomed in and receded. Rue and Kestrel dressed in black at a formal dinner. A ceremony with a Bible.

"Did someone die?" he asked.

Kestrel and Jacques shook their heads in unison.

"Not yet," added Kestrel ominously. "Nick, you promised Meron that you'd take care of both Rue and me, so you have to make Jacques take us away before the Hawk takes Rue," she pleaded before bursting into tears. "You can't let that masked monster take my sister," she sobbed, totally drained by the long eventful night.

"Is there danger of that?" probed Nick.

Jacques nodded and pursed his thin pleated lips as he wondered whether to volunteer information about the two weddings he had performed earlier that evening. He decided not to complicate matters and kept silent.

"You don't even remember about our baby?" wept Kestrel.

"Baby?" whispered Nick, stunned. "What baby?"

Kestrel couldn't hold back. Everything was just too much for her. "My sister is going to be taken away by pirates and I'll never, ever see her again, and if you don't do something soon it will be too late, and you don't even remember about our baby," she wailed.

"He remembers you," offered Jacques, trying to help the confused young doctor.

"Kess, let me tuck you into bed. Jacques and I will deal with the pirates," suggested Nick, softly running his hands over Kestrel's flat belly.

"No!" screamed Kestrel. "I have a plan," she said after a big sniff and a deep breath as she tried to control herself.

"Go ahead," encouraged Nick, not wanting to upset her any further.

"Right now the Hawk trusts that we won't do anything. So why don't we blow a hole in his side. The *Dolphin* is in easy range of the cannons," she stated. "But we maun do it now," she insisted impatiently.

"What do you think, Jacques?" asked Nick.

Jacques shrugged unhappily as he chewed the inside of his cheek.

"I 'ave little honor left. I steal the man's cargo and that is why we are in thees grande mess. I will not let 'im take the small silent one," he sighed, taking comfort from the knowledge of the *Dolphin*'s seaworthy longboats and the close proximity to the Spanish coast.

Rue tossed fitfully, dreaming of the Hawk. She reached across the bunk trying to connect to his warm strength, but there was just an emptiness. She sat up suddenly as a loud explosion shook the boat and orange and red lights flashed through the darkness from outside. She sniffed, smelling the acrid stench of sulfur as another explosion rocked the vessel and she heard the harsh grating of the anchor being raised. She leaped out of bed and rushed to the porthole. A strange cry burst from her mouth as she gazed in horror at the *Dolphin*, the reflection of the flames touching the tips of the waves as the *Étoile* pulled away from the burning ship.

Rue rushed up onto the deck, mewing strange sobs and cries, followed by the black hound. She stood clutching the high bulwark as the burning ship got smaller and smaller until she could not see it anymore. Sobbing wildly, she shinned up a rope to the rigging, climbing as high as she could, her streaming eyes pinned to the burning vessel until it looked like a bright star on the horizon before disappearing. She remained clinging to the spar as the sky lightened and the sun shone, clearing the sea mist. On the deck below Shame sat with her mournful eyes pinned to the hunched figure of her young mistress. She whined her concern before resting a doleful head on her large paws.

Kestrel slept until noon wrapped in Nick's strong arms. She awoke slowly and sighed with satisfaction as she felt lulled by the movement of the ship as it sped through the deep waters. She turned and pressed her breasts against his hard chest and curled one leg between his and breathed deeply of his male fragrance. She made little murmurs of pleasure as she realized how much she had missed the safe comfort of sleeping together. She reveled in the close contact with his long firm body. They had climbed into bed too exhausted to do anything more than fall asleep in each other's arms, their bodies aching from pulling up sails and readying the vessel for a swift getaway after the surprise attack. Much of the work had been done by the three of them, as Jacques felt caution and haste were the best policy, not wanting the watches on the *Dolphin* to become suspicious of any increased activity.

Kestrel rubbed her face in the soft warmth under Nick's chin and wickedly nibbled his velvety earlobe, eager to make up for lost time as her nipples stood erect and tingling, every nerve ending in her body open and waiting. Nick groaned and enfolded her tightly in his arms, trying to restrict her sensual movements.

"Sleep," he ordered, burying his nose in her fresh-smelling hair. Kestrel grinned impishly as she felt his maleness rise and press against her. She wiggled against him, exciting him and herself further until he hungrily kissed her parted lips. Kestrel writhed impatiently as his burning kisses descended to her straining breasts.

"Um," he murmured with appreciation, kissing her hard nipples as his large hands cupped the fullness. "They've grown!" and he grinned lovingly as he remembered the baby. His mouth dropped lower to her still-firm, flat belly. He splayed his hands across her stomach and marveled that his seed grew within the span of his hands.

"Oh, my darling," he sighed as his lips descended lower. Bright, hot sunlight flooded the cabin and dappled the naked caressing lovers as they explored each other slowly, savoring every inch that had been withheld for so long.

"Now, Nick, now," begged Kestrel huskily, and he sheathed himself into the welcoming heat of her, delighting in her uninhibited sexuality as she sighed deeply and moved in unison with his slow strong movements. There was almost a reverence in their first gentle rhythm as they each wanted to hold onto the excitement but were unable to stop the building momentum as they raced faster and faster, their feelings intensifying to incredible proportions as they crested together.

Kestrel held Nick tightly, trying to submerge him even deeper into the whole of her as she felt the deep, wondrous throbbing fade, leaving almost an aching void. She sighed and Nick stared into her passionate green eyes.

"What is it, my love?" he whispered, stroking a tendril of golden hair that curled across her forehead and kissing the tip of her small nose.

"I just didn't ever want it to stop."

Nick grinned engagingly and rolled over on his side, taking her with him as his man-root stayed, nestling its vulnerability within her. He closed his eyes.

"Now sleep," he murmured and Kestrel obediently closed her eyes. "I am always pleasantly surprised when you obey," he added roguishly.

"Love, honor, and obey," muttered Kestrel wickedly.

"What's that?" frowned Nick.

"What you promised me," returned Kestrel, smiling sweetly into his surprised, dark eyes.

"When?"

"When Jacques married us with that black book."

"When?"

"Yesterday evening just before you got your memory back," yawned Kestrel, closing her eyes and settling herself against him for sleep. "Oh," she mourned as she felt him slip out of her.

"Where?" probed Nick, as disturbing pictures of Rue and Kestrel dressed in black flashed through his mind. They were all standing in a red and gold room hung with expensive, luxurious hangings. Three women in black, the Sinclair sisters with Miss Gladys Mackintosh, stood holding delicate wineglasses as liveried servants hovered unobtrusively.

"Shush, I'm sleeping," teased Kestrel, giving a snore and a

chuckle. Nick stared at the wall blindly as he tried to hold onto the elusive images that flashed through his mind. It was as though he looked down a long banquet table covered with silver platters into Rue's wide haunting stare as she sat next to a tall dark masked man.

"Custard!" giggled Kestrel, peeking at his puzzled face.

Pierre shaded his one eye and stared up at Rue, silhouetted against the burning sky as she perched in the rigging. He frowned, knowing something was very wrong by the sadness of her stance. Below, her young hound stared up dejectedly at her young mistress, who hunched like a wounded bird.

"Pierre? Pierre?" screeched Gladys, scurrying on board and looking from side to side in a very bewildered manner.

" 'Allo, my petite Mees Jackette," he boomed lovingly.

" 'Ere, where's the 'Awk?" she yelled, looking north, south, east, and west and not seeing a sign of the *Dolphin*.

"You drink vairee much, my little cabbage, at the marriage, *n'est-ce pas*?" he laughed as she hiked up her voluminous black shiny skirt and mounted the steps to the bridge.

"Wotchit!" she warned, not liking to be thought of as a lush. "I know me limits," she added defensively as Pierre chuckled and affectionately chucked her under her double chins.

"You sleep vairee well, my little cabbage. You no hear the beeg boom-boom?" he laughed.

"What big bombom?" she asked suspiciously, thinking he was making fun of her.

"Of the grande sea battle? *Quand* the *Étoile*, she beat the 'Awk's *Dolphin*?" exaggerated the one-eyed man as he stared fondly at his woman.

"What big battle?" yelled Gladys, exasperated. "And where's the bloody 'Awk?" Pierre clucked and shook his head before blowing out of his slack lips with disapproval.

"It is night. I 'old my little cabbage vairee tight, *comme ça*," he stated dramatically, illustrating by taking Miss Mackintosh in his arms. "*Maintenant*, a beeg boom and I jump out of the bed and I leave my little Jackette and she not care. She not know that I have gone to war?"

"Stop your blarney and tell me what 'appened to the 'Awk," bawled Gladys.

"At the bottom of the sea. The *Étoile*, she fire her cannons *est* boom-boom the *Dolphin*, she go down," recounted Pierre unhappily, unable to keep up his bantering.

"The 'Awk's at the bottom of the sea?" she repeated, totally stunned.

"*Oui*," answered Pierre shortly, turning away from her.

"Don't you wee-wee me!" screamed Gladys, attacking him violently. "My little black lamb was on that boat, and you sunk 'er, too!"

"*Non, non*," exclaimed Pierre, pointing up to the rigging and Gladys shaded her eyes against the sun's glare and looked up at the hunched girl.

Rue stared at the misty line that broke the monotonous limitless expanse, not realizing or caring that she looked upon land for the first time in nearly two months. She was numb and beyond tears. Nothing seemed to matter or penetrate the layer she was wrapped in, not even the mournful howling of her dog Shame. All that existed was a gray futility. A hollow nothingness. She sat hunched and unseeing all day, unaware of the worried eyes that stared up at her.

"Nick, she isn't all right. I have to go and talk to her," insisted Kestrel.

"Leave her alone. Everyone needs their solitude," replied Nick. "I don't want you risking your life. You are with child, my darling," he added, holding her close. Kestrel submitted to his embrace for a few seconds before pushing away from him. "I need some solitude," she said and hurried to the other end of the deck.

Nick swore furiously as he saw Kestrel's lithe figure agilely shinning up the ropes to the network of cobwebs against the angry red sky. He clenched his fists, controlling the temper that raged, knowing if he vented his spleen he could unbalance his wife. He pinned his dark smoking eyes to her slight shape as he felt fear for her and their unborn child.

Kestrel edged along the spar boom toward her sister, who was crouched motionless.

"Rue?" she hailed as she settled herself near, but the dark girl didn't respond. She frowned, noticing the bruiselike smudges beneath the amber eyes. "Rue?" But there was still no response. She didn't know what to do or what to say as her sister's depression bowed her down, even though she was out of the humidity and up in the bracing wind that bellied out the straining sails.

"Rue, look. It's land!" she exclaimed, pointing to the hazy line. "It's Spain! We're nearly home to Father and Lynx and Rowan.

Jacques is going to take us all the way to Scotland," she cajoled, but Rue's blank stare did not change and fear clutched deep in Kestrel's belly. "Oh, Rue, everything's all right now. Nick remembers. He knows who I am and he loves me. He remembers, Rue, he really remembers."

Rue stared dispassionately at her sister, who tried to beam happily. Kestrel lost her attempt at a sunny smile as she looked into Rue's hollow, haunted eyes, seeing deep sorrow. "Oh, Rue, what is it?" she gasped, but her sister looked away.

"Rue? Kestrel? 'Tis nearly dark! Come down!" ordered Nick, cupping his hands around his mouth to project his voice. Kestrel pretended not to hear as she sat side by side with her sister, wondering how to break through the strange silence.

"Kestrel? Rue? Down now!" roared Nick, his temper igniting as it seemed Kestrel waved back gaily.

"Rue, it's time for supper. We have to go down," she said softly, and to her utter surprise Rue rose stiffly and like a zombi started to descend. Kestrel was terrified as her usually graceful sister teetered and tottered.

"Oh, my sainted aunt!" screamed Gladys. "She's going to fall!" And she clutched Pierre's chest hairs painfully.

"Something is vairee wrong," muttered Pierre, extricating his beloved's hand as he held his breath and they watched the perilous descent.

Jacques and Nick gasped as Rue teetered precariously and was grabbed by Kestrel, who nearly lost her balance, too.

"I ain't going to look. Tell me what 'appens," sobbed Miss Mackintosh, unable to tear her eyes away from the heart-stopping scene.

"Dinna move! Stay as you are!" commanded Nick as he started to shin up the hanging ropes toward the two girls. Rue stared down, surprised at the deep voice. Her face was confused as she saw Nick climbing toward her. She looked around wildly, not understanding where she was.

"It's all right, Rue, I'm here," soothed Kestrel, seeing her sister's confusion. "Everything'll be all right now. We sunk the *Dolphin* and that masked mucker'll not bother you again. He's at the bottom of the sea!" she comforted.

A low animal moan of pain burst from Rue's throat and she shook her head from side to side.

"It's true, he's gone," reassured Kestrel, not understanding the cause of Rue's distress. "He's dead. He canna hurt you more."

Rue screamed a raw chilling expression of pain and flung herself away from her sister. The dog stopped howling and there was a sharp intake of breath from all who saw before the silence was broken by the splash of Rue's body hitting the water as it narrowly missed smashing into the side of the ship. Kestrel stood frozen as realization dug in and the black hound below raced back and forth barking wildly.

Nick dived into the foaming dark sea and the people aboard watched with bated breath as he swam toward the dark head that bobbed then sank below the surface of the blood-red water as the sunset bled across the world.

"Oh, no, no," sobbed Kestrel as she realized her sister had loved the masked man. She wiped the tears away from her brimming eyes as she saw Nick dive below the surface trying to find Rue. For a moment there was no sign of life in the molten water that had closed over the dark heads, not leaving a clue that they had been there. "Oh, no!" she screamed, thinking she had lost both husband and sister.

"He has her," rejoiced Jacques as Nick's head burst through the waves as he appeared with the limp shape of Rue and swam strongly back to the *Étoile* with his precious burden.

"What have I done?" wept Kestrel, descending clumsily, her eyes blinded by the pouring tears.

"Do something, you big ox!" screeched Gladys, pulling at Pierre's clothing.

"*Oui*, little cabbage," he soothed, shoving her roughly aside and hurrying to help bring Nick and Rue aboard, as Jacques tried to calm the frenzied hound. From the bowels of the vessel came the high-pitched scream of the horse, Sin, adding to the mass of noisy confusion.

CHAPTER TWENTY-SIX

"I want to see my sister," insisted Kestrel.

"No, Kess, Miss Mackintosh is with her. She's asleep," Nick said as he steered her toward the galley.

"I'm not hungry," protested Kestrel, her eyes filling with tears. "Oh, I don't know what's the matter with me," she sniffed, angrily brushing them away but the tears welled again.

"You are having a baby. It turns even the hardest female into a weeping willow," teased Nick gently. "That's why you should eat so you'll not deprive our child of food."

"She loved him, Nick," sobbed Kestrel, flinging herself onto his chest. "Rue loved him and it's my fault that he's dead!"

"He is not dead. They had longboats and were not far from the Spanish coast," soothed Nick.

"How is Rue really?" she asked, trying to pull herself together.

"Exhausted, that's all. It seems she climbed the rigging before daybreak."

"It's not just that. It's scary, she's like she was when Meron brought her back from the mission," argued Kestrel, her tears starting again.

"It is too soon to say that," soothed Nick.

"I should be dead! First I shoot my own sister and now I kill her lover! How can you love such a person," she ranted and Nick caught her as she stood to rush out.

"Stop!" he warned sharply. "That's enough, Kess, or you'll be out of control and no help to anyone."

Kestrel's eyes widened at his stern tones.

"I love you, Kestrel, no matter what you've done and what you'll do," he stated.

"I dinna blame you for being angry with me," she said in a small voice.

"I'm not angry, Kess, but I will be if you don't eat," he threatened softly. Kestrel obediently put a morsel in her mouth and tried to chew.

"I canna," she cried, dropping the fork with a clunk onto the tin plate as the food got stuck in her throat. "I want to sleep." Nick nodded, knowing she was emotionally and physically drained. He gave her a hug and helped her out of the galley.

"Please let me see Rue?" she begged as they walked along the narrow corridor that rocked from side to side as the vessel rode over the waves.

"Aye, but just a look," he agreed. " 'Tis best she sleep as much as she can." Quietly they let themselves into the cabin and stared down at the dark girl who was sound asleep, curled around her large hound. Shame lifted a sleek head and thumped his heavy tail in welcome.

"It ain't 'ealthy 'aving 'ounds in bedrooms," whispered Gladys hoarsely. "But the poor little motherless thing looked so lonely. She don't look more'n a baby, does she?"

Nick nodded, feeling the same as he looked down at the curled, vulnerable child.

" 'Ow old is she, anyways?"

"She was seventeen on August the sixteenth. I even forgot her birthday," cried Kestrel.

"Shush," hissed Nick as Rue tossed in her sleep. He ushered Kestrel out as once more tears streamed down her face, and he herded her to their cabin where he tenderly undressed her.

"I never thought there would be a day I didn't want to make love," wailed Kestrel dismally.

"We don't always have to make love," reassured Nick.

"Will you hold me until I fall asleep?"

"Of course," growled Nick, pulling her into his arms and marveling at how much she had changed in the few months since he had met her. "I remember not so long ago when you'd steal a horse and go galloping off when you felt bad about something."

"We're on a ship in the middle of the ocean. I canna go galloping off even though I want to," replied Kestrel.,

"You mean you still would?" laughed Nick.

"I dinna ken," returned Kestrel truthfully. "I wanted to before when you didn't know who I was and I broke my whatever-you-call-it—"

"When you broke what?" exclaimed Nick, interrupting her.

"This," declared Kestrel, sitting up and pointing to her collarbone. Nick frowned with concern as he traced the bone, feeling the calcification of the mend.

"How? When?"

"When I got pulled off the rigging by one of the pirates," she recounted. "About four or so weeks ago."

"You heal quickly," breathed Nick as his experienced fingers examined her clavicle. "But no more climbing about like a monkey. I'll not have you and the bairn's life risked. How many weeks pregnant are you?"

"What do you mean?" frowned Kestrel.

"Did I not tell you that you were pregnant?" asked Nick.

"No, I told you," returned Kestrel. "Angus told me if I dinna bleed for two months."

"So it has been two months?"

"Over three now. Why?" she puzzled.

"You last bled when?" questioned Nick.

"End of April or beginning of May. Why?" she spat belligerently. "So you can say it's not your baby and make it a bastard?"

"Whoa there, Kess. What is all this?"

Kestrel glowered at him, hiding her terror under a mutinous expression.

"And you married me in name only!" she yelled.

"Kestrel, stop it," Nick ordered tersely. "Now what is all this?"

Kestrel pursed her lips and didn't answer.

"Is it to do with things that happened before I regained my memory?"

She nodded silently.

"Do you honestly think I could marry you in name only?" he laughed incredulously. "Marry you and not make love with you, my darling?" he insisted, forcing her chin up so she stared into his eyes. "You have a lot to learn about me, my dear," he said huskily, kissing her mutinous mouth.

Kestrel tried to submerge herself in his demanding kiss and block the doubts and fears that tore into her mind. Nick felt her tension and wrapped her in his arms, trying to soothe her to sleep as he cursed his tongue that seemed to have been very cruel. When Kestrel was more secure and better rested, he vowed, he would find out more about what went on during the time he was without his memory.

"Nick, are you sure Rue'll be all right? What if she isn't? Maybe we should sail back and look for the Hawk," worried Kestrel.

"I think we should get to Scotland as soon as possible."

"But Rue loved the man, Nick," protested the distraught girl.

"She canna talk. You are assuming that she loved him."

"She loved him," insisted Kestrel.

"Even if she loved him, I doubt your father would thank me for allowing his daughter to have such an alliance," disagreed Nick gently.

"But if she truly loves him and he's alive we should find him."

"If he truly loves her, he'll find her," improvised Nick.

"Do you really think so?"

"If I lost you I'd search to the ends of the earth," comforted the young doctor, praying Kestrel would soon relax. She was like a highly strung racehorse, he thought, spirited and so easily upset.

"Will your family like me?" asked Kestrel after a long pause as fear of the unknown flooded in.

"My grandfather will adore you, and I shall be very jealous," laughed Nick. "He's a rogue, is Lachlan McCulloch. A seventy-year-old rake. He'll most likely even put you to the blush with his mischief."

"And your older brother?"

"Tarquin? He's a difficult man to describe. You'll have to make your own mind up about him," evaded Nick.

"Don't you like him?" asked Kestrel, her keen senses knowing Nick was avoiding an issue.

"I love him. But he's a private person. Intimidates people who don't really know him," he struggled to explain.

"Oh?" frowned Kestrel, not liking the sound of Tarquin MacKay. "How long before we get to Scotland?" she added, apprehensive about landing in the strange country, even though by blood she was a Scot.

"Probably a week at the most," murmured Nick, idly running his large hands down her warm silky back and caressing the firm curves of her buttocks.

"Where will we live?" asked Kestrel as her fingers lazily felt the hard ridges of muscles across his broad back.

"Shh, enough questions," murmured Nick, capturing her soft lips and muffling her halfhearted protest.

Rue opened her eyes and focused on her dog, whose brown eyes stared sadly at her. She reached out her hand and stroked the black glossy coat. Shame stretched, wiggled closer, and licked her mistress's cheek. Rue buried her face in the hound's warm neck and hugged her as she felt the hollow sorrow well. The Hawk was dead. Her love was gone before she could understand and savor the emotion. Before she could share and dare to show him how she felt.

The numbness had faded and in its place was raw pain. Rue closed her eyes against the sharp agony and fought to stay calm as shuddering sobs tore in. She breathed deeply and angrily threw back the thin sheet that covered her. A croaking snore surprised her, and she turned to see Miss Mackintosh sprawled ungracefully on a mattress, her plump legs outstretched and her rouged mouth open wide. Rue smiled sadly as she noted the piece of velvet clutched like a security blanket in one dimpled red-nailed hand. Everyone was so vulnerable, she mused, and her face hardened as she turned to dress herself in fringed buckskin vest and trews.

Quietly Rue and Shame left the cabin, needing to be above deck in the fresh air. She threw her head back and stretched in the brisk morning breeze as Shame leaped and gamboled, trying to get her to play. Jacques watched the boisterous pup with her dark young mistress from the bridge and sighed fondly with relief at her proud stance. Leaving the wheel to a seaman, he swung his heavy body down, wanting to be near the two spirited young things.

"*Bonjour,* Mam'selle Rue. Your 'orse, he missed you very much. So I give him many attentions so 'e is 'ealthy and nearly 'appy," he reassured her as they walked to the hold together. "*Voilà!*" he sang out, extending his arms wide to indicate the stallion, who snorted and tossed his head up and down as he whinnied a welcome. Rue laughed and patted his nose and he stamped and pawed the floor with one hoof. She leaned her face against his firm girth, wishing the interminable voyage were over so she might leap onto his high back and race out the sorrow and pent-up frustrations that boiled within her. *Soon, my noble Sin,* she thought, trying to silently transmit her hopes to the animal. *Soon we will gallop across wild grasslands in sun and in rain, cle.. ng ourselves.*

Jacques w..ed her for several minutes before quietly leaving, feeling he was somehow intruding. Rue pulled herself onto Sin's back and sat running her fingers through his silky mane. *I will never be cowering and vulnerable again,* she promised herself. *Never, to no one,* she vowed. Not even to her younger sister Kestrel. She would be like her Uncle Meron, free, independent, and alone except for his pinto. The rhythmic motion of the ship brought her to the present and she realized that there would be no familiar wilderness. Soon the ship would stop, and she would find herself in a strange country. She frowned, remembering all the stories her parents had told her that spiraled back to before her first memory. The fact that she was a Scot had been impressed on her since birth, and yet she was going to her native land of Scotland and she was afraid.

Rue tried to picture her father whom she hadn't seen for more than six years. Tall and straight, with a leonine head of hair and eyes like hers. Suddenly the fervent oath made a few minutes before was broken as nostalgia rushed in and she longed for her father's deep voice and strong arms. His warm whiskey laugh reverberated through her and she shuddered. She was going home to her father and brothers, she rejoiced, dismounting from Sin's high back. Deep in thought she walked up to the galley, ignoring the spirited dog that tried to catch the swinging fringes on her clothes.

Rue sat absently eating the dry unappetizing food as she thought ahead to Scotland.

"Rue!" rejoiced Kestrel, entering the galley and throwing her arms around her sister. "You are all right, I'm so glad," she added, her happy expression fading to a frown as her sister sat stiffly tolerating her embrace. "Are you angry with me?" Rue shook her head and turned away. She picked up her unfinished breakfast and put it on the floor for her hound. Nick watched the exchange, relieved that Rue was up and about and seeming no worse for her trauma. There was something very different about his young sister-in-law, he realized. Instead of the poignant, wide-eyed vulnerability that made her look like a startled deer, he saw an alert, hard person.

"Good morning, Rue," he said as the dark girl caught his curious stare and turned a cynical face to him. She nodded curtly, whistled for Shame, and left. Kestrel watched her go, frowning at the swinging door for several minutes as she contemplated the elusive change. She turned a very puzzled face to Nick.

"Breakfast is not very inspiring this morning," he said lightly, not wanting any disturbing discussions so early in the day. "But luncheon will be better. We should be getting to Île d'Oléron within the hour according to Pierre."

"Oléron?" exclaimed Kestrel, all thought of Rue's strange behavior gone.

"Île d'Oléron," corrected Nick, wondering at Kestrel's astonishment.

"My mother and Meron were born at a place called Oléron Sainte-Marie! Is it the same place?"

"I don't know. Why don't we look at a map after breakfast," replied Nick, wishing she would eat as she had not eaten dinner the night before. "I somehow assumed that they were both born in Scotland."

"No, it was something called a nunnery."

"A nunnery? Tell me what else you know of your mother and her twin."

"My grandmother's name was Dolores MacLeod but she died just after they were born," replied Kestrel.

"And your grandfather?"

"I once heard his name mentioned but when I asked my mother she was so angry I hid in the forest for days," recounted Kestrel, shivering at the memory.

"What was his name?" probed Nick.

"You'll not get angry, too?" she returned fearfully.

"Why will I be angry?"

"Why was my mother?"

"Did you ever ask Meron?"

"That was even worse. He didn't yell, but he didn't answer. His face went like a stone and he disappeared for months," she replied, her face clouding once more. Nick's curiosity was piqued as he recalled Meron's evasiveness about the same subject.

"I think everyone has a right to know about their forebears."

"What's a forebear?"

"An ancestor, relative, your grandfather," explained Nick.

"The name was Charles Stuart," whispered Kestrel, unsure of his reaction.

"Charles Stuart," repeated Nick, swallowing hard as he thought it couldn't possibly be the pretender to the Scottish throne, Charles Edward Stuart.

"What's a nunnery?" asked Kestrel, not liking the long silence and intense look on Nick's face and wishing to change the subject.

"A place where nuns are. It's a religious retreat," explained Nick absently, his mind thinking of Bonny Prince Charlie.

"Nuns? What are nuns?"

"Women who devote their lives to their religious beliefs."

"Just women?"

"Just women," laughed Nick. "They forsake the world and take a vow of chastity."

"What has Chastity to do with them?" queried Kestrel, totally confused as she thought of the large painted woman.

"Chastity means abstinence from lovemaking."

"Nick, we met Chastity and I don't think she abstains from lovemaking," disagreed Kestrel.

"Hers is a very ironic name for a woman in her profession. The word *chastity* means not making love ever. Not ever," said Nick with a broad grin on his face as he anticipated Kestrel's reaction.

"Never, *ever*!"

"Never, ever, my lusty wench," he repeated fondly.

"I shall never be a nun!" stated Kestrel.

Rue watched the *Étoile* carefully glide into the small harbor at the northern tip of the small fertile island of Oléron. The kittiwake gulls mewed and wheeled a welcome and Shame, excited by the smell of land, leaped up trying to catch one of the birds. Rue stood at the rail rocking her body with excitement as she longed to put her feet on firm soil after the weeks at sea. She debated diving over the side, but Shame whined eagerly, needing to run free as much as she, so Rue waited as the seamen busily pulled down the heavy sails and coiled thick ropes as the anchor was slowly dropped, the rusty chain creaking on the metal wheel.

Nick and Kestrel stood together watching Rue as the *Étoile* dropped anchor, ready to take on supplies.

"We cast off for Scotland at noon with the tide," shouted Nick as the dark girl turned to look at them. Rue nodded as she wondered how she was going to get her dog down the steep sides of the vessel into the waiting rowboat. She bent and picked up the large squirming dog and placed her on the wide bulwark. Before Nick could understand what she meant to do, Rue dived gracefully into the sea. Shame whined and then leaped into the air after her mistress.

"Not again!" screamed Gladys, her heavily painted lips agape as she trotted across the deck dressed in a very elaborate black dress complete with black veil and parasol. "Pierre? Pierre?"

"She is fine," comforted Nick as he watched Rue swim strongly toward the harbor followed by her faithful dog.

"She ain't ever going to end up a lady be'aving like that," sighed Miss Mackintosh, frowning with horror down the steep ladder to the small rowboats that waited. "Not again! You know I ain't ever goin' ter set foot on a boat again. It ain't natural," she carped as she hiked up her many layers of skirts and clambered gracelessly over the side to the waiting dinghy.

"No move so much, my petite cabbage," cautioned Pierre as

Gladys shifted her considerable weight and rocked the boat as Kestrel lithely descended the long ladder and jumped into the light craft.

"Wotchit!" shrieked Gladys Mackintosh, hanging onto Pierre for dear life. "What on earth are you wearing?" she added indignantly, her eyes popping at Kestrel's beaded Indian dress and high boots. "First time on land for months and she 'as ter get dressed up like some bloody 'eathen!" Nick laughed and pulled Kestrel onto his lap, nuzzling her neck playfully.

"Wotchit!" shrieked Gladys again as the boat rocked gently with the loving movement. "I ain't going to get 'alf drowned again," she warned as she tried to sit demurely under her parasol, setting a ladylike example to Kestrel and hoping to impress Pierre favorably.

"Oh, look," gasped Kestrel as Pierre and a seaman rowed steadily toward the picturesque harbor where the houses were whitewashed and gleaming in the bright sunlight. Brightly colored flowers and fabrics were worn by the people who walked or rode donkeys. "It's beautiful!"

"Asses!" sniffed Gladys, nearly overturning the boat as she craned her neck. "I'll 'ave to watch my step!"

"Wotchit!" teased Pierre as they neared a jetty. Kestrel jumped agilely out onto the stone wharf and tied the dinghy. She stared around curiously and found herself the object of curiosity as children clustered around looking at her strange clothes.

"*Bonjour,*" she greeted them as Nick leaped onto the wharf and helped Miss Mackintosh to disembark clumsily. Kestrel saw Rue was also in the center of a small throng. The large hound shook her wet coat and the children laughed as they were showered.

"We should keep together," ordered Nick gently and Rue looked at him dispassionately. "The tide is in two hours, and we must sail on it," he explained, sensing she was about to rebel.

Rue heard Jacques's raucous voice haggling for fresh fruits, vegetables, and meat, and seeing that Nick had turned away to speak to her sister, she swiftly made her way through the curious group of gaily dressed people to the old sea captain, preferring his company. Nick swore when he turned back to find she had gone, and quickly took Kestrel's hand, not wanting to have to search for her, too.

"There's another island over there," exclaimed Kestrel, shading her eyes.

"That is Île de Re," Pierre told her. "And this beautiful village is called Saint-Denis."

"We didn't look at a map," remarked Kestrel. "Do you know where there is a nunnery?"

"Not here," said Pierre, shaking his head.

"Oléron Sainte-Marie?" she questioned.

"Oh, that is in the mountains, the Pyrenees on the Spanish border many miles from here," explained Pierre.

"Oh, well," shrugged Kestrel.

"Feels ever so funny trying to walk on firm ground," complained Gladys as she tripped and staggered over the cobblestones.

"It still feels like we are on board," laughed Kestrel as they walked through the narrow, crowded streets, followed by an excited hoard of small children.

"What I want is a decent meal before I fade away to just skin and bone," stated Miss Mackintosh, sniffing the air appreciatively. "I smell something lovely."

"There is a petit bistro I know," laughed Pierre. "And I theenk you have the scent of Monique's cooking."

"Monique?" repeated Gladys suspiciously.

"Monique!" she repeated as they entered a beautiful little court-yard where flowers hung in profusion and were met by a shapely sensual woman in her early forties.

"Pierre," cried Monique, throwing herself into the one-eyed man's open arms.

"Monique, *mon petit chou,*" he laughed, swinging her round and round so her ample breasts nearly fell out of her low-cut peasant blouse.

"Monique, *mon petit chou!*" snarled Gladys.

"This is so pretty," declared Kestrel, her mouth watering at the delicious smells that wafted from the open kitchen door as she stared around at the trellised arches covered with fragrant roses. She looked over a low wall and caught her breath at the beauty of the scenery as she gazed down a steep cliff to the sea.

"Monique, these are my dear friends," announced Pierre. "Nick and his wife Kestrel, and this is Mlle. Gladys," he introduced. Gladys haughtily inclined her head as though she were royalty. "This is my niece Monique, Jacques's daughter."

"Oh, I'm ever so pleased to make your acquaintance," gushed Gladys with relief, plopping herself down in one of the wrought-iron chairs.

"Monique, your papa will be here shortly but in the meantime please fill the table with some of your wonderful dishes," urged

Pierre, rubbing his hands together with anticipation and tucking a napkin into his collar.

Kestrel grinned appreciatively as Monique directed several giggling children with laden trays, who piled the table high with fruits of every different color.

"What's this?" Kestrel asked as she picked up an orange, marveling in the texture, symmetry, and aroma.

"An orange," replied Nick.

"It is orange," she puzzled, not sure if she had heard correctly.

"It is called an orange," laughed Nick, taking it from her and deftly peeling it. "Taste." He popped a juicy segment in her mouth and she greedily reached for the rest.

"Delicious," she announced with her mouth full as she reached for pears and plums, also fruits she had never seen before. "What are these and these?"

The endless stream of food continued so that bowls and platters had to be placed on adjoining tables. Several roast chickens surrounded by tender green grapes, large shrimp, every conceivable type of fish, steamed crabs and lobsters, and tender salad greens fought for space on the crowded table. Gladys ate with relish, making funny little smacking grunts of satisfaction as she used two hands to fill her mouth and the juices ran down her double chin. Kestrel tasted everything, in awe of how many foods there were that she hadn't known existed.

"You leave something for me, I hope," hailed a gruff voice and Jacques appeared with Rue and the hound. Nick sighed with relief and pulled out a chair for her, as Jacques disappeared into the house.

"Try this, Rue," offered Kestrel, tossing her an orange. Rue caught it and turned it over and over in her hand not knowing what to make of it. "It's called an orange." Rue put the orange down and it rolled off the table. Shame chased it gleefully, picking it up in her mouth and tossing it this way and that to the amusement of everyone. Rue ate hungrily, delighting in the superbly cooked food and fresh fruits.

"What you think of my little girl, huh?" said Jacques affectionately as he came out of the pretty whitewashed house with his daughter. "She can cook like a man, huh?" he added as he sat at the table and ripped a chicken in two.

Everyone except Gladys and Jacques leaned back contentedly in their chairs, unable to eat another mouthful.

"Monique should cook on the *Étoile*," pronounced Pierre. "What about that, little cabbage, you come with your Uncle Pierre for a little trip to Scotland and then back?"

"With all the children?" replied Monique.

"*Sacrebleu! Non!*" exclaimed Jacques. "*Les enfants!*" he roared and there was a patter of bare feet. Nick stared astounded as the children seemed to keep coming. Kestrel and Rue looked in astonishment at the long line of grinning little faces.

" 'Ow ever many?" gasped Gladys with her mouth full.

"Seventeen," stated Jacques proudly. "And all alive." Kestrel grinned at the line of black-haired, brown-skinned children, noticing there were sixteen boys and one baby girl who was held by one of the small boys. She held her arms out and three little boys clambered on-to her lap.

"Oh, Nick, can we have a lot of children?" she laughed, cuddling the children.

"Not seventeen," replied Nick as several little tykes climbed onto his lap.

"I have the little princess," said Pierre, taking the baby girl, who wore nothing but flowers in her hair.

"Monique, how old is the oldest?" asked Nick.

"Seventeen," said the proud mother, placing her hand on the shoulder of a beaming young man. "I have had a baby every year for seventeen years but now I think I have finished for I have a girl."

"And what a beautiful little girl," crooned her doting great-uncle, holding the gurgling baby over his head.

"Wotchit, Pierre, she ain't wearing a rag and it could splash me best frock;" grumbled Gladys.

"Oh, I know you love the babies," chuckled Pierre, putting the naked, flower-decked infant in her large black lap. Miss Mackintosh gave him what she hoped was the evil eye and tried not to smile at the happy baby girl. Rue stared down at the tiny child cradled in Gladys's black shiny skirt and slowly reached out to touch the soft curls. The child gurgled, grabbed her finger, and smiled toothlessly. Shame sniffed at the chubby child and gave her a big lick, causing the baby to giggle.

" 'Ere, you're a doctor, that ain't 'ealthy," protested Gladys. "Rue, get yer 'ound away!" Rue's face lost its open shining wonder and she extricated her finger from the baby's clasp.

"The dog won't hurt the child," reassured Nick but the damage was done. Rue moved away from the happy communing of the luncheon table with all the suntanned healthy children.

"We have to go so we catch the tide," informed Jacques regretfully. "Monique, where is that man you are married to?"

"Rochefort on the mainland, he'll be back tomorrow," replied Monique, signaling to her children to clear the tables.

"Oh, no! Do something, Pierre! It ain't funny!" seethed Gladys, sitting with her legs wide apart as a stream of liquid strained through her skirts onto the cobbled courtyard and the baby girl kicked her chubby legs gleefully as she relieved her little bladder. Pierre and Kestrel roared with laughter as Nick picked up the dripping child.

"Oh, she is so beautiful," whispered Kestrel, touched by the picture Nick made with the tiny girl between his large hands.

"Seventeen children and all alive. That is unheard of," he said.

"It is this little magical island," pronounced Jacques, taking his tiny granddaughter and kissing her soundly on both cheeks before handing her to her mother.

"I wish we could stay here longer," said Kestrel as they walked back down the steep cobbled street to the harbor. Nick smiled in agreement, appreciating the clean, well cared-for houses and gardens.

"We may come back one day. Jacques, where are your other children?" he asked.

"All near here. My two sons live in Rochefort and I 'ave two more daughters in Rochelle. I 'ad ten children but only five lived to be men and women."

" 'Ave you got any, Pierre?" asked Gladys, hanging on his arm as she tottered over the uneven stones down the steep hill to the harbor.

"Maybe one in every port of the whole world," he laughed.

"You never married, Pierre?" questioned Kestrel.

"Maybe 'e 'as a wife in every port of the whole world also," chuckled Jacques.

"Get away with you!" clucked Gladys indignantly. "I'd like to meet your wife, Jacques. She 'as my 'ealthy respect putting up with a big scallawag like you."

Rue looked at Jacques's weather-beaten face sharply as he turned and stared back up the steep hill toward the white spire of a small church. She and Shame had been with the old sea captain as he tenderly placed a small bouquet of red roses on a neat grave. She took his arm sympathetically as she saw the lined cheek tighten with grief. Her small face mirrored her own sorrow.

" 'Ave I said something wrong?" asked Gladys, looking from Pierre to Jacques.

"My wife is dead," pronounced Jacques a little too loudly as he tried to control himself as his aching loss welled.

"I'm ever so sorry," apologized Gladys awkwardly.

"I 'ave my five children and forty grandchildren," replied the captain, untying the dinghy and handing Rue the rope. "I also 'ave my *Étoile*," he added, pointing to the graceful ship. "So, I 'ave everything, freedom, and family."

Rue sat with her arm around Shame watching the two brothers row strongly out to the ship, not listening to Kestrel and Gladys's excited chatter about their plans for when they reached Edinburgh. She was deeply absorbed in thoughts of death. Her mother's, Jemmy's, Goliath's, her brother Raven's, Jacques's wife and the newest and most painful death of all . . . that of the tall dark masked pirate.

Nick watched Rue's usually straight back slump and he frowned seeing her morose expression.

"Cheer up, Rue. Soon we shall be home in Scotland," he comforted her gently. Her nostrils flared angrily and she turned and stared at him rebelliously. Scotland was not her home. She seethed, her eyes flashing. "Your father and brothers are there," he reminded her as though reading her furious thoughts.

"Oh, my little cabbage, wait until we walk the Royal Mile and I take you shopping on Princes Street," wooed Pierre, winking his one eye as his old muscular arms rhythmically pulled the oars. "Edinburgh, she is a beautiful city, not like Paree, but where is?"

"Scotland," breathed Kestrel, her green eyes alight with excitement. "I can't wait."

PART III

Scotland

Autumn 1782

She dwelt among the untrodden ways
Beside the springs of Dove,
A Maid whom there were none to praise
And very few to love.

WILLIAM WORDSWORTH
"*She Dwelt Among the Untrodden Ways*"

CHAPTER TWENTY-SEVEN

"That is Scotland, really!" exclaimed Kestrel excitedly. "Rue? Rue?" she screamed up to her sister who was perched in her customary place high in the rigging. "There's Scotland!" Rue stared at the rocky coastland that Kestrel waved at.

"We'll be dropping anchor in Leith and sleeping tonight in my grandfather's house in Edinburgh," laughed Nick, enjoying Kestrel's infectious exhilaration and happy to be home himself.

"Look, there's a castle!" shouted Kestrel. "Well, it must be a castle. Is it a castle?"

"Aye," chuckled Nick, swinging her around in his arms. " 'Tis Berwick."

"And that one?" She pointed as more castles came into sight.

"Fast, Dunglass, and Innerwick," stated Nick proudly as he pointed out Scottish landmarks. "And there in the distance is Dunbar."

Rue stared fascinated at the rugged coastline where every few miles a stone castle seemed to spring from the gray cliffs themselves, looking so natural and part of the earth that man's hand could not have fashioned them, she felt. She remembered her mother's reminiscences of her own childhood in a remote castle on the lonely northern promontory of Cape Wrath where the gulls and gray seals reigned supreme by the raging sea.

"My mother lived in a castle with her guardian," proclaimed Kestrel as she wondered if the castle looked like the ones she now looked upon.

"I thought she was in a nunnery," frowned Nick.

"That was only until she was about two. She was brought to Scotland and lived in a castle," sang Kestrel.

"Where?"

"Cape Wrath."

"What?" exclaimed Nick, Cape Wrath in Strathnaver being his clan's land.

" 'Tis far, far north," explained Kestrel.

"I ken my own clan's holdings," replied Nick with a smile.

"Your clan MacKay?" questioned Kestrel with a frown and Nick nodded. "But my mother's guardian's name was Fraser. Duncan Fraser. He was a famous Jacobite outlaw," she boasted triumphantly.

"That's rich!" roared Nick, bent double with laughter. "My paternal grandfather, the chief MacKay, fought for the Hanoverians against the Jacobites. The MacKays have been fighting for the Protestants for the past two hundred years so Strathnaver was an ideal place for a Jacobite outlaw to hide."

"You're not a Jacobite?" she whispered in horror.

" 'Tis 1782, Kestrel. There's no such thing anymore. There hasn't been in your lifetime nor mine. You were born in America many years after the Battle of Culloden."

"I know Scotland should be free."

"Aye," agreed Nick. "But sometimes 'tis not so simple, my love." He looked down at her upturned face, recognizing the angry sparkle in her emerald eyes. "Quick, look before you miss yet another castle. There's Tantallon."

"Sounds French," returned Kestrel sulkily.

"Like your surname, Sinclair. Do you know where it comes from?" he asked, anxious to change the subject and be back to the previous golden joyfulness.

"From Saint-Clair-sur-Elle in Normandy. My ancestor Henri de Saint-Clair was granted lands in Scotland in 1162," she answered, her face still showing signs of mutiny.

"Aye, lands in Caithness adjoining Strathnaver," supplied Nick.

"You are wrong!" declared Kestrel with great satisfaction, feeling superior to her learned husband. "That wasna until 1455. The first lands were in Lothian, in the Lowlands. My ancestors also fought wie Robert the Bruce at Bannockburn. We were also premier earls of Norway and the Orkneys. And I had an ancestor Thorfinn the Mighty who built a cathedral called Kirkwall," recited Kestrel haughtily.

"Wait until you see Girnigo in Caithness, a giant fortress built by the earls Sinclair to keep the Gordons at bay," laughed Nick, enchanted by her earnestness.

"Oh, look," breathed Kestrel as the *Étoile* veered smoothly into the Firth of Forth.

"Across the firth are the castles of Amstruther, Newark, and Ardoss. On the far tip is the town of Crail."

"Crail? That's near my father's lands at Glen Aucht," cried Kestrel excitedly. "Rue? Rue?" she shrieked, wildly gesticulating to her sister. "Crail is over there! Crail!" Rue craned her neck and strained her eyes, looking toward the town she had heard so much about as the ship sailed down the wide mouth of the firth toward Leith.

"This is the Firth of Forth," screeched Kestrel, not sure if her sister had heard. Shame barked and ran back and forth, knowing land was to either side as the gulls mewed and swooped, and fishermen on smaller crafts waved and whistled at the graceful sloop that sped cleanly through the gray-green waters.

"Over there are the castles of MacDuff, Wemyss, and there's the town of Kirkcaldy and to the left is Dirleton," named Nick as Kestrel pointed this way and that with a questioning face. "We'll be docking within half an hour," he added and laughed at the look of indecision on her face as she debated whether to rush to their cabin to dress up in appropriate finery or stay up on the deck in the blood-red sunset running from one side of the ship to the other, not wanting to miss one blink of Scotland.

"We're home!" rejoiced Kestrel at the top of her lungs as she spun around, unable to contain her excitement and keep still. "Oh, Rue, we're home at last!"

Rue stared down at her exuberant sister, wishing she could share her happiness as she turned apprehensive eyes to the bustling, teeming harbor of Leith as the *Étoile* slowly glided into berth. She wrinkled up her small nose in distaste at the overpowering stench that assailed her senses.

"It smells like somebody has died!" remarked Kestrel to Pierre as she stared over the high sides at the debris that lapped in the murky waters.

"When have you smelled death?" chuckled the one-eyed man, thinking she exaggerated.

"Lots of times," retorted Kestrel, surprised by his surprise. "There was a war, remember?" she added sarcastically. "People were killed."

"And you saw them?" asked Pierre.

"Aye," replied Kestrel softly, thinking of the still bodies of Jemmy and Goliath, and Short Arm and the other young braves. Nick saw her sad expression and pulled her close as Pierre's usually benign expression took on serious lines.

"Sometimes I followed my nose in the forest and there were . . . remains. Always horrible, always made me sick. Whether they were Redcoats or friends. Short Arm said not even the greatest warrior could get used to death," remembered Kestrel, thinking of the young Tuscarora's smooth dead face, and burying her nose in Nick's fragrant warmth for comfort.

"A sad thing for such a young girl to have such experiences," grumbled Pierre.

"We better get our things together," said Nick, trying to lighten his tone and taking her arm to lead her to their cabin.

"What about Rue?" asked Kestrel, looking above their heads to her sister, who seemed frozen against the sunset, her eyes pinned to the busy noisiness of the harbor as screaming gulls wheeled and flapped around her.

"Rue!" shouted Nick, cupping his broad hands so he could be heard over the din. "Rue, 'tis time!" he informed her as Shame added her exuberant voice to his.

"Come on, Rue!" screamed Kestrel, and her dark sister tore her haunted eyes from the nightmarish dark shapes of the other sailing ships moored alongside. Each gently bobbing vessel reminded her of the *Dolphin*. She stifled a sob and stared down to her dog who whined and barked, trying to get her attention. She stiffly stood and shinned agilely down to the deck. She patted Shame and looked up into Nick's dark eyes. Pain flooded in and she wrenched her eyes away as the Hawk's eyes seemed to bore into her.

"Have you everything packed and ready to be taken off?" asked Nick, gently wrapping a comforting arm around her shoulders. He felt her stiffen and he gave her a brief hug before releasing her. Rue nodded, unable to look at him as she girded herself and tried to summon courage to leave the safety of the ship and push through the thunderous crowds.

Gladys staggered on deck dressed to the nines in yard upon yard of black velvet complete with an enormous black feathered hat.

"We will be staying at a very, very proper 'otel," she stated proudly with one black-gloved hand on Pierre's sleeve. "And you 'ave to come and dine as our guests. Pierre 'as your address and we'll let you know," she giggled.

"You'll be staying in Edinburgh a while?" replied Nick in surprise.

"A week maybe," chuckled Pierre. "My little cabbage is very— 'ow you say? She can talk the bird from the tree?"

"I ain't talked this one-eyed bird into matrimony yet, 'ave I?" returned Gladys tartly. Kestrel giggled at Pierre's expression.

"Pardon?" he answered with a hand behind his ear.

"Gets deaf any time certain words are mentioned. Wedding, ring, honest woman, church, oh anything to do with being secure in me old age," mourned Gladys with her sense of humor covering up her vulnerability.

"Pardon? Pardon?" repeated Pierre, not willing to have his little cabbage appear incorrect.

"You take care of yourselves, little lambs," sniffed Gladys. "If you need me we'll be at the 'otel . . . um. What's it called, Pierre?"

"Le Spotted Dog," supplied Pierre.

Rue sat in the dark carriage as it bumped over the cobblestones, trying to ignore the love exuded between Nick and Kestrel. She concentrated on the dirty wet streets and the smell of damp leather to block out the terrifying feeling of dread that filled her.

"Why does everything smell so terrible?" asked Kestrel, holding her nose as she wished she had dressed in one of her elegant Charbonnière gowns so she could have made a favorable impression on Nick's grandfather and brother.

"Cities aren't noted for smelling . . . fresh," confessed Nick, appalled by the stench. "That is why one should carry a large or lacy handkerchief liberally doused with perfume," he added, wishing he had the foresight to have such a weapon. "Here we are!" he rejoiced as the carriage came to an abrupt stop before large formidable wrought-iron gates. Kestrel was hurtled forward onto Nick's lap where she curled comfortably and peered out of the window curiously at the uniformed gatekeeper who swung back the heavy barrier, allowing admittance. The carriage jerked forward, the dray's hooves sharply clopping on the wet cobblestones of the drive that wound around well-kept lawns and flower beds until it stopped before a very impressive flight of stone steps leading to an enormous carved door.

Nick leaped out and turned, extending a hand to help Kestrel alight. She stood stunned, staring at the large imposing house and the stream of liveried servants that approached. Nick lifted her down and set her on her feet as Rue frantically watched her horse, Sin, led away.

"Sin will be fine, Rue. The ostler's just taking him to the stables," he reassured. But Rue sprang down and pushed past him only to be grasped by a pair of strong arms.

"Where are you off to, lad?" growled a deep Gaelic voice and she stared up into a wrinkled brown face. She froze, unable to kick and fight anyone so old. She frowned into the deep, nearly black eyes before tearing her gaze away and looking frantically for her horse.

"Well, Lachlan," hailed Nick and the old man's gnarled hands released Rue and she raced behind the large mansion followed by her hound.

"Nicholas MacKay, what are you doing home? Your letter said you were settled in the backwoods of the New World," rejoiced Lachlan McCulloch, hugging his grandson.

Kestrel hung back, watching the reunion of the two tall men as servants carried the trunks up the broad sweeping steps into the house.

"I've brought home a granddaughter for you," laughed Nick, his voice deep with emotion. Kestrel stared bravely up at the tall gaunt old man whose keen black eyes seemed to burn holes in her. Her green eyes widened and flashed as she sucked in her cheeks trying to look sophisticated and worldly. She gasped as a pair of iron hard arms picked her up and hugged her in a bone-crushing embrace.

"Good lad!" approved Lachlan. "No sugar and frills or simpering in this braw lass," he rejoiced, kissing her soundly on the mouth before setting her back on her feet. "What's your name, child?"

"I'm not a child!" stated Kestrel. "My name is Kestrel Sinclair MacKay."

"Sinclair?"

"Of Glen Aucht," stated Kestrel proudly as they walked up the steps into the large well-lit hallway. Lachlan McCulloch turned and surveyed his new granddaughter and nodded his appreciation of her luxuriant golden hair and flashing emerald eyes.

"Aye, then your mother was the Black Cameron twin, bastard daughter of the Bonny Prince," he stated, shocking both Kestrel and Nick with his candor.

"Bonny Prince?" whispered Kestrel. "Prince Charlie? Charles Stuart. That's why . . ." she mused aloud.

"Your father returned several months past wie two braw lads. One black Scot and one red one," stated the old man.

"My brothers Lynx and Rowan."

"Alien names for Scots," snorted Lachlan.

"We're as Scottish as you but born in a different world," returned Kestrel feistily.

"Aye," nodded the old man, his eyes glinting with mischief as he winked at Nick. "Now where's the wee dark laddie?"

"That is my sister, Rue Sinclair," replied Kestrel, turning around and around in delight as she filled her eyes with the large beautiful room hung with many plants. A deep growl caught her attention and an enormous, ferocious-looking dog stretched.

"Dinna touch!" warned Lachlan, but he was too late as Kestrel sank to her knees and petted the wolfhound, who licked the golden girl's face affectionately.

"Whiskey, Kess?" asked Nick, pouring several glasses and enjoying the favorable impression his wife was making on the wicked old man.

"Aye," she replied, lying on her back next to the large dog and staring serenely around the fresh exquisite room. A frantic pounding and scuffling caused the hound to bound to his feet, snarling. Lachlan strode to the door and wrenched it open. In the hallway Rue fought two hefty footmen.

"Stay, Thor!" Lachlan ordered and the enormous hound obediently sat.

"Let her go!" ordered Nick. The burly footmen looked to Lord McCulloch who nodded silently. Rue was released but she rushed back across the hallway toward the front door. "Rue!" Nick roared and the girl froze in her tracks but didn't turn. Lachlan lifted a large weathered hand, staying his grandson as he strode toward the small figure.

"Rue Sinclair?" he said, gently turning her about. He looked down into a face that took his breath away and caused his heart to contract with aching tenderness. Wide amber eyes gazed back without flinching and the most delicate little face steeled itself, showing no fear. The old man wanted to groan and pick up the dark child.

"She canna speak," said Kestrel, defending her sister.

"Her face is eloquent enough," returned Lachlan, holding out his hand to Rue as he would to a frightened animal. Rue stared down at the offered hand and shook her head, pointing at the door. She wanted to place her small hand in his but she hardened her resolve, not willing to be vulnerable. She wanted to be with her horse and hound, not with people.

"She wants Sin and Shame," translated Kestrel.

"Sin and Shame?" repeated Lachlan. "The puir weeun's name is Rue? What dreadful sorrow spawned such names?"

"Sin is her horse and Shame, her hound," informed Nick.

"Rue, you canna bring a great horse into the house," joked the old man, "but maybe your hound. Is it dog or bitch?" he asked, looking at his own animal who lay with his large head on Kestrel's lap.

"Bitch," replied Nick.

"Fredrick?" called Lachlan and a manservant immediately came into view. "Bring the hound in. Now, young lady, would you like a drink or anything," he asked as the servant left, but Rue kept her eyes pinned to the door, waiting for her hound who soon could be heard complaining bitterly as she fought against the restraining leash. Rue angrily tore the offensive bond from Shame's neck and stepped back as Thor stepped up to sniff the young intruder. Lachlan nodded his approval at Rue's understanding of animals as she allowed the two to get acquainted. The older male growled imperious warnings to the excitable exuberant bitch. Shame happily obeyed the older dog, wiggling and barking with adoration, her heavy tail violently wagging.

"Your horse will be well taken care of in my stables after what must have been a long uncomfortable voyage," comforted Lachlan, smiling down at Rue. She nodded tersely and looked away. Something disturbed her about the tall old man, something about his nearly black eyes at the bottom of myriads of wrinkles, something about his commanding presence that weighed her spirit down.

"Where's Tarquin?" asked Nick as they all sat down to a sumptuous meal in a very impressive dining room that was just short of being a banquet hall.

"Went north to his lands several months ago and I've not heard since," replied Lachlan. Kestrel's eyes were big as saucers as she tried to take in everything from the dimensions of the enormous room to the multitude of servants that entered with dozens of covered dishes. She shook her golden head in disbelief at the amount of food. Two whole poached salmons lay head to tail on a large silver salver and several savory pies with golden brown pastry steamed aromatically amid platters overflowing with vegetables and fruits.

"Did you catch these salmon, Lachlan?" asked Nick.

"Of course," answered the old man proudly. "A royal battle we had, too." Rue stared at her plate as Lachlan McCulloch smiled warmly at her. She ate quickly and sparsely, unable to feel relaxed despite the cheerful conversation and affection that flowed from the old man to his grandson.

Kestrel sparkled under Lachlan's attention. She was perfectly at ease enjoying the company and food. Nick leaned back in his chair, stretching his long legs. He was full, and content to watch his beautiful wife with pride as she gracefully entertained his grandfather with stories of Gladys Mackintosh and one-eyed Pierre.

"Any trouble on the voyage? Storms or the like?" asked the old man, his eyes streaming with laughter.

"Pirates," replied Kestrel with gusto and then remembered and turned an anguished face to her sister. "Oh, Rue, I'm sorry," she whispered, seeing the dark, bent head. Rue heard the pity in Kestrel's voice and she straightened her back and glared into the concerned green eyes. Lachlan's aristocratic face hardened and he looked questioningly at Nick, who imperceptively shook his head in warning.

"I'm sure you are tired after your long journey and are wanting nice hot baths and comfortable beds," yawned the old man, pushing back from the still-laden table. "Nicholas, I've given orders for your things to be moved to the master suite. Now you have a bride you need more space, especially since I shall expect some great-grandchildren."

"We've one growing already," informed Kestrel candidly, sticking out her still-flat belly.

"Och, Nicholas, you've found a lass like your own grandmother!' he rejoiced, chuckling and hugging the impulsive girl.

Rue felt suffocated by the golden merriment. She longed to creep away to the comforting darkness of the stables but didn't relish another battle with Lachlan McCulloch's burly menservants. She turned away from the happy threesome and studied the portraits that lined the wooden walls of the gallery they walked through. She recoiled at the dark eyes that stared down from the gilded frames. Many generations of men and women spiraling back several hundred years, painted in various styles; all seemed to scrutinize her. The high prominent cheekbones, hawklike noses, and blue-black straight hair reminded her painfully of the masked pirate.

"Those are Nicholas's ancestors," remarked Lachlan softly as he noted Rue's apparent interest.

"They look like you," laughed Kestrel, holding Nick and Lachlan's arms.

"I look like them," corrected Nick. "There is Black Nick McCulloch," he added, pointing out a very imposing figure who surveyed them with a sardonic sneer. Rue felt cowed by the painted expression that seemed to sear through her to her very soul. She shuddered and turned her back, unable to cope with the ghosts that gazed from the ornate frames. Lachlan's jaw tightened as his keen eyes watched the dark girl even though he appeared to be immersed in Kestrel's conversation. He noted that her slim hands shook as she reached for comfort from her dark hound. His eyes narrowed as she whirled around, feeling his intense gaze, and her small chin was raised defiantly as her nostrils flares as though daring him to feel sorry for her.

"Master Nicholas?" gurgled a warm voice, and Kestrel and Rue looked in surprise at a round, apple-cheeked woman dressed in a mob cap and apron, who stood with her dimpled hands on her ample hips, staring fondly.

"Goody," murmured Nick, holding his arms wide and striding toward the maternal sight.

"Couldna stay in your kitchen, could you, Miss Goody?" chortled Lachlan. "Especially not when you heard that your wee Nicholas had brought home a bonny bride," he teased, ushering Kestrel toward Nick, who hugged the flustered woman. Kestrel found herself embraced warmly and held against the stiffly starched apron that smelled of lavender and fresh-baked bread. Her eyes filled with tears as she was reminded of Angus so far away in the American wilderness.

"And this is Kestrel's sister, Rue Sinclair," introduced Nick gently, and Rue stood well back from the woman and nodded as she kept tight hold on her rambunctious young dog. "Rue, this is my old nurse and now friend, Miss Catriona Goody."

Catriona looked kindly at the guarded expression of the small dark girl and then back to the radiant glow of Kestrel's smile. She raised her eyebrows at Lachlan and a concerned frown touched her round sunny features.

"Your rooms are ready and baths are waiting," she stated with a soft Lowland burr in her voice.

"Miss Goody bosses us all about," complained Lachlan with a twinkle in his eye as they followed the bustling woman along a wide thick-carpeted corridor.

"I have put Miss Rue in the Rose room," said the good woman, opening a heavy carved door to a beautiful bedroom decorated with delicate pink and red posies.

"Good night," whispered Kestrel, giving her sister a hug and feeling her tense and rigid. She stood, not wanting to leave Rue, who looked lost and forlorn. A young maid shyly bobbed curtsies every time anyone, including the dog, looked in her direction.

"This is Annie, who'll give you assistance," stated Miss Goody as she turned to direct Kestrel and Nick to their suite. Lachlan stared at Rue for a long moment, noting the slump of her shoulders as she stood frozen in the middle of the floral carpet, looking totally out of place.

"Is the room not to your liking?" he asked. Rue spun around with a start at the sound of his voice. She looked at the old man, her expression confused and disoriented. "Annie, come wie me," he ordered the maid, who hovered uncertainly. Rue sighed with relief as

he door was shut, leaving her alone in the bedchamber with Shame.
he looked around at the large pretty room, noting the enamel bath
hat steamed a perfumed mist, the thick towels, and the nightgown
hat was arranged across the large bed, reminding her of another
edchamber. She picked up the delicate lacy gown and absently
ubbed it against her cheek as her mind went back to her wedding
ight aboard the *Dolphin*.

Outside in the corridor Lachlan McCulloch spoke earnestly and
uietly to Miss Goody, his housekeeper.

"I've not had time or occasion to speak to Nicholas about the lass.
ll I know is she is mute but can hear, and obviously is filled with a
adness. Go mother her, Goody," he ordered huskily and the woman
odded.

Rue crouched to attack as the door was thrust open, admitting the
mposing figure of Miss Catriona Goody.

"Och, you remind me of Master Tarquin when he was a lad," she
norted, rolling up her sleeves and advancing on the coiled young
igure. "Into the bath wie you," she ordered, wanting to reach out and
omfort the wide-eyed girl. "Now!" she insisted sharply, clapping
er hands together to show she meant business. Rue resisted as the
arge woman spun around and turned down the bed.

Miss Goody smiled to herself as she heard a faint splashing and
urned back and surveyed her young charge with satisfaction. She
nelt beside the tub and soaped Rue's thick hair. Her cheerful, good-
atured face frowned as she saw several crisscrossed scars on the lithe
an back and recognized the signs of more than one severe whipping.
With a well-practiced hand she efficiently bathed, dried, and tucked
Rue into the wide bed, ignoring the young girl's closed, hostile
xpression as she kept up a steady stream of cheerful chatter.

"Sleep well, Rue Sinclair," she murmured, turning the lamp down
o a faint glow and resisting the impulse to push the black hound off
he delicate pink eiderdown, where the young bitch curled close to her
nistress. Rue lay stiffly, wishing the woman would leave, unable to
elax until she heard the door close behind her and knew the
nenservants who disposed of the water and tub were gone.

"Well?" demanded Lachlan impatiently, scaring Miss Goody half
ut of her wits as she thoughtfully descended the back stairs to the
itchen.

"Lord Lachlan McCulloch, you'll be the death of me!" she
hrieked. "Prancing out of the shadows like that."

"Did you find out anything? Did she trust you?"

"How am I to find out anything from a mute child?" scolded the housekeeper as she sat heavily at her well-scrubbed kitchen table. "She's been whipped."

"What?" gasped the old man, sitting on the edge of the table.

"Aye, whipped with a cat or leather thong wie knots. Not lately, for the scars are healed. There's another scar across her belly could be from a knife or gun, I canna tell which. As for trusting me, it was like tangling wie Tarquin after his mother died. I took no nonsense from her but could gie no affection either," sighed the caring woman. "I'll tell you something else, she's not going to stay put, either."

"She's going to sneak out, you think?"

"Aye, and she better be stopped if she canna speak," continued the housekeeper. "Or she'll fall prey to some of the two-legged animals that roam."

"Aye," agreed Lachlan. "If Nick weren't busy wie that bonny wee bride of his, I would get some answers. Maybe tomorrow," he planned, striding out of the kitchen.

"What are you planning?"

"Keeping an eye on Rue Sinclair," he answered shortly as the door swung shut behind him.

CHAPTER TWENTY-EIGHT

Kestrel's mouth dropped open at the opulence of the suite she shared with Nick. She opened door after door, stunned at the amount of room.

"I dinna ken why we need two bedrooms, two sitting rooms, and two other rooms for I don't know what."

"Those are dressing rooms. One for you, that's why all your clothes are there, and the other is my dressing room," laughed Nick.

"I canna watch you getting undressed or dressed anymore?" gasped Kestrel with horror. "Why are there two bedrooms?" she added suspiciously, her consternation growing. Nick grinned down into her disturbed little face.

"Och, Kestrel, now we are back in the civilized world we maun behave wie decorum," he teased. Kestrel stared toward the more feminine of the two bedrooms at the tub of water that steamed, and then she gazed forlornly to the larger bath.

"Do you really think I'd let you sleep so far away from me?" asked Nick, holding her close, unable to bear her woebegone expression.

"Do we need all those people, too?" whispered Kestrel, peeking over his shoulder to the servants, who discreetly waited.

"Good night. I shall be the only assistant my wife will need," he said, dismissing the servants and closing the door impatiently after them. He turned to Kestrel and burst into laughter to find her nearly naked.

"Why do we need two baths?" she asked, stepping into his.

"That's why," he chuckled as he lowered himself into the tub, his long legs each side of his golden wife, and the perfumed water rose and slopped over the rim onto the thick burgundy carpet. He tried to keep a very serious expression as he looked down at Kestrel's intent face while she sensuously soaped him, starting at his neck and sinuously sliding her silky hands down his long lean body. He obediently followed her commands by kneeling and eventually standing so she wouldn't miss an inch of him. Kestrel's free infectious laughter rang out as she stared lovingly at his rearing lathered manhood.

"I'll teach you to laugh at a man's pride, woman," he threatened, lifting her out of the water and charging to the elaborate canopied bed.

"We're all wet and soapy," squealed Kestrel halfheartedly, reveling in the slippery feel of his lathered body.

"We'll clean you inside and out," growled Nick as he fitted himself to her, rejoicing how perfectly they melded together. "I love you, Kestrel Sinclair MacKay," he murmured as their wet bodies made intimate kissing sounds as they surged and thrust against each other.

"I love you, Nicholas MacKay," whispered Kestrel, feeling every part of her open to her dark husband.

Rue listened with her ear to the door of her bedroom before quietly stepping into the corridor with Shame. She peered down the sweeping, winding staircase.

"Where are you off to, lass?"

Rue froze, unable to face the old man who stepped out of the shadows. She frowned down at her hound, puzzled as to why Shame hadn't warned her.

"Dinna blame your young bitch, she's still a pup," he said,

following her gaze. "Come wie me," he ordered tersely, recognizing the mutinous set of her jaw and taking her arm in a steely grip so resistance was useless. Rue allowed herself to be firmly led into a study.

"I prefer this room. 'Tis small and cozy. Now, Rue Sinclair, can you write?" he asked, knowing not to give in to the affection he felt for the valiant little figure. Rue refused to acknowledge. "I take it that you find the question insulting," snapped Lachlan, knowing battle lines were drawn. "Dinna cut off your nose to spite your face, Rue Sinclair. Here's paper and charcoal, write what you need." Rue stared at him hostilely for a long moment before taking the proffered writing materials.

"Aye, I should like to meet your mount," replied the old man after reading what Rue had written. "Come." He extended his hand but Rue ignored it. Lachlan shook his head and clucked his displeasure before opening the door and elaborately gesturing to Rue to precede him.

Together the tall gaunt old man and the slight dark girl walked down the wide stone steps to the courtyard. Rue breathed deeply, thankful for the cool night air. It was still August but the temperature was like autumn, refreshing with just a slight nip in the air and a gentle breeze. She frowned, not understanding the difference in climate.

"We are farther north than you are used to and there's no warm sea currents this side of Scotland," explained Lachlan, understanding her confusion as he pushed open the heavy stable door. " 'Tis all right, Ross, 'tis me," he reassured the sleepy ostler. "Och, that's a fine piece of horseflesh!" he exclaimed as the large stallion snorted and tossed his head in welcome. The old man stood back and watched Rue embrace her horse, her face softening and losing the hard set lines as she rubbed her cheek against him. He delighted in her natural grace as she divided her attention equally between her ebony hound and horse.

" 'Tis time we all rested," he said after about half an hour. "And you're not sleeping in my stable," he added, firmly following her gaze to a pile of hay and steering her to the house. He felt her resistance, but he refused to soften his resolve as he propelled her back up the granite steps and into the small study.

"Och, Rue Sinclair, can we have a truce for the night?" he groaned, looking down into her set little face and noting her clenched fists. Rue glared up at the old man. She had to escape from the cloying caring and cross the firth to Glen Aucht and her family, she resolved, locking her eyes in a battle of wills with Lachlan McCulloch. The old man snorted impatiently and turned away to pour himself a drink.

"You want one?" he snapped. Rue nodded and held out a hand. "You dinna deserve it," he growled, handing it to her so it slopped a bit. He poured himself one and turned to find her intently studying a map. She banged the wall with her fist, indicating he should come closer.

"You're a bossy wee thing, too," he complained, obeying her. "We're here," he pointed, "and your father's estate is here . . . so you can either take a very long ride and cross at Dunfermline or take the Queensferry over to Inverkeithing here," he explained, showing her the various places on the map. "Here is where Glen Aucht is." He sat back and watched her peruse the distances and then search the room with her eyes.

"What is it you want?" he asked wearily and his eyes narrowed as she crossed to the mantelpiece where a well-balanced pair of matched daggers were exhibited. "Can you use them?" he added as she reverently took them down. She looked at him scornfully and turned questioning eyes around the room as if to ask what she might aim at.

"I've never liked that fussy thing," he confessed, pointing to an ornate porcelain figurine of a shepherdess with a multitude of frills and sheep. Rue hardly seemed to take aim before the dagger flew from her hand and the ringletted head was neatly severed. Lachlan pulled at his pleated top lip, not willing to show how impressed he was as he surveyed the room, looking for another target. He leered wickedly, indicating a dusty pheasant with a brood in a very artificial setting. He removed the glass dome that covered the bird and stepped back. Rue stepped forward, not believing what she saw. The bird and her young seemed alive and real and yet were frozen in time. She tentatively touched the soft cold feathers and recoiled. She sniffed, expecting to smell rotting flesh and frowned as she inhaled thick dust. She sneezed and turned inquiring eyes to Lachlan, who was captivated by her innocence.

"Aye, once it was real and alive but now they are stuffed. Barbaric practice, isn't it?" he said, sharing the distaste he saw mirrored on her face. "So what are you waiting on? Kill the puir wee things again," he challenged and before he could blink she had hit the mother pheasant square in the heart.

Lachlan nodded his approval and took a long swig of his drink.

"Well, you certainly have no trouble with a still target. But I wonder how you are at a moving one." Rue straightened from retrieving the dagger and gave him a long speculative look. "You'll not practice on me, young Sinclair," protested Lachlan, raising his hands in mock surrender. "Drink your whiskey," he directed, pointing at her still-full glass. Rue took a long swallow and choked as the fiery liquid burned down her throat, setting her stomach afire. She was used to Angus's rough homemade brew but nothing had prepared her for the real thing. She bent double, as it felt her whole chest area had seized up, restricting her breathing. She gasped and Lachlan roared with merriment and thumped her none-too-gently on the back, forcing her to take a large breath.

" 'Tis true Scottish spirit and needs to be respected," he guffawed, somehow pleased to find a chink in Rue's seemingly impenetrable armor, as tears sparkled her amber eyes and burst down her smooth cheeks. He chortled at her furious expression, knowing exactly what she was about as she stubbornly lifted the glass and drained the whiskey. She thumped the empty receptacle on the desk and stared at him, daring him to resume his laughter. "Aye, and you are also a true Scottish spirit who needs respecting," apologized the old man, desperately wanting to take her in his arms and try to undo the terrible wrongs that he felt she had suffered.

"Tomorrow, my lass, I shall take you to your father in Glen Aucht," he informed her. She stared at him long and hard before scribbling one word and thrusting it at him.

"Why?" read Lachlan. "Because I'm an old man and when you are as old as I, you'll need to feel useful, too," he answered, his dark eyes not leaving her challenging ones for a second. Rue's face tightened as she firmed her resolve never to trust a person again. "Now, I think you should be to bed if we are to leave refreshed on the morrow," he suggested, his keen senses missing nothing.

Rue whistled for her hound and abruptly quit the room. Lachlan stood at the bottom of the wide staircase watching the girl climb the stairs. He sighed heavily before sitting in a very uncomfortable chair after hearing her bedchamber door click shut.

"Lord Lachlan McCulloch?" hissed Miss Goody, who had been guilty of eavesdropping through the study door. "What are you about?"

"You were right, Goody," whispered the old man.

"And when have I ever been wrong?"

"We'll take that up another day. But she'll be off before daybreak, you mark my words," he told her excitedly.

"Then lock her in," replied the old lady with exasperation.

"Aye, and what happened when you locked the lads in?" returned Lachlan. "Out of the windows in two shakes of a lamb's tail and that lass is no lamb. Och, Goody, she's a wondrous fine lass," he mourned.

"Aye, I ken," replied the housekeeper. "I think you should speak to Master Nicholas now. The wee lass is fair exhausted, she'll sleep a bit before taking off anywhere."

"Did I hear my name mentioned?" growled a deep voice, and Nick stepped out of the shadows dressed in just a pair of tight trews.

"I hope you left that golden girl well satisfied, young man," asked Lachlan roguishly and was rewarded by a very sharp slap from Miss Catriona Goody.

"Being the lad's grandfather gies you no right to be impertinent," she scolded.

"Now what is this secret meeting on the front stairs in the wee hours of the morning," asked Nick, giving Miss Goody a resounding kiss on her rosy old cheek.

"Hush!" hissed Lachlan, prodding, and pushing them toward his study. "Now, Nicholas MacKay, we want to know about the lass Rue," he demanded when they were safely ensconced in the small intimate room.

"What do you want to know?" returned Nick, not knowing where to start.

"Who whipped her?" demanded the housekeeper. "Her wee back is crisscrossed wie scars and her tiny belly has a scar from belly button to side."

"I dinna ken who whipped her," replied Nick soberly. "Pour me a dram or two, Grandfather, and I'll tell all I know." Lachlan's face grew stony, knowing his grandson was about to impart something very serious as the lad never called him Grandfather unless he was angry or having trouble with words.

Nicholas drank deeply, knowing the pain he would feel just recounting the tragedy he was about to impart.

Rue listened intently. She lay feeling dwarfed and infinitely lonely in the large bed. She felt hot and suffocated so she padded to the draped windows and threw back the curtains and opened the heavy panes to breathe deeply. She stared out at the moon's reflection as it limned the numerous rooftops that seemed to continue all the way to the horizon. She turned back and stared around the richly furnished room with its rose-patterned wallpaper and fabrics, wishing she was home in the comfort of the rough-wood rambling house in the wilderness, with its homespun plaids and warm furs instead of the rich velvets and plush carpets. As she looked out again over the red-tiled roofs, she thought of the dark green pines and smelled their fragrance, hearing the night calls of the heron and owl coupled with the distant haunting howl of the wolves instead of the raucous singing of revellers staggering along the rubbish-strewn Edinburgh streets.

As Rue stared across row upon row of houses, her mind went back to the mission with its row upon row of crosses in the cemetery, the row upon row of beds, the row upon row of faceless girls all dressed in the same gray identical smock, the row upon row of long furrows in the fields waiting to be hoed. She frantically rubbed her eyes to erase the memory. She idly scratched behind Shame's floppy ear as the young dog picked up her sorrowful mood and whined her concern. She resolved to leave before she made another mistake and relaxed and trusted the tall old man whose eyes reminded her so painfully of another's, whose very presence caused her such pain and furious anger. She wrenched off the lacy nightgown and stared bemused as she realized she had gone to the stables and been with Lachlan in his study dressed so ridiculously. She strode naked across the soft carpet and tugged open the wardrobe and surveyed the gowns bought so long ago, it seemed, at Mme. Charbonnière's. She slammed the shiny wooden doors and turned to the chest of drawers. She rummaged furiously through the neat piles of frilly underwear searching for her trews and shirt, serviceable boy's clothes that wouldn't draw attention to her sex. There were no boy's clothes and small frantic noises burst from her mouth as in frustration she emptied the drawers, flinging the offending garments around the Rose room as she found nothing but stylish female apparel. She snorted with rage as she turned and surveyed the now littered bedchamber. Clothes hung from the paintings, valences, and chandelier. Shame jumped in the air pretending the garments were living prey and growled ferociously as she attacked them, shredding a chemise before pouncing on some silky pantalets and making her kill. She looked up for approval from her young mistress and whined sadly as Rue herself furiously attacked the wardrobe looking for her fringed Indian clothes.

Rue threw herself into an elegant chair and sat with her legs drawn up, staring venomously around the messy bedchamber as her mind seethed with fury. How could she go anywhere without any clothes? Or how could she go anywhere dressed up to the teeth in the latest impractical gown? Well, it was better than riding through the streets stark naked, she determined, as she roamed around the room picking up various items that her young dog had yet to shred as she tried to find something serviceable to wear. There was nothing. Even the simplest dress was made to point out her attractive features, and she cringed as she remembered the hard, hurtful hands that pinched and twisted her in the past. The Hawk's gentle touch was too painful to think about.

Rue pulled the nightgown back over her head, determined to search the stables for some cast-off old clothes. Once again she opened the door a crack and listened intently before tiptoeing out onto the landing and padding down the long corridor to the stairs dressed in the lacy nightgown with a dark cape clutched around her breasts.

On the main floor of the house she heard the low murmur of voices and padded to Lachlan's study where she put her ear to the door. She stepped back sharply, her nostrils flaring before swiftly fleeing out of the front door and down the steps to the stables where her horse Sin awaited her.

Nick halted the heated conversation by grasping his grandfather's arm to silence him as he heard a faint sound from outside. He leaped to his feet but was stopped by Lachlan.

"Go back to your bride, Grandson, and allow me to regain some of my youth," he urged, knowing exactly where to go as he flung the door open and headed for the stables.

"Let him be," agreed Goody, hugging Nick briefly and giving him a push as she urged him back to his bed. "It has his blood pumping young again."

"I dinna ken if you're right," worried the young man. "There's much that happened when my memory was gone that I'm not sure of."

"Go cuddle close to your bonny one. She hasna had it so easy either, if I were to hazard a guess," remonstrated Miss Goody, hugging Nicholas close and loving him no less than if she had birthed him. "I wish your brother Tarquin were here for the wee dark lass," she sighed.

"Quin?" exclaimed Nick, lifting his eyebrows quizzically to his old nurse's suggestion.

"Aye, Quin," returned Goody feistily. "When your mother died, you were really too young to feel the anger, but your brother felt it through his bones and because of the hurt decided never to love again. But we softened him, did your grandfather and I, enough so when your father died in New France it iced his young heart and coated his feelings in steel," recounted the old woman as tears streaked her rosy cheeks.

"That is why I dinna ken what you say!" exclaimed Nick. "Rue doesna need an autocratic, hard man. She needs comfort and loving."

"She's too proud for that," argued Miss Goody. "She'll allow no one near."

"That's why Lachlan shouldna follow," he protested.

"Lachlan will not gie affection even if he feels it, he's too wise for that. He recognizes your brother Tarquin in the wee-un," returned the old woman convincingly. "Let your grandpa have his day, young mon, he knows what he's about."

"I think we should find you some more suitable attire," stated Lachlan, hauling Rue down from her large horse. "You canna go traipsing about Edinburgh in your nightgown." Once again Rue was firmly propelled back to the house and steered up the carpeted stairs back to her bedchamber.

"Och, now, that's quite a temper you have," remarked the old man, surveying the strewn room. He sucked through his teeth as he bent and picked up a beautiful shredded gown. "I should have liked to see you wearing this," he added, his sharp eyes pinned to Rue's rebellious face as she stood clutching the dark cape around her. "If you will be a wee bit patient and stay put, I shall find you some more practical clothes. I take it you would prefer the lad's attire that you arrived in?" Rue nodded emphatically, keeping her face stony and noncommittal, her hands beneath the black cape holding the twin daggers.

"I want your promise that you'll stay here until I return wie clothes for you," demanded Lachlan, not trusting her seeming passivity. Rue's nostrils flared as she allowed a cynical snort to be heard. The old man's temper rose. He remembered what his grandson Nicholas had told him, and his own expression hardened as he grasped her small face in his calloused rough hand.

"I should have thought you've been abused enough, Rue Sinclair!" he stated with icy tones. "That you'd have more sense than to ride out alone flaunting your charms."

Rue felt panic flare and tried to wrench herself away from his steely grip. Lachlan sensed her attack and moved back but not in time as the sharp dagger cleanly sliced across his knuckles. The blood spurted but the old man did not look down. He just pinned his eyes to her coiled figure as Miss Goody bustled into the room and shrieked at the shredded garments that were flung and hung from every conceivable place.

"Oh my goodness," she reproved and then she squealed again as she saw the blood pouring down Lachlan's arm as he held his hand up, asking for silence.

"Put down the dagger!" he ordered, but Rue shook her head as she backed away from the two concerned old people. "Goody, fetch the clothes that Rue arrived in."

"They're wet, soaking, getting ready for being laundered," replied the housekeeper unhappily.

"We need trews and the like. Lad's clothing," barked Lachlan, his eyes not leaving the small crouched figure. "Are there any?"

"Aye," whispered Miss Goody. "Master Tarquin and Nick's from when they were bairns."

"Then fetch what you think will fit . . . boots, too."

Miss Goody bustled away muttering to herself.

"What was that scream?" asked Nick, and the old housekeeper jerked her head to indicate Rue's room before continuing on her way. Nick stood in the doorway of the once tranquil Rose room and surveyed the scene. His lean cheeks hardened as he saw the blood on his grandfather's hand and arm. He casually bent and picked up a torn gown which he wound around his forearm.

"Madame Charbonnière would be insulted," he remarked dryly.

"I'm handling this," spat Lachlan, not removing his gaze from Rue's mutinous face.

"Then take this," answered Nick, throwing the brocade gown at him as he picked up more lacerated material. Rue looked frantically from one man to the other as they both moved toward her. She dropped her hands to her sides, knowing if she didn't she would be disarmed and then would be weaponless. She looked away from the old man not wanting to see the hurt she had inflicted.

" 'Tis just a scratch," snarled Lachlan, pulling his hand away from Nick's scrutiny. "And it was my fault. I lost my temper and judgment."

"Rue, you're among friends and family," stated Nicholas softly, but the dark girl would not acknowledge his words as she stared blindly out of the window. She wished she could speak so she could tell them all to go away and leave her alone. She was so weary she felt she would fall down, but she refused to give one sign.

"Would it not be better to leave in the morning?" suggested Nick. "The ferry doesna run all night."

Rue felt trapped; all she knew was she wanted to get away. Nick looked at the stiff back and wondered what would happen if he reached out to touch her. Lachlan put a hand on his grandson's shoulder and shook his head as he lifted his cut hand in warning.

"Keep the blades, Rue, and climb into bed," he said quietly. "I promise we shall leave at first light."

The girl made no sign that she had heard. Lachlan sighed and sat in a large comfortable chair. "Go to your bed, lad, or that bonny wife of yours will be fashing. It is going to be a very long night."

"I'll sit wie you," determined Nicholas, making himself comfortable in another chair. Rue turned and looked at both lanky men, who rested with their long limbs stretched out, and although she longed to curl up and sleep, her pride forbade her. Shame slept happily, making contented little snores and strange little barks as her tail occasionally wagged as though she dreamed.

"Your puir young bitch needs rest, too. 'Tis quite a journey to Glen Aucht unless you'd thought to leave her here," muttered the old man sleepily, as he yawned and shifted his body more comfortably. Rue looked at the inviting bed but felt that by giving in she would show weakness. She crossed to her dog and sat beside her on the floor as she rested her back against the wall and glared challengingly at the two men who watched her. Once again their nearly black eyes reminded her of another pair, shining through the apertures of the mask. She shuddered and buried her face in Shame's glossy coat.

"She sleeps at last," sighed Lachlan after about fifteen minutes, seeing the slim brown hands relax and limply hang. "So why don't you go to your bed?"

Nick nodded and tiptoed to the door, which was thrust open by Miss Goody, her arms full of clothes and boots, followed by the enormous wolfhound Thor.

"Shush," hissed Nick, indicating the two curled, ebony-haired figures on the floor. Thor yawned and stretched before turning round and round and flopping beside the two.

"Well, isna that a sight," breathed Goody, tottering to the bed and relieving herself of the boy's clothing. "Well, something here is sure to fit and I'm for my own bed," she whispered, quietly leaving the room and shutting the door behind her.

Lachlan stood and stretched before turning down the lamps so there was just a faint glow. He stared down at Rue asleep with the two large dogs and smiled. He settled himself once more in the comfortable chair and closed his own weary eyes.

CHAPTER TWENTY-NINE

Alexander Sinclair stood at the open French doors of his study, staring over the rolling lawns to the Firth of Forth. He had been home for nearly four months after an absence of more than twenty years and yet it seemed time had stood still at his estate of Glen Aucht. Everything was the same, except the people. He had slowly and carefully examined nearly every corner of his ancestral home, noting the nightmarish familiarity of each carved door, marble flagstone, tapestry that warmed the gray stone walls. There was no difference in the large stone lions that guarded the stately home at the end of the long winding carriageway, and yet in the graveyard were the cairns of Mrs. MacDonald and her husband Fergus. The MacDonalds had been as permanent as the turrets and lions, part of Glen Aucht, Alexander's whole life. He looked at their cairns, but his mind was back in the small glen across the vast ocean where Cameron was buried with their children Raven and Rue, beside their dear friends Goliath and Jemmy.

It seemed only one flesh-and-blood person remained at Glen Aucht and that was Ian Drummond, his boyhood friend, who had managed his lands during his long absence. Ian Drummond, who also mourned for the wild, green-eyed Cameron who lay beneath the earth so very far away. Yet, he mused, even Ian Drummond was less familiar than the worn carpets and paneling in the enormous drafty house. The rusty brown hair had thinned and grayed, the strong square shoulders had rounded and the once flat stomach filled to portly proportions.

Alex turned and dispassionately surveyed himself in a glass. He snorted bitterly at the cadaverous, wild-haired, stooped man. His ancient house stayed the same, but the mere mortals had turned to dust. He had walked through every room in his house remembering Cameron's haunting presence that wildly dared every convention as she refused to be part of meaningless social stupidity. He banged his clenched fist against walls, doors, and countless pieces of furniture as he remembered trying to curb his tempestuous bride. He had stared out of the rain-lashed windows at the summer storms that whipped the waters of the firth into a frenzy, expecting to see Cameron astride her horse Torquod race with the wind, defying the thunder and lightning as her faithful black hound Torquil kept apace.

"Oh, Cameron, my wild free love," he grieved aloud, the aching pain never lessening with time.

"Father," ventured Lynx at the open doorway to the study. Alex wrenched his eyes from the cliffside path and spun around. He looked with confusion into his son's own concerned green eyes and pure agony burst from his mouth.

"Let me be!" he ordered harshly, unable to bear the combination of emerald eyes and raven hair that his son had inherited from his cherished wife. He turned back to the open window, knowing his tall son had not obeyed.

Across the rise of land silhouetted against the Firth of Forth galloped a black horse with dark rider, followed by a black hound.

"Cameron!" cried Alex hoarsely, stepping out into the flagstoned courtyard. He breathed deeply and closed his eyes expecting the torturous mirage to fade.

"Who is it?" asked Lynx, standing shoulder to shoulder with his father. Alex opened his eyes and the dark rider approached, black hair streaming behind. The two men stood silently as the large horse neared, effortlessly leaping the stone wall surrounding the rose garden that bordered the courtyard around the house. Lynx stared inquiringly at his father, noticing the white drawn face as the older man backed away.

Rue reined her stallion Sin and looked down at her older brother, her expression guarded as she did not know what to expect. Lynx's eyes narrowed. It couldn't be his sister Rue who had been killed nearly four years before, thousands of miles across the ocean, his young mind reasoned. The small face above him hardened even more, the well-formed mouth clenched in a thin line. The still moment was broken by the glossy black hound, who flung herself on the flagstones at Lynx's booted feet and panted her exhaustion.

Alex stood in the doorway expecting the nightmarish vision to disappear but still the painful tableau appeared before him, reminding him of his loss.

Rue looked beyond her brother to her father, framed in the doorway, and tears of joy burst from her amber eyes. She opened her mouth to call to him, but no sound emerged. She lithely flung her lean leg over the pommel and slid agilely down from Sin's high back as Lachlan McCulloch rode up with several Sinclair men. The riders reined their horses as they watched the dark girl open her arms like a small child and run toward her father, hoping to be swung against his heart for comfort as he used to do so long ago.

"Begone! Dinna torment me so!" roared Alexander Sinclair backing away, and the still onlookers saw the beautiful childlike figure freeze with arms still outstretched for love and comfort. The exquisite face that had been so open and expectant, closed and hardened, and the proud bearing of the small dark lass in boy's clothes slumped for a second.

Rue turned, straightening her bearing, her amber eyes as hard as the fossilized resin of the same name. She leaped upon her stallion's high back and savagely yanked the reins, turning him toward the cliff road above the firth. She galloped away followed by her hound Shame.

The watching people turned as one, expelling their held breath but not making another sound as they watched the furious retreat. Ian Drummond shook his head in disbelief, his face chalky-white.

"I never believed in the supernatural until now," he intoned, walking shakily toward Alex and Lynx. " 'Twas Cameron back from the dead."

"Nay!" spat Lachlan, fury shaking his voice as he approached. "That is your own flesh and blood, Sinclair! 'Tis your wee daughter Rue."

"Rue," breathed Lynx. "I must fetch her back," he added.

"Take this horse, lad," offered Lachlan, swinging himself stiffly from his horse's high back. Lynx quickly mounted the superb steed.

"Lynx, wait for me!" protested Rowan, who had watched part of the painful scene from his bedchamber window on the second floor. Ian Drummond looked from Alex's drained gaunt face and then back to the furious old man.

"Lord Lachlan McCulloch," he greeted formally, somewhat at a loss for words as Alexander strode abruptly away. "May I get you some refreshment?" he improvised helplessly, trying to make up for their host's rudeness.

"Aye, a dram or two," growled the old man, sitting thankfully in a large chair. "Ye're young Drummond, aren't you?"

"Aye, if fifty is young to you," laughed Ian awkwardly.

"Bloody fool!" snorted Lachlan.

"I beg your pardon?" questioned Ian politely.

"I see the gossips are right. You never married because you were smitten wie the Black Cameron, bastard of the Bonny Prince!" chortled the old man, accepting a generous glass of whiskey.

Ian stared down with pursed lips at the mischievous old face before nodding. "Strange that now in 1782 her birthright means nothing, but when she was a child it meant sure death if it were known." He laughed sadly. "Aye, I loved Cameron wie all my heart and when I met her son Lynx, wie his green eyes and raven hair, my heart hurt again. But not as much as just now seeing her daughter astride her black horse wie her black hound." Ian turned back and looked at Lachlan, unashamed of the tears that welled in his gray eyes. "Why did she not say who she was?" he asked hoarsely.

"Rue Sinclair is mute!" stated the old man baldly.

"Mute," repeated Ian, stunned.

"Aye, but she hears. The lass has been sorely abused and the last thing she needed was to be rejected."

"When she rode up I felt I was back twenty years, so I can ken what Alex felt. It was a shock," Ian said in defense of his oldest friend.

"Then it was even more of a shock for a wee lass who's been torn from her family for the last four years. Who's been raped and beaten, has come thousands of miles to her father for comfort . . ." raged Lachlan, unable to continue, and turning to stare out at the tranquil grounds. Ian shrugged unhappily, wishing there were words but sensibly realizing there weren't any adequate ones for the situation.

"It was Rue!" rejoiced Rowan, limping into the room as he hurriedly buttoned himself into his clothes.

"Relax, laddie, your brother has my horse. Sit!" he ordered. Rowan's green eyes narrowed at the command. He perused the ancient man impudently before limping toward the open French doors. Lachlan casually stuck out a long thin leg, neatly tripping the youth. "I apologize for such foul play, especially since you seem to have an injury, but I should like some answers."

"Who are you?" snarled Rowan.

"Lord Lachlan McCulloch."

"You're Nick's grandfather," recalled the golden-haired youth.

"Aye, and now I'm related to you as my grandson is wed to your sister, who incidentally looks much like you. And has as outlandish a name as you do, too," he remarked as he offered a hand to the befuddled young man.

"Where's Father?" asked Rowan, ignoring the offer and painfully regaining his feet under his own steam. Ian shrugged and splayed his hands in despair. Rowan limped to the open door and stared out over the rolling lands of Glen Aucht, looking for a sign of his brother and sister.

Lynx stood up in the stirrups as he urged Lachlan's prized piece of horseflesh after Rue. Beside the tranquil waters of the firth raced the two horses, chased by the tiring young hound who finally collapsed beside the dusty coastal road and panted, her long tongue hanging thirstily as she pinned mournful eyes to the fast disappearing figures. She whined and sprawled limply in the long dry grass unable to run another step.

Lynx drew level with his sister and stared across at her set face, instinctively knowing and feeling the terror and sorrow that pounded through her petite body.

"Rue, it's Lynx," he informed her, but she didn't slow her pace. "Stop!" he roared as he prepared to reach out and grab her bridle. But before he could, she obediently pulled on the rein and slowed her tired horse's pace and the two trotted, panting side by side. Rue slowed until her horse stood still, his sweating girth heaving as his young rider stared across the firth toward Edinburgh. Lynx sat quietly as the wheeling lamenting gulls circled the small fishing boats and a cooling breeze comforted his hot face.

Rue breathed deeply, trying to calm the terrible fear and pain she felt. She had broken her promise, had been vulnerable to her very own father. His words still rang in her ears, numbing her senses to Lynx's loving concern. *Begone! Begone!* screeched with the gulls, hardening her resolve, and she bit the insides of her cheeks and turned a dispassionate face to her brother. Lynx stared into Rue's amber eyes and frowned when he saw her exquisite features were marred by sardonic bitterness. There was a still, pain-filled minute before she yanked her reins and turned Sin back toward Glen Aucht.

Lynx rode sorrowfully beside his strange little sister. He tried desperately to get her to talk to him, to share her fears and sadness, but she kept her small face set and averted and they returned to the imposing granite structure beside the Firth of Forth in silence. Lynx hated the harnessed, manicured lawns of his father's estate, wishing he were back in the untamed wilderness of his birthland with his uncle and Angus. His mind exploded with all he wanted to tell Rue. His arms ached to hold her and give her comfort as he had done when she was a tiny child riding on his shoulders.

Unable to respect the cold barrier between them Lynx reached out and took her bridle, pulling Sin up short. In a flash Rue had her dagger drawn and Lynx stared, shocked at the lethal blade, knowing his sister had no compunction about using it. He sighed deeply and dropped her bridle, kicking Lachlan's horse into a canter across the rolling lawns.

Rue stared at the dagger in her hand and at her brother's tall straight back as he rode away from her. She sat still, wondering what she should do and where she should go before digging in her heels and following Lynx back through the orchards where the boughs creaked, laden with their heavy harvest of apples and pears. There wasn't anywhere to go or anything to do, she thought hopelessly, except to make sure she didn't open herself up for any more hurt.

Kestrel stared lovingly at Nick, who climbed reluctantly into his clothes. Sunlight poured in through the window and a luncheon tray was discarded by the bed.

"I love being lazy." She yawned and stretched, rolling her naked golden body over and over across the bed until she reached him and wiggled onto his lap as he tried to put his boots on.

"This is why we have separate dressing rooms," he teased as she stopped him talking by kissing him hungrily. "Never satisfied," he complained, extricating himself and tickling her so she rolled off him. A furious knocking caused them to frown at each other, and the doorknob was impatiently turned.

"I'm glad you bolted the door," giggled Kestrel. "A few minutes earlier and we'd have been interrupted."

"Who is it!" demanded Nick, angry at the rude intrusion.

"Quin" barked the answer.

"Get some clothes on, my love. You're about to meet my ferocious older brother," returned Nick, kissing her nose and purposefully taking his time crossing to the door. Kestrel quickly buttoned herself into a robe and raised her eyebrows at the impatient knocking that continued.

"Nicholas, 'tis urgent," shouted the deep voice. Kestrel frowned, hearing a familiar ring. Nick opened the door and Tarquin MacKay strode in, totally ignoring Kestrel, who posed hoping to make a good first impression. Her eyes narrowed as she assessed the tall dark man, wondering where she had seen him before.

"Quin, I should like you to meet my wife," introduced Nick with one boot on and the other in his hand. Kestrel smiled hesitantly up into the dark sardonic face that was like her own husband's and yet was very different. Tarquin nodded impatiently and turned back to his brother.

"Where's Lachlan?" he demanded.

"Went wie Kestrel's sister to visit her father at Glen Aucht," he
replied. "Kess, come downstairs when you're dressed," added Nick
as he and his brother left the room.

"How are you, Quin?" he asked as they walked down the thickly
carpeted corridor. As they came abreast of the Rose room, Nick
peered in and frowned, seeing that the previous night's havoc had not
been attended to. Tarquin pushed open the door and surveyed the
disaster. He strode among the remains of the expensive gowns and
stooped to examine the blood on the pale pink carpet.

"What happened here?" he asked as he reached above his head and
pulled a tattered black crepe dress from the chandelier.

"Nothing important," laughed Nick, not knowing how to explain
that he had a rather wild mute sister-in-law.

"Someone got hurt?" probed Quin, eyeing the blood.

"Aye, Lachlan."

"Lachlan, in here?" frowned Tarquin, unconsciously caressing the
soft black crepe. "Who is using this chamber?"

"Kestrel's sister, Rue Sinclair. She is . . . well, 'tis a long story
and I dinna think you should judge her by any of this," recounted
Nick.

"How did Lachlan get hurt?" insisted Quin.

"Our grandfather and Rue had a slight altercation," stated the
younger brother.

"And Lachlan came off the worse for the wear," chuckled Quin,
surprising Nick, who frowned at him.

"Aye," he answered.

"How?"

"Wie a dagger across the knuckles," replied Nick cautiously and
sat stunned at his older brother's reaction as he roared with laughter
and slapped his well-muscled thigh.

A discreet tapping at the door caused both brothers to turn
expectantly.

"Aye?" they chorused, and Miss Catriona Goody popped her head
around the door.

"Why isna this chamber cleaned up, Goody?" asked Nick.

"Your grandfather told me not to. I think he wants the wee-un to
take responsibility for her own actions," explained the housekeeper,
holding her ample arms out to Tarquin. "Well, young Master Tarquin
McCulloch MacKay, where's my welcome after four and a half long
months?" Quin picked her up in his strong arms and whirled her

around until she begged for mercy. He kissed her soundly on both apple cheeks before setting her down on her feet.

"And what do you think of the lass that would do such a thing as this?" he asked, indicating the room, his hooded black eyes pinned to her, demanding an answer.

" 'Tis not my place," protested Goody.

"Come now, Goody, you've always an opinion. Aye, and young Nicky here tells me she even drew a dagger on our grandsire Lachlan, drawing blood," continued Quin.

Miss Goody pursed her lips and sat with her hands folded in her wide lap, refusing to say a word.

"Goody, you mean you'll not gie a good word for the wee dark lass?"

"How did you know she was dark?" exclaimed Nick as he and the housekeeper stared in surprise at the tall lounging man.

"Do you have a good word for her?" Quin continued, ignoring their question. "Maybe Lachlan is right leaving this mess for her to clean. She probably needs a skelping, whipping, or the like to teach her to respect property and person," he jibed.

"If any sets a hand on the wee lass he'll have me to contend wie! She's had enough whippings. If you could have seen her puir wee back!" stormed Goody, her apple cheeks growing rosier with anger as she remembered. "Tell him, Nicholas. Tell your brother what the lass has had to endure," she demanded.

Nick frowned at his brother, who leaned against the rose-budded wallpaper grinning happily at both him and the indignant housekeeper.

"Och, Miss Goody, are you telling me that you have some affection for a wild, destructive, dagger-wielding hellion who dresses in lad's clothing?" he teased.

"Quin, how do you know Rue is dark and dresses as a lad?" questioned Nick.

"Shouldn't a husband know his own wife?" replied Quin, staring with satisfaction at the two astounded faces.

"I knew it!" exclaimed Kestrel, bursting in after listening outside the door. "I knew it!"

"Hush up!" laughed Quin, covering her mouth with his broad hand so her words were muffled. "Where's your sense of fun, Kestrel?" he asked. "Let Nicholas work it out."

"But he canna," protested Kestrel, but nonetheless fell silent under his stern gaze.

"You're married to Rue Sinclair?" puzzled Goody, wiping her hot face on her apron. Nick stared intently at his brother, and his eyes dropped to the black crepe dress that Quin still held. Kestrel followed his eyes and she beamed. Nick crossed and took the ruined gown and held it against Kestrel.

"You have such a one, don't you, Kess?" he asked.

"Aye," she gurgled, nearly bursting with the delicious secret. "Oh, Tarquin, can I gie a wee hint?" she begged.

"Aye," he laughed, and Nick frowned as he had never seen his brother so relaxed and fun-loving.

"Love, honor, and obey," giggled Kestrel as Goody burst into tears and blew her nose noisily.

Nick tried to grasp the elusive fragments that flew into his mind.

"A lap full of custard?" she added wickedly and she and Quin howled with laughter. "He got his memory back but now he canna remember anything of the time he couldna find it," she struggled to explain.

"I dinna ken a thing," sniffed Goody. "Except that you say you are married to the dark wee-un."

"Rue is my wife," stated Quin firmly.

"Then you are the Hawk," said Nick softly.

"I was the Hawk," replied Quin. "Now the war is over I have no need of such subterfuge."

"I dinna ken," puzzled Nick.

"I was working for the Colonists intercepting the British vessels," he explained.

"Then why did you attack a French ship?" questioned Kestrel.

"I intercepted the Gillette brothers, which is vastly different from attacking a French vessel, young lady. The Gillettes have no allegiance except to themselves," informed Tarquin.

"I don't believe you!" retorted Kestrel hotly. "They are good people. They are my friends!"

"I am talking politics, not personal friendship," replied the tall dark man tersely, not wishing to get into a long, drawn-out argument. "Now you say Rue and Lachlan rode out to Glen Aucht?"

"Aye," replied Nick.

"When?"

"At first light," answered Goody.

"So they reached there about nine or ten this morn, and 'tis now about three in the afternoon," figured Quin. "Goody, have a bath sent up to my rooms and also have anything salvageable belonging to my wife sent up also."

Kestrel frowned as Tarquin MacKay strode abruptly out of the room. She turned and looked at Nicholas and Miss Goody, who grinned at each other with pure delight.

"Why are you two so pleased wie yourselves?" she demanded.

"You dinna know Master Tarquin before," sniffed Goody.

"I saw him as a pirate and that wasna so wondrous," returned Kestrel angrily. "I dinna ken why you are just sitting there grinning away, Nick MacKay, when your very own brother shot at us, abducted my sister, and hit you so hard you lost your memory for weeks!"

"You sank his whole boat, Kess," Nick reminded her. "And he does not seem to carry a grudge."

"That's different," she returned feistily.

"Kestrel, Rue loves him," he reminded her gently. "You yourself told me that."

"Then why is he not riding out after her? Why is he going to have a bath?" she demanded.

"Because he may miss her if she's riding back," suggested Nick.

"And he looks very tired and dirty," added Miss Goody.

"Kestrel, I'm going up to talk wie Quin. Goody, show Kess about, will you?" and before either woman could reply, Nick left the room.

Quin lowered his rangy body into the steaming bath and sighed with pleasure. He closed his eyes as the hot water soothed his aching muscles. It was the first comfort since the sinking of his ship. He flexed his arms, remembering the long torturous hours rowing to the Spanish coast as the *Dolphin* torched the thick darkness of the night and the *Étoile* sailed away with Rue.

Nick entered after a cursory knock and stared down at his older brother, seeing the lines of fatigue etched across the handsome face. He sat in a chair with his long legs stretched out in front of him, knowing Quin was aware of his presence despite the closed eyes.

"You look exhausted," he said awkwardly, wanting to reach out but feeling somehow intimidated.

"I dinna think I've had much sleep since you and those French sea rats destroyed my vessel," replied Quin shortly, without opening his eyes.

"Was there any loss of life?" asked Nick, feeling responsible.

"No, just a few minor injuries and a couple of broken arms."

"You made very good time," returned Nick teasingly. "Were you picked up by another ship?"

"Aye, I spent six days aboard the slowest, dirtiest fishing vessel in existence and the last three in the saddle. I've not slept for twenty-four hours." He yawned and groaned, remembering the grueling ride from the south of England. He had changed horses four times, determined to reach Edinburgh before Nick and the Sinclair sisters.

The two brothers sat in companionable silence for a while.

"How is she?" asked Quin.

"Physically, she's healed," replied Nick.

"How was she before?" questioned Quin, sitting forward in the tub so the water slopped.

"When her Uncle Meron found her at the mission, she was emaciated and lacerated," answered Nick, trying desperately to be the doctor as his brother's dark eyes seemed to bore into him. "There is more you should know, Tarquin," he added softly.

"What?"

"Rue has been brutally raped."

"Aye, I know. Not once nor twice but many times it would seem," snarled Quin, savagely scrubbing himself and getting a perverse pleasure in the pain.

"There is more," whispered Nick huskily. Quin's angry movements stopped and he stared intently at his younger brother. "She gave birth to a stillborn bairn."

"When?"

"At the mission when she was no more than thirteen years old," recounted Nick, hurting with the pain he saw in his brother's eyes.

"Oh, God!" swore Quin, punching the water impotently as his stomach contracted with empathy at what Rue had had to endure. "The puir wee Rue!" he cried, his jaw tensing with anger and agony.

Nick sat silently as his brother finished scrubbing himself and stepped out of the tub to dry.

"Aren't you going to sleep?" he exclaimed as his older brother dressed quickly in clean riding clothes.

"I need to find her," Quin whispered hoarsely. "Nick, I see how you love your little wild bride. I feel the same," he confessed.

"I think you have a harder row to hoe," returned Nick sadly. "She has changed, Quin."

"Changed? How?"

"She is closed, hard. For her to stab Lachlan . . ."

"See here?" demanded Quin, baring his muscular arm and showing a long scar. "That is one of the marks Rue left on me."

"One?"

"Aye, the other is where you canna see," said Quin, patting his chest over his heart.

"She is not the same." Nick struggled to explain. "Before, even though she was unable to talk, there was a softness about her, a vulnerability like a faun. Now there is nothing soft or approachable. She trusts no one, not even her sister."

"Why should she trust anyone?" challenged Quin. "The puir child has had to be her own parent since she was thirteen years old. Maybe now finding and being reunited wie her father will soften and undo some of the harm."

"I hope so," replied Nick warmly, reaching out and hugging his brother. "Och, Quin, it has been so long."

"It was interesting to watch my young brother wie out him knowing who I was. You are a fine man and doctor Nicholas, and you have a beautiful bride even though she is somewhat of a handful," he laughed.

"I think my handful will be less than what you're going to have to wrestle wie," uttered Nick prophetically as the two brothers strode down the wide stairway together.

"I think I'll ride out to Glen Aucht after I've had a bite," said Quin thoughtfully.

"Aye, I think that's a good idea. For if Sir Alexander Sinclair is as he was, I'm worried about the reception Rue might receive."

"What do you mean?"

"How much do you know, Tarquin?" asked Nick as they entered a small breakfast room and rang for service.

"That Rue was abused in many ways," answered Quin savagely, unable to put into words the vile ways.

"Rue Sinclair was thought dead for over three years. Her father and brothers don't know she is alive. Her mother never gave up hope but sadly Cameron died before she could see her dark daughter again," explained Nick.

"Come in," called Quin in answer to a discreet tapping at the door, and a manservant entered. "Bring me ale, meat and bread, please," he ordered. The man nodded silently before leaving. "Now, why are you worried about Rue's reception? Surely for her father to find out his daughter is alive after all this time is a cause for rejoicing?"

"He closed himself within himself when his wife died. He couldna even look at Kess because her green eyes and spirited ways reminded him of Cameron. Rue looks even more like her mother wie her dark hair," recounted Nick.

"Surely the man has had time to mourn?" snorted Quin, as servants entered and piled the table with food. Kestrel popped her head around the door.

"Come in, Kess," invited Nick. "We were talking of what sort of reception Rue might receive from your father."

"He is going to be so happy that she is alive," replied Kestrel, looking very wistful. "He always loved her best." Nick pulled her down onto his lap and held her close. Tarquin's eyes narrowed as he remembered Kestrel's confession aboard the *Étoile* when as a child she had tried to save her sister and instead had shot her.

"Have you been out to Glen Aucht?" asked Quin after a long pause, which he had filled by eating hungrily.

"We only got back yesterday," confessed Nick. "You nearly beat us home."

"Did the *Dolphin* sink?" asked Kestrel in a small voice.

"Aye," answered Quin shortly.

"I'm sorry," she whispered.

"Aye, so am I," returned Quin, draining his mug of ale and pouring some more. He chewed and watched his brother gently wind a strand of golden hair around one of his fingers.

"Why didn't you tell us who you were?" she challenged.

"I don't mix business and personal matters," replied Quin.

"Hah!" laughed Kestrel rudely. "Then why did you marry my sister?"

"I slipped. Had an error in judgment!" he parried, not able to explain his impulsiveness in deciding to marry Rue Sinclair nearly as soon as he first set eyes on her.

Rue stood silently at the open door, listening.

"Error in judgment!" shouted Kestrel indignantly.

Quin turned, feeling that he was watched, and stared into Rue's closed, hostile face. He smiled tenderly and relaxed back in his chair filling his eyes with the sight of her. Lachlan stood behind the small dark girl with his broad hand on her shoulder stopping her from fleeing.

"Tarquin?" puzzled the old man, astonished by the soft expression on his sardonic older grandson's face.

"I see you've met my wife, Lachlan," said Quin huskily, slowly standing, keeping his dark eyes pinned to Rue's hard stony face.

"Wife?" blustered the old man, his eyes nearly popping out of his head.

Rue panicked, trying to back away, but Lachlan stood firm.

"Come here, Rue," said Quin, holding out his hands to her. She shook her head as she fought the aching tears that stung behind her eyes. She would not give anyone the satisfaction of showing weakness. She would stand alone needing no one, she resolved. She had ridden back from Glen Aucht unable to feel and on entering the house had heard the deep familiar voice that had reverberated within her, shattering her numbness. She had stood staring at the back of the jet-black head knowing it was the Hawk, and that he wasn't dead. For a moment all her promises of being vulnerable to no one had dissolved—until she heard him utter the words, "an error of judgment."

"I said come here, Rue," repeated Quin.

Rue took a deep breath and spat at the floor by his feet before turning and striking out at Lachlan so she could escape. Quin leaped from his chair and grabbed the back of her cloak, but she twisted out of it and fled, knocking down a shelf of fine glass ornaments with an enormous crash. Shame barked and pranced excitedly as Lachlan sat sharply and cut his hand on the sharp shards that littered the floor.

Rue fleetly raced into the large hall toward the front door only to be stopped by Quin, who in several strides outpaced her. She whirled around with a dagger in each hand.

"Are we to go through this again?" he teased.

"Rue, what are you doing?" called Kestrel. "Stop it, you've hurt Lachlan!"

Rue kept her eyes pinned to Quin, refusing to look at the old man whose hand once again poured blood. Rue hurriedly transferred one of the daggers so she held two in one hand as she felt behind her for the latch on the door. Quin moved quickly and threw her cape over her head before efficiently disarming her.

"Well, these pretty things look very familiar," he remarked. "Your dirks, Grandfather. You're getting careless."

"I gie them to the lass," defended Lachlan. "And before you get your dander up, there are a few things you should know," he added as Rue fought the cloak that blinded her and Quin's strong arms.

"I have my hands full at this moment, Grandsire," said Quin tersely, bundling Rue up like a parcel and heaving her over his shoulder. She lay still, unable to move, shout, or see. "Now what are the few things I should know?" he asked. Lachlan shook his head and indicated he didn't want Rue to hear and be further humiliated by the recounting of the cruel rejection she had received. Tarquin frowned and debated what to do. He didn't trust Rue not to run away the moment she could and yet he was very interested in all that had happened to his young wife.

"Och, Rue, I wish I had a dungeon or the like so you'd stay put until I could get some sense through your stubborn head," he groaned aloud, patting the small rounded bottom that rested on his broad shoulder. He felt her tense every muscle in her body before she started struggling wildly again. He pulled her down into his arms and held her against his hard chest as he would a tiny baby, knowing she could not fight forever.

"Take that off her head," pleaded Kestrel, unable to bear the thought of her mute sister also unable to see. Quin nodded and as Rue struggled he deftly unwound the cape. Rue sat on his lap and panted, trying to get her breath. Quin smoothed the dark hair away from her hot flushed face and froze.

"Nick, for heaven's sake tend to Lachlan's hand before we're swimming in his blood. And may we please get out of the front hall and into more comfortable surroundings?" said Quin lightly although his face was stern.

"You need a few stitches after I have pried out the glass," informed Nick, and Rue sucked her cheeks together and tried to wiggle off Quin's thighs, but an iron hand stopped her. "Goody, I need hot water and my medical bag."

"I'll get the bag," offered Kestrel, scampering up the stairs toward their suite of rooms.

"If you'll excuse us, I think we shall leave you to your operation," declared Nick, watching Rue's face and knowing she felt responsible for hurting the old gentleman for the second time.

"But I have things to relate," protested Lachlan.

"I think I can surmise what happened at Glen Aucht," returned Quin shortly, standing and setting Rue on her feet but keeping a firm hand on her. As soon as Rue felt the floor beneath her feet, she twisted and turned, trying to loose his hand so she could escape. Tarquin sighed with exasperation before swinging her back into his strong arms and imprisoning her once again against his chest. He stared down into her flushed mutinous face and shook his head.

"Rue, you escaped me once, you'll not a second time," he informed her as he purposefully proceeded toward his suite of rooms on the third floor. Rue glared into the deep black eyes, steeling her expression to one of scorn as her heart beat frantically.

Tarquin reached the door to his room and unceremoniously flipped her over his shoulder and opened the door.

"You smell of sweaty horses, my love," he informed her unromantically before ringing for a servant. "So I shall have a bath drawn for you." He sat her firmly in a large overstuffed chair and stared down at her as if he couldn't see enough of her. He feigned indifference though he ached with the pain he felt emanating from her. It was going to be a long haul, he realized, knowing she had lost every ounce of trust. Each inch of her body was tense and rigid as if she were coiled to attack or defend herself, he noted. Her hearing was so acute that he saw the faint shifting of her lithe body as she heard the muffled tread of the servant in the corridor outside.

"Enter," he commanded in answer to the discreet tapping. "I should like a bath for my wife and please ask my grandfather when she last ate, and if 'tis warranted, bring food," he ordered. "No maids are needed," he added and the man silently left.

Quin turned and opened the door of an adjacent dressing room but reached out in one lithe moment, catching Rue as she swiftly headed for freedom. He sighed deeply and shook his head as he would to a recalcitrant child before herding her into the dressing room to examine the contents of an armoire.

"Alas," he mourned cynically, clicking his tongue reprovingly as he surveyed the sparse contents. "Seems you destroyed all of the extremely expensive wardrobe my brother bought for you. This is about the only whole piece of clothing," he observed, holding up a lacy nightgown. Rue froze with terror. "And unfortunately your equally undisciplined sister helped successfully to sink the *Dolphin* where I had many beautiful articles of female apparel."

Rue remembered the bursting wardrobe full of gowns all different sizes with shoes to match. What did he want with her, she wondered, knowing that he must be experienced and therefore have many eager women at his beck and call.

Quin steered her back through the small sitting room and into a large bedroom.

"By rights I should have the master suite, being the oldest grandson, but I think Nick and Kestrel better suited for all those rooms, especially when you tend to disappear, and the smaller the space the easier you are to find."

Noise of servants carrying in the bath and many kettles of hot water could be heard.

"Set the bath up in the sitting room," he called, seeing Rue's terror as she stared wide-eyed at the large bed. There was nothing he could say to comfort her, he knew, and he felt impotent. The only way he was going to gain her trust was through actions. There was a gentle tapping at the bedroom door and a manservant stood there with a laden tray.

"From the looks of all that food, you've not eaten for quite a while," remarked Quin.

"She ate a wee bit last night, so says the master," informed the servant, placing the tray where Quin indicated.

"That will be all." Tarquin dismissed the servants, listening for them to leave and looking down at Rue's rebellious expression. He rubbed his hands together and strode to the door, locking it with keys that he stowed away in his pockets. "Your bath, madam, awaits." But Rue stood with her hands clenched, refusing to move. Her eyes frantically scanned the room, looking for something to protect herself with. On the laden tray of food were two knives and two forks. She averted her gaze so he wouldn't guess what she planned but he quickly strode to the tray and removed the utensils with another of his exasperated sighs.

"Rue MacKay," he said sternly, grasping her shoulders and kneeling so they saw eye to eye. "Rue MacKay, as my wife, I think I should tell you that I have a temper that probably surpasses your own unbridled one. I've not slept for several nights and I am trying very hard to be considerate as I know you've had a painful time of it . . . but I'm fast running out of patience. So get into that bath now!"

Rue sneered at him, daring him to lose his temper, wanting him to explode because anything would be better than his cynical jesting. She gasped as she was picked up roughly. She fought with all her strength as he wrenched the clothes off her. Fear pulsated through her as he tugged her trews down her slim thighs, making her vulnerable. She tried to bite him as she fought to hold onto the protection of the clothing.

Quin stared down at the huddled naked girl and nearly howled aloud with the pain he saw in her wide unseeing eyes. He steeled his expression and ignoring her cowering picked her up and deposited her into the hot scented water. *She has to learn to trust again*, he resolved as he knelt beside the bath and gently soaped her. She sat impassionately like an inanimate doll, allowing him to wash her. He felt no passion, just sorrow, as she obeyed his curt commands, and he wished she would start battling him again as anything was better than such docility. He lifted her out of the water and she stood dripping on the thick carpet looking right through him as though he were not there. He shook his head and sat in a large chair with his long legs apart, holding the thick towel.

"Come here, Rue," he said quietly after several minutes, and she took the three paces necessary until she stood between his thighs. He draped the towel over her dripping black hair and briskly rubbed her dry. " 'Tis a wonder you don't snap like a brittle twig," he snorted as he pulled one of his shirts over her stiff, unyielding body, and threw the lacy seductive nightgown across the room. He picked her up and dumped her in the middle of the large bed where she sat with her eyes unfocused and her jaw clenched.

"Eat," he ordered wearily, placing the laden tray before her. Rue reached for some grapes as Quin poured himself some ale. He watched her as he drank. "That is all you are going to eat?" And Rue nodded without looking at him. She felt a clutch of fear as the heavy tray that had acted like a barrier between them was removed.

"I made you a promise on our wedding night, do you remember what it was?" Rue refused to acknowledge as she kept her gaze blurred and pinned on a mark on the wallpaper. She gasped as he took her chin and forced her to look at him. "I've warned you of my temper, Rue MacKay. Dinna make me lose it!"

"Rue MacKay" echoed in her head. She didn't even have her own name anymore. She felt his hard fingers on her jaw and felt his dark eyes burn. She lifted her hand to strike out at his demanding face that loomed in front of her but her hand was caught in a viselike grip.

"Do you remember the promise I made you?" he insisted. Rue lied and shook her head, needing to hear him repeat the vow.

"I told you that making love had nothing whatever to do with rape and I promised that was one way I would never hurt you," he repeated. "But there are many other ways we can hurt each other," he continued. "I shall make another promise to you. I have had quite enough of knife-wielding tricks. I dinna like being cut or hit, and dislike my own kin being similarly assaulted, do you ken? Any more and I promise you I shall not keep my temper! Is that clear?"

Rue swallowed hard, seeing the anger flare in his black eyes, but she refused to answer.

"Is that clear?" demanded Quin, determined she should acknowledge, but the only sign he got was the flaring of her nostrils as she glared at him. His temper pulsed and he wanted to shake her like a rag. He threw her back against the pillows, somehow knowing she was daring him to lose control.

Quin stood and paced around the room before standing at the

window and staring down to the garden below where Nick and Kestrel played, pelting each other with rose petals and lovingly wrestling on the grass beneath the apple trees. He was jealous of the loving trust between the two and he turned back to his wife.

Rue lay with her eyes closed, cuddled into the pillows where he had thrown her. She looked like a child, not a full-grown, full-blooded woman, he mourned. Where was his sanity? What had he got himself into? He seethed inwardly.

"Christ!" he swore. "I should have adopted you, not married you! What need do I have of such a frightened child?" he lamented, stalking out of the bedroom and throwing himself down in a chair in the sitting room.

Rue lay with her heart hammering at his furious words. She knew she loved him and felt overwhelmingly vulnerable. By his own admission he had made an error in judgment. Tears poured down her cheeks as she wished she could be like her sister Kestrel, able to love without fear. There was only one thing left to do, she planned, and that was to somehow escape from the house and find her way to the *Étoile*. She could stow away, and when the ship was under sail convince Pierre to take her back to her Uncle Meron and Angus. She closed her eyes, unable to stay awake, and dreamed of riding Sin through the winding cobbled streets to the bustling, frightening harbor.

Quin dozed in the chair, his large body protesting at the cramped position. He forced himself to stand and stretch as he wondered once more at his sanity. The bed was plenty large enough for both of them, he decided, yawning as he quietly entered the bedchamber. The sun was setting and the blood-red rays filtered through the window and across Rue's sleeping face. He frowned and leaned forward, seeing the tears still wet upon her soft cheeks. He ran a finger across the salty lines and wished that she would trust him. Carefully, so as not to wake her, he slid under the covers and relaxed his tired aching body gratefully on the comfortable mattress. He turned his head to gaze at Rue's sleeping face on the pillow beside him as he debated whether to pull her into his arms. He turned away from her, not willing or not able to deal with anything else as his fatigue engulfed him and he dropped off into a deep sleep.

CHAPTER THIRTY

Tarquin lay quietly, watching Rue tiptoe around the moonlit bed searching for the clothing that he had stripped off her the previous afternoon. He grinned as she cautiously made her way into the sitting room and bumped into the bath so the cold water slurped noisily and slopped over the side. His grin broadened as he imagined her standing still and listening intently. As soon as he heard her movements start up again, he wickedly gave a loud groan and thrashed about. Her movements abruptly stopped again as she held her breath before tiptoeing and shutting the connecting door. Quin frowned and then patted his pockets, knowing there was no way she could get out of the locked suite as he had the keys upon his person. He heard her try the door that led to the corridor, and he lay still as she cautiously reopened the connecting door and padded across the bedroom holding the boots. She wiggled the door and made a small kittenlike mew of frustration before returning to the sitting room and quietly closing that door.

Quin sat up with a frown as he heard a noise he didn't understand. He listened intently and then swung his long legs out of the bed as he realized she had opened the window. That they were on the third floor reassured him a little as he swiftly strode across the room and grasped the doorknob. He swore as he found the connecting door securely bolted.

"At least she has her wits about her," he whispered to himself as he grabbed his own boots and unlocked the door to the corridor. He locked it behind him in case she decided not to jump and made his way quickly down the stairs.

Quin stood hidden by the apple trees watching Rue agilely edge along the roof. He grinned with appreciation as she systematically tried each attic window until she finally disappeared inside. He nonchalantly made his way to the stables, knowing that would be her next port of call. Her hound Shame was tied to the stall where Sin peacefully munched oats and hay. His own horse swished his tail in the next stall.

"Hobbs, my wife will be coming any minute to get her horse and hound. Do not stop her," he ordered the tired ostler.

"But, Lord McCulloch—" protested the sleepy stableman.

"You heard me, Hobbs. Go back to your bed," Quin interrupted and the old man thankfully shuffled away.

Shame whined and strained toward the stable door as her keen ears heard the almost imperceptible tread of Rue approaching. Quin ducked into his horse's stall, determined to follow his wife.

Rue sucked in her breath angrily at finding Shame once more denied freedom. There seemed something symbolic in the rope, she felt, as she knelt and removed the offending bond. The glossy rambunctious hound leaped excitedly up, knocking her backward into a pile of hay and Rue lay back giggling at the warm loving tongue that cleaned her face. Quin watched the scene through a hole in the wooden partition, delighting in the infectious gurgling laughter and the open happy face. Maybe he should let her go, he thought soberly and then remembered her inability to communicate as well as the countless scars visible and invisible that marred her young body and mind.

Rue led her horse along the long carriageway until she got to the gate. She stared with apprehension at the gatehouse, but not seeing any sign of life, she signaled her hound to sit and warily approached the iron palings. They were too high to get her horse to leap without endangering him on the arrow-shaped spikes. She examined the latch and quietly unlocked it. She froze as the metal rustily protested but no shout or sign of activity issued from the gatehouse, so she swung the wrought iron open and whistling for her horse and hound, she fleetly raced out of Lord Lachlan McCulloch's town estate.

Quin shook his head as he wondered how drunk the keeper of the gate had to be as the horse's hooves clattered noisily and Rue swung herself up onto Sin's high bare back. He waited, listening to the hoof steps receding north before kicking his booted heels into his horse's girth and cantering through the open gates after his wife. He smiled thankfully to himself as he heard the indignant shout. At last the gatekeeper had remembered his post so at least the gates would be secured behind him. Once again, he had to appreciate Rue's innate sense of direction as she headed north through Edinburgh toward the Firth of Forth. He frowned as she veered east away from the ferry to Glen Aucht or the bridge farther west that would also get her to her father's land. He whistled noiselessly between his teeth and he reined as his wife cantered along the narrow dark streets toward the harbor at Leith.

Rue's idea of stowing away was short-lived as she acknowledged she couldn't go back home without Sin and there was no possible way to sneak her horse on board. She reined as she tried to remember where Gladys said they were staying. She smiled, remembering the Spotted Dog and then she frowned, not knowing where it was. She couldn't ask directions, had nothing to write with, and most people couldn't read anyway, she thought dismally. She could ride through the streets looking, she supposed, but after twisting around and peering at the dark, impenetrable winding streets she decided she preferred the openness of where she was. She dug in her knees and walked her horse along the wooden wharves, hating the sharp clatter Sin made and expecting an angry voice to stop her. But nothing moved except an occasional rat or the horrible scream of a cat.

Quin tethered his horse and followed, afraid for her and also wanting to know her plan. He stood in the shadows as she located the *Étoile*, dismounted, and leaving both dog and horse, removed her boots and crept up the narrow gangplank.

Quin yawned as he swung himself up onto his steed's rusty back and galloped back toward his grandfather's house, eager to climb back into his comfortable bed. He groaned as he saw the lighted gatehouse and the angry shape of Lachlan met him as he approached the stables.

"What the hell is going on?" demanded the angry old man, both bandaged hands gleaming white in the waning moonlight. Quin handed his horse to the drooping stable boy and followed his irate grandfather into the house.

"Where is she?" shouted Lachlan, accepting the drink that Quin poured and sitting heavily in a comfortable chair in his study.

"Did she take the dirks again?" frowned Quin, looking to the mantel where he assumed they had been replaced.

"Worse, a pair of duelling pistols as well," answered the old man tersely. "I dinna ken what's so droll," he added as his grandson sat back and laughed.

"Do you want me to cry?" replied Quin, taking a long gulp and getting pleasure from the scalding burn.

"Where is she?"

"Safe," he answered shortly.

"Where?"

"That is my business, Lachlan," he returned. "Trust me, Grandfather," he pleaded as the old man looked hurt and rejected.

"I love that wee lass, Tarquin," confessed Lord McCulloch with tears in his eyes.

"I do, too."

"But you're so young and I'm afraid it might not be enough," burst the old man.

"I am near thirty years of age," returned Quin.

"Aye, but how do you feel about others knowing her before you," tiptoed Lachlan. "In the biblical sense," he added.

"You think rape is knowing anyone?" bellowed the dark young man. "What type of man do you think me?" he demanded, his violent temper fully aroused. Lachlan McCulloch refused to answer as he leaned back in his chair watching his oldest grandson. "You think I have so little manly pride as to hold that against Rue?"

"I dinna ken. All I know is what I have seen of you since you grew to randy manhood and I have seen nothing that gies me comfort where Rue Sinclair is concerned."

"Rue MacKay," stated Quin. He also leaned back in his chair and locked eyes with his grandfather, refusing to defend his past amorous actions. Whether a woman had been a virgin or not had never bothered him, he now realized. An available woman had meant in the past an available woman to be enjoyed. He had never thought seriously about marriage, not wanting to be hurt, as many of his friends and acquaintances had been by overburdened responsibility, infidelity, or death.

"Why did you marry her?" asked Lachlan, softening his tone.

"So no one else would hurt her," replied Quin honestly, without thought.

"Is that all?"

"What do you think?" challenged his grandson.

"Bullheaded lad!" snorted the old man. "I have just a wee bit of advice for you. Will you take it?"

"Depends what it is."

"Remember my hound, Thor's dam?"

"Aye," replied Quin guardedly. "I hope you are not going to liken my wife to a bitch?"

"Aye, I am. She was a beautiful animal but abused. It took care, patience, and love, but she became the most affectionate, loving animal."

"Grandfather, I know you mean well but I really wouldna like Rue to become the most affectionate loving animal," returned Quin.

"Most men would have shot her!" shouted Lachlan, waving his bandaged hands about. Quin didn't answer but just sat quietly waiting for the old man's color to fade from purplish red to a flushed pink before he spoke.

"It would help more if you were to talk of my mother and not your pet bitch," he remarked, his sharp eyes boring into his grandfather's. Lachlan stood and stared out at his well-cared-for gardens that were tinged by the first blush of morning.

"I think we should both get our sleep," answered Lord McCulloch when he could gain his breath.

"Why won't you talk of your daughter, my mother?" challenged Quin.

"Because 'tis my business!"

"Then dinna ask where my wife is, for that is *my* business!" answered Quin. Lachlan turned and his hawklike face was rigid with fury, an older likeness of the young man before him. He released his breath in an angry hiss and sank into the chair facing the younger man.

"You dinna fight fair, Tarquin McCulloch MacKay," he said with a tired smile.

"Do you?"

"Beware that your children don't mirror you too much," laughed the old man bitterly. "Today I witnessed my most painful sin," he confessed after a long pause. "I watched myself, through Sir Alexander Sinclair, reject my most beloved child because she embodied everything I loved in your grandmother and lost. Alex Sinclair couldna accept his beautiful daughter even though it was a miracle that she lived. 'Begone!' he yelled. 'Begone!' And I saw Rue's open hopeful face turn to stone. Her outstretched arms became lethal weapons. . . ." His voice trailed away as the poignant scene replayed in his mind. "When Rue saw her father, she shone. She was exquisite before, but nothing compared to the incredible beauty that radiated when she swung down from her horse and ran to him. I wonder if it was the same with your mother?"

Tarquin looked up, hearing a noise, and Kestrel and Nick stood in the doorway, their arms about each other. He noticed the relaxed lines on his brother's face and the satisfied glow on Kestrel's, and surmised they had just made love.

"What was the same as our mother's?" questioned Nick.

"Where's Rue?" asked Kestrel.

"Come in, pour a drink, and sit," invited Quin quietly. He imagined them in each other's arms and wished he was able to claim Rue in a similar fashion.

"I was telling your brother about Sir Alexander's reaction to Rue's appearance," stated Lachlan awkwardly, busying himself by pouring glasses of whiskey.

"My father's reaction to Rue?" repeated Kestrel.

"He rejected her!" recounted the old man. "It was like he smote her across the face! Kicked her in the belly! Cut out her heart!" he strove to explain.

"My father rejected Rue?" repeated Kestrel, stunned. "No! You're mistaken! It must have been me you saw, not her. He's always loved Rue best!" she protested and Lachlan's old eyes narrowed.

"It was Rue, not you!" he stated firmly.

"He must have thought it was me. He dinna mean to hurt her. He thought she was me," cried Kestrel, tears pouring down her face. Quin lost his sardonic expression as he saw her tranquil face, so beautifully serene from lovemaking, grow wild with guilt and pain.

"Kess, there's no way your father could mistake you for Rue. Your coloring is so very different," consoled Nick.

"Our mother was an independent female, wasn't she, Lachlan?" stated Quin harshly. Kestrel frowned at the sudden change in the conversation. She looked up at Quin's face and shivered at the ruthless lines. She turned to Nick for comfort and saw his beloved features were hardened and somehow remote. She stared at their grandfather and her heart ached as she saw his defeated sadness.

"Aye," he croaked. "She was. She married against me to a MacKay of Strathnaver and I dinna see her for four years. When she returned, you Tarquin were near three years old and Nicholas was swelling her belly. The MacKay, your sire, was dead on the Plains of Abraham. What did she expect? Aye?" he yelled furiously.

"What did you do to your daughter?" whispered Kestrel, conscious of the dark eyes that were pinned to the old man as both grandsons sat tensely waiting.

"I dinna say 'Begone' as your father did," replied Lachlan defensively. "But I might as well have. I opened the door and the larder but not my heart," he continued sorrowfully.

"When did she die?" asked Kestrel after looking at the dark brothers and sensing they were not going to ask any questions.

"Just after Nicholas was born. She just faded away. I couldna hold on to her. A few months before she died we made our peace but what about all those lonely years? All the time I let my hurt pride stop my love?"

"Was it just hurt pride?" asked Quin softly, and Kestrel saw her brother-in-law's stern features had gentled.

"She was too much like her mother," mourned Lachlan. "It hurt so much."

"Rue and Kess are very much like their mother," stated Nick. Kestrel smiled wistfully and he opened his arms to her. She curled on his lap, winding her arms about his neck, smelling the comforting fragrance of him. Quin sighed and wondered when Rue would trust him enough to do the same.

"I think you should go and talk to your new father-in-law," suggested Lachlan. "I've heard tell that the Black Cameron was as wild and free as any Highland lass and Sinclair won her love wie out breaking her spirit."

"I dinna need advice on how to win my wife," retorted Quin.

"Now whose pride is rearing its stubborn head?" laughed the rascally old man. "I just felt that maybe by talking to Sinclair you might get him to see reason."

"Och aye, I'll make him see reason!" murmured Quin. "Now if you'll excuse me I need my sleep."

"But where's Rue?" insisted Kestrel, leaping off Nick's lap and grabbing Quin as he opened the door.

"Safe," answered Quin shortly.

"Safe where? Is she at Glen Aucht?"

"She would not be where she had been rejected any more than you'd be," he returned.

"Where is she?" demanded Kestrel but Quin sighed and exited.

" 'Tis not your business," said Lachlan. " 'Tisn't mine either," he laughed, raising his bandaged hands in mock surrender as he saw the angry glint in her emerald eyes. "I'm not used to all this partying into the wee hours of the morning. I'm for my bed. It has been a long day."

Kestrel submitted to the kiss Lachlan placed on her forehead, her face still creased with anger and concern.

"Rue is my sister," she pouted after Lachlan had left.

"Aye, but now she's Quin's wife," replied Nick gently. "If my brother says she's safe, she is safe," he reassured.

"He's probably got her locked up somewhere!"

"Kess, what's all this anger?"

"I have a right to know where my sister is," she hissed. "What if he's hurt her?"

"Who?" laughed Nick, not understanding Kestrel's mounting fury.

"Your brother, Tarquin."

"He'd not hurt her, I'm sure of that."

"Well, I'm not. He has a hard cruel face," she spat, turning on Nick, whose face tightened with anger.

"I have been told we look very much alike," he stated, his tone cold and menacing as he tried to control his temper.

"Aye, you both have hard cruel faces. And you are both autocratic and overbearing!" she challenged, and Nick refused to answer as he leaned back in his chair with his dark eyes pinned to her. "Well, I have a right to know where she is and if she's all right!" she stated, but he still didn't answer. Kestrel felt her pulse start to race as her husband stared at her it seemed with a mocking half smile on his chiseled face. "And I will go to find her and you shall not stop me!" she declared before striding determinedly to the door, which she triumphantly wrenched open. Nick didn't move a muscle and Kestrel felt a shaft of disappointment pierce her fury. She closed the door firmly after her and stared down at what she was wearing. She definitely couldn't go galloping about dressed in a sheer nightgown and flowing ruffled robe. With one small regretful glance at the closed study door, she turned and raced up the stairs holding her long skirts high so she didn't trip.

Reaching the master suite Kestrel impatiently stripped off her seductive nightclothes and rummaged frantically through the clothes in her dressing room, looking for trews and shirt so she could travel more comfortably and safely disguised as a boy. She threw clothing about as she searched and muttered furiously to herself. If Rue hadn't returned to Glen Aucht where would she go? Where would she go if she were in her sister's shoes? Home to Wee-Angus and Meron, she decided. She laughed aloud as she realized where Rue probably had gone and found the clothes she had been looking for.

Nick lounged in the open doorway to the dressing room, appreciating the sight of his golden naked bride.

"Your tummy's popping out," he remarked idly. Kestrel whirled about with her eyes flashing.

"So would yours be with a baby inside," she snapped, infuriated by the way he stood, nonchalantly leaning with his strong arms folded. She snorted as she stepped into her trews and then stamped her feet into her high riding boots. Nick couldn't help but grin as he wondered if she was going to remember her shirt in her fury. She looked infinitely desirable dressed in the tight dark breeches and dark form-fitting boots, with her firm full breasts thrusting furiously with her rapid breathing as she tried to control her temper and ignore her lounging husband and his mischievous grin.

"Aah," he sighed with exaggerated disappointment as she buttoned herself into a shirt. Kestrel pushed by him, refusing to be goaded as she kept her mouth in a firm pursed line. "Such a pity, I enjoyed watching you get dressed. But now I insist you undress and climb into bed."

"Hah!" shouted Kestrel, flinging a dark cape around her shoulders and hooking it at her throat.

"You obviously want a fight," observed Nick.

"I am going to see my father and brothers!" stated Kestrel.

"At five o'clock in the morning?"

Kestrel glared at him, trying to find a smart answer and coming up short.

"Well?" coaxed Nick.

"I hate you!" screamed Kestrel childishly.

"I've noticed," purred Nick. "Especially your demonstration about two hours ago right there," he added, wickedly picking her up and depositing her on the bed.

Kestrel sat and fumed, unable to find words to describe what she thought of him.

"Kess, do you honestly think I care so little that I'd let you go riding around in the middle of the night?"

"I want to find my sister," she repeated futilely.

"I'll take you to Glen Aucht tomorrow," promised Nick.

"I am quite able to take myself places!" shouted Kestrel. "You make me feel like a child unable to do for myself!"

"Then dinna act like one!" responded Nick and immediately regretted his hasty reply as he saw the mutinous expression flare.

Rue lay in her bunk with Shame cuddled close, watching the strange reflecting lights bounce from the tips of the waves and ripple across the wooden beams of the cabin's ceiling. Her horse was stabled at the tavern called the Spotted Dog where Pierre would see he was well cared for until the *Étoile* moved to another berth for loading. Jacques's old wrinkled face had lit up when she had shyly crept onto the bridge, not knowing what her reception was likely to be. She had scrawled her plea to him and he had nodded and hugged her, releasing her quickly as he felt her tense. In two days they would sail, first to Île d'Oléron and then on to Quebec. Rue couldn't sleep so she tried to conjure up the sprawlng wooden house and the rolling meadow by the clear lake surrounded by the wooded mountains. Wee-Angus's deep gravelly voice singing as he kneaded dough and chopped the wild herbs and onions for venison stew. She and Meron quietly riding through the verdant forests, listening to the birds and animals. Each beloved recollection rang false and hollow as Meron's face became Quin's. She fell into an uneasy sleep only to dream she was in a large crowded banquet room rather like Lachlan's but even bigger. Around her milled hundreds of women all dressed in the gowns she had seen in the wardrobe aboard the *Dolphin*. Every size and style of woman, clad with matching shoes, gracefully glided, and she stood among them tiny and naked. A child with neither breasts nor pubic hair. Quin, dressed elegantly like the portrait of Black Nick in Lachlan's gallery, appreciated each full-bodied, ripe woman who entwined and pressed herself to his tall muscular frame. Rue twisted round and round as there seemed to be a hundred Quins and a hundred women laughing, laughing, laughing at her and then prying and pinching and pulling her hands away when she tried to hide her nakedness from them.

Rue sat up with a cry, sweat pouring down her face as her dog whined her concern and licked the saltiness from her mistress. Rue breathed deeply, trying to calm her racing pulses as the vessel rocked gently with the swelling tide. She sat hugging her knees as she thought on the terrifying dream, and tears slowly dropped, mingling with the beads of perspiration. She straightened her chin and imagined herself regally dressed in an exquisite gown as she confidently walked to meet Tarquin at the end of a long double line of beautiful women. She was taller, more beautiful, more graceful, and more assured than all of them and as she passed them one by one, they shrank into grubby little urchins. She lay back against the pillows with a satisfied smile on her face. She soared, her ebony hair dressed elaborately in the most sophisticated fashion; her breasts were full and rounded, surging above the plunging neckline of her gown. As she passed the women, they deflated their breasts, losing air like punctured bellows. Every inch of her was perfect, from the delicate gloved hand to the properly clad feet, and music played and she could sing so sweetly even the larks stopped to listen. In such a rosy reverie Rue finally fell asleep lulled by her own imagination and the softly lapping waves.

Jacques tiptoed in before going to his own bed and he grinned as he saw her happy sleeping smile, which dispelled the gnawing discomfort he felt in agreeing to take her back to America unbeknownst to Nick MacKay and her own sister. He stood several moments, looking down at the peaceful happy picture she made, thinking of his own children when they were very young. Affectionately he patted the ebony hound and quietly stole out whistling a cheerful Gallic folksong. It was going to be a happy carefree voyage back, he told himself. What he was going to do was right for the small mute girl, he rejoiced, feeling at ease for the first time since marrying her to the Hawk.

CHAPTER THIRTY-ONE

Kestrel awoke as bright sunlight flooded her bedroom. She stretched and turned to cuddle close to Nick but all she encountered was a cold space. She sat up and looked around, a frown marring her still-sleepy face.

"Nick?" she called, looking toward his dressing room but there was no answer. A cold pang went through her as she remembered going to sleep in the gray hours of the morning. She lay back against the pillows, feeling lost and afraid. She had been so angry at not being able to go out and ride out her fears, she had challenged Nick, refusing to listen to reason or love. He had not taken the bait, just coldly turned his back and gone to sleep. Seething, she had gone one step too far by attempting to leave the room. Kestrel rubbed her forearms, feeling the bruises left by Nick's furious hands as he had deposited her back into the bed and locked the doors. She had lain with her back to him, waiting, hoping that he would approach her. The minutes had stretched to an hour and when she had relented and turned around to face him, he was asleep. She had tenderly tried to wake him by tracing the hard lines of his face and pressing herself close to him. She shivered as she remembered his reaction. Nick had sat up and grabbed her wrists in a steely grip.

"No, Kestrel!" he had stated coldly. "Sometimes that is not enough!" he had added, rejecting her. Her blood had boiled as there had seemed something insulting in the way he emphasized "that."

She had made another mistake and hit out at his autocratic face. She looked down at her hand, still feeling the sharp tingle at her hard connection. She had ducked, expecting him to retaliate, but he had curtly left the bed and the room. Pride had stopped her calling out to him. She had cried herself to sleep, quietly so he wouldn't hear from the connecting bedchamber.

Kestrel threw back the covers and swung her legs out of the bed to stare in surprise at the black trews she still wore. She padded on bare feet to the door that joined the two bedrooms and listened. Cautiously she turned the handle and peered in. The large bed was empty. Carefully she tiptoed through all the rooms of the master suite but Nick wasn't there. Anger flared and she stalked to the door that opened on the corridor, expecting to find herself locked in and to her astonishment it opened.

"Morning, Mrs. MacKay," bobbed a maid, who had been standing expectantly outside, waiting for her mistress to waken.

"Are you my jailer?" challenged Kestrel, happy to find someone to take the edge off her temper.

"Pardon, ma'am?"

"Where's my husband?" she demanded.

"He and Master Tarquin rode out very early this day," reported the maid, intimidated by Kestrel's stormy expression.

"Where did they go?" The maid shrugged unhappily. From the lower floor of the house came the deep chimes of a clock. " 'Tis two o'clock?!" Kestrel exclaimed after waiting for more chimes. "Afternoon!"

"Aye, ma'am," bobbed the uniformed girl.

"Two o'clock," repeated Kestrel disgustedly before turning into her bedroom and slamming the door. She stood staring out the window, trying to cool her raging temper. A polite, insistent tapping at the door finally penetrated her fury.

"What is it?" she snapped, irritated.

"May I come in?" growled Lachlan's husky voice.

"Aye!" she answered shortly. Lachlan entered and scowled at her stormy expression.

"I trust you slept well?" he asked mischievously. Kestrel didn't bother to answer such small talk. She nodded curtly and stamped her feet into her riding boots and buttoned herself into a vest.

"Going riding?" he asked casually.

"Aye!" she challenged, daring him to argue with her. Lachlan held up his bandaged hands in mock terror and backed away.

"I trust I have done nothing to incur your formidable rage?" he quavered. Kestrel sneered and breathed noisily through her nose to indicate impatience as she flung a cape around her shoulders and tied her unruly hair back.

"Excuse me," she snapped, trying to pass him and go out of the room but he refused to move. She stared up at him mutinously.

"Nick should be back soon," he said quietly and seriously.

"I dinna care when that mucker returns!" she shouted childishly. "I'll not be held prisoner!" she added, and Lachlan stood aside with an exaggerated bow.

Kestrel stormed down the stairs, aware that the tall old man was right behind. She strode across the large, marble-floored hall, her boots clattering, and wrenched open the heavy front door before the manservant could aid her. Lachlan, following close behind, raised grizzled eyebrows conspiratorially to the uniformed man.

"Would you like to borrow a horse?" he asked impishly as she stared around the large stable. Kestrel wheeled around, her small face nearly contorted with rage, unable to answer politely. She nodded and Lachlan couldn't resist winking at her. "Where are you going?" he asked. Kestrel snorted impatiently.

"Touché," he laughed. " 'Tis none of my business, right?" She gave him a long withering look as she tapped one booted foot as her pulse hammered furiously. " 'Tis just how far you're going so I know which horse would suit you best," he added, making no effort to hide the great enjoyment he was having at her expense. Kestrel walked away from him and looked over his stable.

"Ghillie?" she called and pointed to a very spirited chestnut mare.

"Aye, nice piece of horseflesh, matches your hair too," jibed the irrepressible old man. "But unfortunately she is too wild for a wee lass like you," he lamented, knowing she would be goaded and insist on riding her. The poor ostler looked from the furious golden beauty to the gleeful old man.

"I dinna need all those trappings," hissed Kestrel, preferring to ride bareback with just a bridle. Lachlan nodded imperceptibly to the stableman.

"Saddle my mount wie all the trappings first," he ordered. Kestrel turned on him, nearly foaming at the mouth.

"I dinna need a nursemaid! I go alone," she stated.

"Nay, Kestrel," disagreed Lachlan. "This isna the New World but a large city of which you know nothing, young lady!" he snapped.

"I can take care of myself!"

"Hah!" snorted the old man irreverently. Kestrel's mind planned how to lose the old man. He watched her, grinning at the expressions that flitted across her furious face. "In the civilized world young ladies dinna go galivanting around wie out an accompanying male," he informed her. Kestrel turned her back as she fought to control her racing emotions.

Lachlan sat on his huge gray with a whimsical smile creasing his wrinkled face as Kestrel's high-strung choice reared and danced sideways, trying to lose her unfamiliar rider. The old man nodded his approval at the golden girl's horsemanship as she crooned and used all her energy to show the huge chestnut who was in control. Finally they trotted down the long carriageway side by side toward the gatehouse.

"Do you know where Nicholas went?" he asked idly as they were forced to keep a slow pace due to the heavy traffic on the narrow city streets. Kestrel kept her eyes straight ahead, rocking painfully at the enforced boring pace. "He went to see your father at Glen Aucht," offered Lachlan pleasantly as if she answered politely.

Kestrel wanted to scream and dig in her heels but the thoroughfares were choked with carriages and vendors. Her eyes searched frantically for a way to elude the persistent old man who rode easily and chattered happily. Her mind tried to picture the map that hung in the study. Obviously Lachlan McCulloch thought she headed for her family at Glen Aucht and she should let him think that as long as possible before giving him the slip and finding her way to the harbor at Leith. Jacques and Pierre Gillette had to know where Rue was, she worried. If they didn't, she wouldn't know where to start looking for her sister.

"Keep your eyes open for Nicholas and Tarquin, they should be on their way back by now," conversed Lachlan, knowing it would spur her to make a move. Sure enough, within minutes she veered to one side and the old man chuckled out loud and let her go, being much more familiar with the vagaries of the Edinburgh traffic than she was. He rode easily, keeping her in sight no matter how she dodged in and out. He sighed with satisfaction as she veered east toward the harbor at Leith.

Kestrel congratulated herself as she stared over her shoulder and didn't see the persistent old man. The Firth of Forth sparkled in the autumn sunlight as she rode the coast road toward the busy harbor. She let her eyes stray across the shimmering expanse that separated her and her father's estate. She had never seen it, but countless times when she was growing up she had sat upon his strong knees and listened to the stories from his childhood. She rode the beautiful spirited chestnut, imagining she had crossed the waters and raced along the bank on the other side. She reined her imagination as she neared Leith and looked behind her in case Lachlan had followed, but there was no sign. She smiled nervously as she became aware of the curious stares of the milling, unsavory people. The horse's hooves clattered noisily across the rough wooden planking of the piers as she stared around looking for the *Étoile*. The smells of rotting fish and sewage assailed her nostrils and she grimaced as she kicked the prancing horse forward.

Rue sat on deck of the *Étoile*, keeping herself well hidden but able to watch the busy comings and goings. She gasped as she saw Kestrel astride a large chestnut horse that reared and whinnied in panic as grasping hands tried to pull the golden-haired figure off. Rue reached down to the dagger tied to her thigh and the firearm at her waist before whistling for Shame and running to the gangplank.

Jacques frowned and opened his mouth to shout before looking in the direction she had been staring.

"*Sacrebleu!*" he yelled, seeing Kestrel's bright telltale hair as she fought off her assailants. "Pierre?" he roared, checking his gun and dagger before following the fleet, dark-haired girl and her hound. The one-eyed man stared toward the dock before bellowing with rage and taking chase.

Lachlan rode easily, congratulating himself as he scanned the harbor area. A curse was torn from his mouth as he saw Kestrel and the chestnut horse battling several burly men. As he dug in his heels to push his own steed through the milling throng, Rue and her hound jumped into the fray. Suddenly there was pure chaos as gunfire was heard.

Kestrel lashed out with her crop at the leering, black-toothed faces of the menacing men who pulled at the reins, trying to unseat her. The chestnut mare fought with her, rearing and kicking out with her iron-clad hooves. As Kestrel fought she was only half aware of Rue's slight figure leaping into the fray. There was the sound of an explosion and one man fell clutching his chest, blood spurting and seeping through his fingers.

"Come on, girlie," invited the most disgusting of them, too drunk to be deterred by his fallen comrade. "Och, there's another. One each," he chuckled, rubbing his filthy hands and beckoning Rue to come closer with her dagger. Rue slashed out, catching his forearm so that more blood splashed about. Lachlan forced his frenzied horse into the midst of the fighting mass of people who mostly didn't know why they battled but were so tense or drunk that any excuse was good to relieve their tempers. Another shot rang out and Lachlan reined as a man crashed to the ground in front of him. He stared in astonishment at the one-eyed giant who smiled with satisfaction. The old man lost all sense of time as he became one with the screaming battling throng and his adrenaline flowed. He laughed with glee, feeling thirty years younger and in his prime.

Kestrel grinned in surprise as she recognized Jacques and Pierre roaring Gallic oaths as they used their brawny fists with relish. She gasped as she saw a large man descending on Rue wielding a long knotted rope. She screamed a warning as the heavy weapon slashed, jerking her sister's petite body. A bloodcurdling war cry rent the noisiness and Lachlan charged, reaching for the slight, dark-haired lass as she fought to stay on her feet. He lifted her easily in his bandaged hands, placing her before him on his horse.

"Take her to the *Étoile*, monsieur," panted one-eyed Pierre, pointing to the graceful vessel as he and Jacques backed away from the battling throng.

"Kess!" roared Lachlan commandingly, and gaining her attention he jerked his head toward the narrow gangplank.

"We canna take the horse aboard," shouted Kestrel. "Where is the Spotted Dog?" Jacques nodded, agreeing with her reasoning as they edged away from the lusty fight. No one seemed to notice, or if they did, they certainly didn't care. The fight continued.

"Are you all right, wee-un?" asked Lachlan huskily, seeing blood seep through her thin shirt. White-faced and gritting her teeth in obvious agony, Rue nodded, as waves of cold clammy faintness shivered her.

Rue felt every hoofbeat of Lachlan's horse painfully stab through her as she fought to stay conscious. She didn't want to go to the Spotted Dog even though her horse Sin was stabled there. She stared around deliriously for her hound, and not seeing her, she frantically grabbed Lachlan's sleeve trying to get him to stop so she could slip off the horse and search for her. Lachlan reined, not comprehending her intent and swore as she fleetly eluded his grasp and shimmied to the ground.

Rue gasped with agony and bent double as excruciating pain knifed through. She tried to whistle but could not get her breath.

" 'Tis Shame!" shouted Kestrel, seeing her sister futilely try to summon her dog. She pursed her own lips and whistled, calling the large black pup. A frantic bark and whine wafted through the deafening noise of the battling bedlam on the docks. Pierre saw the blood that oozed through Rue's shirt and felt a split second's anguish before picking her up in his strong arms. He knew he had unwittingly hurt her, but he was unprepared for the shrill scream of agony that burst through her lips. It was the first real sound he had ever heard her utter, and it froze the marrow of his bones. Despite her intense pain Rue fought, determined to save her dog. Lachlan watched her valiant effort.

"I shall fetch your bitch, Rue. Save your strength," he ordered as he kicked his steed back toward the milling throng, followed by Kestrel.

Alexander Sinclair stared at the tall dark young man before him.

"My daughter Rue is dead," he intoned numbly.

"And your daughter Kestrel?" challenged Nick, striding forward. "Alex, you have reason to grieve for Cameron, but what on earth would she say if she knew how you rejected her daughters?"

"Dinna speak of her!" shouted Alex.

"I will!" answered Nick tersely.

"You have no right to," cried the anguished man.

"Aye, Sir Alexander, we have every right. We are now your sons whether you recognize us or no. Cameron entrusted Kestrel to me. Soon she'll bear your first grandchild," insisted Nick gently. Quin watched his brother plead with the sorrowing man as he himself stood silently, trying to understand a man who would close himself off from all who loved him. He snorted cynically as he saw himself mirrored. There was no way he could judge the man, having spent most of his own life behaving in a similar fashion.

"I am married to your daughter Rue. She is very much alive although mute from the abuse she has suffered in the last four years. She needs her mother," stated Tarquin.

"Her mother is dead!" shouted Alex.

"Aye, but her father lives," pursued Quin relentlessly. "My grandfather talks of the wild Black Cameron and how wondrous it was that Alexander Sinclair claimed her love wie out breaking her free spirit. My wife is her mother's daughter and she has been so sorely abused that I wouldna hurt her more for the world," he confessed, fixing his dark eyes to the amber ones that reminded him so painfully of Rue's. "Gie me your blessing and help me," he asked, burying his stubborn pride.

Alex looked into the nearly black eyes of the sardonic young man, seeing himself as a youth.

"I dinna ken if I can help," he stammered.

"Love your daughters," pleaded Nick huskily, seeing his older brother needed a few minutes. "That is how you can help."

Ian Drummond stood in the doorway with Lynx and Rowan eager listeners.

"I dinna ken," protested Alex, unable to cope with the emotions that flooded in. Since Cameron's death he had successfully blocked the sharp torturous reminders.

"If you canna love your children then you never deserved Cameron and may she curse you for eternity!" clipped Ian Drummond, his placid features stony with rage. "Cameron would lay down her life for her loved ones," he challenged.

"Aye, she would," replied Alex softly, staring with misty eyes toward the firth as he wrestled with the pain of his loss. His daughters, Rue and Kestrel, he whispered to himself, knowing that just to look at them would smash the protective numbing layer and the aching void would consume him. *Oh, Cameron, help me,* he begged before turning to the two dark young men. He nodded silently, unable to speak as his eyes caught sight of his sons whose eyes were as green as their mother's. He purposefully strode across the room until he stood in front of them, looking intently into their worried young faces before reaching out and pulling them to him. Lynx and Rowan wrapped their strong arms about their father.

"I'm sorry, lads," he murmured, his voice hoarse with emotion as he realized they, too, had lost their mother and he had been so wrapped in his own grief, he had also denied them a father.

Tarquin, Nicholas, and Ian Drummond watched the three men for a few minutes before striding out onto the terrace, allowing privacy for the emotionally charged reunion.

"I think maybe the mourning is over," said Nick quietly.

"Alexander will never stop mourning Cameron," remarked Drummond. "But I think the man I knew has returned."

Tarquin stared around at the well-cared-for rolling lawns and the majestic stone house that was nearly a castle with its ornate buttresses and countless rooms. He idly walked through the rose garden that surrounded the flagstoned terrace, looking in the windows at the well-furnished formal rooms. It was a beautiful house and grounds, but a little too well manicured for his tastes, he observed, preferring his own much more remote estates of Buchan and Rannoch on the rugged northern coast. He strode through the orchards, biting into a crisp pippin, as he wondered which was the best place to take Rue to gain her trust.

"Are you all right, Quin?" asked Nick, seeing his brother's brow furrowed.

"Aye," returned Quin, tossing the apple core as far as he could.

"You're thinking of Rue?"

"Aye."

The brothers walked in silence, both lost in their own thoughts of their wild brides.

"I have to take Rue away," stated Quin out loud.

"Away from what?"

"All of you. Her father, sister, brothers," he listed. "And Lachlan."

"Aye, I think you're right," agreed Nick. " 'Tis going to be hard to win her trust. Where will you go? Buchan?"

" 'Tis there or Rannoch. Buchan could overwhelm her."

"Aye," agreed Nick, thinking of the cold rambling manse perched on a jagged cliff overlooking the North Sea. "Rannoch is more like what she is used to."

"Tell me of her childhood home," asked Quin, stretching out on the soft grass and closing his eyes against the hot bright sunshine.

"Wild and beautiful. Forests stretching as far as the eye can see. Mountains and lochs. Valleys and rivers."

"Sounds like Scotland," remarked Quin.

"Aye, but so vast. You've never set foot in the New World?" asked Nick, astonished that his older brother who seemed to have traveled the world four or five times over had missed such a large area.

"I have put in at Boston, New York, Charleston, but never had occasion to go into the interior," answered Tarquin as his keen ears heard footsteps reverberate through the ground. He sat up and watched Alexander approach with his two sons. "Good-looking lads," he remarked, liking the strong firm lines of their young faces.

"I met Rowan in a British prisoner of war camp. He had a ball in the hip. Sixteen years old and had been fighting for two years. Lynx, his older brother, was a scout for Clark. His identical twin brother Raven died in his arms," recounted Nick morosely.

"How old is Lynx?" asked Quin, seeing the serious lines of the ebony-haired youth.

"Twenty and Rowan is eighteen. They have done more in their young lifetimes than most men ever do," he replied, standing and brushing dried grass from himself. "You have an enviable estate, sir," he greeted Alex as his hand indicated the sweep of land that rolled to the firth.

"Is Kestrel well?" asked Alex, smiling sadly as he remembered the tousled golden child that used to run merrily through the forest.

"Aye," smiled Nick.

"She is with child, you say?" asked the awkward father, trying to carry on a conversation and not knowing quite how.

"Aye. I estimate that you will be a grandfather by January if not before."

"How is she behaving?" questioned Alex ruefully.

"Could be better," returned Nick, and Alex clasped his hand in a firm grip as he pursed his lips and tears flooded his eyes.

"Tell her I love her," said Alex after clearing his throat.

"Nay, that is for you to do." Alex stared long and hard into Nick's dark eyes and nodded.

"Aye, son, you are right. Where is she?"

"Wie Sir Lachlan McCulloch, my grandfather, whom I think you've met," replied Nick. "At his house in Edinburgh where you and your sons are always welcome. 'Tis a big drafty house wie too many servants so it needs filling up."

Alex felt Tarquin's black eyes burning into him and he knew he had to turn and speak of his dark daughter Rue. The child that had always seemed like Cameron incarnate. He spun on his heel and silently returned the profound look. His nostrils flared as he sensed the handsome, brooding man knew the difficulty he was facing and yet would spare him no quarter. Tarquin MacKay was as ruthless as he had been in his youth. As dictatorial and autocratic, as stubborn and as violent. He shook his head as the years rolled away and he faced himself. Yesterday he had seen Rue for the first time in years. She had instinctively galloped her black horse along her mother's favorite ride followed by a black hound.

"Tell me of my daughter," he asked hesitantly.

"She is alive," returned Quin cryptically. "She has been raped more than once. She bore a stillborn child at thirteen years old. She has been beaten by a cat-o'-nine-tails. She is mute, possibly due to the abuse."

Alex wanted to scream aloud with agony and strike out at the seemingly cruel young man who so casually recounted the atrocities heaped on his child. "You omitted another abomination. Rejected by her father," he snapped. "Where is she?"

"Safe!"

The two men glared at each other, too alike to come to any easy agreement. Lynx grinned, his green eyes flashing with merriment as he saw the father he was used to. He and Rowan exchanged happy looks as they threw arms about each other's shoulders.

"What is it you find so pleasing?" snapped their father but the two didn't answer, just grinned affectionately at him. He tried to scowl parentally but their mood was so infectious that soon his thin face cracked wide, mirroring their expressions that were about to explode into laughter. Alex threw back his head and roared as his busy mind wondered how on earth he could possibly laugh with his beloved Cameron dead. His eyes caught sight of a fleetly moving cloud that raced across the deep blue sky followed by another swiftly moving shape. His laughter stopped and a wondrous expression filled his gaunt face. In his head he heard Cameron's husky, lilting voice urging him to find her through their children. He nodded, his eyes filling with tears as he understood and promised that he would remember her with life and not gray cold mourning.

"I want both my daughters here tomorrow," he ordered firmly. "With, of course, their husbands." He looked challengingly at Tarquin as though daring him to argue, but the tall dark man nodded tersely as his mind planned. He would commandeer the *Étoile* and sail it across the firth to Glen Aucht before continuing north to the seclusion of his estate.

"Refreshments?" offered Alex, waving a hand toward the imposing house and the company of men idly strolled back through the bountiful orchards.

CHAPTER THIRTY-TWO

Tarquin and Nick rode leisurely back toward Edinburgh, pleased with the outcome of the long day. They rode side by side with satisfied grins on their dark handsome faces winking at the women who tried to get their attention from inns and carriages along the way. There was a moment when a particularly fetching wench pouted an invitation at

Quin and though he felt a tightening in his loins, he had not been tempted to bed any women since he had met Rue.

"I'm for Leith," he proclaimed as they left the ferry on the south side of the Firth of Forth.

"Is that where Rue is? Wie the Gillettes?" asked Nick, grinning mischievously. Quin raised his eyebrows and didn't answer. "Let me collect Kess and accompany you? You dinna know what I had to suffer last night because of her worry for her sister," he confessed so engagingly Quin grinned back and nodded assent.

"We'll collect our grandfather, too," he laughed. "Lachlan is determined to ingratiate himself wie our brides. Nick, 'tis strange that we oft so different are together now, truly friends, not just brothers and married to sisters?"

"Incestuous," teased Nick, loving the close camraderie with his brother. "Quin, have you not wondered why our grandfather, the MacKay, ne'er did claim us after our father's death?"

"He denied we were of his blood. He no more accepted our mother than Lachlan accepted our father," answered Quin flatly. Nick turned an inquiring face to his older brother as he noted the bitter tone. "I went to Strathnaver. 'Twas a terrible mistake," recounted Quin, trying to lighten his tone.

"Why?" demanded Nick as they rode toward the McCullochs' town estate.

"He denied our existence. Called me many names," returned Quin, not really wanting to dwell on it. Nick took a look at his brother's set face and fell silent. The short exchange had answered many questions for him. He never truly understood his brother's cynicism or withdrawal behind a cold sardonic front. Now he felt compassion, knowing that the long trip north to Strathnaver had taken a lot of courage.

"When did you see the MacKay?" he asked after a long silence.

"When I was fifteen," answered Quin.

"It must have been what Rue felt when Sir Alex refused to acknowledge her," he offered.

"Nay, I could talk, shout, rant, and rave and Rue couldna say a word," answered Quin savagely. Once again the two brothers rode in silence.

"Quin, why did you marry Rue?" asked Nick, unable to go another yard without asking.

"Why did you marry Kestrel?"

"A promise," replied Nick glibly and Quin turned with a questioning stare. "I promised Cameron. A deathbed vow."

"If I believe that, my name isna Tarquin McCulloch MacKay," scoffed Quin.

"I promised because I already loved and Cameron knew it," confessed Nick as they waited for Lachlan's gatekeeper to give them access. "That doesna answer why you, posing as the pirate Hawk, married a wee mute," he goaded.

"Wee mute!" exclaimed Quin as they cantered down the long carriageway.

"Aye."

"Posing?"

"Aye."

"I dinna ken," confessed Tarquin. "There was something that I canna explain from the first moment I saw her wie a dirk in hand back to back wie Kess, so braw it took my breath away."

"So you married her?" quipped Nick as they swung off their horses and handed them to the waiting ostlers.

"What of you?" returned his brother goodhumoredly.

"Well, she stole my horse, stole someone else's, and shot it. Insulted an Indian chief who had proposed to her and tried to fight the Redcoats single-handed. It was marry her or die of anxiety," joked Nick as they strode toward the gleaming steps that led to the front door.

"Truthfully?" probed Quin.

"I love her and dinna try and get me to explain that one. 'Tis a disease we didna deal wie in medical studies," answered Nicholas seriously.

The ornate carved door was wrenched open before they could reach for it and Miss Catriona Goody stood wringing her hands.

"She's gone!" wailed the poor woman.

"Who?" snapped Nick, knowing the answer. "With whom?" he continued with impatience when the housekeeper could not answer but knowing who his impetuous bride was with.

"Lord Lachlan McCulloch," she mouthed and he nodded resignedly.

"For where?" he asked tiredly.

"To Sir Alexander Sinclair's estate of Glen Aucht," answered the unhappy old woman. Nick and Quin exchanged looks as each knew that if that had been Lachlan and Kestrel's destination they would have met. The answer struck both of them at the same time and they leaped down the front steps and headed back to the stables.

"I should have known I couldna keep Kess locked up," hissed Nick, berating himself for stupidity.

"Leaving Lachlan in charge was your biggest error," returned his brother acidly as they galloped through the gates and headed at top speed for the harbor at Leith. They rode in silence, each lost in his own thoughts.

The sun was setting as they reined their panting mounts on the wooden jetties of the quiet harbor. They stared with consternation at the littered area. Men lay sprawled, higgledy-piggledy across the entire expanse. Some bleeding profusely, some obviously dead or seriously wounded.

"It looks like a war," hissed Nick, his professional eyes seeing gunshot and knife wounds. He got no answer from his brother whose keen eyes searched the harbor for the *Étoile*, then urged his horse toward the flimsy walkway.

"Stay wie the animals," ordered Quin curtly, dismounting and handing his reins to his brother and striding aboard the *Étoile* before Nick could voice a complaint.

Nick prowled the ship aware of the small skeleton crew that watched his every move. Not finding either Rue or her dog Shame he picked up a frightened seaman by the nape of the neck.

"*Ou est* Rue MacKay?" he demanded.

"Spotted Dog! Spotted Dog!" babbled the terrified Frenchman, pointing frantically to the wharf. Quin released him and returned to Nick, who waited impatiently with the two horses.

"The Spotted Dog," he informed tersely as he leaped onto his horse and kicked him to action toward the sleazy dockside tavern followed by Nick.

The brothers threw themselves off their mounts and handed them to the stable boys, not caring whether the lads were able or not to tend their expensive horses as they raced into the main hostel.

The inside was noisy and smoky as men milled and drank and spoke excitedly about the afternoon's melee. Nick and Quin searched for a familiar face or one that showed authority. The brothers parted as each spied who they were looking for. Quin leaped over the bar and accosted the bartender as Nick grabbed a buxom barmaid. The two nearly collided as they lithely headed for the narrow stairs.

"Rue's hurt," informed Nick.

"Kestrel also," replied Quin.

"That canna be right, she's wie Lachlan," he protested.

"He's above, too," returned Quin shortly as they continued up the steep winding steps.

"Which room?" asked Nick, staring at the line of identical doors numbering 1 to 8. Quin shrugged and pointed to the end.

"You start down there," he ordered as he rudely flung open a door, interrupting a lusty couple as they surged together. He ignored the angry shouts as he systematically opened and closed doors until the narrow landing was choked with furious half-naked people venting their spleen.

"There's another floor," hissed Nick, ducking into the dark staircase followed by his brother. They clattered noisily up the wooden steps to be met by Pierre.

"*Bien,* I was to come for you," he greeted, leading them toward an open door where they could hear Gladys's strident, berating tones.

"Just sit yourself down, old man!" she screeched.

Quin and Nick stood at the doorway trying to take in the scene. Their grandfather with a black eye and a bloody rag about his brow, waved his still-bandaged fists at Gladys, who kept him away from the double bed with a large black umbrella.

"Nick," called Kestrel gleefully, leaping off the bed.

"Lie down!" ordered Gladys but the golden girl flung herself into her husband's open arms. Nick hugged her and then held her at arm's length staring with consternation at her beautiful face that also sported a black eye. Quin strode to the bed where Rue lay facedown with a light sheet covering her. Shame sat dismally beside.

"Rue?" he said quietly and she turned her head. Carefully he pulled back the sheet, afraid of what he might see.

"Nick!" he called urgently as he stared in horror at the raised bloody welt that slashed across her back and down her buttocks. Nick handed Kestrel to Lachlan and crossed to the bed. He firmly moved his brother aside and sat next to Rue.

"Rue, can you hear me?" he asked and she nodded carefully. "Tell me when it hurts," he asked, forgetting she couldn't talk as he stared at the violent swollen bruise, afraid that she had sustained some broken ribs or damage to her kidneys.

"Take my hand," whispered Quin. "When it hurts a lot squeeze hard," he directed.

"Does it hurt when you breathe deeply?" asked Nick. "Take a very deep breath."

Kestrel stood clutching Lachlan as Nick and Quin bent over Rue. "It's all my fault," she sniffed. "She was coming to help me."

"Shush," comforted Lachlan, wrapping a long arm about her shaking shoulders. She buried her face in his chest and wept.

"Anything broke?" asked Gladys as Nick stood up.

"Fortunately not, but she's going to be even more uncomfortable in the next few days as those bruised muscles stiffen up," he said shortly.

Quin smoothed the glossy black hair from Rue's brow, smiling tenderly and noting that she still clutched his hand.

"Jacques, do you have any laudanum aboard the *Étoile*?" asked Nick. The old sea captain who stood in the shadows feeling useless nodded eagerly and hurried out of the room. "If we can buffer some of Rue's pain we can move her."

" 'Tis all right," comforted Quin as he felt Rue tense at the thought of being moved. "While we're waiting would someone tell me exactly what happened."

"Aye," agreed Nick, looking expectantly at Lachlan.

"It was all my fault," confessed Kestrel. " 'Tis always my fault!"

"No, lass, it was mine," argued the old man gallantly.

"If you could see yourselves," stated Nick, looking at the battered twosome both with their colorful black eyes.

"If I hadn't tried to lose you and had listened to what you told me, none of it would have happened," sniffed Kestrel, unable to look Nick in the eye.

"What happened!" insisted Quin.

"I was looking for Rue and some men attacked me. She came to my rescue wie Jacques and Pierre," recounted the bedraggled girl.

"Then all 'ell broke out!" continued Gladys with relish.

"And I rode into the thick of it," boasted Lachlan proudly. "Rue unfortunately received the worst of it at the end of a knotted rope. Then Kess and I together battled the bullies who had tied up the lass's pitch. That's where we received these," he pointed at his bruised eye. "You are handy wie your fists, Kess," he added admiringly.

"Let me understand. You rode out here alone?" demanded Nick angrily of his wife.

"Nay, she was wie me," protected Lachlan. "I was right behind."

"Aye, I tried to lose him but he told me not to travel alone," replied Kestrel, honestly feeling a strange cramping in her stomach. Nick's eyes narrowed as he saw her knead her side.

"Do you have a pain?" he asked sharply. Kestrel lied by shaking her head as her face grew pale. "You put more than your own life in danger. Not only is Rue battered and bruised, but doesn't our unborn child mean anything to you?" he continued, his tone controlled and cold.

Quin felt a stab of sympathy for the white-faced girl even though he was also furious with her. She stood with her small chin squared, facing her enraged husband.

Kestrel unfocused her eyes, unable to bear the pure rage he emanated. Once again she was responsible for hurting her sister. The cramping in her stomach became more uncomfortable and she felt panic flare as she realized what it meant.

"My baby," she whispered, rubbing her stomach and looking down.

"Does the child mean nothing to you?" repeated Nick, not understanding

"You're being too harsh, Nicholas," grumbled Lachlan. "Blame me, I was responsible for her."

"I'm sorry," cried Kestrel as she bent double. "I'm sorry, I dinna think. I'm sorry."

"You *are* hurting," Nick hissed, striding forward and picking her up. He laid her on the bed next to her sister as he expertly examined her stomach, feeling the contractions. "Och, Kestrel," he groaned, wishing he could take back his angry words.

"Have I hurt our baby?" she whispered fearfully.

"Lie still and stop fashing," he ordered hoarsely. Rue turned her head and looked at her sister. Tears rolled down both their faces. She reached out her hand and felt for Kestrel's. Quin and Nick looked down at the sisters who lay on the large bed with their hands tightly clasped. "I dinna think we'll be going anywhere this night," Nick sighed as he put an arm about his brother and they walked across the room.

"Is she losing the child?" whispered Quin and Nick nodded soberly.

"Is there aught I can do?" hissed Lachlan shamefacedly.

"Aye, you can let me see your head," answered Nick.

" 'Tis just a scratch," argued the old man. "The harridan over there saw to it."

Gladys gave him a dirty look before turning back to her two charges and sponging their brows with cooling water.

" 'Ow's yer belly, ducky?"

"It stopped hurting."

"You feel damp anywheres?" hissed Gladys conspiratorially. Kestrel frowned and shook her head. "Like you've wet your drawers?" the large woman struggled to illuminate.

"No," answered Kestrel.

"Then if you keep still and quiet and learn to do as you're told, you just might keep the baby," Gladys informed her before crossing to the men. "She ain't losing the baby. She ain't bleeding and 'er pains 'ave gone," she told Nick smugly. "I've done my share of midwifing and the like," she answered the inquiring stares.

Jacques staggered into the room carrying a bag of medical things.

"I 'ave what you asked for and also I brought bandages," he panted.

Nick measured laudanum into a small glass. "Rue, I'm going to have to sit you up so you can drink this," he said gently.

"I'll do it," offered Quin as he wondered about the least painful way to move her. "Roll onto your side, my love," he suggested and Rue obediently moved. She opened her mouth in a silent scream as the lacerated, bruised flesh felt it was being torn from her body. Quin picked her up and held her against him, careful not to touch the injured part of her. "You're very brave, my darling," he crooned as she panted, trying to control her agony. "Now drink this and you'll sleep and not feel a thing," he coaxed and she drank the bitter brew. "'Tis all right. You'll not be moved until you are asleep," he comforted.

Kestrel lay on the bed watching her sister fall asleep in Tarquin's arms. She smiled wistfully as she saw love soften the dark man's stern features and she thought sadly about the events of the last forty-eight hours. She turned to see Nick also watching the still tableau of Rue and Tarquin.

"You'll not stay here, Quin?" worried Lachlan.

"Nay, there is something grimy and sordid here," he replied, staring around with distaste at the drab room. Gladys prickled indignantly, and Tarquin laughed. "Excuse me, Miss Mackintosh, but I'm sure you and Pierre would be much more comfortable at my grandfather's house."

"Really?" purred Gladys, rubbing her plump hands together and turning to the stunned old man.

"Right, Lachlan, that is the least we can do to show our appreciation to Miss Mackintosh and the Gillette brothers," he continued wickedly, ignoring his brother's frown and his grandfather's apoplectic expression. He stared down at Rue, who slept soundly and, feeling Kestrel's eyes, he turned and saw the emerald orbs swimming with tears.

"I am so sorry," she whispered, her voice breaking as she looked at the violent, lacerated bruising on her sister's thin back. "I am always hurting her and I dinna mean to," she sobbed, tears pouring down her face.

"Now what are you saying to upset my little lovey?" attacked Gladys. "This child 'as to be cosseted and kept 'appy if she's to 'ave an 'ealthy baby," she scolded.

"Where do you get all your wisdom, Miss Mackintosh?" laughed Quin.

"When you've run a brothel you know just about everything there is to know of life!" snapped Gladys and was rewarded by a gust of hilarity from Lachlan and an indignant tut-tutting from Jacques and Pierre.

"Now when did Frenchmen get so prudish?" chuckled the irrepressible old man, openly flirting with the outrageous black-attired woman.

"Oh, no," groaned Quin, seeing another escapade he would have to extricate Lachlan from unless he and Nicholas wanted Gladys for a grandmother.

Quin sat cradling the sleeping Rue as Lachlan and the Gillette brothers escorted Gladys down the stairs and went to hail a carriage to take them back to the McCulloch town house in Edinburgh. Miss Mackintosh had excitedly thrown her possessions into several large pieces of luggage, which were now piled expectantly near the door.

"I'm taking the *Étoile*," informed Quin after the door closed behind the other four.

"For what?" exclaimed Nick.

"To take Rue to see her father and then up the coast on my way to Rannoch," replied Quin.

"That's why you extended such a gracious invitation to the Gillettes and Gladys?" laughed Nick and when his brother nodded, added, "Well, thanks a lot. Now I shall trespass on your hospitality and my father-in-law's. Take Kess and me over the firth wie you and I shall stay at Glen Aucht until Miss Mackintosh has either bored or married Lachlan."

"All right," agreed Quin, lowering his voice as Rue gave a shuddering sigh. He put a finger to his lips asking Kestrel and Nick for silence as he sensed Rue was about to speak.

"See the wee Jemmy lass sitting on a stane," sang Rue. "Cryin' n' akeenin' all the day alane. Rise up wee Jemmy lass, wipe your ears awa' and choose the one you love the best and tak' them awa'."

"See the wee Ruey lass sitting on a stane," sang Kestrel, tears rolling down her dirty bruised face. Nick reached out to hug her close, but she rolled away from him, her face hard and angry. "Dinna touch me," she hissed.

"What is this?" sighed her husband, but Kestrel refused to answer, just wrapped her own arms about herself and held herself closely. Quin looked from one to the other and remembered the golden girl's anguished speech aboard the *Étoile*. His eyes narrowed as he realized that she felt she was not deserving of his brother's love.

"Kestrel?" he said quietly and her green eyes flashed at him. "I remember you saying that you were bad and Rue was good. Do you remember that?"

Kestrel didn't answer, her fine nostrils flared as she felt guilty and uncomfortable.

"You also said that it was right that Rue be loved more. Kess, look at me," he ordered softly and he smiled approvingly as she bravely met his eyes. "My brother loves you and you wouldna hurt him for the world, would you?"

"I dinna mean to hurt anyone," sniffed Kestrel.

"You're not bad, lass, just young and full of life. Rash, aye, but bad, nay, and I love you," stated Quin. "Not as a lover but as a brother and you deserve it."

"But why do I always cause such pain?" challenged Kestrel.

"Because that is a part of life," answered Nick. "Kestrel, sometimes you drive me to exasperation but I still love you."

"Last night you wouldn't make love with me," attacked Kestrel as the hurt of the rejection welled. Quin smiled and tactfully glanced away as his sister-in-law's candor amused him.

" 'Tis not always the answer," returned Nick, stiffly aware of his brother's presence for the intimate conversation. "You canna seduce me every time you want your own way!"

Quin softly kissed the top of Rue's dark head, hiding his grin as he wished his wife would resort to such subterfuge.

"I can try, can't I?" snarled Kestrel, trying to hold on to her pride as she instinctively knew Quin was near laughter. Nick gasped and then leaned back and bellowed with mirth. Quin joined in even though he was aware that Kestrel seethed with indignation, not knowing what he had said to reduce the two cynical men to tears of merriment.

"Och, I canna wait for my wee-un to regain her speech," sighed

Quin as soon as he could get his breath. "I have a feeling tha Cameron's daughters share similar diverting turns of phrases."

"Och, Kestrel, you are naughty and really deserve the awfu whipping Rue got on your behalf," stated Nick. "Maybe it is a lesson you had to learn, my love."

Quin shook his head at his brother's lack of tact as he saw Kestrel' face set once again on mutinous lines as she felt shamed at the reproach in front of him. He bit his own tongue that stopped him telling his brother not to berate his wife except in private but knew he would be guilty of the same.

"We have to work it out one to one," he murmured, holding Rue close as he filled with aching joy at having her preciousness between his strong arms. Everything was going to be healing from now on, he mused. He and Rue together, he would teach her to trust and speak again, he promised. Impatient to start as he wished Lachlan would return for Miss Mackintosh's bits and pieces so he and Nick could steal aboard the *Étoile*.

Nick watched Quin with Rue in his arms with feelings of jealousy as Kestrel turned her mutinous face away, refusing to acknowledge hi presence. He was about to remonstrate with her when his blood ran cold at the eerie, rhythmic scream that issued from Rue's mouth as her body jerked in time. He frowned, not knowing if she dreamed o being beaten or raped. He stared up into his brother's agonized black eyes and knew that Quin wondered the same thing.

Gradually the screams died away but still her body was shaken by strange rhythmic jolts that slowly wound down until they ceased altogether.

"If I dinna know her history I'd think she had some palsy affliction," stated Nick. "It makes me wonder about some of the patients who are diagnosed insane."

"Dinna infer that about my wife," snarled Quin.

"Rue is anything but insane," returned Nick. "She is probably one of the strongest people I have ever met. Most people would be mad with what she has endured."

"Oh, them bloody stairs'll be the death of me," gasped Gladys as she staggered into the room and plopped herself down on the nearest chair, which creaked under her weight.

"*Chérie*, I 'ave told you to wait in the bar," huffed Pierre.

"Wait in the bar, 'e says, with all them riffraff!" shrieked the indignant woman. " 'Oo does 'e think I am, a common floozy?'"

" 'Ush up!" hissed Pierre, frantically indicating the sleeping Rue cradled in Quin's arms.

"Whoops, pardon me," grimaced Gladys, tiptoeing clumsily to the bed and staring affectionately down into the dark girl's sleeping face. "Ain't she gorgeous?" she whispered, kissing her fingers and softly touching Rue's soft cheek. "I ain't ever seen such looks on two sisters. I 'ear there's some brothers, too. What I wouldn't give to 'ave an eyeful of them," she chuckled wickedly as she picked up several bags.

"Your *grandpère*, 'e want to know what 'e should do for the 'orses?" asked Pierre.

"Leave them all. I shall take care of them," replied Nick, feeling that Lachlan's and the mount that Kestrel rode would be useful. "They're stabled here?"

"*Oui*," answered Pierre.

" 'E says yes. That's what wee means," translated Gladys, bustling out.

"I feel rather sorry for Lachlan," grinned Nick as Pierre staggered out laden with baggage.

"He deserves it, the old reprobate," laughed Quin. "And if I wasna such a forgiving brother, I'd make you return wie him to enjoy the household wie the unwelcome guests."

"When do we leave?" asked Nick with a grateful grin.

"Within the hour. I'm sure Lachlan will be climbing the stairs to have the last word," remarked Quin ironically, and sure enough he had just finished his sentence when the lanky old man stood in the doorway regarding his grandsons balefully.

"What hae you done to me," he mourned, nearly beating his breasts but realizing they probably would laugh if he did.

"Go hame wie you, Lachlan," teased Quin affectionately.

"How are the lassies?" grumbled the old man, wishing to procrastinate.

"Improving each minute," reassured Nick.

"Take care of them," said Lachlan lamely, edging out of the door as Gladys's demanding raucous voice shook the rafters as she screamed for him.

"You've left all the horses?" asked Quin before the door slammed shut.

"Aye," grinned the old man, trying to sidle back into the room.

" 'Bye, Grandfather," nodded Nick.

"Right," sighed the old man. "I'm on my way."

The door closed and they both held their breaths, expecting the grizzled head to pop back in but Gladys's screeching stopped and they were left with just the usual steady rumble echoing up from the noisy bar.

"How long will the draft last?" asked Quin, shifting Rue in his arms.

"Several hours. I dinna want her to have too much as it can have negative results," replied Nick.

"Such as?" probed Quin with a concerned look at the sleeping girl on his lap.

"Dependency on the laudanum. Congestion in the lungs as breathing is not as in natural sleep," answered his younger brother.

"Well, she'll not need much more once we are aboard the *Étoile*," he said, looking at Kestrel who lay stiffly with her eyes open and unseeing.

"Are you hurting again, Kess?" asked Nick, following his brother's eyes.

"Not as you think," she returned absently. "The baby seems all right."

"And are you all right?" he asked gently. Kestrel made no sound or motion to answer.

"When we leave Kess, I'm carrying you, do you ken?" he stated. Still she lay without giving any sign. "Kestrel, do not get me angry?" he pleaded.

"I have your anger already," she answered dully, feeling overwhelmed by her responsibility in the day's happenings.

"Soon we'll gently sail way from all these troubles," quoted Quin lightly.

"To where?" challenged Kestrel, cautiously sitting up and resting her back against the headboard.

"Across the firth to Glen Aucht," replied Quin casually.

"Glen Aucht?" repeated Kestrel, her eyes opening wide as she recalled the last meeting with her father, months before.

"It will be all right," reassured Nick, seeing her fear and ignoring her efforts to repel him by pulling her into his arms and settling her on his lap. Quin nodded his approval of his younger brother's aggressive action.

"Aye, that's the way," he grinned as he stood and carried the sleeping Rue easily to the door, which he opened, listening intently. "All's clear," he proclaimed and Shame stretched and limped eagerly

oward him. He frowned seeing that the young animal was obviously
urt.

"I think she'll be all right until we get aboard. I'll take a look at her
hen," reassured Nick as he picked up Jacques's medical bag and
ollowed the limping dog and his brother on to the landing. "How will
ve get the horses aboard?" he worried.

"Leave it to me, Nicholas," hissed Quin as they carried their wives
down the dark, steep winding staircase.

"You wish me to help you carry something?" asked Jacques's
gravelly voice. Quin and Nick stared at his mischievous wrinkled face
n amazement. "*Non?* Maybe I should bring the *Étoile* to berth so we
can put the horses aboard?"

"Jacques Gillette, you are full of surprises," laughed Quin.

"I am no fool, Monsieur le' Awk. I will take you anywhere on my
'Étoile. I owe that to you for being part of the sinking of the *Dolphin*
and the taking of your cargo, but my ship is my life," stated the wily
Frenchman.

CHAPTER THIRTY-THREE

Rue awoke as sunlight filtered from the tips of the waves and reflected
in ripples across the cabin. She frowned, not understanding where she
was. She started to turn on to her back but quickly stopped as pain and
memory flooded in. She flexed her legs and arms as she assessed her
injury before propping herself up on her arms and trying to scan
around but all she could see was the wooden wall of the cabin.

Quin watched her wiggle backward on her stomach until her legs
left the bunk and she regained her feet without bending her body too
much.

"Good morning," he said huskily as she stood breathing deeply
from the effort and pain. She regarded him somberly with beads of
perspiration on her face before walking stiffly to the porthole and
looking out. She frowned as she recognized the large gray building
and sloping green lawns of Glen Aucht. Her heart started to race as
she remembered her father's cold rejection and her own stupid

vulnerability. She turned and stared stonily at Quin just as someone rapped softly at the door.

"Your father wants to see you, Rue," he explained as he crossed to the door. She backed away terrified, expecting to see her father, but Kestrel hesitantly peeked in. Her face lit up when she saw Rue out of the bed.

"You're better," she rejoiced, but Rue turned away from her and looked out of the porthole again as though she couldn't believe her eyes.

"Do you think you can walk?" asked Quin. Rue shook her head without turning. She would not go ashore, she determined, furious that her body felt as painfully stiff as though she had been lashed. She turned around frantically looking for Shame but she was not curled in her usual places by or near the bed. She pursed her lips and whistled and there was no answering bark.

"Shame will be all right. She got hurt. Nick splinted her leg," reassured Kestrel. "She's topside as it's impossible for her to manage the stairways."

Rue took a breath and walked toward the door, anxious to be with her hound.

"First you need some salve on your back, and then a shirt or some other clothing," stated Quin. Rue stood like a statue as he liberally smeared the medication across the angry wound and pulled a soft cotton shirt over her tousled black head. "There," he said, stepping back and she walked out of the cabin.

"She is hurting a lot, isn't she?" remarked Kestrel after a long silence, having noted the cool distance between her sister and Quin. Rue seemed remote and hard. The tall dark man nodded before following his wife, leaving Kestrel alone, feeling very responsible.

Rue heard Quin behind her but she couldn't turn without jarring her sore muscles. She seethed inside as she realized she couldn't ride a horse. Sin, she thought, and a pang shot through her as she remembered he was stabled at the Spotted Dog in Leith. Her plan had gone wrong. She would never get back to Meron and Angus. Her fury successsfully anesthetized her as she climbed to the warm sunny deck and made her way to Shame, who limped on three legs to greet her. She awkwardly knelt, keeping her back straight so she could embrace her poor hurt friend. She heard Quin's even bootstep stop behind her and felt his eyes watching her.

"Sin is stabled below," Quin informed her. Rue nodded rigidly and tried to stand but the movement of the boat made it difficult. Quin reached out and helped her but as soon as she had regained her footing she shook free of him. "Kestrel and Nicholas will be staying at Glen Aucht, and after your father has seen you, we will be sailing north." Rue shook her head angrily, wanting to scream her disagreement at his plans. "You have nothing to say about it, Rue," he said firmly and he grinned at her rebellious expression, rejoicing in her fighting spirit which he preferred to her cold docility. "I'm afraid you've run aground, my pet," he laughed affectionately. "You've got your wings clipped for a while and canna run let alone sit a horse to escape me until you're healed."

Rue's hands clawed with rage at his seeming delight in her being maimed. She stared toward the shore, her vision blinded with fury, not seeing the approaching horsemen until she heard her name called and her brothers and father waved. Her eyes widened and she backed away out of their sight, determined to hide, but Quin held her firmly by the shoulders.

"I wouldna fight unless you want to aggravate your wound," he said, softly fanning her fury further. She froze beneath his hands and stood with her face a stony mask.

Alexander strode across the deck of the graceful vessel, eager and yet apprehensive about facing his oldest daughter. Nicholas MacKay had ridden earlier to the house to inform him of the events of the previous day so he was surprised to see Rue dressed and above deck. He stood before her and his welcoming smile changed to a frown when he looked into her set, stormy face.

"Rue?" he spoke gently, and her nostrils flared with contempt as she stared coldly into his gaunt face. "I deserve your scorn, wee-un," he said hoarsely after a long silence.

Kestrel stood watching, unaware of Lynx's arm around her shoulder. Rowan watched from a small way off, his mind back to the terrible day those years before when Rue had disappeared and Goliath and Jemmy had died.

"Oh, Mother," he whispered aloud. "Rue's found and she's safe." He frowned at his dark sister's hostile expression as it reminded him more of Kestrel. He turned to look at his golden sister who watched her father with such longing he began to understand Kestrel's behavior. He quietly crossed to Lynx and Kestrel and put his own arm around her waist.

Alex shook his head, unable to reach past Rue's stony facade. He held out his arms, inviting her to him but she stared adamantly at him, her back pressed against Quin's hard unyielding body, welcoming the

pain that stabbed as it firmed her resolve not to weaken. Alex sadly
stroked her mutinous face.

"I love you, Rue," he whispered hoarsely as she jerked away from
his touch. Alex tore his eyes away from the small rebellious figure
who looked so much like her mother. He looked into Quin's dark
brooding features and a flicker of sympathetic understanding passed
between them.

Kestrel felt panic as Alex strode away from the painful encounter
with her sister and walked toward her. She stared with bewilderment
into the faces of her two brothers, suddenly aware of their presence.
She laced her slim fingers across the gentle swell of her belly as
though to hold her unborn child closer to give her strength. She
looked bravely up at her father, expecting to see disapproval and
censure, but all she saw was pain etched deeply into his gaunt face.
She smiled softly and opened her arms to him. He hesitated for a
moment, looking so vulnerable that tears poured down Kestrel's face.

"It's all right, Father," she sobbed and he wrapped his arms about
her, holding her near his heart.

"Och, Kestrel," he cried, burying his nose in the fragrance of her
vibrant hair. "You've grown into a fine woman. Your mother
would've been so proud."

Rue closed her ears and unfocused her eyes away from her
brothers, father, and sister, who held each other, laughing and crying at
the same time. She felt separate from them as though they had nothing
to do with her. They were not her family. Suddenly she felt surrounded
in the same gray suspension she had at the mission. Standing apart;
never belonging; just holding onto herself in order to survive.

Kestrel observed the solitary figure of her sister and made a move to
go to her, but was stopped by Nick.

"Let her be, my love," he said softly, holding her close.

"I feel so responsible," she whispered, her throat closing with
emotion. "When am I going to grow up and start behaving in a way
that doesn't hurt," she mourned, thinking of Rue's poor back and the
growing child who lay so trustingly in her belly.

"You have already," murmured Nick, thinking of her holding out
her arms to comfort the father who had so painfully rejected her. He
grinned engagingly down at her bewildered little face. He sensed that
in the last twenty-four hours she had made her passage into
womanhood and he rejoiced at her clear trusting gaze.

Rue stood like a small forlorn statue. She heard everything through
a numbing layer although she made no sign of acknowledgment as her

family approached and awkwardly kissed her smooth cheek in farewell. Time passed and she stared unseeing down the long firth, dimly aware of her sister and brothers standing behind talking but she couldn't seem to make the effort to turn. She knew they said good-bye and she heard their feet hesitantly leave the boat. She didn't turn until she heard the anchor being slowly and protestingly raised and the movement of the vessel changed. Then she stared toward her father's estate and to the people who stood watching the *Étoile* sail down the firth toward the North Sea.

Quin left Rue alone, somehow knowing she had wrapped herself in a protective mood. He watched her from the bridge as he directed Jacques on which direction to take. The route along the east coast of Scotland going north to Tain was breathtaking and he hoped it would somehow pierce Rue's numbing shroud.

At nightfall Rue still stood staring across the bubbling wake behind the vessel as though looking to the past instead of ahead to the future, mused Quin, wondering whether to just leave her to her own devices or insist she eat and sleep.

"Rue, the horses and hound need water and food," he remarked, hoping to break through her detachment. Shame whined expectantly and limped awkwardly to the tall man and licked his hand. Quin dropped to his haunches and petted the hurt animal. Rue turned and looked down at the man and dog. Quin grinned up at her and she felt her heart thud excitedly at his loving look. She frowned and looked away, trying to recover her previous detachment as Jacques shouted orders for the anchor to be dropped.

"This is the village of Auchmithie," informed Quin, standing up. Rue shivered, feeling oppressed by his large shadow that towered above her. "Are you cold?" he asked, catching the involuntary movement and seeing her flesh goosebumped on her arms. "Time to tend to your back," he decided, expecting a fight and steering her toward the companionway. Sure enough, Rue tried to resist by digging in her bare heels but she was no match for his strength. "If you'd behave and go below under your own steam, I could carry Shame," he stated idly and she stopped and looked up at him, her small face still closed but with a contemplative air. "Well?" he smiled, and she nodded, averting her eyes as his gaze made her feel naked and vulnerable. Quin picked up the large squirming pup whose right front paw stuck straight out on the board that splinted the broken bone.

"I have some *homard* . . . lobster? For my petite Rue?" cajoled

Jacques as they prepared to climb down to the first level. Rue stared into the kindly, wrinkled face and to Quin's utter amazement walked into the old sea captain's open arms. Jacques looked up into the dark puzzled face and winked one of his bright blue eyes. "I am safe," he explained. "So be warned, Monsieur le 'Awk, be good to the little silent one or she will fly away and find me."

Tarquin MacKay stared down at his wife in the circle of the old arms and he smiled engagingly.

"Thank you, my friend," he laughed.

"You find it funny?" asked Jacques.

"No, not funny, but very encouraging," returned Quin enigmatically as he rejoiced that Rue knew she needed affection and comfort. He had been very afraid that she had steeled herself from needing even that. But seeing her trust and invite the paternal caress, he was reassured. His blood had run cold that morning as he watched her icily reject her own father. The poor man had stood before his daughter for at least three quarters of an hour nearly debasing himself for one sign of affection. Rue had given him nothing except pain. Quin shook his head as he realized the formidable task that loomed ahead of him.

"Well, my petite Rue. We 'ave the lobster, eh?" coaxed Jacques. Rue lifted her head and nodded, and the old seaman held her chin gently as he was stunned by her incredible beauty. "That face, I have never seen such a one."

"First I have to take care of her back," reminded Quin, feeling jealous as the old man rhapsodized over his wife.

"In one hour?" pronounced Jacques. "We shall have a dinner fit for a king!" he rejoiced as he positively danced toward the galley yelling for his cook.

Rue entered the cabin and stared apprehensively at the large bunk and Quin's possessions. Quin followed her gaze and rightly assessed her thoughts.

"Aye, this is our cabin, Mrs. MacKay. There are not many of your things about because you saw fit to destroy them but I did manage to rustle up some cabin boy clothes for when you need a change," he teased lightly with a thread of steel in the timbre of his voice. Without asking or warning her of what he was about, he started unbuttoning her shirt. Rue hit out at him and stifled a scream as she opened the healing wound on her back.

"Hold still," he ordered tersely, pulling the cotton shirt off her and frowning at the blood that welled. "Undo your trews!" Rue resisted, her face whitening with terror. "For God's sake, Rue, do you honestly think I'd rape you wie your back looking like raw meat and your buttocks every color of the rainbow? I assure you I find nothing attractive about the prospect!"

Rue froze at the cruelty in his voice. She stood still as he exposed the result of the knotted rope and applied the salve as her mind rang with all the insults she had saved to protect herself with. *I should have adopted you not married you . . . What need do I have of such a frightened child? . . . Error in judgment.* All rang in her ears now, along with *I assure you I find nothing attractive about the prospect!* She furrowed her brow, puzzled at why she wasn't relieved with such statements.

Tarquin stared at Rue's straight little back, which despite the livid welt and violent bruising was very seductive. He resisted running a finger over the gentle curves and turned away wiping the grease from his hands. Rue waited a few moments to ascertain whether he had finished before awkwardly dressing herself.

"Young Dr. MacKay prescribes soaking in warm water each night to relax those sore muscles and to guard against infection," recounted Quin, as he stripped to the waist and sluiced water across his face in preparation for shaving.

Rue was only partly aware of the following few days and nights. Nothing really penetrated her complacent protection as the *Étoile* sailed languidly north along Scotland's majestic east coast. Her back healed until all that remained was a stiffness as if her skin was too tight. Jacques and Tarquin watched her, both perturbed at her inertia. They had expected her to shin up the rigging like a monkey as soon as she could, but she just stared at the water that bubbled behind the sailing vessel, not wanting to look at the spectacular cliffs to the left or the castles and picturesque villages ahead.

"Tonight we reach Tain," stated Jacques.

"Aye and tonight you'll be free of us," replied Quin, anxious to have Rue to himself.

Rue clung to Jacques, somehow knowing underneath the numbing layers that she was really saying good-bye. She guided Sin down the gangplank with Shame before her on the saddle followed by Quin. She rode a comfortable rhythm, oblivious to the curious stares of the Tain townspeople who called out in welcome to Tarquin MacKay and looked askance at the beautiful woman dressed in lad's clothes.

Rue reined Sin and gazed in awe down the steep jagged cliff to the raging surf that dashed against the rocks with such force a fine mist sprayed on her face and clothes. Quin smiled with relief seeing that at least something seemed to penetrate her armor. Sensing his stare, Rue stiffened and focused ahead on the turreted roof of a gray fortresslike mansion.

"That is Buchan," informed Quin as he wondered whether they should put up at an inn instead of subjecting Rue to the multitude of drafty rooms and aged servants in his isolated retreat. Rue stared up at the gray stone walls as the horses clattered into the large courtyard. "Maybe tomorrow we shall go on to Rannoch. 'Tis a small hunting lodge more like you are used to," he reassured as he watched her stare wide-eyed up the sheer granite walls to the turrets.

Rue dismounted as though in a dream and absently handed Sin's reins to a shriveled, bowlegged old man. She walked slowly up the wide steps with Shame limping behind. The enormous, metal-studded door was opened with a deep agonized creak and she stepped into a vast hall. Quin watched her craning her neck to see the ornate ceiling that soared at least five stories above. She stood and pivoted, unable to believe the gigantic proportions. She cocked her head to one side listening, as she heard and felt a deep rhythmic muffled roar reverberate from the depths of the building.

" 'Tis the sea in the caves below," Quin answered her curious expression. "In the morning I'll take you down and show you," he added warmly. Rue spun on her heel as Shame growled low in her throat looking toward the shadows as several old people stood nervously.

"Welcome, sir," greeted a wizened little man.

"Thank you, Willie," replied Quin, shaking the man's hand. "Rue, I should like you to meet Willie MacTavish, who takes care of Buchan, and his wife, Annie, our housekeeper. Cookie MacGeorge and Granny MacDonald," he added gently, sensing she might feel overwhelmed.

The blood hammered in Rue's ears as she gazed at the old, lined faces, seeing the dried-up censuring faces of the people at the mission.

"I should like you to meet your new mistress, my wife," stated Quin. "She is very tired," he explained, seeing her round haunted eyes and the concerned expressions on the faces of his ancient band of servants.

"And hungry no doubt," fussed Cookie MacGeorge, bustling out to the kitchen, determined to put more flesh on the wee mistress's bones.

"Bed's aired and I'll have hot water sent up in two shakes," promised Mrs. MacTavish, seeing how the "puir wee thing" stood shivering in her shoes.

"I'll see to the fire, sir," planned Willie.

"Well?" asked Quin, hoping for Rue's approval of his huge impractical hideaway, as he carried Shame up the broad carved staircase to the master bedroom.

Rue had never even imagined such a room could exist. Three walls were rounded, with bay windows that hung suspended over the cliff so that salt spray kissed the panes. A huge hearth dominated another wall. It was a large bare space with everything hewn from rock and wood. Quin leaned just inside the doorway, watching the expressions cross Rue's face as she whirled around slowly touching, listening, looking, and smelling. He was enchanted by her evident appreciation of his favorite room, and wished he was a painter so he could capture her enraptured expression.

"Maybe we shall stay at Buchan longer than I planned," he murmured as he watched Rue curl up on one of the wide window seats suspended over the moonlit sea. She stared across the shimmering expanse, smelling the wondrous fresh salt fragrance that defied description. It filled her, seeming to clear all the dark aching places. She was unaware of Tarquin and the ancient servants that filed in with a delicious repast that was tastefully set up on a low table before the roaring fire, lit to combat the sea's damp coolness.

"Rue?" called Quin gently as the last servant left, closing the door. She looked at him with confusion as though just waking. She frowned, seeing the food and wine before the blazing hearth that lit up the large room illuminating a large neatly turned down bed. The dark aching places of her mind returned as she saw the glow in her husband's dark eyes reflecting the burning fire.

A bath steamed seductively, misting the air and softening the dark hard lines of the room. Rue turned back to the sea wishing she could bathe in the buoyant waves instead of the confines of the bucketlike tub. She pointed out of the window to the sea and then to herself, hoping he would understand.

"You want to swim?" he interpreted and she nodded. "Salt can sting a wound," he warned yet he also longed to plunge into the exhilarating surf. Rue nodded her comprehension, and seeing his face light up with boyish delight, she forgot her vow to herself and pulled at his strong hand. Quin threw back his head and laughed. He grabbed several thick towels and allowed the excited girl to drag him from the room.

"No, Shame," he ordered the limping dog, who made an effort to follow, and the hound curled back by the warm hearth.

The moon silvered the fine sand of the secluded cove that Quin led Rue to and she quickly divested herself of her clothes and walked slowly into the sea, loving the feel of the firm wet sand beneath her bare feet. Quin wondered if he dare take the same freedom and plunge naked into the rippling waves. Deciding there was plenty of time for such pleasures in the future, he stripped off his shirt and boots, but still clad in his tight breeches he dived into the refreshing water.

Rue swam through the moonlit waves, delighting in the awakening crispness despite the first sharp stinging in her healing wound. She felt scoured clean by the waves that lapped around her as her firm hands fragmented the moon's reflection. Feeling at peace for the first time in ages, she turned and floated on her back staring at the clear night sky with its myriads of stars. She heard a faint splashing and Quin swam strongly until he was near her and then floated on his back. He longed to hold her cool silky body against him but was afraid that he would frighten her. He saw the white flash of her teeth as she smiled at him and he reached out a hand to her. Mischievously she splashed him before neatly diving under the water.

Quin laughed and gave chase, able to see her pale body below the surface and easily catch up with her. Though he longed to wrap his arms about her sleekness, he contented himself with just swimming beside her, marveling at her graceful agility.

Laughing and out of breath they raced up the sand to the towels, shivering in the crisp autumn night air before running briskly back to the large hearth in the inviting room with the windows that overhung the sea.

Rue ate heartily, feeling her skin tingling from the bracing salt and the roaring fire. She was relaxed and comfortable wrapped in one of Quin's enormous robes. She leaned back drowsily sipping wine as she stared dreamily into the red embers wondering why she felt disappointed in Quin not catching her. She had wanted him to, she mused, and at the realization stark terror stabbed her.

Quin watched her peacefully serene face change to agitation and then rage. He raised his eyebrows comically as she glared at him.

"What have I done now?" he laughed, fanning her fury so she stood and stomped to one of the window seats and curled up looking over the dark sea. She shivered, feeling cool away from the fire. The sea now looked lonely and menacing.

"Come here, Rue," said Quin, seeing her shiver and clasp her knees, hugging her body close, it seemed, for warmth. She pretended not to hear as she recognized his autocratic tone. She watched him stand and cross the room to her as she fixed her eyes thoughtfully on his well-formed mouth, remembering her first kiss aboard the *Dolphin*. As he neared she stood, trying to appear tall and womanly, but he towered over her. Quin picked her up and set her on the window seat, not wanting her bare feet on the cold floor. He wrapped a blanket around her.

Rue submitted to his ministrations as she looked down at his stern face. Quin looked up, feeling her intense gaze. Their eyes locked and slowly he reached up and pulled her onto his chest as his mouth took possession of hers.

Rue's limbs seemed to turn to liquid as she felt the length of her pressed to his hard body. The pressure increased, forcing her lips apart and she opened to him, her breath coming in short gasps as she felt every inch of her come alive. She returned his kisses savagely and pushed herself against him, delighting in the new sensations that coursed from the depths of her.

Quin carried her to the pillows by the hearth, his mouth still locked to hers as their tongues warred for dominance. He laid her down as his hands pulled away the blanket and robe searching for her silky breasts as she clung to him. Gently he uncoupled his mouth as he undressed her until she lay naked before him.

"Hush, my love, I'll nae hurt you," he soothed huskily, seeing panic flare in her eyes despite her erect nipples. He was glad for his tight restricting breeches that kept his aroused member safely contained as he devoted himself to caressing and bringing love to Rue's abused body.

Rue stared up into his dark eyes that reflected the dancing flames in the hearth and Quin's own inner fire, as his mouth descended to hers again. She arched up, trying to connect to his warmth, but he gently pushed her back as his hands explored, tantalizing and bringing excitement.

"Yes, my love, yes," he answered as she writhed and made small noises of passion.

Rue tensed as his hands caressed lower and she pressed her legs together, expecting painful clawing hands to rip into her.

"No, my darling," he murmured, stroking her thighs and kissing her most intimate place.

Rue had never felt or imagined such exquisite sensations existed as Quin fondled her aroused young body. She arched as she crested, crying aloud her intense pleasure. Wave after wave of inexplicable ecstasy shook her until she lay exhausted, feeling the faint echo beat deep inside.

Quin stared down at Rue's glistening young body with a gentle smile softening his features. He willed her to open her eyes and when she did, he grinned roguishly down at her trying to conquer the terror that built inside. Rue looked up solemnly, she opened her legs, indicating he should position himself between them. Quin shook his head.

"No, Rue, not yet. One lesson at a time and when we really make love it'll not be a duty," he said, interpreting the reason for her invitation, and covering her tempting young body with the blanket so he'd not be seduced into something he would regret. He congratulated himself, for not in his wildest dreams did he think they would have progressed so rapidly, or that she would exhibit so much passion.

Rue rolled onto her stomach and lay staring broodingly into the fire as she idly scratched behind Shame's floppy ears. She was all mixed up and wished she could voice her questions. She swiveled around and stared questioningly at Quin, who leaned back against the cushions watching her and sipping red wine. She felt a quiver inside at his loving expression and frowned, remembering his admission about marrying her.

"Tell me?" suggested Quin. "Try," he encouraged, but Rue turned away reaching for her own glass. She took a sip of the rich earthy wine and a deep breath as she tried to voice aloud.

"Why?" burst from her lips and Quin sat up as she turned with a look of pure astonishment on her face.

"Say it again," encouraged Quin as she just sat staring at him in shock. She heard the word that had somehow burst through her lips and the joy she first felt now turned to fear.

"You asked me why," prompted Quin, seeing her face stiffen with terror. Rue nodded silently, her lips firmly pursed. "Why what?"

She shook her head, refusing to attempt speech again as she mimed writing, hoping he would fetch paper and a pen. Quin was aware of what she demanded but he shook his head, feeling that she would talk when she had to. Rue frowned angrily at his denial. She shook his arm, demanding that he look at her as she mimed writing again. Again Quin firmly shook his head.

"'Tis late, Rue," he yawned and drained his wineglass. She stared at him hostilely, her amber eyes flashing as he regarded her with a slight smile on his face. Rue looked away confused, not understand-

ing how one minute he could be so gentle and able to arouse exquisite
sensations that shook her body to its very core, and the next be so
cruel as to deny her the means to communicate.

"Are you coming to bed?" he asked, but she refused to acknowledge that she had heard. Two people could play the same cruel
games, she decided. Quin stood and looked down at her rigid back as
she sat turned away from him. He sighed deeply before piling wood
on the fire and stretching out on the large comfortable bed, leaving her
to her own devices.

Rue felt abandoned as she heard his steady breathing, knowing he
slept. She pulled a blanket around herself and curled up on the
cushions with Shame but was unable to sleep as the events of the long
day whirled in her mind. She stared toward the bed as she wondered
what the tall dark man really wanted with her. Maybe he did love her
as Nick loved her sister Kestrel, she mused, remembering warm
loving looks and his gentle hands and mouth that caressed her whole
body bringing joy instead of the expected pain. But as she tried to
relax joyfully with that thought, doubts crept in. He thought of her as
a child; a hindrance; had married her by mistake; should have adopted
her; she remembered bitterly. But why then was she with him? Why
had he kissed her as a man kisses a woman? she questioned, wanting
to believe that she was loved as a woman. She sat up and hugged her
knees as she remembered opening her thighs to invite him between.
He didn't want to love her as a woman, she concluded as her mind
raced back to the mission. When she was a child, she had been abused
as a woman and now she was a woman she was used like a child.

Rue felt so desolate, hollow and cold, that she wished she could
find the numbing protection that she had during the journey from Glen
Aucht. Once again she had opened up and now felt lost and alone.
The fire died down and Shame wiggled closer to her shivering body
for warmth.

Quin awoke and stared bemused at Rue's hunched figure before the
ember's glow. He swung his long limbs from the bed and resignedly
left the comfortable warmth.

"You're a stubborn female," he sighed, picking her up and easily
quelling her struggles with his strength as he carried her back to the
warm bed. Her toes were icy so he enveloped her in his arms and held
her close to the heat of him. "Sleep," he ordered as she tried to
wriggle out of his hold. "Stop!" he roared threateningly as she
continued. He smiled sleepily to himself as she froze at his stern
voice. He kissed the top of her unruly head and closed his eyes.

Rue tried to stay awake but the comfortable bed and Quin's warmth soothed her exhausted body until she slept tucked neatly into the large man's hard stomach.

CHAPTER THIRTY-FOUR

Rue awoke to bright blinding sunlight as the reflection from the sea poured through the windows. She sat up and stared around at the empty room. The remains of the last night's meal had been cleared away and a jug of hot water steamed by the bed. How could she have slept through everything, she wondered, jumping out of the high bed and running to look out of the window. She caught her breath at the magnificent view.

Quin stood in the doorway watching her stand on the window seat, her arms spread wide, with the sun glinting on her glossy hair. He quietly crossed to her, wanting to see the expression on her face. Her eyes were wide and shining, her mouth open and smiling as she gazed enraptured by the breathtakingly beautiful vista.

" 'Tis nearly as beautiful as you," he said softly, placing his hands each side of her slim waist and lifting her down to hold against him. He felt her stiffen and turned her around so he could look deep into her guarded amber eyes. Refusing to be repelled by her apprehension he slowly lowered his head and softly kissed her lips. He stifled a grin as he felt her clench her lips, refusing to participate. He increased his pressure slightly and teased her with his tongue until he felt her breathing quicken and her mouth open to him.

Rue once more felt the pleasurable sensations start to build and a deep exquisite aching start to burn. Quin reluctantly raised his head and stared down into her passion-veiled eyes.

"Pull on your clothes and after breakfast we'll ride over the cliffs," he said huskily. Rue shook her head and lifted her lips toward him, wanting to continue kissing, but Quin just laughed and gave a quick kiss on her uptilted nose and crossed to his riding boots, knowing he was very aroused. Rue shook her head, unable to do anything but stand full of confusion and pain.

"Och, Rue," groaned Quin, reading her reaction correctly. "I'm not rejecting you, my love. Come here," he added, opening his arms, but she turned her back and stared over the shimmering sea. Each time she allowed happiness in she was hurt, she reminded herself, unable to do anything but shake her head in disbelief at her stupidity. Quin sat sadly staring at her straight little back, wishing he knew what was going through her mind as he tried to select just the right words to reach her.

"Rue, I want to make love to you very much . . . but I am afraid," he confessed. "I dinna want to hurt or frighten you," he continued as she made no sign she had heard. "Do you ken?" he asked, walking slowly toward her. Rue heard him approaching and spun about, her furious expression daring him to come closer. His black eyes smoldered and his face was set on stern lines as he berated himself for his impulsive behavior. Seeing her looking so vibrant and beautiful, embracing the brilliant morning, had made him throw caution to the wind, not realizing how near the edge he was. He had spent the night with her in his arms, barely able to sleep for the all-consuming need he had for her.

Rue turned her back, unable to detach herself from his intensity. She fought to cover herself with the protective armor but all she felt was his pain join with hers. She wished he would leave so she could sort out the jumbled emotions that warred within her. But when the door slammed announcing his departure, she felt no relief, just an aching loss as the decisive sound jarred her senses. She dressed quickly, eager to be outside riding Sin so the wind could sing in her ears, drowning out all her nightmarish anxieties and fears.

Quin watched Rue ride across the crest of the cliff as he sat on the wide window seat of their bedroom, idly scratching the bored hound, who longed to be free of the splint and racing outside with her young mistress. They had been at Buchan for nearly a week and there had been no progress. It was as though that promising first night had never occurred, he mused bitterly as the sky darkened and the thunderclouds built. He wondered now if his hesitancy that first night had been a mistake. He turned back and surveyed the room, noting the large bed where she chose to sleep alone each night.

There was a discreet knock and Willie MacTavish entered with an armload of logs for the fire.

"You've a special wild filly there, Master Tarquin," observed the old man as they stood side by side watching the dark figure on her black horse silhouetted against the stormy sky.

"Aye," answered the brooding young man.

"Someone tried to break her," stated the shrewd MacTavish. "Was it you?" he asked sharply, knowing the young man's ruthlessness when he was crossed.

"Never!" hissed Quin, shocked that one of his oldest friends would think such a thing. "I would never try to break her."

"Not on purpose you wouldna," returned the old man laconically. Quin barely heard him as he stared off in the distance, feeling the earth's tensions crackle and stretch until the sky was rent with lightning. The old man noted the set of his young master's jaw and sensed another storm was brewing. "She's wrapped in more than silence," he remarked, before noisily raking the ashes in the hearth.

Rue raised her face to the strong biting rain that scoured her skin and soaked her luxuriant hair that streamed heavily down her back. The storm was nearly passed; just distant rumbles and a faint shimmering on the horizon remained. The rain poured, dimpling the sea, and the ground put up the sweetest smell that was the same both sides of the vast ocean, she mused, feeling at ease with her solitude. All that existed was the elements and the rhythm of the horse beneath her.

Quin reined his horse and sat back in the saddle watching his wife's seemingly serene face raised to the rain. Sin whinnied in greeting and Rue's eyes flew open. She stared in shock at her husband's sudden appearance as he seemed to loom out of the sheets of rain.

Rue gazed at him, unaware of the scalding tears that poured with the icy rain down her cheeks. She shivered, feeling cold and vulnerable, unable to deal with her tumultuous emotions. When she was alone, she felt able to cope. When she knew to expect his presence, she was able to somehow steel herself. But to be caught unaware caused the pain to surge.

Quin gasped at the sudden transformation as Rue's serenity was smashed at his appearance. He saw her expression of calm changed to great agitation and then to pure pain. Without conscious thought, he reached across to comfort, plucking her off her saddle into his arms, cradling her and wrapping her in his cape.

Rue desperately tried to shroud herself, detach herself as she heard Tarquin crooning his love for her with very uncharacteristic words as he kneed his horse toward the shelter of Buchan.

" 'Tis all right, my darling love. Cry, that's right, cry, my sweetheart," he urged over and over again. Rue tried to stop the sobs that built and built like a rising storm, threatening to totally submerge her. Over and over again in her head she fought with herself. *No, no, no, no.* She would not give in to the mounting pressure that was in danger of consuming her.

Quin dismounted, handing the reins of the two horses to the concerned old groom, and with Rue in his arms strode through the pouring rain into the house and up the stairs to the intimate privacy of their room, determined to break through her wall of silence.

Rue was unaware of anything as she tried to cling on to the very edge of sanity. *No, no, no, no!* screamed in her brain.

"Let it out, my own dear heart, let it out," begged Quin, holding her close as he sat before the blazing hearth.

"NO! NO! NO! NO!" screamed Rue aloud and Quin's blood curdled at the stark anguish that rang, seeming to reverberate off the cold stones of Buchan.

"Aye, you maun, my darling," he pleaded. "You canna be a prisoner any longer. There's too many years of tears locked inside. Let them out."

"No!" howled Rue.

"Let go!" he shouted, giving her a shake. Rue's shoulders shook as she closed her mouth in a tight line trying to stop the terrifying flood that threatened.

"I . . . I . . . canna . . ." she stammered and a low sobbing moan burst from her mouth and like a very small hurt child she cried and tried to explain her pain all at the same time. "They hurt me! Mama! They hurt me! Mama! Mama! Father! They're hurting me!" she screamed. "Stop them, Mama! Stop them!"

Tears poured down Tarquin's lean cheeks as he held Rue close, hearing her plead and beg for help. His blood ran cold as he listened to the numerous atrocities she had been subjected to. Something had snapped inside of Rue; the barrier was broken and she was unaware of him except as someone she called out to for help. In the hour or more he held her, he became her mother, father, brothers, sister, Jemmy, Angus, Meron, and Goliath; all those who been taken from her that autumn four years before. She relived those first heartrending screams on that awful day when she saw Jemmy and Goliath killed, and her own little girl's body had been violated. Even more chilling was her expressionless monologue as she recounted the many brutal rapes by the pious farmers who hired her from the mission. Gradually her voice petered out and she lay exhausted in his arms, her body still shaken by deep shuddering sighs. He rocked her gently, wanting to get her out of the wet clothes that steamed in the fire's heat but not wanting to agitate her further.

"Rue, I shall do all in my power to make up for those years," he promised, tenderly brushing the damp tendrils of dark hair from her flushed face. Rue stiffened in his arms and stared about their bedroom with confusion as fear started to pound her blood.

" 'Tis all right, my sweeting," comforted Quin as he felt her rapidly beating heart resound through him. Rue shook her head violently from side to side as she was filled with a terrible dread. It seemed her last protection had been ripped away from her.

"Everything is going to be all right, my darling. I love you and no one will hurt you again," he crooned. Rue pursed her lips, willing herself to silence as she heard his words. She shook her head, her amber eyes large and luminous in her small white face.

"No" burst through her tight lips as she desperately tried to salvage some protection. "You should not have married me," she stated in stilted tones. "You should have adopted me!" she spat as she tried to push herself off his lap but he held her firmly. Quin nodded silently, remembering his frustrated words when he thought her sleeping.

"Aye, I said that," he admitted. "But I dinna adopt you, I married you."

"Aye, 'twas an error of judgment!" she challenged, words feeling strange and disjointed in her mouth. Quin threw back his head and laughed as he hugged her close as he realized why she had hoarded each negative statement he had made.

"I know when I fell in love with you," he informed her with a very roguish expression. "When did you fall in love wie me?" He felt her tense in his arms. "Well?" he prompted gently after a long pause. "Please tell me you love me," he whispered, gazing into her tear-streaked face.

"I love you. I always did," she stated, her eyes filling with tears. "It's strange and frightening to talk," she confessed, wrapping her arms tightly about him in case it was an illusion.

"I think we should get out of these wet clothes," suggested Quin as a great shudder shook Rue's small frame and she burrowed against him. Rue smelled the beloved scent of him and pressed her nose into the warmth of his neck. Tentatively she kissed the softness, feeling the pulse under his ear increase. Rue reached up and pulled his dark head down, trying to capture his lips.

Quin drowned in the sweetness of her kiss, determined to keep his passions reined, but Rue pressed against him with a kind of desperation, offering herself.

"Love me," she begged. "As a woman."

"Aye, my love. I'll claim every inch of you," he promised huskily before kissing her hungrily and carrying her toward the bed. He felt as nervous and as insecure as a callow youth as he undressed her, his large hands fumbling and clumsy with the wet materials. He gazed down tenderly at her small face, which stared back, unable to hide her fear.

"There is nothing to be afraid of," he comforted, not wanting to alarm her further by removing his trousers and showing evidence of his need. He lay down and pulled her on top of him as he kissed her lingeringly.

Rue tried to relax and drown in the sweet dominance of his warm firm mouth. She felt the length of her body pressed against his muscular frame and excitement started to build as she felt her breasts tingle and her breathing quicken. She opened her mouth to his thrusting tongue, feeling another pressure push against her core, straining for admittance.

Quin rolled on his side, panting for breath and trying to control his raging passion.

"I have to get undressed, sweetheart," he said gently. Rue felt desolate and terrified when Quin left the bed. With her brain blinded by passion there was no time for thinking, but now lying naked and cold waiting for the inevitable coupling, she felt mortal terror.

"Now, my own love," crooned Quin, climbing back into the bed and pulling her against his nakedness. Rue stiffened in panic as his man-root pressed against her. Images of hurting, thrusting members tore through her. "Kiss me, my darling," he urged, sensing that once her passion was reawakened, her fear would recede.

Rue closed her eyes and opened her mouth under his, waiting for the painful stabbing that never came. Instead, delightful sensations ran through the whole of her, bringing joy and excitement until she pressed against him trying to be one.

Quin eased her onto her back and positioned himself between her firm thighs. He looked down lovingly at her, willing her eyes to open before he thrust into the center of her.

Rue strained upward trying to connect to his warmth as she felt him poised. She stared up into his smoldering black eyes and thrust her pelvis, trying to drive him into her. Keeping their eyes locked, Quin smiled and slowly sheathed himself, claiming his wife.

Rue couldn't believe the exquisite ecstasy that filled her as Quin entered her. Slowly at first, relishing each loving thrust into her excited young body, delighting in the way she rose to meet him and then unable to stop as the pace increased.

They were swept together into a whirling vortex of incredible feelings that built in intensity, culminating in an explosion of such ecstasy that it left them both straining breathlessly against each other. Rue sighed deeply and held Quin tightly as she marveled at the exquisite echoes that still pulsated deep within her.

Quin rolled onto his back, holding her firmly so they remained intimately coupled. He gazed up at her flushed face under her tousled ebony hair. She smiled wonderingly, her eyes round with awe at the magic they had just shared. The joy and relief she felt caused a husky giggle to well and she threw back her head and laughed. Quin's jubilant voice joined with hers and he cupped her firm buttocks, pressing her closer so he didn't slip out of her. They lay together peacefully for a long time before Quin broke the silence.

"I think we should ring for luncheon. Are you hungry?" he asked, unable to take his eyes from her open joyous face. She nodded and wiggled mischievously to let him know what she was hungry for. "I need sustenance. This is hard work, woman," he growled as he felt his still-sheathed member stiffen. He lay back with a roguish look of resignation, seeing Rue's delicate nostrils flare as her lips parted and she started to move sensuously against him.

Much, much later they lay still entwined. Quin stared down at Rue's sleeping face, revelling in her incredible beauty and the passionate nature that had been finally unleashed. The sun was setting and the room was bathed in a warm rosy glow. Shame whined and tried to climb onto the high bed but was hampered by the clumsy splint. Carefully Quin tried to extricate himself and leave the bed without waking Rue but she giggled sleepily and held him tightly.

"We'll have puddles on the floor and I'll be dead of exhaustion and starvation," laughed Quin, burying his face in the warm sleepy fragrance of her before tickling her to break her hold.

Rue watched Quin leave the room carrying Shame before she climbed out of the bed and pulled a nightshirt over her head. Taking her hairbrush she crossed to the wide window seat where she sat, rhythmically trying to bring order to her unruly hair and tumultuous thoughts. She stared over the blood-red sea as she thought of the afternoon of loving. She shook her head at the mystery of how something that had been so painful and abhorrent could also be such exquisite ecstasy. The shadows lengthened and she wished Quin would return as Mrs. MacTavish and the bevy of ancient servants bustled in. Rue felt awkward and very young and she tried to sink into the dark window seat so she was unobtrusive as she looked back over the sea, imagining disapproving stares dig into her back. Terror swept in and she was suddenly back in the cold gray mission with the ancient missionaries. She pressed her thighs together feeling the hollow aching pain, knowing the shrewd old eyes knew she had been thrust into.

Quin frowned as he entered, seeing the dejected slump of her shoulders that seemed to take no pleasure from the festive feast he had directed his servants to set up. A large bathtub steamed a perfumed mist in front of the blazing fire. The last old person scurried out, giggling excitedly, and Mrs. MacTavish stood in the doorway.

"That'll be all. Thank you," dismissed Quin, not taking his eyes from the huddled shape of Rue.

"Hae a wonderful evening, your lairdship and ladyship," said the old woman quietly, her eyes full of compassion for the small quiet figure on the window seat. She and the other servants had heard the anguished cries earlier in the afternoon and had clustered together, not knowing whether to interfere or not, but her husband Willie MacTavish had sent them all about their business. She closed the door and smiled softly, having noted the tender expression on her young master's usually stern face.

"What is it, my love?" asked Quin as the door shut after Mrs. MacTavish. Rue turned and smiled but he noticed it didn't reach her eyes, which remained haunted and sad. She shook her head and crossed the room to the steaming bath. Quin frowned at her embarrassed awkwardness as she stripped off her shirt, hiding her body from him, and stepped quickly into the tub, her arms folded across her breasts.

"Rue, dinna lock me out," he pleaded softly but she avoided his gaze and shook her head dismissingly. "Talk to me," he urged, taking the sponge from her hands. Rue opened her mouth and then closed it again. "Try," coaxed Quin softly, lathering her back, noting the faint scars.

Rue didn't know how to even attempt explaining the feelings that clawed within.

"I . . . I . . . I . . ." she stammered and then savagely she punched the water so it splashed, soaking Quin. "I feel cowed . . . beaten and cowed like a dog! To your servants . . . I have no dignity . . ." she struggled. Quin shook his head in disbelief.

"You are the most graceful, dignified . . ." he started to reassure.

"I . . . feel dirty . . . and grubby . . . and filthy . . . and beaten," she shouted, interrupting, and she gasped as Quin gave an agonized groan and pulled her out of the water to hold her wet soapy body close. "No! Dinna pity me!" she spat, pushing him away.

"Right!" he agreed, and dumped her back in the bath so she sat suddenly and stared up at him with surprise, not knowing what to expect as he turned away from her and poured a glass of wine. He stood by the blazing fire, staring at her with a strange half smile on his handsome face. She gazed at the length of his long firm body, remembering the feel of it against the length of hers. Quin's expression broadened to a seductive grin as he saw her nipples stand erect.

"I'd like a bath also," he stated idly as she shimmied her body under the rapidly cooling water. Rue looked around for a towel within reach. Quin followed her gaze and grinned engagingly back at her. She pointed but he cocked his head to one side comically, with an inquiring look and when she still said nothing, just shrugged and sipped his wine. Rue smoldered, knowing he knew exactly what she wanted. She stood and haughtily stepped out of the bath, and suppressing a shiver as the cold air goosebumped her flesh, she walked across the room with as much dignity as she could muster. Quin shook his dark head in mock despair as she wrapped the thick warm towel about herself.

"When someone wants something, one should ask," he recited with mischievous pomposity as he stripped off his clothes and sat in the cool water. "Would you fetch that pail of water?" he asked, pointing to the steaming object he desired. Rue regarded him thoughtfully before picking up the pail of cold water and pouring it over him. Quin gasped as the icy flood took his breath away. Rue giggled at his astounded expression and then threw herself down on the pillows before the hearth and laughed until her stomach hurt.

Quin sat in his bath unaware of the temperature as he grinned, appreciating her gurgling laughter. He leaned back with a satisfied smile on his face as he congratulated himself on his unerring instinct in the selection of a mate. They still had a long way to go and there were many scars, but how he loved her. Rue looked at him, her eyes still streaming as she gasped for breath. Quin rose out of the water like a phoenix, and strode toward her, his arms outstretched like wings dripping water, until he stood above her.

Rue watched him approach, filling her eyes with his perfect male beauty. His well-defined face with its thick thatch of black hair, his golden body from his broad shoulders to his tapered waist and slim hips and long muscular legs. Her eyes came to rest on his center where his man-root moved fluidly with his strides and then stiffened under her burning gaze. She raised her eyes to his as she dropped the towel that covered her own arousal.

They came together slowly, savoring each precious second, committing, claiming, bonding, promising everything to each other in an act of love on the pillows before the blazing hearth.

"Rue, you have the most inborn dignity and pride," he said huskily, wishing there was another way humanly possible to get even closer as he realized he couldn't possess enough of her. She rubbed her little nose against his aquiline one before reaching over the laden table and picking up a bunch of succulent grapes. She lay atop him, glorying in the strong hands that splayed across her, keeping them intimately joined, and leaning on her forearms she fed him the juicy fruit, one by one. The amused twinkle in Tarquin's dark eyes caused a great excitement to grow and churn in Rue but she kept her face prim and impassive.

"When someone wants something, one should ask," she parroted, feeling him stir and grow within her. He regarded her somberly and nodded.

"Aye," he agreed. "Pass the chicken, please."

Rue smiled sweetly, and before he could guess what she had in mind, she rolled off him as she reached for the dish, leaving him rearing in anticipation.

"Och, wee woman of mine, you'll pay for such wickedness," he threatened, rolling onto his stomach and grabbing her. He roguishly bit her bottom and pretended to chew with relish, smacking his lips as she squealed with a mixture of shock and hilarity. They rolled together like two carefree youngsters, absolutely delighting in each other.

The ancient band of servants at Buchan smiled contentedly at the antics of the laird and his beautiful young wife as the golden autumn passed in loving play and the first snow clouds piled on the horizon. They nodded their approval as they observed the softening of the harsh lines on Quin's handsome face, and the confidence that caused Rue's hesitant voice to become surer and more fluid. Each old person from the MacTavishes to the rolypoly Cookie MacGeorge would have laid down their lives for their tiny unconventional mistress whose infectious husky laughter warmed the frosty morning air.

Rue collapsed with mirth into the enormous pile of leaves. Quin picked her up and tossed her high before catching her against his broad chest and kissing her parted lips so her laughter spurted out in rude little noises.

"No more," pleaded Rue, her sides aching and tears of happiness sparking her amber eyes and coursing down her flushed cheeks.

"To bed," he ordered and Rue collapsed again with merriment.

"We've only just got up," she gurgled when she could manage a couple of words.

"Right," remembered Quin, holding her tightly in his arms as he fell backward into the great pile of leaves. They lay quietly staring up at the clear profound sky, breathing deeply of the crisp fresh air. Rue felt complete, wishing the golden days would never end.

"Winter's nearly here," sighed Quin and he frowned as he felt her stiffen in his arms. "What is it?" he asked, but she shook her head adamantly, and grabbing a handful of leaves, threw them at him, trying to return to the carefree play of before, but there was no returning as he lay silently watching her pile the leaves on him. Panic flared and Rue saw the tension knot his jaw. She tried to laugh but an ugly sound burst through her lips. She let the light frail leaves float from her hands.

Rue recoiled from Quin's dark intense stare; she shook her head mutely, unable to deal with the dread that filled her before turning her back on him and staring blindly over the shimmering sea.

Quin stood, angrily brushing the leaves off himself and savagely running his fingers through his hair. Suddenly the autumn leaves were dry and dead, abrasive to his flesh, and he crushed them to dust in his hands. He watched her, feeling a warning crackle surround her, telling him to stay away. It was the set of her head and shoulders. He debated reaching out to her but was deterred. The past weeks with Rue had been more wonderful than he had ever envisioned and yet there were times when she withdrew to a place where he couldn't reach her. Several times he had awakened in the night to find her staring over the dark sea looking so solitary and isolated it was as though she were surrounded by an invisible moat.

Rue stared over the endless sea wishing she still had the protection of silence. Now that she could talk, she had a responsibility to share her feelings, but they were too raw, too inexplicable. Quin's mentioning of winter had caused a terrifying rage to explode within her and she wanted to howl that nothing else existed but that moment, that place, and the two of them, because to admit to the existence of other times, places, and people was to remember too much. It was to remember the long cold winter in the mission waiting for a spring that never came.

Quin was about to turn away when Rue turned to him. He made no sound or motion though he longed to sweep her into his arms when he saw the raw pain mirrored in her eyes. Her mouth opened and closed and her small hands clenched and unclenched as she tried to express herself.

"Can . . . Can . . . *now* last forever . . . for just a little while longer?" she begged stiffly and Quin frowned as he strove to understand.

"Now?" he repeated and she nodded emphatically. "Aye," he agreed, understanding, and opening his arms wide to her. Rue stared at him, loving him so much it hurt and coupled with a terrible sense of loss. What if she lost him? What if she screamed and screamed for him and he never came? She stood poised, her face drained of all color and then flung herself into his arms with such force they fell back into the generous pile of leaves.

"What is it?" Quin asked, concern sharpening his tone. Rue shook her head, not wanting to talk, and covered his mouth with hers, kissing him desperately so she could block out the painful images. Quin held her close and returned her kisses, wishing he could erase all the hurtful dark corners, and determined that he'd let time stand still for her for as long as he could.

Quin and Rue were so immersed in themselves and the leaves they were oblivious to the approaching hoofbeats as Lachlan McCulloch rode up. He reined his horse and stared with undisguised satisfaction at the couple entwined in each other's arms.

"Well, well, well. Willie MacTavish said I'd find the two of you here," he finally boomed, rather regretfully feeling that he should make his presence known before the rising passions got out of hand and possibly embarrassed someone, but certainly not him.

"Lachlan!" exclaimed Quin, blinking as though he dreamed his grandfather's substantial presence. Rue blew the leaves away that obscured her vision and stared up at the gleeful old face.

"Och, what a bonny lass," chortled the old reprobate, feasting his eyes on her radiant cheeks, sparkling eyes, and soft lips that were flushed from the very thorough kissing she had just received.

"What the de'il are you doing here?" asked Quin, stunned and still lying in the leaves with Rue in his arms.

"Thought you might like some company," prevaricated Lachlan, sensing his grandson was angry at the intrusion. "Was worried about your wee wife . . . and so was Gladys," he ended lamely as Miss Mackintosh's strident tones could be heard. Quin, about to stand up, fell back with the most incredible expression of disbelief on his face.

"Lachlan!" he postulated, unable to say anything else.

" 'Twas the Mackintosh woman's idea," informed the old man defensively. " 'Tis a plot to make that rascally, one-eyed pirate jealous."

"Pierre Gillette is here, too?" roared Quin.

"Not yet," replied Lachlan unhappily. "I wish he'd hurry up."

Quin opened his mouth to give vent to his spleen but Rue collapsed across his chest, her lithe body shaking. He flashed a furious look at his grandfather and gently turned her over expecting to see fear and tears. Rue gazed up at him, her eyes brimming as she choked with laughter.

"Och, Lachlan," she howled, fighting for control. The tall old man frowned, his mouth dropped open with amazement, and he peered down comically at her, causing both Quin and Rue to convulse with merriment.

"She spoke!" he exclaimed incredulously before joining in their mirth. "Say something else," he demanded when they all could talk and Rue shrugged shyly, not knowing what to say. "Well, 'tis guid she doesna talk too much. Confoundedly bad trait in a woman," approved Lachlan as they strolled back to the house. "That Mackintosh woman talks too much," he added as Gladys's voice could be heard ringing through the cool air.

Rue walked between the two tall men realizing that the autumn was over as a sharp wind blew whirling the leaves and crisping them with a frosty rime.

"How is everyone at Glen Aucht?" she asked bravely, knowing it was time to face other places and people. Quin proudly smiled down at her, his profound dark eyes sparkling suspiciously with tears.

CHAPTER THIRTY-FIVE

Alexander Sinclair smiled wistfully at his family, who were assembled around a large Christmas tree in the main salon at Glen Aucht.
Outside, snow blanketed the sloping lawns to the firth but inside there
was a golden warmth that had not existed for many years. For a
moment his mind was back in the sprawling wooden house in the
wilderness of America and his ears rang with the echoes of children's
voices as he and Cameron watched their offspring happily gathered
around another tree. The twins, Raven and Lynx, the golden heads of
Rowan and Kestrel, and the quiet dignity of Rue, all glowing, joyous
children. All so long ago. All in the past.

Alex's hand prickled as though he held Cameron's small silky one
in his roughened palm and he raised his amber eyes to the present,
knowing his love was there in spirit. His heart ached as he gazed at his
grown children, seeing the painful voids left by Raven and Rue.

"Dinna shroud yourself in regret, hold on to the joy," he mouthed
to himself, hearing Cameron's musical voice gently berate. He
watched Lynx, so dark and tall, impatience glowing in his emerald
eyes so painfully like his mother's. Lynx, wild and caged in the small
confines of Scotland, yearning to return to the vast, untamed land of
his birth where his identical twin was buried. The rangy youth of
nearly twenty-one prowled the hearth unable to be still.

"Sit, Lynx, you make me dizzy," cried Kestrel, who longed to be
able to move so lithely but was hampered by her enormous shape.

"She's just jealous, Lynx," teased her golden brother Rowan, who
had fallen totally in love with the estate of Glen Aucht. Alex smiled,
knowing his youngest son would become Laird, leaving Lynx to roam
the wilderness unfettered.

"Aye, I'm jealous. I don't think I shall ever ride, swim, walk, or
even stand up again," she mourned, trying to be humorous about the
situation.

"It was the only way I could think to harness her," sighed Nick.
"Keep her so fat she couldna even waddle," he added, ducking a

well-aimed pillow. "She'll not be able to ride around wie half-naked braves wie a belly like that," he continued as Kestrel heaved herself to her feet with great difficulty and advanced on him.

"I'll show you what harnessing is," she threatened before collapsing on his welcoming lap so he groaned with exaggerated pain as though being flattened, before wrapping his hard arms possessively about his wife and their unborn child.

The French doors were suddenly thrown open and the wind howled menacingly as three dark figures seemed to be blown into the warmth. Quin wrestled with the doors, closing them against the inhospitable elements as the black hound Shame shook the snow from her glossy coat and Rue silently surveyed her assembled family, her eyes seeking her father.

Alex stared in amazement at the small exquisite woman who looked so much like his Cameron. He stood unable to say or do anything as her amber eyes assessed him, sharing more pain than he felt was possible. He wanted to welcome her into his arms, but she was a woman, no longer his little girl. Her eyes blazed, somehow warning him to keep his distance.

Rue looked at her father, seeing the reflection of the fire in his once-vibrant hair, remembering how he had looked before she was forced into premature womanhood. She frowned, not able to find the father she knew. He had been tall and strong, handsome and brave, able to soothe every hurt and always, always there to love and protect her. He had been her first hero, her first love. Her eyes filled with tears for bygone days when she had been a carefree, cherished child in their wooden house by the forest. She brushed the tears away angrily as a multitude of conflicting emotions tore through her. She had been so sure that her father's love would save her; so sure he would always be there to protect her; so sure that no matter where on earth he was he would hear her. She had screamed and screamed for him until all she could do was open her mouth in silent agony.

"I called you but you didn't come," she pronounced slowly, deaf to the sharp intake of breath from her siblings as they heard her speak.

"I am here now," replied Alex, remembering Cameron's words as she heard the mournful howl of the wolves and stared out at the vast wilderness, knowing their dark daughter was alive and needing them.

"Mother isn't."

"Aye, she is, my daughter. She is in you," he answered, his voice cracking with emotion. "And that is how you survived, my darling."

"Oh, Father, it hurts," cried Rue, running into his outstretched arms.

"I know. Och, how I know," groaned Alex, holding her tightly, wondering how he could have been so bound by his own grief that he had hurt Cameron's precious children even more. " 'Tis so good to hear your voice," he rejoiced, staring over her ebony head and smiling mistily at the rest of his family, who sat crying and grinning as they watched the reunion.

"Sometimes it's more comfortable to be wrapped in silence," confessed Rue and then she giggled huskily as Lachlan's deep voice and Gladys's cockney tones shattered the emotion-filled stillness.

Quin nursed a generous goblet of whiskey, delighting in the joy that lit the Sinclair faces as his beautiful wife was lovingly embraced by her brothers and sister.

Rue stared with awe-filled eyes at Kestrel's enormous stomach as her golden sister sprawled contentedly across Nick's lap.

"Feel it kicking," offered Nick, proudly splaying his large hands across the firm round expanse.

"It doesn't look real," exclaimed Rue, laughing and crying at the same time before very gently placing her small hand on her sister's stomach. "I felt it, Quin. I felt it kick," she cried with wonder.

"Oh, Rue, it's so good to hear your voice," sobbed Kestrel. "I've missed you so . . ." She stopped suddenly and froze in an awkward position, holding her breath.

"Och, Kestrel MacKay, trust you to break your waters while you were sitting on my lap. My best trews, too," complained Nick as the wet warmth flooded, saturating him and the couch.

"What's happening?" worried Kestrel, trying to see past her large belly to the source of his discomfort, as Nick stood lifting her easily in his strong arms.

" 'Tis our bairn getting ready to be born," he reassured. " 'Tis perfectly natural, nothing to worry about," he added as Rue gave a small gasp and turned alarmingly white as she remembered the birthing pains that had torn her child-body in the cold comfortless mission.

"How can we help?" asked Quin, wrapping his arms about Rue as he read the terror in her wide amber eyes.

The door burst open and Lachlan and Gladys entered in the midst of a raucous argument.

"Och, I wish that one-eyed buccaneer would shake his bones a wee bit," he roared and then stopped in astonishment, staring at his youngest grandson who stood holding his very pregnant and still-dripping wife. "You're soaked, lad," he stated baldly.

"Very guid, Lachlan. You're a very observant mon," Nick remarked tersely before striding across the room.

"Where are we going? I don't want to miss anything," complained Kestrel.

"We're going to have a bairn and when you've done that, you can come back," teased Nick.

"The baby's coming?" squealed Gladys.

"The baby!" chorused Rowan and Lynx as Alex sat grinning from ear to ear at the noisy happy confusion that reminded him of bygone days with his large energetic family.

"But you said there would be pain and I have none," retorted Kestrel.

"None?" puzzled Nick, stopping in mid-stride, half in and half out of the room.

"I'll be the midwife. A birthing's no place for men," stated Miss Mackintosh, rolling up her voluminous black sleeves as there came a thunderous knocking at the front door.

"I'll bring my own child into the world, thank you, Gladys," returned Nick. "You haven't had even a wee twinge of pain?" he questioned.

"No," answered Kestrel, craning her neck to see what the cause of the commotion was as servants ran here and there in the hall. "Aaaaah!" she squealed, straightening in his strong arms as the first labor pain hit and Pierre's Gallic voice boomed throughout the vast house.

"Where ees my leetle cabbage?" he shouted.

"Thank God!" rejoiced Lachlan.

"Pierre!" screeched Gladys.

"No. Not yet. I don't want to miss anything," lamented Kestrel as Nick strode purposefully out of the room.

Kestrel lay on blankets and sheets by the blazing fire of her bedchamber.

"I'm more comfortable here," she panted. "The bed was too soft."

"Will it be much longer?" asked Rue, wiping her sister's brow with a cooling cloth as she thought on her own interminable painful labor.

"Canna tell," replied Nick tersely, and Quin grinned seeing his younger brother was no longer the unflappable doctor. He laid a strong brown hand on Kestrel's hard belly.

"I estimate at least another hour if not more. Our niece or nephew is definitely positioned but in no great hurry," he remarked sagely, trying to keep a straight face as Rue and Nick looked at him in astonishment.

"And how many bairns have you delivered?" snapped Nick.

"Three," grinned Quin. "And about twenty calves, several foals, and a litter or two of piglets."

"Don't make me laugh," giggled Kestrel. "Can we play cards or something to pass the time . . . so I don't get bored?"

"Och, Kess, how can you talk of boredom in the middle of having a baby?" laughed Rue, trying to push her own painful memories away.

There was a tentative knocking at the door and Lachlan, Alex, Pierre, and Gladys popped worried faces around the door after eavesdropping and hearing several giggles and gurgles. They stood astounded at the sight that met their eyes. Kestrel lay on the floor by the blazing hearth, her enormous stomach being used as a card table. Every few minutes or so the game would stop as the card table contracted and cards flew in all directions and the fourth player groaned loudly.

"Out, everyone," ordered Nick, officiously waving the curious cluster away.

"Nay," disagreed Kestrel vehemently. " 'Tis my bairn."

"Ours!" contradicted Nick.

"Ours," corrected Kestrel, stopping as another pain took her breath away. "And everybody is very welcome to watch my . . . our baby being born," she finished in a rush as her slim thighs obeyed the age-old ritual as they raised and parted and Pierre hurriedly excused himself.

"You are doing lovely, lovey ducks," hastily approved Gladys, before chasing after her one-eyed lover, not trusting him out of her sight for a moment.

"Nicholas, guide your bairn into the world," urged Quin, seeing his younger brother was more the nervous father than the objective doctor.

"But we haven't finished the hand," gurgled the irrepressible Kestrel seeing the anguish in her handsome husband's eyes and knowing he suffered for her pain. "It doesna hurt . . . much!" she reassured with a squeal.

Nick positioned himself between his young wife's legs, and although he had helped in the birthing of countless babies, it was the first time he was personally involved. He watched Kestrel's love nest stretch until he feared she'd be rent in two. Her warm core where his manhood had thrust lovingly and lustily was distorted beyond recognition.

"Nick! Nick, hold me!" screamed Kestrel, afraid because she couldn't see his face.

"I'm here, my darling," comforted Nick, motioning his brother to take his place. "Quin, one day I shall guide your child into the world while you comfort Rue," he promised, holding Kestrel's hand and whispering loving encouragement into her ears as she strained with all her might.

Quin watched the baby's head crown and then he grasped the slippery shoulders. "One more push," he directed.

Rue's eyes filled with tears as she watched her husband deliver her sister's child. Tenderness that she thought would split her heart with aching knifed through her as he held the still bloody baby in his large brown hands.

"My niece," Quin said softly, placing the tiny child, who was still attached by the thick engorged cord to her very young mother, on her still contracting belly.

"I give you Cameron Sinclair MacKay," pronounced Kestrel weakly as she ran her hand through her tiny daughter's ebony hair and gazed lovingly up at Nick.

"Cameron," repeated Alex, staring down at the tiny black-haired baby lying between his golden daughter's naked breasts.

"Aye," whispered Rue, standing close to her tall husband as healing tears poured down her face.

"Aye, and if she's anything like the daughters of Cameron, heaven help us all," chuckled Lachlan as the tiny scrap of life clenched little fists and gave out an angry squall.

Seize The Dawn

by Vanessa Royall

For as long as she could remember, Elizabeth Rolfson knew that her destiny lay in America. She arrived in Chicago in 1885, the stunning heiress to a vast empire. As men of daring pressed westward, vying for the land, Elizabeth was swept into the savage struggle. Driven to learn the secret of her past, to find the one man who could still the restlessness of her heart, she would stand alone against the mighty to claim her proud birthright and grasp a dream of undying love.

A DELL BOOK   17788-X $3.50

At your local bookstore or use this handy coupon for ordering:

 DELL BOOKS
P.O. BOX 1000, PINE BROOK, N.J. 07058-1000

SEIZE THE DAWN   17788-X $3.50

Please send me the above title. I am enclosing S _____ (please add 75c per copy to cover postage and handling). Send check or money order—no cash or C.O.D.'s. Please allow up to 8 weeks for shipment.

Mr./Mrs./Miss _____

Address _____

City _____ State/Zip _____

A woman's place—the parlor, not the concert stage! But radiant Diana Ballantyne, pianist extraordinaire, had one year before she would bow to her father's wishes, return to England and marry. She had given her word. Yet the moment she met the brilliant Maestro, Baron Lukas von Korda, her fate was sealed. He touched her soul with music, kissed her lips with fire, filled her with unnameable desire. One minute warm and passionate, the next aloof, he mystified her, tantalized her. She longed for artistic triumph, ached for surrender, her passions ignited by Vienna dreams.

A DELL BOOK   19530-6 $3.50

Vienna Dreams

by JANETTE RADCLIFFE